TETHERS OF THE PRESENT

GARETH IAN DAVIES

CONTENTS

To my father, Graham Davies,
who taught me some risks are worth taking.
No regrets, Dad.

Excerpt of email recovered from closed account, owner untraceable. Destination account also closed and untraceable.

From: (address withheld)
To: (address withheld)
Subject: St. Louis 2024-01 #2
Sent: 2024-01-10 01:56:46 UTC

...the Intrusions. That there is agency behind the phenomena is not a new belief, of course, but is a fringe one, with alarming associations. To hear it expressed by someone so high in the organization is shocking.

Before I continue, I must apologize for the tone of my last email. You must know that I have the utmost respect for you, and I regret my choice of language, if not the sentiments I expressed. I have made my opinion clear about the schoolteacher and her associates, and so have you. Please forgive my rudeness. I chafe at my association with our business partner, and there is not much more I can teach my protégés, or at least little more I think they can learn. If I am forbidden contact with those who so easily undid all our hard work at the condo complex, then I am not sure of my ongoing purpose in St. Louis.

I hear activity in London is increasing, perhaps a fresh start there could be arranged...

CHAPTER ONE
FIRE ALARM GUY

A bitter wind howled around me, tossing innumerable snowflakes like icy daggers against the raw skin on my face. I stretched one hand forward in a vain attempt to shield my eyes, blinking eyelids I could no longer feel. Each step was harder than the last. I needed to reach what I had come here to find, before I succumbed to the cold and darkness.

And this frozen nightmare wasn't even an Imprint. This was downtown Chicago at the tail end of winter.

A street corner materialized before me, the fitful red glare of traffic lights on State Street battling the blizzard to keep rush hour traffic in some kind of order. I stumbled into a huddled mass of unwilling pedestrians awaiting their walk signal, and took the opportunity to peer up at the street sign. Ontario Street. Dammit! I'd gotten turned around again, the familiar landmark of the river bridge to the south lost in the snow. Cursing my wayward sense of direction, I shuffled back the way I'd come, weaving around others seeking the sanctuary of a bar, a restaurant, or most likely an 'L' station to take them home, somewhere warm and dry. Winter in this city was not for the faint-hearted.

The gods of the walk signal smiled upon me as I reached the next and final intersection, and I hurried east into the teeth of the winter storm. Halfway down Ohio Street, I spied a familiar white neon sign flickering above a brass-framed revolving door, and I plunged into the lobby of the Great Lakes Hotel.

For long seconds, all I could do was stand and bask in the almost tropical warmth pumping out of the lobby's heating vents, well-disguised amidst the black and gold art deco fixtures. Ahead of me, just past the elevator bank, a host stand guarded the entrance to a chic whiskey bar. Jess and I hadn't tried it during our stay the previous summer, but I hadn't been the hotel's most popular guest that weekend.

Jess. I scanned the lobby, but it appeared she hadn't beaten me there. Just inside the entrance, a brawny security guard in a padded black winter jacket remonstrated quietly with an unkempt younger man who, despite wearing at least two woolen hats and several layers, looked scarcely half his size. At the front desk, a young father checked his family into their room while his partner slumped on a nearby couch, cradling one sleeping toddler while an older girl clutched her leg. I wondered what had brought them here in February - no, it was March now, today was March 1st - but certainly far in advance of spring break. If they were here for a vacation, I hoped their itinerary didn't involve anything outdoors.

The mother turned her wary gaze on me, and drew her daughter closer. I found an unoccupied space against the opposite wall and fixed my attention on the revolving door. Did she think I was homeless too? Was my mere size and complexion a threat? Or was it simply the protective instinct of an exhausted parent in an unfamiliar place? I stifled my resentment and tried to find some sympathy, but I was glad when Jess tumbled, shivering through the revolving doors and into my arms.

"Mmmghh," she growled, her entire face buried in the now toasty fabric of my coat, my arms enveloping her in a fierce embrace. Her gloved fingertips dug into my back, kneading my spine, which actually felt quite pleasant.

"Glad you could make it," I said, after she raised her face to look at me. Her lips were cold when I kissed them, a faint taste of mint remaining from her lip balm.

"Why did we move here again?" She side-eyed the turbulent snowfall outside as if it had personally offended her.

"St. Louis gets cold too, you know."

She barked a laugh. "We've been here over a month, and it's like this *all the time*! I've forgotten what the sun looks like."

"That's because you're a night owl, coding or gaming or whatever it is you do on your laptop at two in the morning."

"And whose fault is that?" she retorted, but she was grinning now. "Someone won't leave me alone when they get back from their evening shift." Her hands fisted in my coat, and her eyes held a playful glint.

"Well, if it's solitude you want," I began in mock indignation, but she kissed me again, clutching me against her. I kissed her back for as long as I thought decent in public, then held her at arms length and assumed what I hoped was a businesslike expression. "Are you ready?"

"Sure," she said, standing up straight and adjusting her work backpack. I heard the clink of two water bottles colliding within. "Let's do this."

Let's do this. It was becoming our catchphrase.

The family had completed their check-in while Jess and I greeted each other. The security guard helped the father load their luggage onto a cart, while the mother cajoled their older daughter to stand up for one last effort. She gave me and Jess a curious look as they passed us on the way to the elevator. I nodded back and thought of my sister Fiona, and her vow that she wouldn't travel again until her youngest was in kindergarten. This couple was brave. I sure hoped they weren't staying on the eleventh floor.

"Come on," said Jess, tugging at my sleeve.

I took a deep breath and pulled myself together. We had a job to do. "Hi," I said to the young black woman behind the front desk. I remembered her from our last visit. Her dreads were almost down to her waist now. "I'm D, D Rodriguez, and this is Jess Evans. We have an appointment."

She stared at me, brow furrowed for a moment, and then her face relaxed. "I remember you. Fire alarm guy."

Jess snorted.

"Um, yes, that was me," I said, embarrassed. "That's kind of why I'm here. I spoke to Devin on the phone earlier."

"Devin!" she called, still regarding me with something like fascination. I tried not to squirm.

A black door, sporting an "Employees Only" sign in the middle of a frosted glass window, opened to our left. The man who emerged, studying us through thick-rimmed glasses, wasn't much older than the front desk clerk. He wore the same black polo shirt emblazoned with the hotel logo on its chest, and stood only a little shorter than me, mostly due to his towering Afro. We recognized each other too, but I hoped he wouldn't call me "fire alarm guy".

"D, right?" he said, shaking my hand after a slight pause, not quite meeting my eyes.

"Yes. I'm glad to be back here under better circumstances." Because last time I'd avoided a felony charge, but still got slapped with a $1000 fine for pulling the alarm when no fire actually existed. Not in the present day, anyway. I'd made a lot of people unhappy, including the one I was now talking to. "Do you remember my girlfriend, Jess?"

"Of course." Everybody remembered Jess. He shook her hand too, but her face was stone. She'd been more irritated by the fine than I had. "Come on back. We can talk in my office."

He held open the Employees Only door, and we filed into a square room half the size of the lobby, but which felt much smaller. Ranks of black steel file cabinets marched across the back wall, framing an enormous wooden desk to the right. A flat-screen monitor, keyboard and mouse battled at least three coffee mugs amidst untidy stacks of paper on the desk surface.

"Sorry for the mess," Devin said as he sat in the battered desk chair, throwing one hand up in futility while inviting us to sit with the other. The building's heat had caught up with me, and I shed my winter coat before perching on one of two mismatched plastic folding chairs. It had a distinct tilt to the right, as if the office wanted to cast me back into the lobby.

"Thanks for seeing me," I began. Jess kicked my shin and I suppressed a yelp. "Us. And giving us a chance to make things right. I expect you're busy, or at least I hope you are."

Devin's lips twisted into a humorless smile. "Not as busy as we'd like to be, at least not for the right reasons. That hasn't changed much since you were last here. Barring a miracle, I'd say we have weeks instead of months."

No pressure then. "I'm sorry to hear that. Have you had any more... trouble with the eleventh floor?"

"We don't rent rooms on eleven if we can help it. Fortunately, or unfortunately, we're rarely busy enough to need them. We did for a couple of weeks over the holidays. One couple asked to move rooms as soon as they checked in, and canceled when we told them every other floor was full. Two other groups checked out early, and left bad reviews. It hurt. But no-one pulled the fire alarm."

I grimaced. He looked tired, or perhaps just resigned to the hotel's fate. Maybe it was too late. I knew how it was in the hospitality industry. It takes a lot of hard work to build up a good reputation, and only a handful of bad reviews to tarnish it. But late or not, I was determined to do what I could to help. Fine notwithstanding, I had a debt I wanted to pay.

"Like I said on the phone, I think I can help you. I wasn't prepared last time, but I have a lot more experience with these things now. I'd like to try, to..." To what? Be that miracle? It wasn't so long ago that I'd assured others that Rosalind was the miracle worker. I missed her, but this was my show now, mine and Jess's.

Devin watched me in silence, face impassive. I couldn't tell if he thought I was crazy or just wasting his time. But the fact that we were here, sitting in his office, suggested he was desperate enough to entertain crazy. He glanced at Jess, who appeared content in the role of quiet sidekick, at least for now.

"So what are you planning to do? An exorcism or something?"

I fought back a sigh. "No, not really. We don't believe in ghosts, or at least not in what most people think of as ghosts: spirits of those who haven't 'moved on'. We think these are recordings, memories of real events that have been imprinted on the buildings where they occurred. We're still learning how that happens, but we do know how to erase these Imprints."

Jess stirred next to me, but if she'd wanted to comment on our woeful understanding, she disguised it by shedding her own coat. A sleek black polar fleece covered whatever lurid tee shirt she might be wearing, yet another reason she despised winter.

Devin's gaze lingered on Jess. "That sounds like an exorcism to me, from a practical standpoint."

"It is. Just without the bibles, crosses, and holy water."

He nodded. "What do I have to lose? Is there any risk? There's no one staying on eleven right now. Do we need to warn other guests?"

"No. The only risk is ours." I kept my voice level, but the fear that had gnawed at me all day intensified. I'd almost got lost in a building's memory once, unable to shake free from a trauma so reminiscent of my past. Rosalind had saved me then. She'd trained me, taught me everything she knew, but she didn't know everything. And, for the first time, she wouldn't be here to help me. I was walking the rope without a safety net.

"Okay." Devin stood, and we took his cue. "I guess I'll let you get to it. How long will it take?"

I shrugged, picking up my coat and slinging it over my shoulder. Jess did likewise. "It's hard to tell. An hour, give or take?"

"I'll come find you if it's been much longer than that. Good luck, I guess."

"He thinks we're insane," Jess murmured as we waited for an elevator. Her smile suggested she was more amused than offended.

"He wouldn't be the first," I said, between deep, slow, calming breaths. "And probably won't be the last."

An ominous mechanical clunk preceded a tuneless chime, and the elevator doors parted. The riotous decoration of the car beyond failed to distract me from how small it was. In. Out. Breathe.

Jess took my hand and led me inside. As the doors closed, we turned to face each other, our chests rising and falling in unison. Calm. Focus. Strength. Awareness.

Time to face my demons once again.

We watched the red digital display count the floors and waited for the now-familiar sense of otherness. Sure enough, just as '10' replaced '9', I felt a tightness in the air and a rising heat. When the car stopped, I filled my lungs with the stuffy air of the elevator and braced myself. The doors opened and we walked into an oven.

Or so it felt like. We emerged into one end of a narrow corridor, its ceiling and walls painted beige above a dark blue patterned carpet. There weren't quite enough overhead striplights or maybe I was projecting a heat haze, but the far end of the short corridor seemed obscured somehow. Waves of heat beat against me, and I coughed as soon as I inhaled the smoky dry air. Despite my preparations, I struggled to quell my surging panic. What good was deep breathing when the very air choked you?

"You okay?"

Jess laid a hand on my arm, and I covered it with my own. "Do you sense anything?"

"Sure. It smells like someone's doing hardcore electrical work. This place stinks of ozone."

I sniffed. Nothing. The reek of smoke, of burning walls and furnishings, was too strong. "Anything else?"

She frowned. "Air's a bit thin, but maybe I'm just nervous."

"I don't blame you," I muttered. On the wall, about halfway down the corridor, I could make out a scarlet pull alarm. It called to me, a siren song defying reason, seductive and deadly. I stuck my free hand in my jeans pocket. "Okay. The longer we stand here, the worse it'll be. I'm gonna walk slowly down the corridor until I can find the source. Come with me if you want, but don't do anything unless I ask. This memory is strong."

"I know, I know," Jess said, unable to mask her irritation. This was only her third Erasure since she'd somehow acquired the sensitivity to detect Imprints. She burned with curiosity, and it didn't help that questions were piling up faster than we could answer them. Foremost of which was why she could suddenly sense what she couldn't before.

"Observe as much as you can," I said as I took my first steps forward, as much to keep myself calm as anything else. "The more information we gather, the better chance we have of understanding it."

She nodded, and then her face spasmed with disgust. At the same time, the temperature soared and I closed my eyes, afraid they'd boil in their sockets. I knew I was standing in a quiet, empty hotel corridor while a blizzard raged through the streets outside, but it felt like I'd walked into the sun. Or close to the sun. The sun was on my right. I turned my face into its glare, the skin of my face blistering and peeling, and cracked my dissolving eyelids as much as I dared.

I stood before the door to Room 1105.

"This is it," I said, taking Jess's hand. "This is the source of it all."

She tensed. "Do we need to get into the room?"

"I don't think so. It's so strong, I think we can find the Catch from here. Look for a pattern in whatever you're sensing."

The Catch: what I thought of as the focal point of the Imprint, the invisible hitch in the fabric of the universe that tethered the memory to the structure of the building. I had to reach through the waves of devastating heat, while my body shriveled and burned, and find that point. Find it, and release the memory.

Knowing what to do was one thing. Doing it, entirely different. It was so hot! Choking smoke billowed around me, filling my lungs. I couldn't breathe! How could I find the Catch if I couldn't breathe? Focus. Listen. Look for the smallest candle flame amidst this roaring inferno, this smothering tempest of fire and death and...

There.

It was there.

The flicker of light and heat that started it all, pale and cool and hard as diamond.

"Did you find it?" I asked Jess, surprised at how hoarse my voice was.

"I... maybe?" Her face twisted in revulsion, and she shuddered. It was time to end this.

As my body failed, smothered by smoke and ruin, I reached out with some part of my awareness, latched on to that flicker, and pushed with all the force of my buckling will.

My ears popped and the universe exploded.

And then reassembled instantly, into a dark, sparsely-furnished apartment, lit only by the fierce glow of a space heater that squatted on the floor near one of the curtained windows. Too near. A lick of flame sprouted from a corner of the heavy fabric, then spread upward and sideways, slow at first, then gathering pace. The angry red light of the heater flickered as smoke billowed around it. I heard coughing, quiet, from an adjoining room, and watched in horror as the flames reached the walls, the ceiling. Chest-wracking coughs and cries of alarm punctuated the air, and a young couple staggered into view, wide-eyed, mouths covered with scraps of clothing. They stopped and gazed in terror as their home burned, the woman clutching her partner's arm, frozen to the spot. He looked around frantically and yelled something I couldn't hear. *Get out!* I thought, willing them to hear me. *Just get out!*

I've never been sure if I can interact with these memories. Sometimes I've convinced myself I can, but Rosalind believed our pleas and soothing words were simply part of the process of releasing the memory. This was the riskiest part. By removing the Catch, the memory was mine, ripped from the building's Imprint and flooding my mind and senses. If I lost focus, got too caught up in the emotion and trauma, I couldn't channel it away. If I couldn't expel it, to disperse and fade, the memory would consume me.

The young man pushed the woman towards their apartment's front door and ran back into the other room. Rivers of fire streaked across the ceiling, and chunks of burning plaster fell in a deadly rain, catching a lumpy old couch on fire and smoldering atop the stained carpet. The woman hesitated by the door, staring wide-eyed after her partner even as she doubled over coughing.

It's not worth it, I urged her. *Whatever he went back for, whatever valuables you think you need to save, nothing's more valuable than your lives.*

"My baby!"

Oh shit.

My resolve wavered, caught up in her fear, not for herself, but for her child. I couldn't hear an alarm, didn't know if help was coming. What was taking him so long? I tried to follow him, to will myself into wherever their child was, but I couldn't move. I tried to will the apartment door open, to speed their escape, but that didn't work either. They needed to get out!

Open the door, while you still can. Open the door so you can flee when he comes back with your baby, so you can call for help. Open it!

Still looking towards the other room as the hungry flames reached toward its entrance, her hand grasped the door handle and turned it, turned it ever so slowly. The door resisted, and she dropped the crumpled shift she'd used to cover her mouth, then yanked at the handle with both hands. Her body convulsed as smoke writhed around her. A gap. More. The widening crack of dim, yellow light battled the apartment's ruddy glow and promised safety.

C'mon, dude!

Just as the woman collapsed to her knees in a fit of coughing, door half-ajar, the man lurched from the other room, swatting smoke and flame away with one arm while cradling a wailing infant in his other. He made it to the door, somehow heaved his partner to her feet, pushed her through the gap, and almost fell through it as he followed her.

The scene crumpled like a sheet of paper tossed into the flames.

And I was on my hands and knees in the corridor outside Room 1105 of the Great Lakes Hotel, dry-heaving, head pounding, throat so dry I couldn't even remember what water tasted like. Jess curled up on the floor beside me, retching, one hand stretched toward mine. With my failing strength, I reached out and took it, our fingers entwining. We stayed like that for an age.

CHAPTER TWO

UNUSUAL SOLUTIONS TO UNUSUAL PROBLEMS

I recovered first, clawing Jess's backpack towards me from where she'd dropped it, and rummaging inside for our water bottles. I drank one slow mouthful, wary of cramping my stomach, then pressed Jess's bottle into her hand. She looked up at me through watering eyes and wiped her mouth, before propping herself against the wall.

"Easy!" I said as she spluttered after her first drink. She waved off my solicitous hand.

"I know," she croaked, then coughed again, the heel of one hand against her forehead. A bead of perspiration dripped from the roots of her black bangs and ran along the inside of her wrist. I hauled myself up and sat next to her, sipping precious water and glaring at the door to Room 1105. The low rent apartments had closed for good in 1983, the blaze having devastated several units on this floor and the one above. Two people had died, asphyxiated in their sleep, before the fire department could respond to extinguish the flames. I didn't think the victims were the couple we'd just seen, or at least I hoped not; I'd read nothing about a baby.

I shivered and took another drink. Research could only prepare you for so much. There were horrors in every building's past. I wondered for the thousandth time if I was doing the right thing. "Feeling any better?"

Jess took a long, shuddering breath and turned her face toward mine. Her dazzling emerald eyes were bloodshot, a vaguely unsettling effect, and she gazed at me as if searching for something. "Was it really that bad? Or are we just out of practice?"

I shrugged. "Probably both. I was prepared, especially after the last time we were here. But that was still... intense." I frowned. The word didn't do it justice. "It's been a while, and that was our first time without Rosalind."

She scowled and looked like she wanted to comment, but drank more water instead. I glanced at my phone and made a swift calculation. We'd been up here for almost forty-five minutes. Crazy.

"Come on," I said, forcing some pep into my voice as I climbed to my feet and extended my hand. "Let's go report our success, with heads held high. That was the point of all this."

Muttering curses, Jess pulled herself to her feet, and we wobbled back towards the elevators. Someday, we'd have to figure out why Erasures affected us the way they did. For what seemed largely a mental exercise, the physical after-effects were all too real. I suspected Jess already had theories.

Devin was waiting in the lobby, chatting with the security guard. They turned to face us as we emerged from the elevator, far steadier on our feet than when we'd entered. A question hung in the air, unspoken.

"That should be the end of your problems," I told them, projecting all the confidence I could muster. "As far as the eleventh floor goes, at least."

The two men exchanged looks, and then the security guard nodded and squeezed past us on his way to the elevator. I frowned.

"Isaiah is the only one on staff who notices anything on eleven," Devin explained. "Nothing like some of our guests, apparently."

"And you want his confirmation that we've done what we've claimed." I tried to keep the irritation out of my voice. Devin had no good reason to take my word for it. In his place, I would do the same. It still bugged me. Rosalind, my mentor from St.

Louis, rarely encountered such skepticism. But then she wore authority like a mantle.

"Can I get you something?" Devin asked after the silence became awkward. The lobby was otherwise empty, and he seemed hesitant to leave us alone. I shook my head, then turned to Jess, but her eyes were far away, brow furrowed in thought. I took her hand and squeezed it; she gave a small shake of her head, but squeezed back. Later, then.

Devin and I, at least, were both grateful when the elevator's ping announced Isaiah's return. The burly security guard stared at me and Jess with a strange expression, mostly curiosity, but with a hint of something else. I wanted it to be respect, but I think it was wariness. Not fear. Not at all.

"Can't feel nothing up there," he told Devin, eyes not leaving mine. "Walked the floor twice. It's quiet sometimes, but something's always there. But it ain't anymore."

Jess drew herself up, emerging from her trance and favoring them with a dazzling smile. "Like we said, that should be the end of your problems. You can start renting those rooms now, without worry. I hope it helps you."

Devin grimaced and glanced at Isaiah, who took his cue and returned to his post by the revolving door. "I don't know if it can fend off the inevitable," he said, taking off his glasses and rubbing his eyes. "But even with our reviews, we're almost fully-booked the week of spring break. I guess we'll find out then. Thank you. For trying, for... doing whatever you did. I know we didn't discuss payment."

It was a statement, but I heard that question too. And I was ready with our answer. "There's no fee, this time," I said, reaching into the inside pocket of my jacket and extracting a business card. I offered it to him, and after a moment's hesitation, he took it. "We just moved to town. We think we can help people, such as yourself. For various reasons, we won't advertise our services on conventional media channels. But if you know of anyone, personally or professionally, who could use our help, please refer them to us."

It sounded just like it had when I'd practiced in front of the mirror that morning. I hate marketing, especially self-promotion. It was all I could do not to cringe.

"'Unusual Solutions to Unusual Problems'," he read, after putting his glasses back on. He smiled grimly. "Sounds about right. I'll keep you in mind."

"I told you that was a good name."

Jess grinned at me as we settled into our seats on the CTA Red Line train. We'd avoided the worst of the evening commute, when workers fleeing the Loop packed the cars. Even the platforms made me nervous, both the narrow wooden structures bracketing the elevated stations and the bleak concrete islands of the subway. Either way, I shrank from so many people in such a confined space. The rails themselves held an inexplicable fascination, and my fear of falling on them set my pulse racing every time. But it was almost 7pm, and save for a few happy hour stragglers and others heading north for a Friday night out, we had both the platforms and the train mostly to ourselves.

"I still think it's a bit of a mouthful," I said, wrapping my arm around her shoulders as she burrowed against me. A dark-complected young woman sat opposite us, cocooned in almost as much winter clothing as the two of us combined. A thick scarf wrapped around her chin and partially covered her lips. She met my eyes without expression, then her gaze drifted up to the advertisements above our windows.

"Nah, the words have a good shape to them. Just that, and your name and number, it's perfect. Discrete and to the point."

"A good shape to them?"

She shrugged. "That's what my friend Alex said. He just started a User Experience job back in St. Louis."

"You told him about what we do? We've got to be careful, Jess."

"I *am* being careful," she said in a long-suffering tone. "I didn't say anything about what we do. I just asked him to look at our business card design. He's a friend. He helped me a lot during Shift_Dev."

I recalled her anecdotes about the software mentorship program that helped find her current job and new career. She might have mentioned an Alex, but I was terrible with names. "Still. I guess I'm just wary. We don't know who the players are in this town. Or if Steven Rourke hears about it and makes more trouble for me, and those I care about."

Jess took my hand, and I could feel the bones of her fingers through our thick winter gloves. I squeezed her shoulder in return.

"You did what you had to," she whispered. "You stood up for your friends. For Rosalind."

Which was all true, but I still felt guilty. The people at Hickory had been like a family to me. Far more than most of my actual family.

The young woman got off at the next station, and since no-one replaced her, I stretched my legs out. Damn, I was tired. Jess looked drowsy too. The last thing we needed was to fall asleep and end up at Howard, the northern terminus. We were only traveling two more stops.

"Tell me what you saw," I murmured. "During the Erasure."

Jess didn't reply at first, and I drew back to see if she had, in fact, fallen asleep. She grunted, and her head followed mine. "I'm thinking," she protested.

"Did you feel the heat? Smell the smoke? It was so strong for me."

She shook her head. "No, none of that. I expected to, since the Imprint was the memory of a fire. But all I could smell was ozone. And I could barely breathe, like all the air was being sucked out of the corridor. If any other guests sensed all that, no wonder they canceled and left."

"Huh. I wonder why we reacted so differently. I wonder what Rosalind would have sensed. She always claimed to hear more than anything else. Always told me to listen." To the quietest voice in the room.

"We're different people, D. We all sense normal, everyday things differently. Maybe the differences are more extreme with Imprints."

"Maybe. Did you see the burning room? The people in it, trying to escape?"

"I saw a woman standing by a door, holding it open. It was difficult to see. There was a lot of smoke."

"You didn't see the guy? You didn't see him run into the other room to rescue their baby?"

"Their baby? No! I... well, I was distracted. Did you sense anything else? Anyone else?"

"Anyone?"

"I don't know. I could have sworn there was someone else there with us, watching the memory. Just for a second."

I frowned and looked at her again. Her eyes, fixed on the almost featureless darkness blurring past the glass, looked haunted. I hadn't sensed anything like that.

"It's like we all get our own slices of the memory," I found myself saying. "Our own viewpoints."

She sighed and relaxed. "There's still so much we don't know. Like, I could have sworn we were up there for ten minutes, fifteen tops. But it was more than twice that. Where did all the time go? Why were we so dehydrated, so nauseous? Why were we so weak we could hardly move afterwards?"

I rested my head back against the cold glass of the window. I'd asked those questions so many times, of myself and of Rosalind. I had no answers, or at least none that weren't speculation. It hadn't bothered me when first grappling with the idea that someone else experienced the strange phenomena that had plagued me for years. I'd been elated that this person, Rosalind, could help me endure and even eliminate them, help me take back control of my life for the first time in decades. Understanding it all had been a bonus. But Jess had never been satisfied, and I was coming around to her view. What had I gotten myself into? What had I gotten us into?

"This is North and Clybourn," announced the automated PA, as the darkness outside gave way to the eggshell white tile walls of our station. With obvious reluctance, Jess detached herself from my body heat as the train jerked to a halt. I collected myself. I preferred to stay on the train until Fullerton, even though it was a longer backtrack to our apartment. There was a patch of chilling cold on the North/Clybourn platform that had nothing to do with the winter storm. I endured it, and I didn't know if Jess noticed. She'd never said anything, and I'd never asked.

The storm's fury was milder here on the southern edges of the Lincoln Park neighborhood. It was still freezing, and we trudged as fast as we dared through two or three inches of powdery accumulation. A handful of restaurants clustered around the busy intersection, promising warmth as well as dinner, but we were too tired for more than a frozen pizza back at our apartment. We hurried north for two long blocks along Halsted Street, bustling with early Steppenwolf Theater traffic, then turned left into a series of narrow side streets lined with parked cars and snow-covered trees. Brick apartment buildings stood shoulder to shoulder with private townhouses, some under active renovation. Many of the larger homes had been converted to apartments, especially as you got closer to the elevated tracks of the Brown Line. We rented the upstairs unit in one such house, and it was there we collapsed into the welcoming embrace of our battered couch.

My phone rang almost immediately. I considered ignoring it, but Jess was still fighting with the blankets, so I dug it out of my jeans pocket and looked at the caller ID.

It was Rosalind.

"How did your Erasure go?" she asked after we exchanged greetings. I missed her voice, its genuine warmth and unpretentious British accent. I hadn't heard it since we moved to Chicago a month before.

"Good, I think," I said. I started to give her a summary that quickly sprawled into a blow-by-blow account of what Jess and I had seen and done at the Great Lakes Hotel. Rosalind didn't seem to mind, and was especially curious about Jess's perceptions and how they differed from mine.

"Well, I'm sure that's something of a relief," she said at last. "I know how much your prior experience at the hotel rankled. If you have, in fact, solved their problem for good, that is an excellent way to start your Chicago career. Unusually or otherwise."

We laughed, including Jess, who was eavesdropping with her head nestled on my shoulder.

"I hope so. We'll see if we get any referrals. I... miss it. And miss you. How are you and Martin? How is retirement, from Erasures at least?"

There was a pause, and when she spoke again, her good cheer had vanished. "We're fine, all things considered. Actually, there's another reason I called. We're flying up to Chicago tomorrow morning. Bit of a last minute trip. I hoped we might catch up with you and Jess in person, if you have time. I know it's late notice."

"Oh! We'd love to see you," I said, trying to remember my work schedule. "Jess is off all weekend. I've got the dinner shift tomorrow, but I'm free Sunday evening if that works."

There was a muffled conversation at the other end of the line, and I heard Martin's voice. I couldn't make out any words, but he sounded stressed. What was going on?

"Sunday evening works," Rosalind confirmed at last. "Thank you. I'm afraid we have a favor to ask, but there is much we need to explain first. It's time to dredge up some ghosts from our own past.

"It's time to tell you about Daniel."

Chapter Three
A Huge Favor

The neighborhood of Lincoln Park, sandwiched between Lake Michigan and the Chicago River, takes its name from the lakeside park that stretches north from the original border of Chicago. The first mid-nineteenth century settlements flanked the Green Bay Trail, now known within its borders as Clark Street. Kashubian immigrants from northern Poland established a vibrant and long-lasting community as the century turned, and DePaul University built their campus in the heart of the neighborhood. Following the decay of the Great Depression, conservation battled gentrification in the drive towards urban renewal. The Young Lords, a transformed street gang within the flourishing Puerto Rican community, boosted the area's civil rights credentials in the 1960s and 1970s, staging demonstrations and sit-ins to preserve their homes from the wrecking ball. Towards the end of the millennium, young professionals, coveting Lincoln Park's semi-suburban appeal and proximity to downtown, brought their money with them. Upscale retail corridors and trendy nightlife spots thrived, and, so we heard from more than one leasing agent during our January apartment hunt, drove property values through the roof. Supposedly, there was a block not too far from us, which was the single most expensive in the city.

"I'm still kinda surprised we're living here," I told Rosalind and Martin, as we settled around our table at a tapas restaurant just north of Armitage Avenue. My new coworkers had recommended the place for both the food and the eccentric ambience. Subtle lighting illuminated half a dozen rooms of different sizes and decor, thrown together with no obvious plan in mind. I almost got lost going to the bathroom. The place was packed, impressive for a cold Sunday evening.

The Hills looked tired. We'd hugged out our greetings by the host stand, all still bundled in our winter finest. Now they both slumped around our corner table and spared only a passing glance at their menus. The crow's feet around Rosalind's eyes were deeper than I remembered, and shadows blotched beneath. At least her nose had fully healed from its break the previous October. Martin appeared lost in thought, often scratching at a beard that was much fuller and grayer than before, although he nodded at all the right places in the conversation.

"We didn't really know where to look when we first came up here," I said, leaving Jess to order our food. "I'd already got my job lined up, but Jess was still looking. Her grandparents all live in the area, but in the western and northern suburbs, and I didn't want an hour each way commute. When she got her gig in The Loop, we knew we wanted to find a place close, and the dojo you recommended is just down the street; Sensei Ryuichi is awesome by the way! But we struggled to find an apartment we liked and could afford. We thought Lincoln Park was out of our reach."

"Yet here you both are," Rosalind said. "Order for us too if you don't mind, Jess. So what changed? Factoring in earnings from your Erasure side business?"

"Ha! I wish. No, actually it was all Jess's grandfather."

I'd only met James Evans once, during our infamous birthday weekend trip last year. That was when I'd not only pulled the fire alarm at the Great Lakes Hotel, but also started a fight at Jess's other grandparents' favorite restaurant. Unlike the charming Kenyan expat couple who'd brushed off my hotheadedness and welcomed me as their beloved granddaughter's boyfriend, James had been cool and aloof during our more refined and, frankly, boring meal the following evening. Jess assured me he wasn't always like that. She worried about him, living alone in the Evanston house he'd shared for so long with her grandmother, who'd died three years before.

"He knows people who own rental property around here," said Jess. "One had a vacancy, and he offered to chip in for the rent. I think he still feels guilty for not coming down to St. Louis when Dad had his heart attack last year. Said he couldn't find someone to look after his dogs."

My hand covered hers. "Whatever the reason, we're grateful. It's a really nice place, for the two of us. We'd have had you over for dinner, but it's a bit tight for entertaining. And we're still unpacking."

"And finding furniture," muttered Jess.

Rosalind's smile was sympathetic. "Moving in together for the first time is stressful, especially if you've moved to a new city, or a new country." She turned to her husband, and Martin chuckled, almost the first sound he'd made since we sat down. They'd married and moved from England to the USA soon after graduating college, thirty years before. I now had a faint inkling of just how hard that must have been, yet they were still together. Clearly, they were doing something right.

"It is," I said. "But we've been stressed out for a while, especially since Hickory burned down."

I had to take a swig of water. Just mentioning that event left a bitter taste in my mouth.

Our server, a hassled-looking young woman with a pleasant but efficient manner, chose that moment to stop by and take our order. Jess kept it simple: seafood paella, a pitcher of sangria, and a half dozen tapas.

Rosalind looked like she wanted to say something, but she waited for me.

"I know it was Steven Rourke. No one will ever prove it, of course, just like no one will prove his connection to the notes or all those Imprints. But I knew his threat wasn't empty.

And offering to bankroll the rebuild when my boss's insurance couldn't cover it all, as long as I wasn't rehired, is totally Rourke's style."

"He's a thug," snapped Martin, surprising all of us, including himself I think.

"He's much worse than a thug," said Rosalind, her lip curled in distaste. "He's a smart, powerful and knowledgeable man. We must tread, and speak, carefully, my love."

Martin scowled, then turned away, studying the framed piece of violent modern art that hung beside him. He was quieter than usual, and I wondered why. Jess poured four glasses of sangria, but kept her own counsel.

"I'm sorry for bringing that scumbag into your lives," I said. "I know I'll never be free of him, even here. I hope he leaves you alone now that you're retired from erasing Imprints."

Rosalind looked me in the eye. "How could I retire? Knowing what I know about that man and his acolytes. And there are those who rely on me still."

I thought Martin shot a glance at me, but I was too busy gaping at Rosalind to be sure. "You're still... practicing?"

She chuckled, but it failed to lighten the mood. "Interesting choice of word. Makes me sound like a lawyer. Yes, I'm still practicing, with the same discretion I always have. He cannot operate unopposed. Although, I suspect there are other agencies in play."

"What other agencies?" Jess leaned forward, eyes intent.

"I'm not sure yet," Rosalind replied, her thoughtful gaze meeting Jess's. She sipped her sangria. "I think you and I should have a conversation about that soon. You possess research skills I do not."

"Are you talking about Rourke's associate?" I asked, heading off Jess's pursuit of the bait Rosalind offered. "Jamal, or whatever his name was? The guy who left me the note to call him, before we went to Chouteau Village?"

Rosalind's eyes lingered on Jess, then she turned back to me. "Perhaps. I can't find much about him, but I'm convinced he represents interests other than Rourke's. I want to know what those interests are. I once told you I'd never found any information, scarcely more than wild speculation, about what I do, about imprinted memories or erasing them. But I confess I never looked that hard. I think a part of me was afraid of what I might find. It still is, if I'm being honest. I just fear my ignorance even more now."

"I'm sorry," I said as I digested this. "I'm sorry for moving up here and leaving you with that burden. But when Mike told me he had a friend in Chicago who needed a grill chef, it was the best job lead I had." It was true, but that wasn't my only reason for leaving St. Louis, and I think she knew it.

The food arrived, a variety of aromas tugging at my appetite. We passed the tapas around, selecting our own mouthfuls from each plate. Martin dug in, but Rosalind passed on all but the bacon-wrapped dates. She accepted a towering spoonful of paella, but only picked at it.

"Not to beat a dead horse, but I do wish you hadn't moved away," she said at last. "I was quite looking forward to playing the role of armchair mentor. And I miss the company. But I understand, and perhaps it's for the best. There's actually something you can help us with, since you're here. If you're willing."

Martin looked like he wanted to speak, but decided against it, forking paella into his mouth and not quite meeting my eye. I detected an undercurrent of tension between them that our pleasant reunion could no longer disguise. Each mouthful of excellent paella tasted blander than the last. Rosalind set her fork down and dabbed at her lips with a napkin, then folded her hands together.

"D, you asked me once about our son, Daniel," she said, lowering her voice but leaning forward. I could just hear her over the piped 90s playlist and the enthusiastic conversation at a neighboring table. "I wasn't ready to share that part of my life with you then. It's... painful. Painful for me, painful for Martin, painful for our marriage. You and Jess have become good friends, and we've already gone through much together. But I still wouldn't tell you any of this if we were back in St. Louis, three hundred miles away. You see, Daniel's here. In Chicago."

She paused, but I couldn't think of anything to say. I exchanged glances with Jess, but her expression gave nothing away.

"Daniel ran away from home when he was seventeen. He'd threatened to before, but always came home later that day. Not this time. He vanished. We didn't sleep for days, scouring the city for clues as to where he might be, visiting everywhere we knew he liked to go. We talked to everyone he knew, friends and those he'd once called friends, their families and friends, anyone who might tell us anything. No one knew, or would say. He was a ghost.

"We called the police, of course. That first morning when we discovered his empty bed, unslept in, and after the school denied he was there. It's a sickening feeling, and it never leaves you. The police tried to help, but it was soon clear that Daniel had left the city. He was gone."

She dropped her eyes and took a great, shuddering breath. Martin wrapped one arm around her shoulders, his expression grim. I pushed my plate away. I'd quite lost my appetite.

"Why..." started Jess, then pursed her lips.

Rosalind looked up, expectant and vulnerable. I'd never seen her like this, and it bothered me more than I thought it would.

"Why were you so sure he'd run away?" Jess forced the question out, as if she feared to ask. "Why not an accident or... or worse?"

"We looked," Martin said, his high voice much gruffer when he was quiet. "We called all the hospitals, all the police stations too. First in the city and county, then further out, into Missouri and Illinois. Nothing. But he'd packed a bag, the rucksack he'd just bought with birthday money. He meant to leave, and not return."

Rosalind flinched, then raised her eyes again. "I pray you never endure what we did then, what we've endured since. I'm told that some runaways want to be found, but not Daniel. A friend of ours suggested hiring a private investigator. I resisted. I was in denial and I didn't want a stranger that deep in our personal affairs. But the need to know was too strong, so I did it. And they found him."

Jess's hand slid into mine under the table. Perhaps she reeled as I did from this flood of revelation. I recalled the sunny morning in St. Louis's Botanical Garden when I'd confessed to killing a man, and how the Hills had met that with acceptance, if not understanding. If they felt anything like the pain and embarrassment I'd felt then, I pitied them.

"Danny was in rehab in Colorado, just outside Boulder," Martin went on, his voice dull. "Drugs were one of the things we fought about, before he left. We flew out immediately, but he refused to see us. He was eighteen, we couldn't force him to and knew it might hurt more than it helped. At least we knew he was being cared for. He left soon afterwards, disappeared again, and that's been the pattern ever since. Rosalind's PI will find him at another rehab facility, we go there and he refuses to see us, then he disappears a few days later."

"You want to know why we persist in trying to see him, when he clearly doesn't want to see us." Rosalind was talking to Jess, more weariness than defiance in her tone. Jess hesitated, then nodded, and Rosalind gave her a curt one in return. "I understand. It's foolish to repeat the exact same behavior and expect different results. We agonize over it. All I can say in our defense is that we're his parents. We love him. We miss him. And we have to keep trying."

Whatever had happened in the past, I marveled at their dedication and simple love for their son. I couldn't suppress the decades-long bitterness towards my parents, who'd done quite the opposite. "Is that why you're here? Daniel's in rehab somewhere in Chicago?"

"He is." Rosalind offered a weak smile. "We would have visited you at some point, and I still hope to do so under happier circumstances. But yes, we learned last week that he's been here since last autumn. We had little hope he would see us, and we weren't disappointed. But this time he left us a message, more than a simple refusal. He told us he had work to do here."

"Work? That could be good, right?"

"Perhaps. We don't know. This rehab facility is associated with an organization called 'The Scales of Equilibrium'. We hadn't heard of them, but they appear to be some sort of New Age movement. And that may not be a bad thing for Daniel but..."

"We're worried," Martin finished, downing the last of the sangria I hadn't noticed him drinking. Rosalind turned to him, eyes brimming, and he squeezed her shoulder. I noticed the server approach our table and waved her away. Jess caught my eye and nodded.

"What can we do?" I asked.

Rosalind wiped a tear from the corner of each eye and looked at me with a grateful smile. "Thank you, both of you. This may be pushing the bounds of our friendship, but we have a huge favor to ask of you."

"Name it."

"Can you keep an eye on him for us? Not spy, definitely not spy. Just check up on him whenever you can. Private investigators are expensive and, well, they're not family. Or friends. I'm done with the pity, with the understanding and reassurances of strangers. This is our cross to bear, and if we must share the burden, I'd rather it be with only our closest friends."

Martin glanced over at Jess, but Rosalind's eyes held mine, beseeching. I didn't know exactly what we were letting ourselves in for, but what else could we do? After all she'd done for me, for us, surely it was the least we could do. Wasn't this what friends were for?

"Of course," I said, pouring myself and Martin another glass. "Tell us more."

Excerpt of email recovered from closed account, owner untraceable. Destination account also closed and untraceable.

From: (address withheld)
To: (address withheld)
Subject: Chicago 2024-03 #1
Sent: 2024-03-04 22:28:09 UTC

…even colder, but the view looking out over Lake Michigan is breathtaking.

There are developments already. The cook has destroyed at least one Tether and appears to be trying to establish himself in much the same role held by his mentor in St. Louis. Faustyn tells me they've dealt with this kind of thing before, not surprising for a city of this size and age. Chicago's Intrusion background remains high, almost rivaling New York. No wonder we have discovered some of our best field agents here (and you know me far too well to accuse me of sycophancy). I do wonder if Faustyn et al have run up against someone possessing so much raw strength as our cook. Is Fisher ready to try out Astbury's new countermeasures? And lest we forget, the cook's partner gave cybersec quite the scare last month. I hear those servers have been safely decommissioned.

Do we have anyone lined up for St. Louis yet? The schoolteacher surely needs monitoring, at least…

Chapter Four
IS THAT YOU?

Still bleary-eyed after dismissing our morning alarm, I cracked our bedroom's window blinds to check the weather and flinched. Not two feet away, perched on the wooden rail of our narrow balcony, a sleek gray cat regarded me with an imperious stare.

"Can you make any more noise?" Jess complained, yanking the comforter up over her head. I wondered when she'd finally come to bed. To sleep, that is.

"Sorry. There's a cat on our balcony."

Jess mumbled something indistinct.

"Can't hear you, Jess," I said, peering through the window again. The cat was grooming itself, as if satisfied with the disruption it had caused.

"Jasmine." Jess emerged from her cocoon, grinning. "She likes it up there."

"Jasmine? How do you know its name?"

"Her name. She's the Millers' cat. You know, the couple downstairs, our neighbors you never talk to?"

"I've talked to them," I said, and it was true. Technically. Even used more than one syllable once. Jake and Erica Miller were both attorneys, young and ambitious, probably renting the downstairs apartment while deciding which million-dollar home to buy. I only ever saw them when leaving for or returning from work. I'd just about got *their* names down, I couldn't be expected to know anything about their cat.

"Why don't you give her some leftover chicken?"

"We can't feed someone else's cat!"

"Why not? I feed her all the time. She loves it, don't you, Jasmine?" Jess peeled the comforter away from her lean, coffee-toned body with a languorous stretch and rubbed her eyes. For all that she complained about the cold, you'd think she'd wear more to bed.

I looked away. We really didn't have the time. "What if it has a special diet or something?"

"*She* would know," said Jess, rummaging in the refrigerator for last night's leftovers. "It's fine."

"I don't think you'd care, would you?" I asked Jasmine. She fixed me with a baleful glare, and I stepped away from the window. I was talking to cats now.

While Jess fixed up Jasmine with contraband breakfast, I headed for the shower, stumbling through a minefield of half-full duffel bags strewn across our bedroom floor. We'd only had room for one dresser in the U-Haul, and our bedroom's single built-in closet barely held our respective work clothes. Jess wanted to go to IKEA, but I'd been putting it off.

I hadn't shared space full-time with another adult since Missouri Eastern Correctional. Twelve years in a jail cell with a series of unwilling roommates hadn't prepared me for living with someone I wanted to be with. I liked everything in its place, a holdover from protecting my few belongings from others. Jess understood, but thought I was obsessive. She tolerated me cleaning her dishes, but forbade me from picking her clothes off the floor. It was never an issue back in St. Louis, when she occasionally stayed the night in my apartment. We were living together now, 24/7. This was our relationship's next big test.

Most weekday mornings, we got up together, when I was scheduled for the lunch shift. Jess had the option to work from home up to three days a week, since her software development job at Paragon Insurance involved her sitting in front of a laptop. However, most days she went into the office. "I don't want to be stuck in the apartment all the time," she told me. "Besides, it's easier to learn on the job if you can work with people face to face. There are only so many virtual meetings I can take." She preferred going in on days when I worked the lunch shift, so we could ride the train together. I couldn't argue with that, but my stress rose as we danced our morning routine and tried to leave on schedule. Her job's start time was flexible, mine was not.

Jasmine's second breakfast notwithstanding, we left as planned that Thursday. Bright sun heralded a warmer day, teasing the possibility of spring. Hesitant birdsong and the hum of distant traffic were punctuated by the metallic rumble of elevated trains. We walked to the Armitage (Brown Line) station in companionable silence, hand in hand, Jess studying her phone and me the streets. I felt safe here, now that I was getting to know the area, but I wasn't going to take unnecessary risks.

"Are you still coming by after work?" Jess asked as I stood to leave the train, one stop before hers.

"Sure," I said, after the briefest of pauses during which I hunted down the memory of me agreeing to that. "As long as I don't get conscripted into the dinner shift again." I appeased Jess's raised eyebrow by stooping and kissing her.

"Text me," she said, smiling, and then patting me on the butt as I shouldered my way toward the train car's open doors.

I arrived thirty minutes early for my lunch shift, but I was still adjusting to the kitchen at Trattoria Cappelli, and extra prep time helped. I really needed this job. I couldn't fault my old boss, Mike Szemis, for not rehiring me after Hickory was rebuilt. He and his ex-con staff had become family to me, and although I hadn't started the kitchen fire, my choice had lit the fuse.

Mike was awkward and apologetic about Steven Rourke's offer and attached condition, but I understood. "A buddy of mine runs an Italian bistro in Chicago," Mike told me. "He's looking for a new grill chef. I recommended you, and he's willing to take you, sight unseen, if you're interested. It'd be different from what you've done here, but you're more than capable. And I think you could do with a fresh start."

He'd been right. Luca "Chef" Cappelli was a thin man whose oiled-back black hair framed a pale, angular face. The rumors that he slept in his chef whites were probably untrue, but I had never seen him out of them. He ran his kitchen with skill and efficiency, expecting the highest standards from every member of his staff, even when he'd turned them loose on their station their first day. I'd sweated less when receiving my prison sentence.

"Morning, D," he called out as I entered the staff room to swap my winter coat for my own whites. "Tamsyn called in sick. COVID again. Take a test and stay outta my kitchen until it's negative. If it is, I need you to pitch in on meats today."

"Got it, Chef," I replied, opening the medicine cabinet and selecting the topmost of a stack of free, government-issued rapid tests. I hated the things, hated rummaging around my nostrils with a swab, afraid I'd dig too deep and it'd get stuck or poke my brain or something equally idiotic. I also knew a negative result meant little - you needed a proper PCR test to confirm that - but all Luca wanted was the absence of a positive result. At least he acknowledged COVID was still a thing.

After not testing positive, I scurried back into the kitchen to begin my own station prep, anxious to impress. Luca walked me through marinades and seasonings, and the cutting, cooking and plating of our most popular beef and chicken dishes. My head spun as I tried to absorb all the details. This kitchen was more than twice the size of Hickory's and lunchtimes were busy, more dependent on office workers than guests of the towering chain hotel to which it was attached. Even with Tamsyn out, there were nine of us bustling through service, weaving our culinary tapestry. I coped, just. I overcooked a couple steaks, and dropped a tray of lemon-marinated chicken on the floor after a clumsy collision with Alessandra, the sous chef. I delivered my grilled vegetables without flaw, but my mistakes irritated me. Luca shrugged it off, but I wondered if I'd get another opportunity to work meats or anything other than the grill.

I was tempted to make an excuse, and slink home afterwards, instead of meeting Jess at her office, but that wasn't fair. She'd been wanting to show me something there for over a week, and being damn mysterious about it. So I stuck my hands deep into my coat pockets and trudged the four blocks south to where Paragon Insurance's crimson stone national headquarters towered over its neighboring office buildings.

"What's the matter?" Jess said at once, holding me at arm's length after kissing me in greeting. We stood by the visitor's desk in an airy two-story lobby. Rush hour approached, and the first trickle of employees leaving for the day passed us by, as I tried not to slump in dejection.

"Work stuff. I've had better days. How's yours going?"

"Lovely. I spent two hours hunting down an error in my code, only for Conor to glance at it and find a missing equals sign. Wanna come see the scene of the crime?"

I cocked my head. "For real? I mean—"

"It's a metaphor, ya goof," she laughed, dragging me towards the elevator bank. "Although... Well, see for yourself."

As always, when entering a building for the first time, I was on high alert for any disturbing sensations that signified an Imprint: fluctuations in temperature, scents or sounds only I could perceive. Once or twice I thought I detected something, but the feeling vanished as soon as it came. This was the problem with a phenomenon that manifested only in my mind, and those of a few others: there was no obvious way to prove any of it.

We arrived on the seventh floor, where Jess badged us through a glass door and led me into the cube farm that encircled the elevator bank. Rows of chest-height, fabric-covered walls marched either side of us, all the dull silver shade I associated with laptops, printers and other institutional technology. A handful of monitors peeked above their enclosures, their owners using a standing desk. We passed some highly-decorated cubicles, rows of red staplers or plastic figurines scattered over desks, walls lined with travel pictures, and, in one case, a towel with the inscription "Does this smell like chloroform to you?" Most sported no more than a family photograph or an inexplicable technical diagram, and my mood soured again. These were cubicles, not cells, I reminded myself.

"Here we are!" Jess announced.

If you sliced the building in two at the elevators, her cube was bang slap in the middle of the northern half, as far from any windows as you could get. The L-shaped desk supported two monitors, keyboard and mouse, and her black mesh chair boasted enough buttons and levers to control the Starship Enterprise. She'd made more effort than most to brighten the decor, hanging posters of bands or characters from some of the games she played. A selfie of us on last year's Lake Michigan speedboat ride took pride of place above her desk phone. She grinned at my expression. "It's not that bad. And it beats bartending any day of the week!"

"If you say so," I said. "Do they let you out for meals or bathroom breaks?"

"Only if we behave. Otherwise, they come around with bowls of gruel and a chamber pot twice daily."

I laughed despite myself and looked around. I'd seen a couple people immersed in work, but none of the neighboring cubes were occupied. The faint tapping of a keyboard was the only sound I could hear. "Where is everyone?"

"This floor is all IT, so some are working from home. Most of those who came in have left already, trying to beat the worst of the commute. I think Conor's still around somewhere." She scowled, and I suppressed an urge to roll my eyes. I'd heard enough about her arrogant (but, grudgingly admitted, brilliant) boss already to last me a lifetime. "Anyway, this isn't why I brought you up here. Do you sense anything yet?"

I stared at her and lowered my voice. "So that's what you wanted to show me? You think there's an Imprint here?"

"Either that or my nose is ultra-sensitive to bleach, or whatever they clean the bathrooms with, because no-one else can smell it. And..." She grimaced, picked up a sheet of paper with scrawled notes, and set it down again.

"And what?"

"Do you ever hear wind chimes? Just at the edge of hearing, but loud enough to be creepy."

"Can't say I have. No-one else hears them, I assume?"

"None that I know, although I stopped asking after the second funny look. I use the bathroom at the other end of the floor now."

I licked my lips. After the day I'd had, I really wasn't in the mood to deal with an Imprint, if that's what it was. But I couldn't ignore it either. Jess was going through what I'd endured ever since returning to St. Louis after doing my time. She wasn't as sensitive as me, not yet anyway, but this wasn't the first time she'd complained of weird feelings or disturbing sensations as she explored our new home city. The fact that she had some idea what they were only helped so much. No wonder she was so keen to learn how to do what I now could.

"Okay," I said, taking her hand. "Show me."

She smiled her gratitude, then led me through the maze of cubes towards the far end of the floor. The wall to ceiling windows curved around on both sides, but were interrupted by a standalone white wall before they met. Lining the other side of the wall was a refrigerator and a long marble counter, sporting a sink and a half dozen machines for making coffee, tea, kombucha, or whatever drink satisfied an employee's caffeine fix. Opposite the beverage station, a short corridor led to the restrooms, and a third door at the very end I guessed to be a janitor's closet.

It was cold down here. I felt it before we passed the last row of cubes, and the hackles rose on the back of my neck. Goosebumps prickled my skin, and my teeth chattered as the restrooms came into view. If I closed my eyes, I could swear it was snowing, the first exploratory flakes from an oncoming storm kissing my face. I sniffed, but couldn't smell anything unusual, just stale coffee and a hint of something floral, an institutional air freshener perhaps? I half-convinced myself I heard Jess's wind chimes, but so faint I wouldn't have noticed if I hadn't been trying so hard to hear them.

"You feel something too, don't you?" Jess asked as we halted a few steps from the corridor. Her nose wrinkled as she studied my face.

"Oh yeah," I muttered, blinking invisible snowflakes from my eyes. "It's f-freezing."

She frowned. She didn't feel the cold, just like I couldn't smell the bleach. We should take notes on this stuff, but I didn't need notes to remember other occasions when I'd experienced this: a bungalow in which an old woman grieved for her husband, a rooftop on which a pregnant girl contemplated the unthinkable, and a hospital ward where a man wrestled his own grief.

"Jess," I whispered, gritting my teeth to prevent them chattering. "What do you know about this place? Has anyone ever tried to harm themselves here? Worse?"

"No idea. Like I said, no-one else I've talked to notices anything strange. And the company doesn't include that kind of information in the Employee Handbook. Why are you thinking about self-harm?"

"There's a pattern to these sensations. Took me a while to notice. Something sad happened here."

"Look at you using your analytical skills!" She grinned, then licked her lips, twirling her lustrous dark hair around her fingers. "What do we do?"

"What, now?" I looked over my shoulder, but failed to see any signs of life from the cubicles not hidden by the beverage station.

"Why not? You could come back, if you think you can discover any info I haven't been able to. Or if you're not ready."

I frowned at the hint of challenge in her voice, and then I understood. "You want to tackle the Imprint yourself. Jess—"

"I know it's dangerous. Both you and Rosalind have said so. I know. And maybe I can't do it alone, not yet. But I want to try."

I took a deep breath. Inhaled. Exhaled.

I knew Jess. If I refused to help her now, she was likely to try it herself one day. And how much help would more research be anyway? Rosalind would urge caution, would remind me of the perils of attempting an Erasure without anticipating as many of the possible memories as we could. But in Chouteau Village, the old hospital turned condo complex, we'd had to rely on what types of memory were more likely. Was that really different from my suspicion that this Imprint was tied to a memory of extreme sadness or despair?

Assuming I was right.

"Okay, Jess. Here's what I want you to do. I want you to try to find the Catch."

"That focal point you keep talking about?"

"Right. Every Imprint has one, the source for all the weird stuff you're sensing. If you can find and release it, it unblocks the memory."

"That's it? Like picking a lock? That's how you erase them?"

I laughed, without humor. "No, then the hard part begins. When you unblock the memory, it pours into you. You have to channel it away, dissipate its energy. If you can't..." You get stuck in the memory, watching it repeat endlessly. Unless someone else is there to bail you out.

"So how do I find this *Catch* of yours?" she asked, staring at the restroom corridor and clutching a fistful of hair.

I scratched the stubble on my chin. "First of all, relax. Let go of your hair. Breathe. Rosalind told me to listen for the quietest voice in a classroom full of kids, but she always heard far more than I ever did. What's stronger, the smell of bleach or the sound of wind chimes?"

"The smell. Definitely."

"Hmm. Close your eyes. Does it come from somewhere specific?"

Her brow furrowed. "No, it's all around me."

I closed my own eyes and concentrated on the phantom snowflakes swirling around me. There weren't enough for me to see the source yet.

"We need to get closer. Keep your eyes closed, I'll guide you. Concentrate on that scent, try to find a pattern, a point where it's much stronger or weaker. Ready? Here we go."

As we took slow steps towards the corridor, something strange happened. Well, something even stranger than the already strange things happening. As I extended my awareness and probed for the Catch, I sensed something else, something more immediate than the cold, something that blotted out the snowflakes near me. It was alive in a way they weren't, and I was sure it was directed by a will not unlike my own. It felt familiar, and I remembered the unexpected and unknown well of strength that had saved me during our showdown with Donovan and Lana at Chouteau Village. I had thought then that it might be Rosalind, clinging to consciousness as she sprawled on the floor. But what if...?

I reached out as I had that day and tried to connect, to harness this reserve of strength for my own purpose. As I did, Jess gasped and I turned to find her gaping at me.

"What...? Is that you?" she whispered.

"You feel that?"

"Yeah." She closed her eyes again, and so did I. Her will, some projection of her consciousness that occupied the same space as these Imprint phenomena, coiled around mine. I embraced it, yielding to her instinctive tapping of my own strength, even as I honed in on the Catch myself. There were no words exchanged, no thoughts read, but this was unmistakably Jess. Everything I knew about her personality, her passion and curiosity, her temper and vulnerability, had a shape; this shape. I molded myself to her, and she shifted to accommodate me in return, both physically and mentally. It was the most intimate moment of my life, and for several, eon-spanning heartbeats, all I could do was bask in it.

I could smell the bleach now, sharp and nauseating. Wind chimes clanged, and a blizzard of snowflakes stung my flesh. Yet amidst this riot of sensation, it was easy to find the source, a point off to my left where the air was purer, quieter, warmer. I sensed Jess struggling to recognize it, overwhelmed and not a little frightened, but then I felt a stab of excitement.

"I see it!" Her voice was loud and clear, but unnecessary. I knew she saw it. I didn't need words to confirm what I could feel just as clearly.

Push against it, as hard as you can.

No. No, that's not right. It's...

Instead of pushing, instead of directing our combined wills into that twist in the universe and forcing it apart, she tugged, like she was hooking a fish on a line.

And my ears popped, the familiar release of pressure interrupting my surprise. A universe in chaos yielded to a row of sinks below a mirror that stretched to the ceiling. Opposite were a pair of stalls and three urinals: we were inside the men's restroom. Our viewpoint hovered close to the stark fluorescent ceiling lights, so high that we could peer over the tops of the stalls and spy the room's lone occupant. He sat on a closed toilet seat, hunched over, cradling a cell phone, wiping tears from his eyes.

"Mama! I'm coming home tomorrow, mama. Please, hold on!"

His voice was deep and plaintive, his accent and complexion suggesting South Asian origin. We felt his sorrow and desperation as if they were ours. They had been ours, when Jess got the call that her father had suffered a heart attack and was en route to the hospital. Our first instinct was to comfort this poor man, assure him that his mother would—

No. That's not right either.

Disoriented, I remembered there were two of us watching this memory. And Jess, well, this was her show.

"Mama, please!"

I realized I was holding my breath, waiting for Jess to do something. At first, nothing changed, then slowly the light dimmed, the distant son of a dying woman faded, his pleas vanishing into whispers obscured by the ringing in my ears. Darkness came. Breathe! I couldn't breathe! I'd forgotten how to breathe, but I remembered how to panic and—

I was on my hands and knees, gasping for breath, staring at Jess panting before me. Behind her, coffee pots and kombucha taps. Above us, warm office lights. No stench of bleach, no chimes, and certainly no blizzard. Nothing. The Imprint was gone. Erased.

"What?" I croaked. "Jess, what the fuck did you *do*?"

CHAPTER FIVE
A CHANCE MEETING

No matter how we each interacted with Imprints, the after effects were the same: nausea and dehydration. Once we'd caught our breath enough to stand, Jess and I slumped against the office beverage counter, nursing bottles of spring water she'd stashed in the fridge earlier.

"Whoever stole one of my waters better hope I don't find them," she muttered, then coughed again.

I shrugged. I had more important things on my mind. "Could you feel me, my... presence?" I murmured, once I'd forced enough water down so my tongue didn't stick to the roof of my mouth. I was aware of Jess's body next to mine, her alluring curves promising another kind of intimacy. That I could deal with. My mind still reeled from what had just happened.

"I felt something," she said. "I wasn't sure at first. I mean, you were standing right next to me. What was that?"

"I don't know. That doesn't usually happen."

"It never happened with Rosalind?"

"No." Although once, while erasing an Imprint of the memory of an orgy... but no, that hadn't been the same thing at all. "The only time I ever felt anything like that was at Chouteau Village, after Rosalind fought Donovan and they were both unconscious. I didn't know what it was then, but I think I know now."

Jess slipped her hand into mine. "I was so worried. Rosalind was out cold, and you were almost catatonic. Something pulled at me. It was like being drawn into an embrace, but all in my head. I was scared, but it felt... right. Then I saw that kid on the hospital floor, and everything blurred, and I came to huddled next to you, and *you* were out cold and—"

"It's okay." I set my water bottle down, took both of her hands, and turned her to face me. She shuddered, but sank into my arms as her breathing slowed. We hadn't talked much about her first encounter with an Imprint. We'd both been too concerned about Rosalind, and Steven Rourke, and that his associates deliberately imprinted memories on that building and likely others. Discovering Jess's sensitivity was one more surprise, and Rosalind and I had focused on tempering her eagerness as we figured out how to bring her into the fold. I hadn't taken much time to consider how experiencing that first traumatic memory had affected her, alone, everyone who knew anything about it sprawled unconscious around her.

"Why now?" She leaned backward to look me in the eye. "I didn't notice anything like that at the hotel last week, or any of the times we went out with Rosalind in St. Louis before we moved. Did you do anything different?"

I shook my head. "Other than I wasn't really prepared. Maybe... maybe it had something to do with the memory."

Jess's brow furrowed. "Something that connects us, perhaps? I remember feeling something like what we just saw in the ER, that night Dad had his heart attack and I thought I was going to lose him. But, D, when was the last time you talked to your mother?"

"Not since I went inside," I said, and marshaled my emotional defenses against the old wound. My mother had remarried soon after I was born, and while my stepfather wasn't a bad man, he prized his two daughters above his stepson. It hadn't taken long for Mom to follow suit, and the gulf between us widened throughout my childhood. Our last conversation, if it could be dignified with the term, had occurred via telephone handset either side of a glass window. It was a far cry from what we'd just witnessed, a son's tearful plea to his dying mother thousands of miles away.

"Hmm." Jess narrowed her eyes. "Do you think it was how I erased the Imprint?"

"I don't know. We were sharing senses, but I couldn't tell if you used my strength. And you approached it differently. I still don't know what you did there, to channel the memory away. I usually talk them through it, comfort them."

Her frown deepened. "I know you do. But that didn't feel right. I mean, who are you actually talking to? I just thought if the memory had life through me, through us, that we should starve it of attention, starve it of... of—"

"Starve it of air?" I finished for her, remembering my struggle for breath. "That sounds awfully dangerous, Jess."

"I know." She sighed and ran a weary hand through her hair. "I need to think about it. Let's grab my stuff. I can think more clearly at home."

I agreed with that. I wanted my own time to think. We collected our water bottles and rounded the corner of the beverage station wall.

"Oh shit," breathed Jess. "It's Conor."

Standing next to her empty cube, pale blue eyes squinting at his phone with a frown, Jess's boss was of middling height, slim, and rakishly handsome. A tousled mop of ginger hair framed a freckled, light-skinned face, the perfect amount of designer stubble covering his square jaw. A long-sleeved, collarless black shirt hung untucked over dark blue jeans, both accentuating an athletic physique. I guessed he was about thirty, just older than Jess, but a few years younger than me. Once I would have tensed and entered jealous boyfriend mode, but I liked to think I was better than that now.

"Hey, Jess," he said, looking up at last and flashing a winning smile. His eyes flicked towards mine, and the smile might have faltered for the briefest of moments. "You must be D."

"That's me," I said, taking the hand he offered and shaking it. Firm grip. "And you're Conor."

"Guilty. I guess our reputations precede us. Jess giving you a tour?"

His tone was light, but I detected a hint of challenge. I wondered if I betrayed any of the exhaustion I felt from the Erasure. Jess, packing up her laptop in wary silence, looked as immaculate as ever. "Kinda. I don't work tonight, so I thought I'd stop by so we could take the train home together."

"I get that," he said, nodding. "Looking out for each other, good. I've heard a lot about you, glad to finally meet you in person."

I glanced at Jess, who tossed her long black hair and smirked. "What, I'm not allowed to talk about you at work?"

"Didn't think there was much to say. I'll assume at least some of it is true." Conor chuckled and Jess winked, hoisting her bulky black and silver backpack over her shoulders.

"Did you need something before we leave?" she asked him, her voice suggesting he probably wasn't going to get it if he did.

"Nah, just making the rounds before I get out of here myself. Can't leave too early, gotta wait to pick up Esmeralda from gym class. My three year old," he told me with a rueful grin. "Toddler gymnastics. Hard to watch. Kinda farcical to be honest. My wife's idea, but I try to make an effort. Gotta look out for the ones we love."

"Amen to that. Good to meet you, Conor. I imagine we'll run into each other again."

"Count on it! Jess is doing great work, we're glad to have her. She's full of surprises."

As he strode off into the cube farm, I couldn't help but wonder exactly what he meant by that.

I don't often cook anything extravagant at home, but I needed a methodical task to occupy my hands and conscious mind. I decided to make jambalaya using Andouille Sausage and shrimp from the freezer. While I chopped, seasoned, seared, and simmered, I let my subconscious wrestle with what had happened during the Erasure at Paragon. Jess did laundry and cleaned the bathroom, and we avoided conversation until we sat down at our wobbly kitchen table to eat.

"I want to try connecting with you again," she said, chasing a slice of Andouille with her fork. "I want to see if it works when there's not an Imprint involved."

Reluctance battling my curiosity, I agreed. We looked across the table at each other and reached for that connection, willing our minds or perceptions or whatever they were to link. Nothing. We closed our eyes, performed breathing exercises, even stood and practiced *kata* to no avail. Frustrated, we took to bed, our bodies achieving what our minds could not. Yet while our physical intimacy was as intoxicating as ever, we both hungered for more, for the intimacy of spirit.

We both had theories, but had little chance to discuss them. I worked two double-shifts in a row, and while I acquitted myself better subbing on the meats station, my heart wasn't in it. I wanted to find another Imprint and test our newfound ability. But no one called looking for Unusual Solutions to Unusual Problems.

"We'll figure it out," Jess reassured me. "In the meantime, perhaps you can keep your promise to Rosalind."

Ah yes, that. I had to find Daniel Hill.

We had lunch with Jess's maternal grandparents every Sunday. I enjoyed their company, their loving and playful relationship, and their devotion to Jess. I would have much preferred to lounge once again in their small but immaculate home in Oak Park, but, as Jess pointed out, I didn't know how long it might take to catch sight of Rosalind and Martin's estranged son.

"I'll go hang out with the oldies. We can talk about you behind your back," she said with a grin. "They're on your way, so you can drop me off and say Hi. I might even make you a to-go box."

Rosalind had given me an address in Glen Ellyn, twenty miles due west of the Chicago Loop. According to its simple one-page website, the Themis Center billed itself as a private clinic for treating those with addictions to drugs, alcohol, violence, and just about any anti-social condition you could imagine. They offered no credentials or testimonials, simply an email address and a phone number for inquiries. Martin advised us against such contact.

"From what we discovered, they run a full background check before deciding whether to even return your call. They flat out refused our request to speak to Daniel, which was their prerogative, if that was his wish. But we learned that the Center's residents do community work on Sunday afternoons. Cleaning up trails, that sort of thing. We tried to catch a glimpse of him, without success, but that might be a place to start."

I dropped Jess off, waved to Gathii and Atieno, her grandparents, from the car, and headed back to the Eisenhower expressway for what amounted to a stakeout.

There was an awful lot of traffic for early Sunday afternoon. Perhaps the balmy spring day was to blame, bright sunshine shredding the morning cloud cover, a gentle breeze sapping little of its warmth, mocking the previous weekend's blizzard. We'd heard the Eisenhower was always busy. It was the main artery through rundown west Chicago and out into a series of municipalities, which began to look less like suburbs and more like quintessential American small towns that had grown up together and now jostled for space like teenage siblings. I had to cross two north-south interstates before I reached Glen Ellyn, abandoning the Eisenhower for the five lanes of Roosevelt Road. I began to get a sense of how much larger the Chicago metro area was compared to St. Louis. Back home, the road west would have petered out into two lane highways and farmland long before.

According to Gathii, an avid student of his adopted city, Western settlers built their first homes in what would become Glen Ellyn in the 1830s, including a tavern for the stagecoach route between Chicago and western Illinois. A railroad soon followed, and the village grew around the new train station and lake, which residents created by damming a local stream. Soon afterwards, they discovered mineral springs in the area, and visitors from Chicago flocked to this charming health resort. Even now, long since absorbed by the big city's suburban sprawl, Glen Ellyn retained much of the charm and character of that old spa town. I found myself gawking as I drove north up Main Street, missed my turn, and turned around in what had rapidly become a neighborhood of elegant homes, giving Lincoln Park a run for its money.

My destination looked like an old hotel nestled within the cozy downtown area. Its northern facade looked over the railroad tracks at the eastern end of the Metra station. Three stories of dark red brick and a modest, iron fence-wrapped parking lot occupied half the block, shared with a florist and a former restaurant. The paint on the original hotel sign, jutting over the sidewalk, had long faded. The only identification was a letter-sized poster on the inside of the glass-paned double front door. Bland, white on green text proclaimed "Themis Center" along with a phone number and a symbol I couldn't make out from my car as I crawled past.

I parked in the half-empty station lot, and considered my options. Knocking on the front door seemed too direct. I spied a coffee shop on the other side of the tracks, and investigation turned up a seat at a counter running the length of its front window. I ordered a large dark roast, and then, because I was missing Atieno's lunchtime spread, a feta and spinach panini. Basking in the seductive aroma of roasting coffee beans, I settled down to wait.

For over an hour, nothing happened. I stared at the clinic, occasionally glancing at my phone to make it a little less obvious, but no-one entered and no-one left. I counted four cars in the parking lot, but its gate remained closed. According to my phone, the Illinois Prairie Path trail ran in front, parallel to the tracks. It was busy, couples and families grabbing lunch or ice cream—yes, it's above freezing now, let's all eat ice cream—and stretching their legs in the spring sunshine. Several cyclists coasted by, as did a handful of joggers. I felt a pang of guilt: I'd gone out running exactly once since our move. No one gave the Themis Center a second glance. A line formed at the counter behind me, and I'd just started worrying about overstaying my welcome when the Center's front doors opened and a dozen or so people spilled out. They all appeared to be men, but a mix of ages, ethnicities and physiques. All wore neon orange vests over t-shirts or light jackets. A tall, bald, powerfully-built white guy addressed the group, then exchanged a quick word with a shorter, darker-skinned man, before leading the group east down the trail, followed by his shorter companion. There were no physical restraints, but I knew a chain gang when I saw it.

I'd memorized the picture of Daniel Hill that Rosalind had sent me, the picture I'd kept referring to while drinking my coffee, but squint as I might, I couldn't tell if he was one of the group. They were too far away, and the picture was blurry, having run out of pixels as the software zoomed in. I was looking for long dark hair and a scraggly beard, possibly eyeglasses. Rosalind's PI had mentioned something about a limp, and as the men passed from sight behind a fence, I thought I saw one walk with a more halting gait. Was it Daniel? Even if it was, I'd seen nothing worthy of a report. I'd have to follow them.

I discarded my trash, then hurried along the last block of small town retail, looking for a chance to cross the railroad tracks. Once I did so, I caught a flash of orange to my left and slowed down, just another guy out for an afternoon stroll. I mingled with elderly couples and families with strollers, who regarded the cyclists and joggers with mild apprehension. Some regarded me the same way, and I realized I was the only non-white person in sight not wearing an orange vest. The Themis group had split into two about fifty yards ahead and were combing both sides of the trail for litter, each filling their own black trash bag. I shaded my eyes, my sunglasses forgotten back in the car, and tried to pick out Daniel. I needed a closer look.

I walked as slow as I dared, the train tracks to my left, while an auto repair yard, a squat apartment building, then single family homes paraded to my right. I feigned interest in the brick patios and multi-colored plastic jungle gyms visible above simple chain-link or wooden fences, if there were fences at all. People appeared unconcerned about their security around here. I saw other trail users cast curious looks at the cleanup crew, most of whom ignored the attention. It allowed me to do the same as I drew level, and although I dared not check my phone to be sure, I thought I recognized Daniel as he rose up after tugging an empty Doritos bag free from a bush at the end of someone's yard. He stared at the house, a white two-story with a wraparound deck cradling a hot tub, and grimaced before shuffling forward, scanning the ground before him. He looked healthy enough, his limp barely noticeable, but there was some-thing about him that bugged me, something about his posture or empty expression. I stopped and retied my shoe, sneaking glances in his direction, but couldn't put my finger on it. Maybe if I walked up the trail for a bit, then doubled back, I could get another look.

"D? Is that you?"

I froze, then turned toward the tracks. A scrawny white guy, whose dark tan, scruffy beard and sock hat couldn't disguise the tattoos covering his face and neck, crouched not ten feet away. One hand remained inside his black trash bag as he stared at me with an intensity I remembered all too well.

"Train?" I stood up, letting my arms hang loose at my side, my feet shoulder width apart. The last time I'd faced this man unarmed had not been pleasant.

"It is you! Holy shit, D! What are you doing here?"

He stood too and peered up at me. He was much shorter, but that didn't make him any less of a threat. Two nearby orange vests watched us, wary of him, me or both of us. I wondered what they knew about their companion.

"I might ask you the same thing, Train," I murmured. I didn't know if Daniel was watching, but I didn't want to risk the attention. "I'm visiting family. Needed to get out for a walk."

He grinned, but the hard white line of scar tissue on his cheek twisted it into a leer. "Ain't family great? Mine didn't want nothin' to do with me after I got out last time. Got a job with a buddy up here, deliveries and such. Just couldn't lay off the joy juice." His grin morphed into a grimace, then his eyes flickered in alarm just as a large shape loomed in my peripheral vision. I spun, muscles tensing, but it was only the bald headed man who'd led the group from the clinic. He spared me an appraising glance, then imprisoned Train with a smile that didn't reach his eyes.

"Friend of yours, Bryan?" His voice was deep and grating, like two boulders rubbing against each other.

"It's cool, Lyall," Train mumbled. "D's from inside, from last time." I wished he'd stop saying my name.

"Ah. A chance meeting then." As the man, Lyall, turned to me, I noticed a tattoo behind his left ear, a set of uneven scales with what looked like a ball on the lower side. He didn't extend a hand, nor did I offer. "My apologies. Our residents are keen to do their part for the community, but they're each on a larger journey of self-discovery. We're careful about their contact with those from their former lives."

It was my turn to grimace. After twelve years inside, I'd avoided most family and friends after my release. I raised my hands, palms out. "I get it. I'm not trying to interfere or anything. I think we were both shocked to see each other."

"I can imagine." Lyall nodded, looking thoughtful. "But Bryan needs to keep up with his fellow travelers. Plenty of litter to be cleaned up, unfortunately."

Without a word, Train shuffled off in search of more trash. I couldn't think of anything else worth saying, so with a tight nod to Lyall, I rejoined the trail and headed back to my car, wondering if Daniel was watching me.

It only occurred to me later, driving back on Roosevelt Road, that it would have been better cover had I kept walking east instead.

Chapter Six

Hold on, Baby

"So who is this Train guy?" Jess asked, as we drove to IKEA. I wasn't really in the mood to shop for furniture, but I'd promised we'd stop by on our way home.

"He was at Missouri Eastern Correctional."

"You knew him?" Jess's tone was cautious. She knew how much I disliked discussing my twelve years in prison. I'd never sheltered her from those dark memories. How can you hide a third of your life? It was where I'd not only learned to cook, but also to enjoy it. That, and reading as many books as I could from the prison library, was what I'd clung to. The rest? My distrust of strangers and avoidance of crowds stemmed from my jail time. Some things Jess had a right to know, and only she knew them. But she rarely asked me about it anymore, and I certainly never volunteered information. That chapter of my life was over, and I had no desire to turn its pages again.

"Knew of him, mostly. Went by Trainwreck, or Train. Had a bad reputation, even for Eastern. Vicious son of a bitch. It was his second time inside. Aggravated assault against a cop. Alcoholic, I think. Sounds like he still has issues with that."

"He's from Chicago?"

"No, somewhere in downstate Missouri. He worked for some bigshot down there, I don't know who. Don't care either. Train and I had a little tussle one day, and I stayed the fuck away from him after that."

We turned into the IKEA parking lot and cut that conversation short. I texted Rosalind to call me later, then plunged into Scandinavian bliss. Or torment, depending on your point of view.

It wasn't so much the buying of furniture that I dreaded. I amused myself and, I think, Jess by creatively mispronouncing the Swedish names, despite which we acquired a sleek white dresser, a bookcase, and a pair of end tables. But then we had to put it all together. I doubt we'd have had much of a problem were I not still unnerved by my encounter with Train on the trail.

"Why don't these damn things line up?" I grumbled, kneeling amidst the debris of dresser parts, and frowning at two pieces of white-veneered wood that refused to connect.

"I told you, you put that last piece on backwards," Jess said with fraying patience. She sat cross-legged against the wall, brandishing the wordless instruction booklet like that was going to help.

"That's the only way it would fit!"

"No, look, the circular cutout has to go on the bottom, otherwise it's gonna look stupid. Plus, I think you used the wrong screws: Bs instead of Cs."

I bit my tongue. Getting angry at Jess wouldn't help. "What's the difference?"

"About half an inch, from the looks of it."

"Fuck sake. Would it kill them to color code 'em?"

My phone rang as I started to disassemble the backwards part, and I seized the opportunity to take a break. It was Rosalind. "Hi, D! I hope I'm not interrupting anything."

"You are, and bless you for that," I replied, pretending not to see Jess roll her eyes.

"Oh dear. Well, I'm returning your call. Did you...?" She left the question hanging, as if she didn't dare ask.

"I saw him, Daniel. I checked the picture you sent when I got back to my car. I'm certain it was him." I told her about my stakeout of the Themis Center, up to the point I recognized her son. I said nothing about Train or Lyall, the intimidating chaperone.

"And he looked healthy? I suppose happy might be too much to ask." Relief and longing poured through the cell phone connection. I'd rarely heard such raw emotion in Rosalind's voice.

I hesitated, remembering my impression that something was off about Daniel Hill. But it had been fleeting, nothing worth adding to Rosalind's considerable worry. "He still had a bit of a limp," I replied. "I didn't see him long enough to assess his state of mind, and I certainly didn't talk to him."

"That's probably for the best," Rosalind said in something closer to her usual measured tone. "Sounds like the Themis Center frowns on residents interacting with the public."

"Definitely." I remembered Train's alarm when he saw Lyall coming to intercept our conversation. The more I thought about it, the more it weirded me out.

"Well, thank you. A brief sighting of our son may not sound like much, but it means a lot to us. When you have time, we'd love to hear more."

"Of course," I said, trying not to sound awkward. I didn't think I'd get away with another casual encounter on the trail.

"Good. Now, is Jess there? Do you mind if I have a word?"

I passed my phone to Jess, and she offered me the dresser instructions in return. Stifling a sigh, I resumed furniture assembly. Perhaps Rosalind's gratitude settled my mind, but once I corrected my previous mistake, I quickly completed the dresser. I heard Jess talking, but I wasn't paying attention. By the time I tightened the last screw, she was telling Rosalind goodbye.

She stared at my phone for a few seconds, lost in thought, then offered it back to me. "Nice job, hon," she said, examining our new dresser, pulling the draws out one by one. "Obviously, you work better without me hovering over you."

"We both know that's not true," I said, stealing a kiss. "What did Rosalind want?"

"She's run into a wall with the Scales of Equilibrium, the organization behind the Themis Center. She asked me to help."

"Doesn't she have a PI doing that?"

Jess shrugged. "Maybe she just wants more eyes on them. They're as shady as this other lot."

"What other lot?"

"The ones working with Steven Rourke back in St. Louis. The ones imprinting memories. Whoever they are, they're good at covering their tracks." She scowled, pulling open another drawer as if looking for answers inside.

A sudden thought occurred to me. "Do you think they're up here? In Chicago?"

"There are Imprints up here, aren't there?"

"Right, but is every Imprint intentional?"

"I don't know. But if they have a presence in St. Louis, I'd bet they have people up here too. I'm sure we'll run into some eventually."

It was a sobering thought, but I suppressed my paranoia. It wouldn't be a problem unless we were erasing Imprints, and for several weeks we didn't encounter any. Jess spent a few late nights with her laptop and energy drinks, but got grumpy and defensive whenever I asked her about it. So I stopped asking.

Instead, we pieced together more of our new life in Chicago. We explored our neighborhood and celebrated the milder spring temperatures by laboring on our first run for months. We trained twice a week at our new dojo, a hole in the wall on Armitage Avenue. Sensei Ryuichi was Japanese and in his sixties, but I'd learned not to underestimate anyone dedicated to studying martial arts. He'd watched impassively when Jess and I first demonstrated our skills, then recommended we sign up for as many classes as we could manage.

Our downstairs neighbors, the Millers, invited us over for drinks one evening. Jess was far more comfortable than I was. They were both staffers for prosecutors at the Cook County State's Attorney's Office. Jasmine, their cat, did her best to put me at ease, twining around my legs until I sat on the couch, then sitting by my feet and fixing me with an imperious stare.

"She likes you," said Jake with a chuckle. "You must have fed her before." It turned out Jasmine had been born at his parent's old farm to the northwest of Chicago. Jake looked like a farmer, stocky, broad-shouldered with rugged good looks, but there the resemblance ended. "I was the first of my family to go to college. Farm life wasn't for me. My folks were so disappointed they sold up before I'd even finished law school. Another sacrifice to suburban expansion."

Erica, pale and slight but with eyes of steel, turned out to have St. Louis connections. "I grew up in Clayton," she told us. Jess narrowed her eyes, and I could see that classic St. Louis question forming: Where did you go to high school? Erica continued before Jess could ask. "My mom's a criminal defense lawyer with Barrett and Wolf, one of the most prestigious firms in the city. My older brothers are prosecutors in the area too. It's our family business, I guess you could say. I couldn't wait to move to Chicago, to get away. I wanted my own space, to leave all the ghosts of my childhood behind."

I nearly spat out my beer.

We hadn't forgotten about Imprints and Erasures, but it was still something of a shock when I got a phone call on my way to work on the last Friday of March. I'd just stepped off the train, hanging back while my fellow commuters crowded the escalators up to the street. I didn't recognize the caller's number, a 312 area code, and would have passed it off to voice mail, except Jess had urged me not to do that. "You put your number on our business card," she reminded me. "You need to answer your phone."

So I did, with a cautious "Hello?"

"Is this D Rodriguez?"

I had to press my phone against my ear to understand the low, rumbling voice. "It is. How can I help you?"

"Unusual Solutions to Unusual Problems? If that's you, then you might be the only person who *can* help me."

I cupped my hand over my mouth to be heard over the thundering echoes of the departing train. "You know Devin? From the Great Lakes Hotel?"

"Friend of a friend. She told me what they said you did. Is it true?"

"That depends on what they said, Mister...?"

"Smith. Jericho Smith. She said you took care of their ghost problem."

I looked around, but the platform had emptied out. The only person within earshot was an old white man wrapped in a tattered winter coat, slumped with eyes closed against a nearby pillar. I walked toward the escalators just in case. "We don't believe in ghosts, Mr. Smith. We believe there are other explanations for these phenomena." Man, I was starting to sound like Rosalind.

"What explanations?" Jericho's question sounded honest, curious, but I realized I didn't have a good answer. Something to work on.

"Why don't you tell me about your problem?" I countered. "Then we'll see if we can help."

The problem turned out to be unhappy tenants in a three-story apartment building on Austin Boulevard, the north-south street dividing Oak Park from the west side of Chicago. The Austin Community Area to the east was one of Chicago's largest, and had thrived alongside its suburban neighbor until after World War II. Then, as elsewhere in the city and nation, racial steering triggered white flight into the suburbs. For a while, middle class black Americans thrived in the neighborhood, but as money left and drug-related gang violence grew, many of them left too. Businesses closed, services deteriorated, hospitals shut down. The Chicago Transit Authority even closed the L station on Central Avenue; its skeletal island platform still stood amidst the Eisenhower expressway, a bleak reminder of past prosperity.

Oak Park, famous for the architectural influences of onetime resident Frank Lloyd Wright, resisted the policies responsible for rapid racial change. Even now, the village discouraged the display of "For Sale" signs for houses within its borders. White Americans, their businesses and their money, stayed. The village's evolution towards more ethnic diversity was more gradual and harmonious than Austin. Jess's grandparents had moved to their modest but immaculate two-story home in 2002, and loved it. Gathii claimed it was on the same block as Ernest Hemingway's childhood home, and it was only minutes away from the Frank Lloyd Wright Home and Studio. He took me there at the first opportunity, although Jess begged off, claiming she'd seen it "dozens of times before."

1017 North Austin was no such architectural marvel. Three stories of light brick squatted a few steps back from the sidewalk behind a lifeless stone courtyard, each floor presenting a pair of dark sash windows to the street. We'd found no specific records for the building, but guessed it dated to the early twentieth century and had always been a multi-family dwelling. A bank of six steel mailboxes nestled against the robust front door, its glass covered with security company decals. Uninspiring, but it looked in good condition, no chipped paint or rotted wood in sight.

Jericho Smith, an enormous black man who looked like he'd just retired from the NFL as an offensive lineman, met us out front on a bright, frosty Sunday morning. Gold gleamed from his ear lobes and awkward smile, and flashed from the hand he extracted from his calf-length winter coat. We shook, and after a moment's hesitation, so did he and Jess.

"You folks find a place to park okay?" he asked, glancing behind us as if searching for our car. His deep voice had a hitch, as if someone had taken a sheet of sandpaper to his larynx.

"Actually, we took the L," I told him. "Green Line to Austin. Not a bad walk from there."

"Really? Too cold for me. And not everyone likes that walk." Jericho scrutinized us through narrowed eyes, likely making guesses about our backgrounds. I hadn't felt any less comfortable during our fifteen minute walk from the station than in Lincoln Park. The faces of the people we'd passed were black instead of mostly white, but they'd regarded us with the same polite disinterest, if they'd acknowledged us at all. Jess's complexion was darker than mine: her maternal grandparents emigrated from Kenya, although James Evans's ancestors had brought their mining expertise to Pennsylvania from Wales in the early nineteenth century, and his wife descended from several generations of German farmers who'd settled in northern Illinois. My mother's family had been stalwarts of the American Irish community in St. Louis ever since there'd been one, but my father was Cuban and, well, that was all I knew. All I'd ever received from him was my complexion, plus my middle and last names. Both Jess and I were used to not quite fitting in anywhere, and any undercurrent of racial tension that might exist in this borderland between rundown Chicago and its well-to-do suburban neighbor was little different from our daily experience.

"It's fine," I said, and gestured towards the apartment building. "Are the tenants home?"

"Shouldn't be. I told them pest control was coming to fumigate. Brought some nasty-smelling shit with me." He grinned as he prodded the black duffel bag at his feet. "I'll save that for after you do whatever it is you do."

I returned the grin and hoped our own landlord was less deceptive. Jess caught my eye and raised an eyebrow. I took the hint and composed myself. "Why don't we go inside, see what we're dealing with?"

He nodded and led us to the front door, his duffel bag clanking as he lifted it. A movement in my peripheral vision made me look up, and I glimpsed a pale face observing us through one of the second floor windows, vanishing immediately. Clearly, not everyone had bought Jericho's pest control line; I hoped he didn't poison whoever it was. I considered saying something, but then we crossed the threshold into a dimly lit lobby. A dark wooden staircase stretched upwards on one side, and a short corridor led to the ground floor apartments on the other. The floor tiles and the painted walls and ceiling were uniform bone white, and sepia-toned framed photographs of old Chicago adorned the walls. If Jericho was going for a creepy, haunted house vibe, he was well on track.

And it didn't need it. Before the front door closed behind us, the chill in the air changed character. I could feel warmth pour from the vents by our feet, hear the dull growl of the basement furnace battling the latest cold snap. The chill I felt now was different, as if something invisible reached for me, probed beneath my coat, prickled my skin. I hugged myself, rubbing my arms to no effect. There was a sour taste to the air, and I imagined myself licking blood from a wound.

"What do you think?" I asked Jess. Her face twisted in revulsion, nostrils flaring as she pointed upstairs. I agreed, although I could only smell a slight mustiness. The Imprint was above us, and I thought I could guess the kind of memory we were dealing with. I turned towards Jericho, who watched us curiously. "How long have you owned the place?"

"Six years. Never had no problems 'til last year. Three tenants moved out, complained about drafts and weird smells and shit. I can't feel or smell a thing. But it looks like you do."

I nodded. "Yeah. We need to go up."

"Probably to the top floor. Those units were the ones folks left."

We crept upwards, Jess and I side by side, and Jericho following. Stairs creaked in protest at our combined weight, or maybe just for atmospheric effect. Wraith-like tendrils of cold air tugged at me. Jess cupped an ear and paused as we reached the second floor, and I realized I could hear something too: someone yelling or screaming in the distance. In other circumstances, I might have suspected one of the tenants was watching a horror or disaster movie, but I'd encountered sensations like these before. I wasn't looking forward to dealing with them again.

"Jesus, this is rank," muttered Jess as we finished our climb to the third floor landing. She cast a disgusted look at the chocolate brown door to apartment 302 and shook her head as if trying to ward off a buzzing insect. "Can't you guys smell that?"

"What do you smell?" I said, fighting down a wave of nausea at the bitter taste of iron cloying my mouth. Jericho hung back several steps below the landing, watching us with a mix of curiosity and alarm. I couldn't blame him.

"It's like the inside of the boys locker room right after a high school football game. Only ten times worse. I can't get it out of my nose."

I almost asked what she'd been doing in that boys locker room, but fought off the distraction. And I didn't want to voice the fact that I could taste blood and lots of it, not with Jericho in earshot. "You hear something too, don't you?"

"Yeah. Yelling, lots of yelling, but I can't make out any words." She laid a hand on my arm and looked at me with wide eyes. "This is more than I've ever sensed before. Far more. Am I just getting better or... or is this a really bad one?"

"I don't know," I said, covering her hand with mine, trying to project a calm I didn't feel. If I was right, then the last time I'd tried to deal with a memory like this, I'd almost lost myself in it. "Jericho," I called over my shoulder, eyes not leaving Jess's, "are you sure you don't know of any violent events in this building's past?"

"No, but that don't mean there weren't any. The big gangs never really got out this far, but bad shit goes down every-where."

I took a deep breath, watched Jess do the same, then she gently disengaged from my hand and straightened her back, resolute. "Can we deal with it out here, like last time? Or do we need to go inside?"

Good question. I slowed my breathing still further, closed my eyes, and searched for the source of it all. The Catch was definitely in apartment 302, but I couldn't pinpoint it. Part of me didn't want to, I knew, scared of what I would find once I released the memory. Jericho's mention of gangs reminded me of my past trauma. But I needed to face those demons sometime, and it might as well be now.

"I think we need to go in," I said. "Unless you've found the Catch." She shook her head. I turned, but Jericho was already climbing the stairs and fumbling through a chunky ring of keys. Without a word, he unlocked the door, then stepped aside.

In its heyday, the spacious apartment might have been elegant and well-appointed. Tall ceilings and wide doorways filled the rooms with late winter sunlight, but the crown molding was chipped, the hardwood floors scratched, and the sparse furnish-ings shabby. I didn't absorb any more detail, because within a few steps of the doorway I gagged on phantom blood, and the screaming in my ears rose to a deafening pitch. Jess stumbled into me, and after I propped her up, we both gazed at the living room's bay window, shrouded by crimson drapes admitting a single shaft of sunlight to slice the dust-heavy air.

"It's there, somewhere," Jess muttered thickly, then coughed and dug her fingers into my arm.

"Yeah," I agreed. "Breathe, Jess. Reach toward it, whatever you sense. Let's see if we can find each other again."

We hadn't tried since the last Erasure, and I prepared for dis-appointment if we couldn't connect, but there she was. As soon as I embraced the Imprint, I felt her spirit, her will, reaching for the Catch and then for me. We met and danced, wrapped in each others' emotions: joy and relief, but also revulsion and fear. After what seemed an age, we remembered we had a job to do, and searched for the Catch. We found it in front of the window, an infinitesimal speaker blaring out screams of horror and anguish.

"Me or you?" I whispered.

"You."

I focused our attention on that almost invisible point and pushed.

And was blocked.

It was like walking through a doorway and face-planting into glass. I recoiled, and Jess grunted. We stared, stunned, at where we knew the Catch must be. Something was in the way.

What the hell?

I reached out more cautiously this time. Nothing was different from every other Erasure I'd been part of until I tried to apply pressure against the Catch. The barrier wasn't cold and rigid like glass, but yielded and shifted slightly as I probed from multiple angles. Jess tried her technique, hooking the Catch instead of pushing it, with no better luck. I remembered the last Imprint I'd faced at Chouteau Village, the one with two Catches: was this just another variation used by the people creating these things? If so, why? More importantly, how could we deal with it? I felt sure we needed a sophisticated approach, that we should retreat and regroup, tell Jericho we'd return later with a better plan. But I was irritated. It was bad enough to expect the memory's release to be all I could handle. I didn't want to work extra hard to get at the damn thing. So I gathered all of Jess's strength along with my own, our bodies trembling as if pumped full of adrenaline.

"Hold on, baby," I rasped, and threw it all against the barrier.

There was a moment in every Erasure, as the Catch disintegrated, where the pressure changed, my ears popped, and everything sounded weird for a while. This was an explosion, an instant where the void sucked us forward, followed by a wall of sound whipping across us. We staggered backwards, our feet tangling, and I flailed for the door frame to stop us tumbling to the floor. Our foreheads met as we clutched each other, regaining balance. Jess's eyes were wide with shock. Her lips moved, but I couldn't hear anything over the ringing in my ears. Her spirit coiled around mine in a defensive posture, though who was defending who I couldn't tell.

Seconds passed, maybe minutes, before I could think clearly again. The ringing faded until I could just make out Jericho's dull rumble behind me, his words indistinct. I held Jess at arm's length and raised my eyebrows in inquiry. She nodded once, and we turned back towards the bay windows.

Somehow, the Catch was still there. This surprised me less than when I realized I wasn't using sound to pinpoint it; the screams were no more than a distant buzz. The rank stench of stale sweat poured at me from the same place. The gag-inducing metallic taste was sharpest when I focused in that direction, and I just wanted this to be over. Marshaling our forces again, I pushed and the Catch gave.

Night fell. Thinner drapes failed to cover the windows, but Austin Boulevard's streetlights appeared reluctant to penetrate the room. I couldn't blame them. A black man in a red Chicago Bulls jacket sagged on the only chair, illuminated by a shadeless floor lamp. Bruises and blood covered his face, and his wrists were tied behind his back. He was young, maybe still in high school, and he was terrified. Arrayed in a semi-circle before him stood three older men. The two on either side could have been twins, both bald and thickset, one wearing a gold jacket, the other a black vest showing off an upper body rippling with muscle. Muscle he'd just used, as he nursed the knuckles on his right hand. The man in the center was taller, leaner, short hair braided in cornrows, an immaculate beard framing a handsome face. His eyes glittered with malevolence as he brandished a roll of twenty dollar bills in one hand and a clear plastic bag of white powder in the other. I couldn't hear him speak, but I understood the gist: "You stole from me, and now you're going to pay." Suddenly, without me seeing how, the drugs and money vanished, replaced by a wicked-looking switchblade knife.

"No!" gasped Jess, fingernails digging into my arm. Shock, fury, and fear flooded our connection. Had I not prepared myself for this kind of memory, it would have shocked me too. I exhaled slowly, trying to reassure her, but also myself. I wanted this one, to prove I could handle it, but I held back, nursing our strength. Jess squeezed my hand, and that was all I needed.

No, I told the man with the knife, or his memory. *Leave him be. You've made your point.*

"You stole from me." I saw his lips frame the words as he advanced, one of the thugs seizing their captive by the shoulders. The youngster thrashed, kicking out in vain, and the thug clubbed him savagely around the head. The bearded man grabbed him by his shirt and pressed the knife to the skin of his throat, teeth bared.

He's just a kid! I fought a rising desperation, recalling another ruthless drug kingpin I'd once worked for. *You don't know why he did it, if he did. You don't know who depends on him, who he'd leave behind. He's just a kid.*

The bearded man licked his lips and turned the blade flat. His captive stared back, unfocused, still stunned from that last blow to his head.

We all held our breath.

Don't you have family too?

A spasm of disgust twisted the bearded man's face, and he flung the youngster away. Pocketing the knife, he strode from the room without a backwards glance. Then the light fractured, everything dissolved with a dull roar, and Jess and I collapsed in a heap on the present day floor.

Excerpt of email recovered from closed account, owner untraceable. Destination account also closed and untraceable.

From: (address withheld)
To: (address withheld)
Subject: Chicago 2024-04 #1
Sent: 2024-04-02 17:09:22 UTC

…no further ill effects and recommended she rest from her duties for at least two weeks.

I doubt Fisher will listen. She has all the fearlessness and, frankly, foolhardiness of the young. Listen to me, I sound like an old man! But I seem to spend as much time monitoring her as I do the cook and his girlfriend. As far as I can tell, they emerged unscathed from the entire episode. They left the apartment building under their own power, and sufficiently impressed the apartment building owner that he's telling everyone he knows. We're picking up an increase in chatter about their abilities, discreet thus far, although that could change in a heartbeat. Faustyn is alarmed, and I believe he has reached out to you. Penny for your thoughts?

Of course, if we can get the Shields to work, this may all be a moot point…

CHAPTER SEVEN

NOT JUST PYTHON AND PERL

Jess was unusually quiet all the way home.

At first, I put it down to fatigue. I was bone-tired, more than I remembered being after any previous Erasure. We'd taken several minutes to sit upright, let alone stand, and I could barely summon the energy to assure Jericho that, no, he didn't need to call 911. We drank water and waited for life to trickle back into our limbs. We hadn't eaten that morning in an attempt to minimize any mess. That likely contributed to the relentless throbbing pain in my temples, and her muttered curses suggested Jess struggled likewise.

Jericho refilled our water bottles and offered to drive us home. I twice caught him looking at us and shaking his head, as if in disbelief. When I finally struggled to my feet, clutching the door frame for support, he barked out a laugh and told me our performance rivaled that of any faith-healing preacher, speaking in tongues. "Or," he said softly, after I grimaced in response, "this could be real after all. Shit, man."

Shit, indeed.

Jess heaved herself upright seconds later, and rested one hand on my back while we gingerly descended the stairs. The movement appeared to help, and she disengaged after we emerged into the cool light of day, wafted by a stiff breeze carrying hints of burning diesel. "Let's take the bus," she whispered, pretty much the only words she spoke until we shuffled into our apartment and collapsed onto the couch. We'd contemplated recovering at our usual Sunday lunch venue, but Jess didn't want her grandparents to see us like this. So while she dozed, I threw another frozen pizza into the oven and debated whether I had time for a shower before heading to work.

"Has that ever happened before?"

Her sudden question startled me out of my oven timer-watching reverie. "Not to me. And Rosalind's never mentioned anything like that."

"It makes you wonder..." Jess drifted back into her own thoughts, then locked eyes with me. "What did you do, exactly? It felt like you just took all our strength and threw it at the wall."

"That's more or less accurate," I said, trying not to sound defensive. It had worked, hadn't it?

She frowned. "That was risky. We don't know what that blockage was. What if it had reflected back on us? You can't just use brute force and hope for the best."

The piercing tones of the oven timer interrupted me before I could snap in response. I rescued the pizza, carved off a pair of slices, and brought plates back to the couch.

"There's no manual for this," I said, my tone calmer than I felt. "We have one mentor who admits she doesn't know all the answers. We have to adapt on the fly."

"I understand that," she said, eyeing her pizza dubiously before taking a bite.

"I made a call. Was it the right thing to do? It cleared the blockage, allowed us to erase the Imprint. But I hear you. We need to think of other ways to tackle it, should it happen again."

Her hand reached out and cupped my cheek. It sent tiny electric shocks down my spine.

"At least you did something," she murmured, caressing me briefly before turning back to her pizza. "And I knew you'd want that memory. I know how hard that was for you. That poor kid! Do you think they...?"

"I don't know," I said, after her question hung in the air, raw and unfinished, for several heartbeats. "We might be able to find out if we can find the right records. I hope not. Did you see the bearded guy walk away?"

She shook her head, brow furrowed. "The scene faded in and out. I saw his knife. And I saw the other guy hit the kid. Fucking bully!" She picked the pepperoni off her remaining slice, then set her plate on the end table. "How has Rosalind done this for so long? What has she seen and what has it done to her? What price will we have to pay?"

"What do you mean?"

"I mean, I don't think we can just binge on water and pop ibuprofen and count ourselves recovered. This has a mental toll too. We don't know anything about the true risks, and it bothers me.

"You know me, I believe I can do anything if I put my mind to it. Not the things others want me to do, but what *I* want to do. Sixty percent of Shift_Dev students burn out, did you know that? I made it. I was determined to make it, to get a better job doing something I enjoyed, and I did that. I wanted to find someone I could spend the rest of my life with, someone I truly loved and respected, and I did that."

I froze, the last bite of pizza forgotten an inch from my open mouth.

She continued without acknowledgment. "When I saw that other kid on the floor at Chouteau Village, when I first experienced these visions that you and Rosalind experienced, I wanted to do what you guys did. I wanted to do it as well, if not better than you. How fucking cool would that be? All my life, I've been reading books and playing games where characters have magical abilities, escaping the boring, frustrating normal world, dreaming of wielding some arcane power to do good. To save the day. And this was it, finally, my dreams were coming true!"

Moment by moment, heartbeat by heartbeat, she returned to herself, and looked me in the eye. "But all magic has a cost. And we don't know what that is yet. Don't you think we should find out?"

The thought occurred to us often over the following weeks, as spring dislodged winter's grip on Chicago.

Business was booming. Any doubts I'd had about starting and sustaining an Erasure side hustle were dispelled as soon as we met Jericho Smith. Assured by his tenants that the strange phenomena had disappeared, he'd appointed himself as our de facto marketing department. With a discreet word here, and gentle encouragement there, Unusual Solutions to Unusual Problems discovered a base of customers ready and hungry for our services. "This is cool, man!" Jericho chortled one night when I returned his call during break. "Folks are lapping this up!"

I was conflicted. I appreciated his help and enthusiasm, but I didn't want to become a carnival act. Nor did I want our side hustle to cause trouble with our day jobs. I took my responsibilities at Trattoria Capelli seriously. Chef Luca demanded punctuality and perfection, and I was determined to give him that. Jess was even more ambitious. When she wasn't bringing work home with her, she'd experiment with new programming languages on her personal laptop, nestled against me on our couch while I watched the baseball game. I found the language names amusing - JavaScript, Python, Perl, Go - and half-suspected her of making them up.

The extra income from Erasures was welcome, however. For one thing, there were karate lessons to pay for. More Erasures meant more mental and physical stress, and we didn't need Rosalind to explain how study and practice of the martial arts could help. We loved our new dojo: the classes were smaller, the students more serious, but the camaraderie far outstripped Gateway to the West back in St. Louis. Our progress was better for it. How much of that was due to the absence of a certain ex-college buddy and his attentive girlfriend, I couldn't say.

We were busy and constantly tired, but life was pretty good almost four months after moving three hundred miles to a whole new city. I missed Hickory, and weekly phone calls did little to make up for Rosalind's in-person tutelage and our developing friendship. She promised to visit once school was out for the summer, and I made a mental note to seek out Daniel again. If the Erasures were going smoothly, I would've been happy enough.

But they weren't.

We'd tackled Imprints at private homes, a florist, a car dealership, a dental clinic and a high school. Sometimes everything went well, according to what we now associated with routine. We'd identify candidate memories through research, narrow them down onsite based on specific sensations encountered, locate the Catch, and release the memory using either Jess's technique or mine. More and more, however, a mysterious barrier blocked our access to the Catch. Each time it was stiffer, more resilient, harder to penetrate. When we could establish our intimate and powerful mental connection, when we wielded our combined strength, we could break through, but only via brute force. We'd found no way around the barrier, or another technique to defeat it. The more force we used, the more we hurt afterwards. We'd both had to call in sick after our last success, and that couldn't continue.

And we couldn't always establish our connection. Jess thought it might be related to the nature or strength of the Imprints, but what came so easily most of the time had failed us utterly twice. Alone, neither of us could deal with the barrier. Our failures had been galling and embarrassing. I became convinced we were being targeted, that whoever imprinted these memories was aware of our activities and was deliberately trying to thwart us. Who they were I didn't know, but Jess muttered darkly about "those shady bastards" whenever I brought it up.

As I steeled myself for another weekend of back-to-back Erasures, Jess threw me a curve ball. "Conor's invited the team to his house tomorrow night for a party," she told me as we walked home from the dojo. "Spouses and partners welcome. You still have Friday night off, right?"

"I do." I'd hoped to relax, maybe review our Erasure research, maybe watch a movie. Socializing was the last thing on my mind. "And you want to go?"

"The timing isn't great," she conceded, squeezing my arm. "We don't have to stay long, but I should make an appearance. And I'd rather you come with me."

I tried not to drag my feet on the sidewalk. This was important to her, and it really wasn't much to ask. "I'll come," I promised.

Conor McKee and his wife owned a two story brick townhouse in Wrigleyville, a few blocks west of the Chicago Cubs baseball stadium. The Cubs were in town, fresh from splitting a four game series in St. Louis, and I tried not to grind my teeth as we pushed through the swarm of blue-clad fans, clogging the train and spilling out of Clark Street's bars and restaurants. I skipped wearing my Cardinals ball cap, but I half-expected someone to out me as a fan of the Cubs' arch rivals. I wasn't in the mood for jeering, however good-natured, and was happier than ever to leave the heart of the crowd behind as we slipped down a narrow side street. Remnants of an early afternoon shower glistened on the flowering bushes decorating tiny front yards, and shafts of warm evening sun fought through the towering trees that marched down either side of the road. Wafts of grilling meat and bursts of laughter surrounded us, as friends and families celebrated the end of another work week, congregating on patios and balconies. I wanted to be back in my own apartment. I was on edge, although I couldn't have said why.

"Jess! Come on in!" Conor cried, beer bottle in one hand as he beckoned us inside with the other. "D, right? Good to see you again. Welcome to our humble abode."

It didn't look that humble to me. Gleaming white walls were sprinkled with dozens of framed family photographs, mostly Conor with his wife and daughter, in some pictures a baby, in others a toothily-grinning toddler with a wild mop of ginger hair. A white plastic gate protected the bottom of a straight staircase upwards, while to our right a double doorway opened onto an immaculate living room that looked like it'd been transplanted from an IKEA showroom. It was standing room only, and although a few people called out to Jess, she just waved back and led me into the kitchen. Bright, airy, heavy with Scandinavian influence, surfaces cluttered with snacks and appetizers, it was still too stuffy for me, and I eyed the door onto their back patio.

"Help yourself," said Conor, gesturing at the spread as Jess slid a tray of toasted ravioli into a free spot on the kitchen island. "Beers are in the coolers, or soft drinks in the fridge if you prefer. Most of the team is here, even Marcus."

"Dear God," muttered Jess, and Conor grinned.

"I'll catch up later," he said, glancing at me. He looked like he wanted to say something else, but changed his mind. "Michelle's outside, with Esmeralda. I'm sure she'd like to meet you both."

I let Jess fill a plate while I dug a wheat beer for her out of a massive gray cooler not quite tucked into a corner. I chose a bottle of water for myself - I drank beer for comfort, and I wasn't comfortable - and escaped onto the patio. The backyard was deep but narrow, framed by walls of brown brick. A massive oak tree guarded one far corner, shadowing an elaborate wooden playground set. I could only glimpse children through the line of adults encircling the playground, drinks and plates in hand, but I could hear the squeals of delight well enough. An unused fire pit squatted in the center of the patio's dark gray flagstones, and a glass top wicker dining table stood nearby. A middle-aged white guy with a ZZ Top beard sat backwards on a chair at one end, cradling a beer bottle and watching the scene expressionlessly. Despite the day's warmth, he wore jeans and a navy blue hoodie, the slogan on its front obscured by the chair.

"Which one's Michelle?" asked Jess, ghosting alongside me in trademark fashion.

"No idea," I said, exchanging her beer for the food plate and counting heads. "I'd say we have a one in three chance."

"Jess?"

She stiffened, then turned to face the man at the table. "Hey, Marcus," she said in a voice capable of juggling explosives.

"Come to pay homage to Princess Esmeralda? Take a number." Marcus gestured toward the playground set with his bottle, then took a swig and grinned. "Who's this character, then? Your honor guard?"

"This is my boyfriend," Jess said, laying a fleeting hand on my arm. "D, this is Marcus. Been on Conor's team for a couple years. Best coder I know."

"Ah, you're young," chuckled Marcus, although he straightened up in his chair. He seemed friendly enough, but his eyes danced around and didn't quite meet mine. "And what do you do for a living, D? I don't really care, but I'm told it's the polite thing to ask in these awkward social situations."

"I'm a cook," I said, somewhat taken aback. I didn't elaborate, since there seemed little point.

"Ah," Marcus acknowledged with the slightest of shrugs, then scratched his upper arm absently. The ensuing silence had just become uncomfortable when it was rent by a banshee's shriek.

"Jessie, Jessie, Jessie!"

A whirling dervish of ginger hair in a pale blue dress erupted from the crowd in the garden and hurled itself at Jess's legs. She staggered, spraying beer over my neck and chest as she flung out her arms to regain balance. "Whoa there, demon child!" Jess laughed, sinking to her knees and hugging the excited toddler, who I guessed was Conor's daughter.

"I take it you've met," I said, dabbing at my neck with a patch of T-shirt that wasn't already soaked.

"Oh yes. Conor brought Esmeralda into the office last week, and I made the grave mistake of giving her candy. We're fast friends." Jess smiled indulgently as Esmerelda bounced on her toes. The kid had more energy than the rest of the party combined.

"Swing me, Jessie!" she begged, tugging at Jess's arm. "Please!"

"Very well," Jess said, standing up with an exaggerated sigh and allowing herself to be led away. The ring of adults parted to allow passage. A slim woman with short blond hair, who I recognized as Conor's wife, mouthed an apology, and I smiled back.

"Little rugrats rule the world," declared Marcus with a hint of a sneer. "At least while there's still a world for them to rule. Won't be much left by the time she can do anything about it." He lifted his chin in challenge.

"Seems like we're doing better than we were." I knew better than to take the bait, but my limited small talk vocabulary left me few options.

He barked humorless laughter, swiveling to face me. "What planet do you live on? The one we plunder with impunity, because of greed or some holy mandate, and claim will just heal itself? Every day we bring hundreds of thousands more people into the world and expect to sustain them. We talk about going green and make trivial concessions to the rape of the land, the pollution of our oceans. Nah, things are getting worse, not better."

Jess's laughter floated over the patio, and I wished I could take a turn pushing Esmerelda's swing. Marcus's attitude irked me.

As much as I thought about such things, I didn't disagree with him, but I found myself unwilling to let him believe he'd scored a point.

"I heard they made real progress at the last climate summit. Committed to more emission reductions, even got China and India onboard. I know Russia's a loose cannon, but--"

"Ah, don't be naive. It doesn't matter what nations do. They're not the ones running the show."

Don't ask him. You don't have to ask him.

"Who is, then?" *Dammit, D.*

"Well that's the question, isn't it?" His eyes sparkled, the showman finding his mark. "Forget about the Illuminati, the Templars, Q, and all that crap. Forget about the church, or whatever religions indoctrinate the masses. Forget about the media, they just parrot what they're told. They're all just fronts, diversions. You have to go deeper to find the truth."

I forced myself to take a long drink of water, and almost choked. If this was what I could expect from Jess's work parties, I would beg off next time.

Marcus glanced around and lowered his voice, so that I strained to hear him even if I didn't want to. "Ask yourself who benefits from those climate summit decisions. Ask yourself who stalls reforms. Ask yourself who allowed the Industrial Revolution to grow unchecked the last few centuries."

I searched in vain for Jess. I thought I glimpsed Conor watching me through his kitchen window, but when I turned he was talking to someone I couldn't see.

"Uncomfortable, isn't it?" Marcus asked with a mirthless smile. "Ah, I'm no better. Look at what I do for a living: churn out code for some dispassionate insurance company in the heart of a lifeless city. For all I know, they're part of it. Of course, that's not all I do. There are ways of fighting back—"

"D!" cried Conor, appearing at my elbow and startling me. Jess must have told him how much I hated that. "I see you've met our resident Python and Perl savant. Just beware of his anecdotes."

A look passed between the two men, something different from a manager/employee vibe. Marcus licked his lips, then shrugged. "Not just Python and Perl," he muttered, then turned around in his chair and paid me no further attention. I'd been dismissed, and even though I didn't want to talk to him, that irritated me.

"No, not just Python and Perl," Conor said, frowning. Then he looked up, catching the same movement I did. Jess strode toward me, her smile full of mischief, clutching Esmeralda's hand in one of hers.

"Princess Esmeralda requests the honor of having her swing pushed by my valiant knight in shining armor," she announced. "That would be you, D."

"Lead on," I said.

Chapter Eight

THIS WON'T WAIT UNTIL MORNING

The Erasure on Saturday morning - a suicide attempt via drug overdose in the alley behind a Near North sports bar - went well. The Erasure the following morning did not.

Perhaps we were still tired from the first one, but we had trouble connecting. Jess's presence flickered in and out as my mind reached for her. Without that, the barrier between us and the Catch might just as well have been the steel door to a bank vault. Jess speculated, not without amusement, that I was uncomfortable in a "house of ill repute", but the establishment was closed at the time. Besides, I was no prude, even if I'd never visited such a place myself. Its owner, a dark-haired woman with heavy makeup and an Eastern European lilt, took our failure in stride.

"Perhaps our problem is too unusual even for you," she said as she showed us out. I gritted my teeth as I politely acknowledged the possibility. The silver lining was that avoiding the strain of another Erasure might prevent more screw-ups at work: my nostrils still hadn't banished the scent of burned asparagus from the night before.

Hoping to achieve something that day, I sent Jess to her grandparents with my apologies and headed to the Themis Center for another stakeout. I texted Rosalind to let her know, but I was swirling the dregs of my caramel frappuccino before she replied.

'Grading. Might have something for you later.'

Whatever "later" meant, it was after I packed up and left without seeing any signs of life from the clinic. Jess drove me to work, and stopped trying to cheer me up long before we got there.

I recovered my mojo during Sunday's dinner service, and so was in better spirits when I read Rosalind's reply after collecting my phone from the break room.

'Selene's Books. Tuesday 7pm.'

I scratched my head. *'What about it?'* I texted back.

'Not sure' came the reply, several minutes later.

"It's a New Age bookstore in the West Loop," Jess told me within thirty seconds of me relaying this exchange after I got home. She brandished her phone as evidence of her search result.

It still wasn't second nature to me to use mine for that purpose. "New Age, huh? Wasn't that what the scale people were about?"

She giggled. "Scales of Equilibrium. They're not reptiles, love."

I waved her off. "So what's happening there at seven this Tuesday night?"

She frowned in concentration, tapping and swiping silently for a while before tossing her phone onto the end table in disgust. "No idea. Their website is barebones, not even mobile-friendly. Pretty shoddy for selling anything in this day and age. Maybe I can offer my services as a freelancer when we go there."

"When we go there?"

"Sure. I think we should go. I haven't discovered much about 'the scale people', and Rosalind obviously thinks it's important. Although, it would be lovely if she'd elaborate."

I agreed, but no elaboration or further contact of any kind was forthcoming before Tuesday evening. I texted a couple times and called once, without response. I considered contacting Martin, then decided I was being paranoid. Rosalind could look after herself. She was probably just busy preparing her high school girls for their end of year exams.

The West Loop was close enough to Paragon Insurance that we decided to walk to the bookstore after work. We were missing karate, so the exercise was partial compensation. We followed Madison Street west, over the Chicago River and under the freeway, into a former manufacturing neighborhood. Not unlike Washington Avenue back in St. Louis, gentrification had transformed aging, disused warehouses into upscale condos and boutiques, sprinkled generously with trendy bars and eateries. I picked up an edgier vibe than Lincoln Park; the north-south cross streets faded into uncertain darkness as we headed west. Young families with strollers were already packing up and heading home, leaving a handful of dog walkers and bored young professionals to keep us company. I was second-guessing our decision, and resolving to call a Lyft for the ride home, when we arrived at Selene's Books.

I didn't know how long the bookstore had been in business, but it looked like they'd taken over the lease from a very different kind of store, and hadn't had time or inclination to redecorate. The faded pastel decor and sparse aluminum and glass fixtures reminded me more of soaps and perfumes, although to be fair, books comprised barely half the merchandise. Crystals, tarot decks, and a bewildering selection of incense dominated the space, or at least the half that hadn't been shoved aside by rows of plastic folding chairs. These faced an ornate wooden lectern whose front had been engraved with stylized vines and flowers: it looked as valuable as everything else in the store put together. We arrived a few minutes early, but either the audience was hanging back until the last minute or the speaker was going to be disappointed. Four men huddled around the lectern, faces away from the door. I glanced in their direction, then focused on our cover story. Because of course, we had a cover story.

"We need a reason to be there," Jess insisted during our walk. "We're not sure what's happening, so we need a legit goal to fall back on. I'm fascinated by homeopathic remedies and the impact astrology has on them."

"You are?"

"I sure am. You're the long-suffering boyfriend who wanders the store bored out of his skull. I figured you could manage that role."

I chuckled and she grinned back. "It'll also give you reason to be curious about whatever we're there to see. Be prepared."

"Yes, ma'am," I saluted, clicking my heels as we waited for a walk signal.

So while Jess assumed a suitably dreamy expression and pestered the regretful saleswoman who'd approached her with obscure and, frankly, incoherent requests for suitable books, I wandered. I didn't have to feign boredom. With the exception of a half-shelf of sensational titles describing how extraterrestrial wisdom was responsible for all major accomplishments of human civilization - next to a sign advising "For advanced reading, please ask!" - everything in the store was absurd, dull, or both. I picked up one unremarkable crystal after another, resisting the urge to throw them against a wall to see if they would shatter. A few of the tarot decks were borderline pornographic, but I imagined other bored boyfriends thumbing through the cards and hastily set them back down. I was relieved when, with the staccato hum of an activated PA system, the presentation began.

I must have been more absorbed in the merchandise than I thought, because few chairs were empty. Most of the audience were men, unlike the customers I'd seen so far, but they were a diverse bunch, young and old, white, brown, and black. In the back row, I saw the group I'd seen huddling around the lectern earlier. Only now I could see their faces, and with a shock, I recognized two of them: Train and Lyall, my fellow ex-con and his bald chaperone from the trail in Glen Ellyn.

I whipped my face away and froze, heart hammering. I didn't know exactly why I didn't want them to see me, only that my intuition urged against it. I was abruptly conscious of my size and complexion. Throw in my ponytail, and I was easily recognizable. Trying to convince myself I was being paranoid, I picked up the nearest book, not even reading the title, and pretended to study it. And I listened.

"Welcome, brothers and sisters, present and future," said a rich, melodious, Ivy League voice, a voice designed for political speeches or church sermons. "We gather in fellowship, to explore the bonds of goodwill, to embrace Gaia, to seek healing for the damage that has been, and still is, inflicted. We seek connection with the Earth, the wisdom of our ancestors, the blah of the blah blah blah..."

Good Lord, Rosalind. What did you send me to?

My attention drifted, and it was all I could do to drift physically too, to not stand immobile and look like I was hanging on every word. Each one washed off me like oil on teflon. I caught sight of Jess, seated at a small table, huddled over a stack of books, frowning at what she was reading. Or, perhaps, what she was hearing. I tried to listen, but it was as if my brain's nonsense filters had engaged and refused to stand down. Okay, D. Bored boyfriend. Only so much patience. Time to act the part and hover.

"Hey babes, won't be much longer," Jess said with a distracted smile, but her eyes flashed towards the table's other chair. I sat, I hoped with an air of resignation, and risked a glance at the speaker. He looked like a college professor: white, medium build, trim beard and receding gray hair, eyes blinking often behind rimless circular glasses. Surprisingly small hands clutched the lectern, and turned over page after page of prepared notes. For all his unassuming appearance, something about him drew the eye and the ear. His audience was riveted. No one appeared bored, and some of the store's other customers had stopped to pay attention. The only one not spellbound was Lyall, who stared in my direction.

I don't think I flinched. I forced my disinterested gaze to pass over him without a noticeable hitch. But my skin prickled, as if in response to the intensity of his gaze. I couldn't look at him again, not once. I focused on the speaker, whose voice rose in pitch as he reached his conclusion.

"There is a path!" he cried, stabbing the air with his index finger. "There is a way back. It won't be easy. It will take courage and sacrifice. But with your help, it *is* possible. Thank you."

He took a dramatic step back from the lectern. The moment hung, then the audience burst into applause. Before I knew it, I was joining in, earning a strange look from Jess. I shrugged and looked at my Fitbit.

"Yes, I think it's time we headed out," she announced. Looking with some distaste at the stack of books in front of her, she selected the slimmest volume and took it to the cashier. I risked a glance at the audience to find most of them lining up before a nearby table, upon which neat stacks of books sat ready for signature. Lyall and Train were nowhere to be seen.

"Honey, I'm gonna use the restroom," I told Jess, for some inexplicable reason affecting a Southern drawl. She looked at me in bewilderment, then shook her head and smiled at the cashier, who passed her a paper bag containing her purchase. I slunk off before embarrassing myself further.

The men's restroom hid behind racks of pungent incense in the far corner of the store, close to the signing table. I wanted to get in, get out, then regroup with Jess on our way home. The door opened as I reached for the handle, and I was face to face with Train.

We stopped and stared at each other. He cast a nervous glance behind him and licked his lips.

"Buy his book," he said.

I blinked. "What?"

"Allen Weston's book. The man who just spoke. If it looks good to you, buy it." Then he brushed past me without another word.

The restroom was a one urinal, one stall affair. I stared into the chipped mirror above the sink, ran my hand through my thinning hair and along my ponytail, and tried to slow my pounding heartbeat. Perhaps I should've waited, found facilities in a nearby bar, but too late now. I took a deep breath, moved to the urinal, and was standing over it when the stall toilet flushed and out walked Lyall.

For a man, this was a nightmare scenario. I was at my most defenseless, caught literally with my pants down. My thoughts flashed back to the previous summer, when I'd started a fight with a racist customer in a restaurant men's room. I was in no position to fight now. What would Sensei do? I suspected Sensei was smart enough not to put himself in this situation in the first place.

Lyall stepped up to the sink, and began washing up without acknowledging me. I held my breath, almost daring to believe he was so deep in his own thoughts that he hadn't recognized me. But, as he grabbed a wad of paper towels from the wall dispenser, he turned towards me, a crooked smile on his face. "Chance is a funny thing, isn't it, Mr. Rodriguez?" And then he walked out of the restroom.

My heart was getting some serious cardio this evening. I took my time finishing up, steadying my nerves. How had Lyall known my name? Had Train told him? Was the Themis Center, or whoever ran it, that concerned about their resident's chance meeting with an old acquaintance? The Scales of Equilibrium, I reminded myself, some sort of New Age movement. Sounded more like a cult to me.

I emerged from the restroom with as much caution as my flight instinct allowed. Out of the corner of my eye, I saw Lyall and Train huddled with another two men behind the signing table. Their expressions were bland, and neither looked in my direction. The speaker sat at the table signing copies of his book, chatting with customers in a low voice. I was about to hurry past, to find Jess and get out of there, when I noticed the top book in the nearest stack was tilted at an angle. *If it looks good to you, buy it.* Before I changed my mind, I snagged it as I went by. Jess, waiting by the cashier with a fading display of patience, raised her eyebrows.

"I'm curious," I said defensively.

"So many are," said the cashier, ringing up my copy of *The Gaia Contract* by Allen Weston. "Do you want a bag?"

I declined and ushered Jess to the door. We were two blocks away from the bookstore before I remembered I'd been planning to call a Lyft. I stopped short in the middle of the block and looked around, blinking stupidly.

"D?"

I focused on Jess, who eyed me with some concern, then looked down at the book in my hands. On an impulse, I rifled through the pages and a slip of paper fell out, wafting away down the sidewalk. Cursing, I gave chase and held it up to the nearest streetlight. It was a bookstore receipt, but someone had scrawled a message on the back.

Help me. IPP 5/26 3pm.

"You're sure it was Train who left the note?" Jess asked, as we hustled east towards the nearest L station.

"Who else would it be?" I puffed, gripping her hand and scanning the streets ahead, behind and to either side. There were still a few dog walkers out, and some people sheltering in doorways from the fitful rain. Not enough to overhear our conversation, but too few to disguise us. I tensed at every passing car, preparing to defend us if anyone jumped out. "He practically begged me to buy a book. Seems too big a coincidence."

"Fair." Two more blocks to the Morgan station. Jess counted on her fingers. "'5/26'. May 26th? That's the Sunday after next. What's 'IPP'?"

"It has to be something we both know. The trail in Glen Ellyn was called the Illinois Prairie Path, so that would be my guess."

"Look at you!" Jess sounded impressed, and I didn't know whether to feel pleased or offended. "So what kind of help does he want?"

"I have no idea. Or if I even want to help him."

We climbed the stairs to the platform and left the puzzle on the street below. Maybe Rosalind would have an idea, since she'd sent us to that bookstore in the first place.

I texted her, but didn't hear back before I decided on an early night. Jess joined me, which while pleasurable didn't help me sleep at all. We coiled naked on top of the covers, while our window A/C unit labored against thick, warm air that begged for a storm that wouldn't come. I was just drifting off when Jess's phone pinged twice. The second time, she gently disengaged to check it, and I turned away on my side as she sat up with a muttered curse. The sound of her feet padding towards the bedroom door was the last thing I remembered for a while.

Until she shook me awake, hissing my name.

"What?" I mumbled in protest, squinting up at her face hovering inches above mine.

"Get up!" Her voice was low, urgent, and her fingertips dug into my shoulder. "This won't wait until morning."

"What won't wait? I've got a double shift tomorrow."

"Exactly. That's why you've got to see this now. I can't tell you, I need to show you."

I hauled myself up to sit on the side of the bed and rubbed my eyes. Once they regained focus, I inspected my phone on the bedside table. 01:18. Outside, thunder rumbled.

Jess dragged me into the living room and sat me on the couch. I blinked and grumbled to myself, until she told me to stop. Her laptop rested on the coffee table between two open cans of whatever energy drink she was into that week. She sat next to me, grabbed the laptop, and used the fingerprint sensor to wake it from sleep mode. It did so sluggishly, and I couldn't blame it.

"So there's this Discord server I've been following, ever since I started trying to learn more about Imprints and Erasures. It's one of those paranormal investigation chat rooms. I think the moderators might be involved with those sensationalist cable TV shows, or at least they're big fans of the 'real life ghostbuster' scene. People report anything - and I mean anything - weird that might be a ghost, and then anyone and everyone chimes in with their theories. You wouldn't believe some of these conversations, some folks are batshit crazy!"

"Jess. What—?"

"Sorry, off topic. Too much caffeine." She took a deep breath before continuing. "I started noticing this one user asking more rational questions, but never offering opinions about what the phenomenon might be. Sometimes, they'd ask the OP to message them directly. I realized a month or so ago that when that happened, I'd never see another post from the OP again."

"OP?"

"Original poster. So of course I tried to track down this user, 'eg0n3287'. Their public profile was blank, of course, and it took me a while, but I finally found an email address. I went after that address and... well, you won't care about the details, but you'll care about these. I saved them off into a local file, just in case. Take a look."

She turned her laptop to face me, and I squinted at the screen. Everything was set to dark mode, which I disliked, but I wasn't going to get into that right then. She maximized her text editor's window, and I could see the file was a series of emails with dates going back to May 2022, two years ago. None had any sender or recipient information, and their subject lines were bland, places and dates such as "US Midwest 2022/2". Jess had highlighted sections of each email in bold text, so I skimmed the rest of the text and focused on those.

'*Moving further south, there are some concerning developments in St. Louis.*'

The first email sounded like a company report, as did the second. My tired brain couldn't understand the relevance, but I assumed Jess did. I read the third one, and that's when it started to click.

'*Or maybe our business partner is the source of my discontent, for he continues to exercise what he considers his prerogative in directing my activities. If our very different motivations did not so neatly coincide for our mutual short-term gain, I would be more than happy never to deal with the man again. As it is, he apparently has a familial connection to the second freelancer, which complicates my study of the first.*'

I reread this passage, twice, as suspicion burrowed its way out of my subconscious. "Are they talking about Steven Rourke?" I asked Jess in a hushed voice.

She smiled her approval, but just said "Keep reading." So I did.

'*I'm still not sure what to make of our freelancers. It is clearly as much a mentor-protégé relationship as that which I have with my own students. Equally clearly, they have little to no idea of the risks involved, and not just to themselves. The mentor's level of control is undeniably impressive, quite on a par with my own. However, I fear for the student.*'

I checked the date. June 10th of last year. Right after my first attempt to erase an Imprint with Rosalind's supervision, at a hardware store on South Grand Avenue, almost ended in disaster. "Little to no idea of the risks involved"; that was an understatement. I'd feared for myself too.

The next email mentioned "the idiotic note" and "the relapse at the hardware store", which sounded ominous, and I thought I had my guy. I'd received several notes that summer, the last a simple plea to talk and a phone number. I'd never followed up, but we were all sure its author was an otherwise silent, bald black man by the name of Jamal, an associate of my nemesis Steven Rourke.

The next sentence stopped me cold.

'*Our latest student locked her first Tether earlier today, guided solely by my other student.*'

I looked up at Jess to find her watching me intently. "Donovan and Lana?"

She nodded. "It has to be. He was training them to imprint memories all around St. Louis. Working with Rourke, helping him make a killing in the property market." I flinched, but she didn't seem to notice. "Have you figured out who he is yet?"

"Jamal? The guy at the 5K in Forest Park, who I later saw with Rourke."

"Yeah, you'll love this next one."

I read on with increasing horror. September 16th, just after that race. "He knows Rosalind's a teacher! And he knows you've been snooping around on the internet. Oh Jess! How much does he know about us?"

She sniffed. "I quite like the term 'insightful inquiries', actually, much better than snooping. I'm flattered."

"Better than 'all brawn, not brain'," I muttered. It wasn't the first time someone had underestimated me, but it rankled.

'*Are you certain we shouldn't make an overture? Allies are surely better than adversaries.*'

"What do you think this means?"

"They're arguing about how, or even if, to contact us." Jess skipped ahead to another email. It sounded like the argument had gotten feisty. She took a deep breath as she scrolled down. "This is the one you really need to see."

The email was dated March 4th, and the subject line was "Chicago 2024-03 #1".

'*The cook has destroyed at least one Tether and appears to be trying to establish himself in much the same role held by his mentor in St. Louis. Faustyn tells me they've dealt with this kind of thing before... I do wonder if Faustyn et al have run up against someone possessing so much raw strength as our cook. Is Fisher ready to try out Astbury's new countermeasures? And lest we forget, the cook's partner gave cybersec quite the scare last month.*'

"Shit," I breathed. "They followed us to Chicago!"

"He did at any rate," said Jess. "Sounds like they've got an established operation here, and whatever it is, it's far greater than enriching the grubby hands of local real estate moguls. He seems quite impressed with us, doesn't he?"

"Excuse me if I don't bask in the flattery. What does he mean by 'countermeasures'?"

She rested her hand on mine. "Oh I think we can guess, don't you? Read the last email."

"They were there!" I cried, horrified, a minute later. "They watched us get on a bus back to the L station! Who are these people?" I looked around our apartment in a rising panic. Was it bugged? Were concealed cameras watching our every move?

"I don't know. I wonder... well, I'm wondering a lot of things. We need to talk to Rosalind as soon as possible. She needs to know they're watching her, especially if she's back in the Erasure business. We need to be extra careful, D. Clearly, we don't understand the risks, and that's just the top of a long list of things we don't understand. We don't know who we can trust, so let's trust no one. But..."

"But what, Jess?"

"Do you still have Jamal's number? I think it's time we gave him a call."

CHAPTER NINE
THAT'S QUITE ENOUGH

We bickered about calling Jamal all week.

"How can you urge caution and say 'trust no one', then turn around and chat with the guy who trained Donovan and Lana?" I complained after the third time Jess asked if I'd called Jamal yet.

"Because they know about us and I want to know about them," she replied, her calm exterior failing to mask her irritation. "I'm pretty sure they know I hacked into their emails; that server's offline now. We're just prolonging the inevitable."

"I want to talk to Rosalind first. This affects her too."

"Fine, if she stops ghosting you."

Every argument came back to this, and I was losing ground. Rosalind's silence since her tipoff about Selene's Books disturbed me more and more. No matter how busy she was grading exams, she could surely spare a minute to answer one of my texts or voicemails. I'd finally caved and texted Martin too, with no better luck.

Push came to shove on Friday morning when Jericho called as we were leaving our apartment for work. "You know that high school we went to last month?" he rumbled over my tinny speakerphone. "Either the problem moved to another part of the school or they got a new problem. They want us to come back this weekend if we can swing it." He sounded delighted. We'd agreed on a finder's fee for potential Erasures, and the implications of a second Imprint in the same building as one we'd just erased didn't seem to bother him.

"It's gotta be Sunday," I told him, before Jess could say anything. She bit her lip, but nodded.

"Cool, cool. I'll text you the deets when I get 'em."

"You want to try another Erasure without calling Jamal?" Jess said immediately after I hung up.

"Dammit," I growled, and dug out the folded note from my wallet. It was a 314 area code - a St. Louis number. I left my phone on speaker and dialed.

"The number you have reached is no longer in service," proclaimed the recorded message, somewhere between apology and judgment.

Jess glowered at me like it was my fault, then sighed and hoisted her backpack. "Let me know if you hear back from Rosalind."

The call came on Saturday night, during the busiest dinner service I'd yet worked at Trattoria Cappelli. Fueled by a gorgeous warm and sunny evening, with schools poised for their summer breaks, customers packed our dining room and sidewalk patio until closing. It was one of those services where everyone in the kitchen clicked, where we forged our own kind of connection, and we all emerged exhausted but elated. Chef Luca cracked open bottles of Peroni for everyone, on the house. I collected my phone just before midnight, and noticed I had a voicemail.

I didn't recognize the number, a 636 area code, which suggested suburban St. Louis. I wouldn't have answered the call anyway, reasoning they'd leave a message if it was important. Sometimes those turned out to be impassioned pleas to change my internet provider or fix my credit history, so I wasn't in a rush to listen. I waited until I was seated on the train with a good view of my surroundings, then pressed the play button and held the phone up to my ear.

"D, this is Rosalind." Her voice was low and urgent, but I recognized it before she said her name. I only know one woman with a British accent. "I'm calling from a friend's house. I'm fine, but I fear my own phone may have been compromised. Martin suggested I invest in a burner, but that's rather too spy thriller for me.

"I know you're probably at work, so I'll keep this short. I have reason to believe you will soon be contacted by a representative of the HLF. I implore you: do not talk to them without first talking to me! If you don't get this message before 11pm, text me when you'll be free tomorrow, and I'll try to get back to my friend's house. Sorry to be so cloak and dagger. Give my love to Jess."

I replayed the message, cupping my hand over my ear to ensure I heard every word over the train's rattling. Then I hurried back to our apartment and thrust my phone at a sleepy Jess, curled up on the couch with a half-empty bowl of pretzel snacks.

By the time she'd heard Rosalind's message, she was wide awake. "Told you this lot were shady," she cried, sitting up straight and grabbing her laptop. A fire kindled in her emerald eyes. "Now, Google, who the hell are the HLF?"

I collapsed into the seat next to her and watched her fingers blur over the keyboard. The first results were for a nutrition company whose stock ticker symbol matched the letters; they seemed unlikely to be involved in Imprints and Erasures. Other hits included airports and railway stations, international literature festivals, and a handful of funds and charities associated with American Islam, cancer research, coma treatment, and the British national lottery. Nothing seemed to fit.

Thirty minutes later, Jess shut the lid of her laptop and yawned. "Would it have been too much for her to spell it out?" she moaned.

"Maybe she doesn't know what it stands for," I said. "Or didn't want to say it over the phone. She seemed a bit..."

"Paranoid? Just because you're paranoid doesn't mean no one's out to get you." Jess smiled, but it was a weak effort. I lost my battle against my impending yawn.

"Why don't we get some sleep?" I suggested. "I've got the day off tomorrow. I'll text her in the morning, we'll knock out that Erasure at the high school, then we'll go see your grandparents. I'm sure we'll catch up with Rosalind soon, then she can explain what the hell's going on."

I texted Rosalind as soon as I woke, but didn't hear back before we met Jericho outside Garfield Park High School at 10 am. By that point, it was too late.

Another storm had rolled through overnight, leaving behind a cool breeze. Across the street, in Garfield Park itself, trees scintillated in the sunlight, and joggers, bikers and dog walkers were out in force. It reminded me of Tower Grove Park back in St. Louis, of my old apartment, and a life much simpler than the one I lived now. Not nearly as rich, though, I reminded myself, and the homesickness passed. Mostly.

"Hey, my brother," cried Jericho, clasping hands with a tall, gangly man with a receding hairline and gold hoops in his ears. He wore dull gray overalls, steel toe work boots, and an enormous ring of keys hitched to his belt.

Despite his smile, he didn't look as pleased to see us as Jericho was to see him. "Hey man," he said, nodding to me and inclining his head towards Jess. "Did you tell 'em?"

"Yeah, sorta." Jericho's grin faltered as he turned back to us. "DeShaun can't pay you this time."

Jess bristled, but I laid a hand on her arm as I met DeShaun's eyes. No hostility, but wariness and the tilted chin of defiance.

"You don't think we fixed the problem last time," I said quietly. A statement, not a question.

He shrugged, but didn't look away. "Principal's office is good. But now there's something worse in the gym. I can't stand going in there. It bothered some students and parents, even our star point guard, at the playoff game. He said it was freezing and it hit 75 that night." He licked his lips. "Whatever you did, I think you just chased the ghost from one place to another. Don't think I should pay twice for the same job."

"That's okay," I told him. "It's not the first time something like this has happened." I was thinking about 1500 Locust, of my old friend Colton's apartment where I'd first met Rosalind, and of the apartment directly above it where, five months later, I'd performed my first solo Erasure. But then I remembered something else, from one of the emails Jess had shown me, about a "relapse in the hardware store."

"We good?" Jericho asked, possibly wondering about his finder's fee.

"We're good," I confirmed. "Let's check out the gym."

Jess mumbled something I didn't catch, but fell into step beside me. DeShaun led us inside through a windowless side door. I assumed it locked itself behind us. Even on a sunny Sunday, fluorescent ceiling lights bathed every corridor and classroom in stark, cold light. Evidence of the almost-over school year surrounded us: students' work hung outside classrooms, while calendars and prom fliers competed for attention in the common spaces. The basketball team had made it to the state tournament, only to lose a thriller in the semi-final. I wondered if that was the game DeShaun had just mentioned.

I started to sweat as we climbed a switchback staircase. It opened onto a wide corridor and a set of blue double doors which faced us in the opposite wall. Their head height windows were dark, unfriendly, and somehow ominous. My eyes watered from the sudden acrid stench of bleach, although it was tempered by a sweeter, muskier scent, a whiff of smoke, and a metallic taste at the back of my tongue. I thought I could hear muffled screaming, as if someone was buried under the rubble of a collapsed building.

"This is it," said DeShaun, eyes narrowed as he studied us. "But I guess you already knew that."

I nodded and turned to Jess. "Do you smell bleach?"

She shook her head, nostrils flaring. "More of a burning smell. It's like walking past a road crew when they're laying down fresh asphalt. I swear I can hear shovels grating on stone, or something like that." She grimaced. "Sweat, of course. I guess that could be natural."

"Huh. I certainly get the heat." A timely bead of sweat dropped from my eyebrow, and I wiped my forehead with the back of my wrist. I tried to prepare myself for what awaited us on the other side of this door, but there were so many different sensations. What memory could be associated with them all? I couldn't remember anything about the gym from Jess's research, so whatever happened here wasn't public knowledge. Trends and probabilities, as Rosalind had often said. Still annoying.

"Want me to unlock the doors?" DeShaun asked.

"Please. But let me open them."

"Okay." He selected one of his many keys, slid it into one of the door handles, and turned it with an audible click. "I guess we'll wait out here."

I nodded. "Ready, Jess?" I reached for her as I spoke, finding her immediately, closing my eyes at the thrill of our intertwining consciousnesses. She didn't need to answer me, I knew she was just as ready. We breathed in time, slow and deep. I cracked my eyelids so I could grasp a door handle in each hand, then concentrated on the sensations pouring from the gym, searching for the Catch. Too much, there was just too much, too confusing. I swore snowflakes were stinging my face while sweat coursed down my cheeks. "Let's do this," I murmured, and heaved the doors open.

Sometimes, opening a door catalyzed an Erasure, even coincided with removing the Catch. But not this time. Suppressing my disappointment, I took a cautious step into the gym, then another. The only light came from doors in each side wall. Shadow-wrapped bleachers flanked the basketball court, and the nearer hoop towered above and a few paces in front of me. I stopped, and Jess clasped my hand in hers. It was my turn to lead, but she was there to help or bail me out if anything went wrong. We pooled our strength and sought the Catch amidst a torrent of conflicting sensations.

It was the basketball hoop.

At least, that's where the snowflakes and waves of heat came from, where all the different scents seemed strongest. I had a sudden, absurd desire to dunk a basketball as I removed the Catch, but I'd only been a mediocre player. Better I just did what I was good at. I focused on the Catch, took another deep breath, and pushed.

And was blocked - a stellar defensive play by the other team.

We'd half-expected this, another mysterious barrier erected between us and the Catch. Jess let go of my hand and walked slowly around the hoop, probing for any edges or weaknesses, anything that would allow a more sophisticated attack than a frontal assault. I guessed her physical movement helped her visualize what our other combined senses were telling us: the barrier enclosed the Catch in a not quite perfect sphere. Her frustration surged through our connection. The damn thing was seamless.

I resisted the urge to look around, to find whoever was responsible. The skin on the back of my neck prickled. They were there somewhere. They had to be. *Show yourselves, you cowards! No? Right then. Let's see what you're made of.*

"Brace yourself," I whispered, and threw our combined strength at the barrier. It yielded, contracting around the Catch, but protected it still. I bore down, gritting my teeth with exertion, to no avail. I could feel our energy draining, and if I pushed too far, I'd struggle to deal with the released memory. But I was damned if I was going to let these people stop us again. I beat upon the wall, steady, relentless. It gave more ground, but held.

"D!" Jess hissed in warning.

"All... you've... got," I groaned. I pulled back, as if defeated, felt the barrier start to rebound, then stabbed at it savagely.

The world exploded. Then, even as I flinched from the dazzling, deafening chaos, it reassembled into the gym again, but a gym now brightly lit and crowded with people. This was the memory, the tattered remains of my consciousness realized. The memory...

These bleachers were smaller and looked rickety. No pennants adorned the walls to celebrate trophies, allowing the white paint to glare unobstructed above a gleaming wooden floor. Forty or fifty boys stood in a large circle, facing inwards. They were young men really, probably sixteen or seventeen, with all the variety of shape and size that unsynchronized puberty could offer. All wore sober black pants and jackets, white shirts and navy blue ties. All stared in fascination at the circle's center, where a short, middle-aged man with dark hair and a neatly clipped mustache stood grasping the ears of two other boys. One, sporting a GI buzz cut and a defiant scowl, was of a height with his tormentor. The other was half a head taller, and his unruly mop of blond hair flopped over furious eyes as he was forced to stoop. The man, likely a teacher or principal, addressed the ring of boys, but as was often the way with these memories, I couldn't hear the words, merely a low buzzing that blended with the echoes of the barrier breach. Suddenly, every boy in the circle took off their belts. Some appeared hesitant, exchanging nervous glances with their neighbors. Others had a predatory glint in their eyes, clutching the buckle and a length of leather around their wrists. Just when I understood what was happening, the teacher thrust the two boys away with a swat on their rumps. "Run!" I recognized him cry, and they ran, one behind the other, around the inside of the circle. And as they passed by, their classmates whipped them with their belts.

Shocked and drained as we were, I still clung to Jess's spirit, and she recoiled with a horror I shared. No matter how much the runners waved their arms to ward off the blows, they were quickly overwhelmed. Even those who'd been the last to unbuckle their belts, half-hearted in their first lashes, grew bolder as the victims staggered around the circle, screaming in pain. Many were teeing up and stepping into their blows, as if years of animosity were spilling over into mob rage. And presiding over the carnage, hands folded over his chest, the teacher smiled with smug satisfaction. I felt sick.

Why are you doing this? Even I had trouble hearing my inner voice, and I wasn't sure who I was addressing. The scene was glitching, the signal fading in and out, and I struggled to focus. I couldn't think, and a panic I hadn't experienced in months stirred within me. I couldn't think! I couldn't remember anything I'd learned from the dojo. I couldn't remember anything Rosalind had told me. I couldn't think!

And then the memory reset, the two boys again standing alongside the teacher, grabbing them by their ear lobes.

This was bad.

I'd only experienced a replaying memory once before. The first Imprint I'd tried to tackle by myself had hit so close to home, evoking my own very real and painful memories, that I'd been powerless to stop it. I dreaded to think what would've happened had Rosalind not been with me, stepping in to erase that memory.

Rosalind wasn't here now.

I tried to summon whatever reserves of strength I had. What we had. My connection with Jess had frayed, and I couldn't sense her physically at all. I couldn't breathe, only panic. The casual cruelty played out again before my eyes, dozens of young men exacting petty revenge or simply swept up by bloodlust. I could only ask *Why?* Over and over, but no one answered, no one gave me a reason, even one I didn't want to hear. My chest hurt. Why couldn't I breathe? *Why? Dear God, why?*

"That's quite enough, Dickinson."

The teacher's head snapped up, looking not at me, but over my shoulder at someone I couldn't see. Belts dangled in hands frozen in fear or guilt, and the two runners collapsed to their knees, tears in their eyes and welts rising on their skin.

"It's my job to discipline students—"

"It is your job to teach. What do you think you are teaching here?"

"It's my job."

"Let us hope not for much longer. How many lives have you already ruined?"

The teacher stared back in defiance, then his expression crumpled and he covered his face with his hands. The scene dissolved, fragments falling around me like volcanic ash.

I came to in the corridor outside the darkened, modern-day gym. I lay on my side, limbs splayed in all directions as if I'd had some kind of fit. Kneeling over me, his dark-skinned face the picture of concern, was the man I recognized as Jamal.

CHAPTER TEN

THE HENRY LYONS FOUNDATION

I would've flinched, but I couldn't summon the energy. I could barely blink. "Jess," I croaked, the syllable splintering into chest-wracking coughs.

Jamal laid a comforting hand on my shoulder as my body animated itself, my conscious mind powerless. My head hurt, not just from the usual dehydration-based headache - and man, my mouth was so dry I couldn't feel my tongue - but a dull throb on my right temple suggested it had collided with something. The floor, I guessed, judging from the way I was lying. Had I collapsed while channeling the memory away?

But that hadn't been me at all, had it?

My stomach churned, but retching was going to hurt far more than coughing. I closed my eyes and focused on slowing down my breathing and heart rate. I heard Jamal's voice, but not what he said. Shoes scuffed on the floor, and someone was dragging a body. It wasn't until I heard a sob, followed by a muttered "D!", that I opened my eyes again. Jess sat slumped against the wall next to the gym doors, her hair matted with sweat, eyes dull, a damp patch discoloring the front of her Japanese Breakfast t-shirt. With exaggerated care, as if learning to use her body for the first time, she lifted her hand and wiped her chin with the back, inspecting the residue before wiping it on her shirt.

Jamal squatted down and pressed a water bottle into her hand. "Drink," he told her, lifting her forearm. She stared at him with obvious distrust, but completed the motion. She sipped, coughed, then sipped again. Satisfied, he turned back to me, pushing circular rimless eyeglasses further up his nose. Sweat beaded on his almost bald scalp, a close-cropped fringe of gray protecting his neck and ears. His black golf shirt might have wicked away any other perspiration, but his labored breathing told me what I needed to know.

"It was you," I said, and forced myself to move, to push my chest off the floor, to start the daunting process of sitting up. He extended his hand, but I ignored it. I was going to do this myself. He watched without expression as I labored to drag myself upright and sit alongside Jess, then he passed me my own bottle. Water never tasted so good.

"You've had a very close call," he said at last. His voice was precise and cultured, with an accent I couldn't place. Minnesota? Canada? "Drink. Recover your strength. We have much to discuss, but only when you are ready. Please excuse me for a moment."

He rose with a grunt of exertion and walked towards a knot of people standing a few yards down the corridor. Jericho watched me with concern, and I flexed my fingers at him in what I hoped was reassurance. DeShaun listened to an older man I didn't recognize. Slim and tall, the speaker wore a sharp charcoal black suit that wouldn't have looked out of place in the memory from the gym. Neatly-trimmed, snow-white hair and beard framed a ruddy, angular face, and I had the wild thought he looked like Santa Claus's lawyer. *You've been very naughty this year, D. No candy for you.*

Jamal interrupted the conversation and spoke into the suited man's ear, while Jericho and DeShaun exchanged puzzled looks. Santa Claus's lawyer nodded, then gestured towards another figure I hadn't noticed yet, a pale, dark-haired woman sitting propped up against the opposite wall about halfway between us. She wore a black Kill Hannah t-shirt and leather pants of the same color that hugged her slim legs, before tapering out at Doc Marten boots. She held her head in her hands, resting her elbows on hunched up knees, and metal glinted from half a dozen ear piercings. She appeared to be breathing as heavily as I was.

"Who are these people?" I muttered.

"Isn't that your buddy Jamal?" asked Jess. Her shoulder rested against mine, and I felt suddenly aroused. This was not the time. I struggled to control myself.

"I think so. But what's he doing here? And who are the others?"

"Isn't it obvious?" Jess began, but Jamal returned before she could elaborate, the other man alongside him.

Jamal squatted again, but his companion remained standing, gazing down at us with disapproval.

"Feeling any better?" Jamal asked.

"Slightly less shit than before," I said, and his lips twisted as if practicing for a smile later.

"You should know by now that any extension of your psyche when interacting with Intrusions, tethered or otherwise, comes at a cost. Dehydration and fatigue are just the most visible. You're lucky we were here."

I didn't disagree, but I wasn't going to give him the satisfaction of saying so.

He glanced at Jess, then back at me. "The custodian would prefer we continue our discussion somewhere off premises. Our presence makes him understandably uncomfortable."

I glanced at DeShaun, but he was busy arguing with Jericho, probably about us. A nasty thought occurred to me. "Are you police?"

Jamal blinked. "God no! At least, not in the sense you mean. How's the head? You cracked it pretty hard on the floor when you fell."

As if summoned by his question, the pain at my temple flared, and I massaged it gingerly. I could already feel the goose egg rising. I wondered if I had a concussion and how I would know. "I'll manage," was all I said.

"Are you going to introduce us?" interrupted Jess, gesturing with her water bottle.

"Certainly," said Jamal, inclining his head. "My name, as you might have guessed, is Jamal. Jamal Peters. This gentleman is Faustyn Lazarowski, who runs things here in Chicago." I looked up at Santa Claus's lawyer, who favored me with a curt nod.

"Mr. Rodriguez, Ms. Evans." Faustyn had a scratchy voice that suggested he needed to quit smoking. "You have caused quite a stir in my town. I'd like a conversation of my own, once Jamal has finished with you."

"And to our right," Jamal continued, after pursing his lips, "also recovering after you destroyed her latest shield, is Izzy Fisher." The dark-haired woman's only movement was to curl all but the middle finger of her right hand into a fist. Jess snickered.

"Lovely," I said, stretching cautiously. Life was slowly but surely returning, although I was still lightheaded. The building's weight pressed down on me, all its memories, imprinted or otherwise, bottled up in one classroom after another. I needed fresh air. Once again ignoring Jamal's offer of assistance, I climbed to my feet. I was most of a head taller than him, but as wobbly as I was, I completely failed to intimidate. I reached for Jess and, gritting her teeth, she clasped my hand and hauled herself upwards.

Jamal exchanged a meaningful look with Faustyn, who turned away without another word and walked over to Izzy. He tapped her on one hand and was rewarded with an irritated wave.

"Give me a minute, would you?" she protested in a hoarse voice, rubbing her eyes.

"Are you hungry?" Jamal asked us. "The Billy Goat is just down the street. Or you can grab a drink if you don't want to spoil your appetite for lunch at Jess's grandparents."

"How do you know about my grandparents?" demanded Jess once the three of us had sat down at a sidewalk table outside the Billy Goat Tavern. The crowded restaurant occupied one corner of a busy intersection at the western end of the West Loop. No one paid us much attention, including our server. "You'd better leave them the fuck out of it."

Jamal, sitting opposite the pair of us, was unruffled by Jess's belligerence. "I assure you, we have no intention of involving them in any way, Ms. Evans. We merely know that you visit them most Sunday afternoons. We have been watching you for some time."

"Watching us how? And why? What were you doing at the school, and how did you know we were there? Oh, and stop calling me Ms. Evans, it's creeping me out."

That brought a smile to his lips. "Jess, then. I suspect you know the answers to at least some of those questions."

I landed one fist on the table, barely hard enough to rattle the crockery, but his smile disappeared. "Who is 'we'?"

Our server, a sullen high school age girl with pink hair and a silver nose ring, chose that moment to bring us glasses of water and take our order. If she detected any tension around our table, she didn't show it, but maybe it suited her vibe. Jamal ordered bacon, eggs, and hash browns, while Jess and I shared an order of fries. Neither of us was hungry, but I hated not ordering food at a restaurant.

DeShaun had stood by impassively as we left his school with Jamal. He probably regretted ever inviting us there, even if the Imprint or Imprints had finally been dealt with. Jericho left at the same time, but despite all his furtive glances, I couldn't catch his eye. I wondered if we'd hear from him later, or again. Faustyn escorted Izzy from the building, lending her his arm for support. "I'm taking her home," he'd told Jamal, and she'd spared us a venomous look on their way out. Her heart-shaped face was attractive for all that, despite or maybe because of the heavy eyeliner, and she was younger than I expected, maybe just out of college. I wondered how long she'd been doing this. Whatever this was.

"So?" I said, after our server disappeared inside the Billy Goat.

Jamal steepled his hands, peering over them as if collecting his thoughts. "I wanted to explain all this last Fall, back in St. Louis," he said quietly. "Others, to whom I defer, wanted me to wait. You should understand that before I begin."

I waved at him to get on with it.

"One hundred and fifty years ago, an Englishman called Henry Lyons established a foundation to promote the scientific study of paranormal phenomena, what the common man referred to as ghosts or spirits. Or demons or fairies et cetera, depending on cultural and religious background. Henry was a wealthy man, the only son of Albert Lyons who owned a number of lucrative steel foundries in the British Midlands. Albert could afford the best education for his son, and Henry was a diligent and capable student. He eventually earned a degree in chemistry from Cambridge University, where he met his future wife Anne. Through her, the upstart industrialist gained a grudging acceptance in polite society. He returned to the Midlands with his new bride to run his father's company. Albert was ailing, probably cancer although the records are unclear. Henry leveraged his network wisely, and by the time Albert died, Lyons Steel was a bastion of British industry. The company practically ran itself."

This sounded like a rehearsed speech, one he'd given before. My eyes drifted to the passing traffic as I waited for him to get to the point.

"Along with Anne, who had also studied chemistry at Cambridge - although the University did not allow women to sit exams back then, much less award them degrees - Henry also brought home a fascination for the occult. The Victorians, even those at the highest levels of society, were mesmerized by seances, ouija boards, and all things supernatural. This interest built upon a rich heritage of folklore and arcane religious beliefs, giving the illusion of scientific method to those who considered themselves above common superstition. Henry and Anne were determined to go beyond that illusion, to analyze these phenomena with all the skills their education had given them. And they had plenty of phenomena to study."

Jamal's history lesson was interrupted by the arrival of our food and a pot of coffee. I stole a glance at Jess; she was rapt. She loved this stuff. Me? I'd seized on the name "Henry Lyons" and his foundation. HLF.

An inner voice chastised me. *You were supposed to talk to Rosalind before anyone from the HLF.*

Assuming he's part of the HLF, another pointed out. *Besides, I tried to text Rosalind. Not my fault she's been ghosting me.*

The first voice had the last word. *Have you checked your phone recently?*

Good point. I slid my phone out of my jeans pocket and surreptitiously glanced at its cracked screen. At least one text from Rosalind. Shit.

I couldn't do anything about that now. I'd have to respond later. I replaced my phone and tried to pick up the threads of Jamal's monologue.

"The Henry Lyons Foundation barely survived World War Two," he said. He paused every few sentences to fork more egg, bacon and potatoes into his mouth, chewing and swallowing rapidly. It was hard to watch. "The Lyons family itself did not, both grandsons perishing in the conflict. But the science prevailed and the phenomena not only persisted, they increased. The loci shifted. New leadership expanded our reach until it was truly global by the end of the twentieth century. We continued to learn, and while researchers disputed the details of each others' conclusions, most began to view the phenomena as harmful, as Intrusions into the natural world."

He took more time over his next mouthful of breakfast, and it gave Jess an opening.

"Intrusions? From where?"

"We're not sure. There are many theories, some more plausible than others. Their study is in its infancy. Personally, I like the analogue of invasive species, of flora and fauna transported intentionally, or otherwise, from one continent to another, not only thriving in their new home, but outcompeting native species. We don't yet understand all the pathways, but it's clear these things don't belong and that they're dangerous if unchecked. Other theories attribute some agency behind it all, but..." He scowled, then sipped his coffee.

Jess leaned across the table, her expression earnest, and dropped her voice. "Is it aliens?"

Jamal held her gaze in silence, perhaps wondering whether she was mocking him. She blinked first. "I can't tell you it's *not* aliens," he said, pouring himself another cup of coffee. "But I don't think that's the most likely explanation. What I do know is that documented Intrusion activity over more than a century indicates a fivefold increase over that time, with a strong correlation to the deterioration of humanity's collective mental health."

"Wait, wait, wait," I interjected. "I'm no scientist, but how do you measure that? If your organization has been spreading over the world in the last few decades, of course you're going to record more... Intrusions or whatever. Are you trying to tell me they're solely responsible for our mental health crisis?"

"Not solely, no." His tone cooled. "I said 'correlation', not 'causation'. And we adjust the activity measurements for geography and population density. We know how to do science, D."

"Let's say you do," said Jess, reaching under the table and squeezing my hand. "Let's say your science is solid. Is it published anywhere? And what about you and your friends at the high school? Are any of you scientists?"

Jamal sniffed in amusement. "What reputable journal would accept papers on what they regard as paranormal activity? No accredited academic institutions would ever peer review our material. That is as true today as it was a century ago. Our researchers have always accepted it. Or perhaps endured is a better word.

"Twenty years ago, one of them developed a model for predicting Intrusion activity worldwide. Enough of its predictions were verified for us to adopt it as a practical tool, under continual refinement. This model predicted a steady increase in Intrusions globally, and our observations match that. It also predicted an imminent upsurge in Chicago activity - this city is one of the prime loci. St. Louis surprised us two years ago, which is why I went there, but the data I gathered influenced the Chicago prediction, which so far is proving accurate."

"So you and your buddies are just gathering data," I asked, not believing that for a second.

"Oh heavens no! We're defending our world against the Intrusions. We're fighting back!"

He said it with such conviction that I almost laughed. It was surely only a matter of time for Jess to trot out her Ghostbusters quip. But she was frowning instead of smirking.

"How does imprinting memories defend the world?" she asked, her voice deadly serious. I sat back in my chair, suddenly feeling out of my depth.

"Imprinting memories," he murmured. "Yes, that's not a bad way of thinking about it. The majority view is that isolating the Intrusion, as manifested by sensations unattributable to the current physical world, prevents its influence and spread. We call them 'Tethers' incidentally. Done right, they eliminate the impact on anyone in the vicinity."

"Tell that to DeShaun," I scoffed. "Tell that to Jericho and all the people we've helped here and back in St. Louis. You and your Imprints or Tethers or whatever you wanna call them made my life hell." Another memory jogged me. "And I don't buy your altruistic, save-the-world line either. Most of the Imprints you created in St. Louis were to help Steven Rourke expand his property empire. I call bullshit."

Jamal weathered my vitriol without flinching, then took off his glasses and rubbed his eyes. "I can understand your point of view. Sometimes we're obliged to work with those we dislike. Not everyone who can manipulate these phenomena is part of the Foundation, far from it. We're still not sure why some people are sensitive to them, and others are not, although there are theories. What we do know is that some people create, or more rarely break, Tethers using instinct alone, sometimes at great personal cost. Others learn a measure of control, and some even profit from it. Your own Mrs. Rosalind Hill is one such freelancer.

"In early 2022, a property developer in St. Louis began making what he likely thought were discreet inquiries about 'hauntings to order'. We've seen this before. A freelancer, usually without training, partially tethers an Intrusion to a house or hotel, somewhere curious people are willing to pay to visit. It's good for business. A leaky Tether focuses the phenomena so that those who are sensitive, people like us, are far more affected. Others may not notice anything at all. Sound like a ghost to you?"

"See?" Jess said, squeezing my hand again, really hard. "That's what Rourke was doing! I knew it!"

"He wasn't doing it." I withdrew my hand and massaged it under the table. That had hurt.

"No," confirmed Jamal. "But he found people who could: Donovan Brooks, who almost killed himself attempting his first Tether, and Lana Gunderson. They wouldn't have survived long. If they knew or cared who their employer was, I can't say. They took his money, and did his bidding. But only after I trained them. Believe me, doing business with a man like Steven Rourke didn't sit well with me, but it wasn't my first marriage of convenience. We need foot soldiers, men and women who can tether Intrusions in their home cities. Donovan's and Lana's early efforts were poor, leaky: in other words, perfect for scaring undesirable residents away from their homes, or temporarily devaluing a property for lucrative purchase. I'm not proud of that. But Donovan is a top-notch tetherer now, and Lana isn't far behind. I'm sure they'll still create a few leaky Tethers to keep Rourke happy, but they'll more than make up for that with all the good they'll do."

I pushed the almost empty plate of fries away from me. My nausea was back. I caught Jess's eye, and it had a glint in it too.

"I understand you have history," Jamal continued, his voice softer. "Had I been able to contact you sooner... Well, that's water under the bridge. And I could do little about your familial connection with Steven Rourke, D. For what it's worth, I think the man respects you."

I snorted. "I don't care what he thinks of me. He's tried to ruin my life twice now. Fuck him!"

A young couple scowled at me as they pushed a stroller past us on the sidewalk. I raised my hands in apology.

Jamal nodded. "I understand. I do. But he's not the only one who respects you, and neither am I. Your progress has attracted attention at the highest levels of the Foundation, as has the tutelage and ability of Rosalind Hill. As for you, Jess, you're also giving our IT department fits—"

"Good!" Jess interrupted, with a Cheshire cat grin.

"As well as earning a compliment from Emma Astbury herself, the creator of the model I told you about."

Jess beamed, but I felt far less flattered. "So what?" I said. "You've given us your history lesson. You've explained why you were in St. Louis and working with Rourke. You've told us about this model and all your theories - so what? You want us to stop? Go back to being good little citizens and stay out of your way?"

For the first time, he showed genuine emotion, jaw dropping and eyes wide in astonishment. "Why no, isn't it obvious? We want you both to join us!"

CHAPTER ELEVEN
THE WHOLE PICTURE

I'm walking through a redwood grove, statuesque sequoia trees towering above me. Beams of sunlight stab through hazy air in the distance. There's no trail; I follow the merest hint of a path through the scrub lapping the roots of these titans of the forest.

Is there a reason I'm here? I forget.

I come across a dell, an almost circular depression carved from the ground, as if by a gigantic ice cream scoop. The ground here is barren, not so much as a weed, just fine red-brown earth. A black iron gate stands in the center.

I walk down and stand before the gate. It's taller than it looked, taller than me. Set in a solid rectangular frame connected to nothing else I can see, it consists of a series of thick iron bars, a handsbreadth apart. At hip height on one side, there's a square panel with a keyhole in the middle.

It's a prison door.

I stare at the door. Through it, the dell looks identical to my side.

I look closer and see my reflection.

I'm dressed, not in the prison jumpsuit I half expected, but in a long-sleeved tunic and loose-fitting pants of the purest white. I'm clean-shaven and my hair is cropped short, my ponytail gone. The edge of a chest tattoo pokes above the collar of my tunic, but not enough that I can guess its design. I raise my hand to draw the fabric aside, and then I notice the gate behind me.

I whirl to confront it.

There's nothing there, just the other half of the dell. Just the other half of the dell - the redwood forest has vanished. So has the sky.

I turn back to the gate. And see all the other gates, stretching into infinity, like I'm standing before a carnival funhouse mirror.

I've got to get out of this place.

I reach for the lock, fighting a rising panic. Before my fingers can close around it, they hit a barrier. There's a flat, transparent barrier in front of the gate. It feels cold. Like glass.

I've got to get out of this place!

I hurl myself against the gate. It shudders with a sound like a gunshot. Hairline cracks mar what I see now is a window painted with the image of an iron gate. I back up, take a deep breath, then run at it, closing my eyes and covering my face with my arm just before impact.

Glass shatters around me, splinters ripping through my tunic sleeves. I stumble to a halt on the other side and inspect the damage. Torn fabric and a few spots of blood. Could've been worse.

It is worse.

The gate is still there.

Or it's another identical gate, the next in an infinite series. Shards of glass pool around my feet. I see nothing behind me. It doesn't occur to me to go around the gate. My path leads through it.

I go again.

And again.

My arm is torn to ribbons.

Again.

I blink blood from my eyes. My hands are smeared with it.

Again.

There is no dell, just an endless succession of gates.

Again.

And again.

I will die in this cage.

I jolted awake in darkness, head pounding and heart racing. I lay sprawled atop my bed, its covers mostly thrown off. Sweat soaked the sheets and pillow case, making them damp and unpleasant. Jess was nowhere to be seen.

I glanced at my phone as I fumbled for the glass of water on my nightstand. Not quite 4 am. Terrific.

Unlike most of my dreams, good or bad, this one refused to fade. The image of the shattering glass gate haunted me. I wiped my face with my forearm, discovering only sweat, not blood, and that my skin wasn't shredded to ribbons. My stomach twisted and I half-fell out of bed, ending up on my hands and knees, panting and trying not to vomit.

I heard a groan from the bathroom. Its door was ajar, and I could see Jess's calves and feet. It looked like she was lying down. I wanted to check on her, but I dared not move just yet. Not yet.

When I came to again, I was curled up on the carpet. Predawn light filtered through the edges of the window blinds. A muttered curse followed the thud of something falling on the floor. I pulled myself up on the edge of the bed and saw Jess rise with her phone in hand. Its soft light illuminated her frown as she swiped the screen, and played with her naked curves. I clung to the sight, alluring and familiar, and nothing to do with dreams or any other weird shit.

"You okay?" she asked at last, looking over at me. I couldn't tell if she was amused or concerned. Perhaps both. "I didn't want to wake you. The bed's a mess. Definitely gotta change these sheets."

I propped myself up onto my knees and took stock. Breathing: normal. Heart rate: normal. Perspiration: absent. Still a faint headache, but nothing that some ibuprofen couldn't handle, I hoped. The vivid recollection of a nightmare: not sure what I could do about that.

"I'm fine. You? Did I wake you?" I remembered seeing her legs in the bathroom earlier.

"Nah, I might have woken you," she said, shaking her head in disgust. "Worst nightmare I've had in a while. I gave up trying to fall back asleep an hour ago, just took a shower. Still can't get the dirt off me."

"What?"

She grimaced, running one hand through her damp hair. "I was crawling through tunnels in the dark. Like pitch blackness. I just knew they were tunnels, and I could feel the dirt on my knees and in my fingernails as I clawed my way forward. I can still feel it, even if I can't see it. And I don't know what I was crawling from or where I was crawling to, but the tunnels kept getting tighter and tighter and..." She shuddered. "Did you have nightmares too?"

"One," I said, and told her about the endless parade of glass gates. Somehow, recounting it to Jess took the edge off.

"I wonder what it means," she murmured once I'd finished.

"Does it have to mean anything?"

"Well, we both had a day yesterday. Could be just that."

She tossed her phone onto her bedside table and stretched, arching her back as her hands reached for the ceiling. I glimpsed her new tattoo, a Celtic knot running in a band around her upper left thigh, and suddenly my libido roared to life. I crawled across the bed and drew her down towards me. She hesitated for a moment, then pushed me savagely onto my back, straddling my hips. She threaded her fingers through my hair, before tightening them in a fierce grip. I gasped and dug my fingers into her arms, her back, her thighs, and we pressed urgent kisses upon each other as she rode me. I climaxed just before she did, then she collapsed against my chest. We lay there, panting, until my alarm went off.

"Fucker," I growled, stretching a half-hearted hand towards my phone and coming up short. Jess laughed, and climbed off me, swatting the hand that tried to stop her.

"Come on, you need to take a shower." She cast me a flirtatious wink as she danced out of my reach. "I'll go make coffee."

The shower refreshed me, as did the bright sunlight pouring into the bedroom after I opened the blinds. It was still going to be a long day. And I had to steel myself for a conversation with Rosalind later.

We'd exchanged texts after Jess and I left the Billy Goat, but she couldn't get to her friend's house that day. I planned to call her there during my break in Monday's dinner shift at work. We'd have ten minutes at most, so I needed to distill the high school Erasure, and subsequent meeting with Jamal, while also giving her time to share.

"I bet she's been contacted too," Jess said, popping another frosted mini wheat into her mouth. She refused to pour milk on her cereal. "I wonder who by, and if she heard the same story we did."

"Whatever Rosalind heard, she thought it worth giving us a heads-up before we talked to them," I said, pouring myself a second cup of coffee. I'd hardly noticed the first. "I don't want to do anything else until we've heard what she has to say."

"You don't want to watch Jamal imprint a memory? Or tether an Intrusion, or whatever he calls it?"

"I'm not saying I don't. Although, are those the same thing? I'm lost in all the jargon. Imprints, Tethers, Intrusions..."

Jess frowned for a moment, then dumped the remaining mini wheats onto the table. She spread them evenly, then tapped one as she spoke. "I think an Intrusion is the base phenomenon, something that drags memories from the building's past into the present day. Let's say this mini wheat represents an Intrusion. Some people might notice it, most wouldn't. It may be harmless, but the Henry Lyons Foundation thinks otherwise. They're worried about it spreading, becoming stronger." She gathered the remaining pieces closer to the first, then scooped them up and dropped them back in the bowl. "So they tether it, concentrate the memory, and lock it in place. Imprint it."

"In the bowl?"

"In the bowl, yes." She picked up a mini wheat and ate it, somewhat ruining the analogy. Jess hated analogies.

"So Imprints and Tethers are the same thing - got it. And somewhere on this bowl is a Lock, something that keeps the cereal inside. The Catch?"

"I think so. A cover, perhaps, that forms a tight seal around the rim. And the quality of that seal determines how much people like me, you, and Rosalind can sense. Apparently, all the Imprints we've encountered so far had crappy seals. Aren't you curious to see Jamal do it right? To watch him make an undetectable Imprint?"

I was. Countering our skepticism about joining the HLF to imprint memories, when I'd spent the last year erasing them, he'd offered a demonstration. "With enough practice, you can both do the same," he'd promised. "Do you remember the hospital where you visited your friend Rosalind, after the, uh, unfortunate incident at Chouteau Village? Why do you think I was there, while Steven Rourke paid our respects? How many Tethers would you say exist at that hospital? Did you notice any?"

I'd wondered that myself. Surely, a hospital's rich history of trauma was fertile ground for all sorts of Imprints. The Chouteau Village condo complex had once been such a hospital, and Rosalind and I had barely survived our Erasure mission there. But during my visits to Barnes Jewish Medical Center - once to visit Rosalind with her broken nose, and also after Jess's father's heart attack a month before - I'd only detected a background hum of memory. It was on our long list of unanswered questions. Now, Jamal explained it by claiming he was so good at his job that I wouldn't notice any Imprints that were there. Cocky? Or confident?

He'd picked up the bill at the Billy Goat, but only after leaving us with more food for thought. "What do you think happens when you destroy a Tether? The Intrusion is still there. Sometimes it's muted for a while, sometimes for a long while. Other times, especially if it's part of a cluster, it comes back as strong or stronger almost immediately. Sometimes as strong as a leaky Tether. I believe destroying Tethers weakens our defenses against whatever Intrusions represent, like removing the cast before a broken bone has healed properly."

"I wonder if Rosalind's gotten a demonstration, and what she thinks." I stared at the bowl of cereal while Jess finished eating it. If I were to sweep the bowl and its contents off the table, letting it all smash on the floor, would even more mini wheats miraculously appear by the time we got home from work? It sounded like something from another nightmare.

"I'd like to know too," Jess said, hoisting her backpack onto her shoulders. "But I'm worried."

"About what exactly?"

"That we've been making things worse. That we've got this all wrong, that these memories or Intrusions *should* be locked away."

"You're not seriously considering changing sides?"

She frowned. "Sides? I don't see it like that. I think we're all trying to figure out what these phenomena are and what to do about them. And the HLF has been working on that problem for a lot longer than we have, or Rosalind has. Jamal's trying to share what they've learned over more than a century of study. I think we need to hear him out."

"I thought we had heard him out," I said, trying not to sound sulky.

"We need the whole picture, D," she said, tossing her hair. That meant she was done arguing. "We need to know what damage we're causing by erasing Imprints."

"How do we know they're not causing damage by creating Imprints?"

"Great question," she said, smiling as she opened the apartment door. "The first of many I want to ask once we hear him out."

Despite my best efforts, I felt off all day, almost dissociated from what I was doing. I held my own in the kitchen, made no major mistakes, but it was as if I watched someone else do the work. Not every day in the life of a line cook was exciting, but I'd never found it so dull before. At one point ,Chef Luca took me aside and asked if I was okay. I summoned a reassuring smile and pleaded a sleepless night. I couldn't wait to slink down to the break room, dig out my phone, and dial the number Rosalind had given me.

"Hello?" answered a female voice. I recognized enough Midwest accent in that one word to know it wasn't my mentor.

"Hi, uh, this is D. Can I speak to Rosalind, please?"

There was silence, followed by murmured voices I couldn't understand. Then, "Good evening, D! Sorry about all this, but until we meet in person, I wanted to speak without reasonable fear of being overheard. Are you alone?"

The break room was empty. Luca didn't like us closing the door, but I peered into the short corridor outside and saw no one. "I think so. What's going on?"

Rosalind took a deep breath. "What isn't going on? I'm just glad the school year is over, it's terrible we're so short-staffed. I'm sorry I haven't been communicative recently. Did I manage to catch you before you heard from the Henry Lyons Foundation?"

"Actually, no. Jess and I ran into them yesterday."

"Damn." As mild as it was, I couldn't remember when I'd last heard her curse. "I know we don't have much time, but can you tell me about it? What did they say?"

That was my cue. I'd been refining my story all day, as if preparing for a test, and now the examiner had started the clock. I summarized the Erasure, the shield and Jamal's rescue, his companions and history lesson, his claims about Intrusions, Imprints and Tethers. I omitted, for now, his attempt to recruit us. The tale still took longer than I wanted, and I glanced anxiously at my Fitbit as I finished.

"I see," was Rosalind's first reaction to the information dump. "You mentioned these barriers or shields to me before. I'm afraid I haven't had time to think about them. I... I'm delighted you were able to overcome them and not get lost in the memories they protected."

"I think we were losing ourselves yesterday," I said, and an aftershock of panic rippled through me. "I hate to say it, but Jamal saved us."

"And presumably completed the Erasure."

I blinked. "Or re-imprinted the memory?"

"Maybe, but I don't think so. From what I've been told, it doesn't work that way."

"What have you been told?"

"More than I can tell you in the time we have, I'm afraid. Suffice to say that imprinting a memory is a methodical process, and releasing a memory during an Erasure destabilizes the system. The one isn't a simple reversal of the other. Jamal would have had no choice but to complete what you started."

"And he knew how to?"

"It seems so. I can imagine several reasons why he should, but it doesn't sound like he shared any. Did he try to recruit you?"

I paused, but couldn't think of a way to avoid answering that question, and I didn't want to lie to her - that's not my thing. "He did. We haven't signed up."

She barked a humorless laugh. "Good. Please don't do anything until I get there. Martin and I leave for England tomorrow. His father can't manage by himself anymore, so we're moving him to a home and, well, there's been a lot of drama. I'm dreading it, frankly, but at least it will be over and done with. We're not sure how long we're staying, hopefully no more than a week, but we're flying back through Chicago and plan to stay for a few days. We can catch up then, about many things."

That included Daniel, I presumed. And I had little or nothing to report on that front. I still didn't understand why she'd sent us to the New Age bookstore.

"So should we just avoid Jamal until you get here?" I heard a door close in the corridor outside and checked the time. Someone was going to come looking for me soon, if they weren't already.

"Not necessarily," she said, after a long pause during which I almost repeated the question. "Listen to what he has to say. Just remember he is but one man in an organization that supposedly numbers hundreds or possibly thousands. You're getting one side of the story, and there are other points of view. The Henry Lyons Foundation is not as united an organization as he might lead you to believe."

Chapter Twelve
SAVING IT FOR YOU

I've never liked exams, even though I'd performed well in them throughout most of my school career. They made me anxious for hours, sometimes days before. Stress headaches had become so common during high school that I'd bought family-size bottles of ibuprofen to get me through. Other pharmaceuticals took their place in college, at least until they got me expelled.

I'd never felt less prepared than when we arrived at the dojo for our blue belt exam the following Tuesday evening. We'd earned our yellow belts back in St. Louis, shortly after the Chouteau Village Erasure, and had been well on the way towards blue when Hickory burned and we uprooted ourselves to Chicago. I expected that almost a month's gap in study would give us more time to prepare, but Sensei Ryuichi wasn't having it.

"The world does not take time off," he declared two weeks earlier when informing us of our examination date. "Karate does not take time off. Why should you?" He insisted we were ready, and pushed us hard to prove it.

Had that helped us at the high school Erasure? I graded ourselves a 'C'. Top marks for destroying Izzy Fisher's shield and the Catch, but our complete inability to then release the memory lost a lot of points.

We did much better on Tuesday, and earned our blue belts.

Afterwards, we treated ourselves to ramen at the restaurant next door, still basking in our success and Sensei's approval. I texted the good news to Rosalind as promised, although it was the middle of the night in England. She'd left a voicemail wishing us luck, her reluctance to use her own phone not extending to karate.

We were blue belts!

"Are you happy?" Jess asked, stirring her noodles as they cooled.

"Of course I am! Aren't you?"

She smiled, but it didn't quite reach her eyes. Odd. She'd been as pleased as I was when we entered the restaurant. I lowered my voice.

"You okay, Jess? Is something wrong?"

She chewed and stared at something over my shoulder, as if marshaling her thoughts. "I am excited about our blue belts," she said at last, meeting my eyes. "And I love that we did it together, that we're together, here in Chicago. But I miss seeing my St. Louis friends. I'd love to celebrate with them too, hug them, laugh with them. God help me, I even miss my family. You can keep in touch online and via text, but..."

She left the thought unfinished. I took her hand in mine. "I know it's not the same. I know you miss them, miss St. Louis. Your entire life was there. I'm sorry I dragged you all the way up here."

That earned a laugh, although she wiped a sudden tear from the corner of her eye. "You didn't drag me! I wanted to come, to start fresh in a new city, with a new job in a real career, living with the man I love. I knew what I was giving up, and I'm cool with it. I just miss the people sometimes, especially when things get a little overwhelming. Don't you?"

Did I? I hadn't had much of a social life outside of Jess. I'd grown up in St. Louis, but lost touch with most of my childhood and college friends - and family too - during twelve years in prison. Very few people ever came to visit; my half-sister Fiona was an exception, and we still talked regularly. I missed Mike and TJ and the crew at Hickory, but I was too embarrassed by what, and who, I'd brought upon them to keep in contact. No, apart from Fiona, Rosalind, and Martin, of course, the only other person I talked to occasionally was Colton Lynn. If I hadn't run into my old high school buddy and fellow ex-con while buying coffee one spring morning, I wouldn't be sitting in a ramen bar in Chicago now. I wouldn't be worrying about a mysterious secret society trying to tell me what to do about the weird phenomena plaguing my life.

"D?"

I started, returning to said ramen bar. "Sorry. You got me thinking. Do I miss it? Not much, if I'm honest. A handful of people, sure. But I had more to escape from than anything keeping me there."

Her smile was sad, but at least it was genuine. "I know. I don't regret it, I don't. But I'm glad we're going to visit soon."

"How can we miss Kenya Day?" I grinned.

"I'd never hear the end of it," she agreed, rolling her eyes. "But I plan to see as many of the old crowd as I can too."

"Sure, and they're always welcome to visit us in Chicago. I guess we're both struggling to make new friends here."

She shrugged. "We're not that social, are we? We talk to the Millers downstairs, but we don't have much in common. I guess karate is social, but it's an older crowd. I like a couple people at work, but work is weird at the moment."

"How so?"

"Conor and Marcus had a big argument last week. Monday, I think. They were in Conor's office, but screaming at each other so loud everyone could hear them. Marcus stormed out afterwards. I assumed he'd quit, or Conor had fired him, but he's still online. He joins meetings and responds to messages as much as he ever did. Conor hasn't said anything - it's like he's pretending it never happened. None of us have the courage to ask, and we're all walking on eggshells."

"Marcus was the guy with the beard, right? At Conor's party?"

"Yeah. Great coder, but I definitely get a conspiracy theory vibe. Creeps me out."

I chuckled grimly. "Creeped out appears to be our vibe."

Jess was running late. Conor had called an emergency staff meeting just as she was leaving on Thursday afternoon. I prowled around our apartment, glaring at my phone at least once a minute for an update that refused to come. It was almost 3pm, and if we waited much longer, we'd be swallowed whole by rush hour traffic. Finally, I grabbed my keys and ran down to my car.

I'll pick you up outside Paragon, I texted.

I don't know if my decision saved time or stress, but I was doing something, if only gritting my teeth through stop-and-go traffic. There's a reason we took the train to work. My phone pinged as I sat at a red light five blocks north of Paragon Insurance.

Sorry, love. Meet you out front.

"Sorry," she repeated after she tossed her backpack into the trunk, then slid into the passenger seat. She smoothed down her knee length black skirt, her grudging nod to workplace professionalism. "That was painful."

I didn't respond immediately, concentrating on slipping through cracks in the stream of vehicles clogging the downtown Chicago streets. I sighed with relief when we reached the Eisenhower expressway, joining the daily exodus towards the western suburbs. It was slow, but it rarely ground to a halt. I hoped.

"What was painful?"

Jess looked up, thumbs poised over her phone screen. She'd been tapping away ever since buckling her seat belt. "Marcus quit. Threatened some sort of legal action. We had to scramble to remove his access to all our code and files and whatnot. It's chaos in there."

"Why did he quit? Was it related to that argument you told me about?"

"That's what we're all guessing, but Conor refused to say. There's something else, and I haven't told anyone this. Marcus sent me an email, right before the meeting, maybe the last email he sent before his account was deactivated. Here, look."

She waved her phone toward me just as I slammed on the brakes to avoid another Very Important Driver, their red pickup cutting me off to save a few precious seconds. I punched my car horn and swore, then swore again when the Very Important Driver flipped me off.

"Can't read your phone, Jess," I growled, forcing myself to brake and let the idiot squeeze through other gaps in traffic that were barely there.

"Fine," she snapped, clutching the grab handle above her door and sounding irritated. "It just said 'Don't trust Conor.'"

"Huh. Maybe it was personal then. Marcus seemed pretty temperamental."

"Yeah, but... I don't know. He was always so long-winded in his emails. Maybe he knew he didn't have much time. But it bothers me. I wish I knew if he sent emails to anyone else."

I couldn't think of a response, so we lapsed into a brooding silence. At last, we peeled off onto Roosevelt Road, the same route I'd taken to Glen Ellyn to spy on Daniel Hill. We weren't going nearly as far today. A right and another right, and we entered an almost empty parking lot surrounding a nondescript single-story office building in Oakbrook Terrace. Jess told me that Chicago's smallest suburb was called Utopia until 1959, but the many office towers and hotels clustering around five lanes of asphalt must have been someone else's idea of paradise.

Two cars parked near the dark glass doors of our destination, a gleaming white Acura sedan and a mud-stained green Jeep. I parked next to the Acura and we scurried toward the meager shade in front of the building entrance, the blacktop radiating almost as much heat as the sun. I dug my phone out to text Jamal, but the entrance doors swung open just as we reached them. Jamal, wearing a scarlet polo shirt and khaki slacks, ushered us inside into the air conditioning, then locked the doors behind us. I flinched, then berated myself. Not every door closed a cage.

"Welcome to the national headquarters of Lyons-Strickland Logistics," Jamal said, gesturing to the dim and shabby reception area in which we now stood. A sun-bleached, U-shaped mahogany desk occupied most of the space to our right, unattended and unadorned except for a dusty computer monitor and a conference phone handset. To our left, an assortment of uncomfortable-looking chairs huddled around a glass coffee table. A handful of prints hung on the walls, most scenes of the Chicago of yesteryear, most crooked. Whatever Lyons-Strickland Logistics was, the company looked like it had fallen on hard times.

Faustyn Lazarowski rose from one of the chairs as we entered, wearing the same dark suit and dress shirt as he had at the high school. I felt underdressed in my t-shirt and jeans. I hadn't expected him to be there, and said so after we exchanged polite greetings.

"I'm mostly here to observe," the Henry Lyons Foundation's top man in Chicago admitted in his scratchy voice. I kept waiting for him to cough, but he never did. "But also for backup. The forces we manipulate are unpredictable."

"Speaking of which," said Jamal, standing next to him. "What do you sense right now?"

Good question. Jess's brow furrowed as she closed her eyes. I took a deep breath and closed mine, searching without sight for any hint of scent, sound, or anything else at odds with our observed environment. I sensed nothing at first. It was a shade warmer than most buildings, but since it appeared unoccupied, maybe they were saving on air conditioning costs. The longer I stood there, I convinced myself of a background hum, a jumble of unusual sensations not distinct enough to identify. I was sure something was there, although would I have noticed if I hadn't been so focused?

I opened my eyes and met Jess's. She shrugged. "I can't feel anything."

"Maybe something real faint," I told Jamal. "I could be imagining it. It reminds me of standing in the ER at Barnes Jewish Hospital. I knew there had to be lots of intense memories there, but instead of Imprints, I just got a kind of hum."

He exchanged an unreadable look with Faustyn. "Interesting. Very few recruits notice anything, even when they suspect something is here."

"You think we're recruits, do you?" said Jess, raising an eyebrow.

"Potential recruits, then. Let's go through to the main space."

He swiped a keycard over a reader and opened one of a pair of solid wooden doors opposite the entrance. We filed into a cavernous room that occupied the rest of the building. Personal offices and conference rooms lined the perimeter, surrounding several rows of cubicles. Jess muttered a curse at their beige, chin-high walls, and I shuddered, not at any sudden strange phenomena, but at the prospect of working in such a place. In some ways, it appeared little better than Missouri Eastern Correctional.

"At a guess," Jamal said, "how many Imprints would you say are in this building?"

"Imprints?" Faustyn said, puzzled.

"It's what they call Tethers. I don't think it's a bad term actually. Well?"

I shrugged. "No idea. I still don't pick up much. Sometimes they're pretty localized. I don't sense anything until I'm almost on top of them." I looked at Jess, and she mirrored my shrug.

"Take a walk around then, see what you can find."

So we did. I decided to follow Jess, and we ducked inside each unoccupied office and dingy conference room, before snaking our way up and down the rows of cubes. Most had phones and computers, but few showed any signs of personalization, just a sports schedule here or a beach vacation photo there. Jess's floor at Paragon, similarly unoccupied, hadn't felt nearly as empty. Neither of us detected any of the weird smells or temperature swings we associated with Imprints. I thought I caught a hint of musky heat as I stepped into one of the bigger offices, but then the HVAC kicked in and swamped whatever might have been there.

"Nothing?" Jamal sounded disappointed when we finished our sweep of the floor.

"Not really," I said. Jess shook her head, strangely quiet. I bit my lip. "There might have been something in one of those offices, but I couldn't sense enough to be sure."

"Which office?" Jamal asked, and I gestured. His mouth tightened, which I'd come to realize might represent a smile for most people.

"How many are we up to in here?" he asked Faustyn, who thought for a moment.

"Somewhere in the low twenties, I believe." Jess did a double take, and I gaped at him. Twenty Imprints? Here? And I couldn't sense any of them?

I didn't want to believe it. Surely he was joking.

"Like I told you," Jamal said, likely guessing what was running through my mind. "Done right, Tethers are undetectable, even to those as sensitive as yourselves. This is one of our training facilities. We own it via a shell company and occasionally bring in some of our remote workforce to maintain a façade, and appease our landlord."

"Why here?" asked Jess, breaking her silence. 'What's so special about this building? Why does it have so many Intrusions, or whatever you call them? Or can you create Tethers from unremarkable memories, not just traumatic ones?"

"Good question!" Jamal beamed, a rare burst of emotion. "Or rather, questions. It's possible to tether an 'unremarkable memory', as you put it, but it's rarely necessary. There's always a correlation between the local Intrusion density and the availability of intense memories. We suspect that might be a factor in where the Intrusions occur, on a fine scale. Our global model is based on other data."

"What other data?"

Jamal glanced at Faustyn, who pointed at his watch. "Another time, Jess. I want to show you how we tether such an Intrusion. Follow me."

She scowled at the brush off, but held her tongue. I was still trying to process the rest of his answer, and I didn't notice until we stopped that we stood outside the very office I'd paused by earlier.

"Another damn Barker?" Faustyn muttered.

Jamal's lip curled. "The man was as reliable as he was despicable. You sensed something here, D?"

"Yeah." I concentrated, but it wasn't until I crossed the threshold that I caught it again, barely noticeable above the background hum. "A whiff of perfume, maybe? What about you, Jess?"

Her head cocked at an angle as she reached my side. "Something... whispering? It's hard to hear above my own breathing."

Jamal nodded. "Good. We've been aware of this Intrusion for a few weeks now. We've been saving it for you. Observe."

I wanted to know what he meant by "saving it for you", but Jess silenced me with a clasp of her hand. I focused on Jamal, who did nothing but squint. It was like watching Rosalind at work.

"What did you just do?" demanded Jess suddenly, and a moment later sultry heat coiled around me and a musky scent assaulted my nostrils. In my mind's eye, translucent and superimposed on the empty office before me, I caught a glimpse of a ruggedly handsome, middle-aged man standing behind the desk. He wore a white collared shirt, a scarlet tie, and a smirk, as he looked down at the long blonde hair of a young woman kneeling in front of him. I didn't need to see the ends of a leather belt bracketing her head to understand what she was doing. The vision collapsed, as if Jamal had taken it in his hands and scrunched it up into an impossibly tight wad of paper. Most of the heat and scent disappeared, but not all. I could still feel the beguiling warmth, smell the heady perfume, not as intense as before, but much stronger than when I'd first entered this office during our initial circuit.

This was an Imprint. It reminded me of a house in Kirkwood and an awkward, devout couple, embarrassed by sensations they couldn't explain. An unusual problem, to which Rosalind and I had provided an unusual solution.

"That is a crude, Single-Point Lock," said Jamal, showing no sign he'd expended any effort. "It's what we might expect from a novice, even for such a low-grade Intrusion. The Tether prevents the growth of the Intrusion, but there are side-effects, as I'm sure you can tell."

"Oh we can tell," Jess said, running her fingers through her hair. "How did you do that? How did you know what memory to use? Where did it come from?"

Jamal withstood her torrent of questions, then nodded in approval. "As to how, the technique can be taught. It requires willpower and mental dexterity. The memory itself is a property of the Intrusion. Think of it as some force penetrating space-time and dislodging a past event into our current time-line."

"So now what?" I asked. As fascinating as all this was, my body was responding to the caress of the heat and the allure of the musky perfume. I could feel Jess tense beside me, which didn't help. The other two men were either made of stone or sensed something far less arousing. "Do you leave this as an example to others of a bad Imprint?"

"We could," said Jamal. "You could destroy it, 'erase' it as you say. The Intrusion will return eventually, here or elsewhere within the building. Many Tethers in one place weakens resistance to further Intrusions. Instead, I want to fix it. I want you to see how effective a proper Tether can be."

He set his feet further apart and took a slow, deep breath. I focused on what I called the Catch, and he a "Single-Point Lock", the tiny, invisible point that sealed the memory. I knew what to expect. Without a shield, I could easily erase this Imprint. I felt Jess's spirit probing alongside mine; she could too. Instead, we watched and waited.

Our approaches to dealing with a Catch were different. I liked to gather all my willpower and focus it like a laser beam at that one point, to break it apart. Unsophisticated, perhaps, but effective. Jess preferred to hook it somehow, tug at it and tease the blockage loose. Jamal's method was more like an unfolding than a tug, more deliberate and sophisticated. One moment the Catch was an infinitesimal point, then it expanded like the rapid unfurling of a flower's petals. Instead of the rush of memory, I only caught glimpses: a pretty blonde wearing heavy mascara, a striped minidress, and a seductive smile, reaching for the man's belt buckle; his hands clutching her head while she took him in her mouth. As soon as they appeared, the images were snatched away, but instead of a rapid squashing, I sensed structure, a series of deliberate folds that constrained the vision, the heat, and the scent. I tried to follow, but it was too rapid, and then it was over. One final fold, and I couldn't sense anything. I couldn't even tell where the Catch was. It was a magician's trick, taking an object in plain sight and making it vanish in front of our eyes.

Jess was open-mouthed, and I stared at Jamal in astonishment. Even though this was exactly what he'd promised, neither of us could believe it. It was, and I hesitated to even think about the word, magical. Jamal had the decency to be panting a little. Faustyn passed him a water bottle, and he took a deep swig.

"Well?" he said, wiping his mouth with the back of his hand.

I spread my hands and shook my head. Jess whistled and shook hers. Jamal smiled.

"That is how to tether an Intrusion with a proper Single-Point Lock. They have never been known to leak or fail.

"So, now are you interested in joining us?"

Chapter Thirteen
Stay Away

"I want to talk to Rosalind first," I insisted. Jess lapsed into another brooding silence. I couldn't tell if she disagreed, but didn't want to do so in front of Jamal and Faustyn, or was still processing what we'd just witnessed. "She has a lot more experience with this. And we still have questions. This seems like a good thing, but what are the side effects? What is this model, this data that drives what you do? I feel like I brought my car in for service, and you're trying to sell me a new one."

Faustyn grimaced, but Jamal just nodded. "I apologize if we're giving you the hard press. I promise I'll try to answer all your questions before you commit either way. Talk to Rosalind. As I understand it, she should have all the same information as you by now.

"I do have one more thing to show you, before you make your decision. And, please, no more 'unusual solutions' until you do. After that... well, we'll cross that bridge when we come to it."

I shrugged. We hadn't heard from Jericho all week. It wouldn't hurt to take a break until we'd had a chance to discuss everything.

As we left, I was surprised to see Faustyn head toward the Jeep; that seemed more Jamal's style. Jamal chuckled when I said so.

"Faustyn's an off-road kind of guy. Used to race dirt bikes back in the day. His wife made him stop when he almost snapped his right leg in two: there's more steel than bone in that limb. Now he drives his Jeep into the wilds of Wisconsin or Michigan whenever he can. Not really my scene. You?"

I shook my head. "Never ridden a motorcycle. I knew a kid in high school who died on one, decapitated when he skidded under an eighteen-wheeler. No thanks."

The Jeep roared into life, and Faustyn gave us all a curt nod before driving off. Jamal paused, his hand resting on top of his open car door. "When do you think you'll talk to Rosalind?"

"She's visiting family in England right now," I told him, then wondered if that was too much information. "She and her husband are supposed to fly back on Sunday. They're stopping over here, so I expect we'll talk then."

Jamal's eyes widened before sending a sly glance towards the Jeep. He lowered his voice, even though we were quite alone. "She's coming to Chicago? I'd like to meet her, if possible. It might be good for her to see what I want to show you too."

"We'll see," I said. I got the impression he wouldn't want Faustyn to know about his meeting Rosalind, and I wondered why. I remembered her telling me the HLF weren't united. Was this part of it?

Jess and I spent the first half of our drive home lost in our own thoughts, while the radio sang to itself. After a few rapid-fire text messages, she laid her phone flat in her lap and stared out her side window. Daylight pulled back from the city like a receding tide.

"More work nonsense?" I asked at last as we passed through Oak Park.

She didn't react at first, then sighed and scratched the bridge of her nose. "Yeah, this is all a bit overwhelming."

I reached over and squeezed her hand. "A lot's happened this week. A lot's happened today. We need time to talk it over together, before Rosalind gets here."

"I agree." She paused. "D?"

"Yeah?"

"In all the time you've been dealing with Imprints, even before you met Rosalind and started erasing them, did you ever get the impression there was something, or someone, there? More than just a memory?"

The question bothered me. I'd never believed in ghosts, in sentient spirits, vestiges of dead people haunting our world. Even after encountering the strange and disturbing phenomena that plagued certain buildings back in St. Louis, I still rejected that explanation. I'd felt vindicated when Rosalind also dismissed it, claiming that what we observed were merely recordings. Although interacting with those recordings helped complete the Erasure, she maintained this was a metaphor for the mental process involved. I believed her. I *wanted* to believe her. No spirits or ghosts were involved. But sometimes, sometimes I doubted.

"Why do you ask?" I evaded.

"Don't you dare laugh, but I felt like someone was watching me, while Jamal was fixing his Tether. I got goosebumps all over."

"It wasn't Faustyn?"

"No, he was too embarrassed by the memory of a blowjob to even look at me. This was someone else. Some*thing* else. You didn't feel it?"

"No, not this time. But I'd be lying if I said I'd never felt anything like that before. Maybe it's just paranoia. We're messing with our minds here."

"Maybe," she said, and stretched, cat-like, in the passenger seat. She was lucky not to cause an accident. "Every time we learn something new, we discover something else we don't understand. There's far more to this than we know, and I think there's more to this than the Foundation knows, or is letting on. We need to be careful."

I couldn't have agreed more.

Rosalind kept her texts short and to the point. She and Martin were flying from London Heathrow to Chicago O'Hare on Sunday, arriving mid-afternoon. They planned to spend "a few days decompressing", staying at "our usual hotel", and would love to have dinner with us that night, preferably not too late. I looked up the flight time and was shocked it was almost nine hours. Add six hours for the time zone change, and even an early evening meal would be midnight England time after a grueling day of travel. She must want to talk to us as much as we wanted to talk to her.

I usually worked Sunday evenings, but switched shifts with Alaska, the newest and youngest member of the Trattoria Cappelli kitchen. She was Luca's niece, but he showed her no favor, and to be fair, she didn't ask for any. Fresh out of culinary school, shy and serious, she listened more than she spoke, and I for one had never had to explain anything twice. I liked to think I was as good a student.

"We could do the tapas restaurant again," I mused, once conversation had turned away from the chaos at Paragon on Friday night. Conor had asked Jess and her teammates if they'd received any "unusual communications" from Marcus before he quit. She agonized over Marcus's last email, but still kept it to herself. I didn't see why she should be so secretive, but I hadn't said so. My mind was on Rosalind's visit and the Henry Lyons Foundation.

"I think they'd prefer somewhere near their hotel," said Jess. "You're sure you don't know where they're staying?"

"If Rosalind told me I don't remember," I admitted, suspecting she'd mentioned it during their last visit.

"We'll figure it out. We just need to make sure we're back in time."

"From your grandparents?"

"No, from the rendezvous with your buddy Train. That's this Sunday, right?" I stared back at her, and she raised an eyebrow. "That doesn't look like a remembering face."

"Shit." I'd totally forgotten.

I still had the bookstore receipt Train used to scrawl his note. I opened the drawer of my bedside table where it, and Allen Weston's book in which he'd concealed it, had languished since we returned from Selene's Books.

Help me. IPP 5/26 3pm.

Almost the same time as the Hills' plane would be landing.

"You still have no idea what help he wants?" asked Jess, squinting at the note.

"I haven't thought about it. I don't know if I *want* to help him."

"You're going to meet him though." It wasn't a question.

I sighed. "There's a sort of unwritten code about these things. He's asked for help. I don't know what I can do for him, but I need to hear him out."

Jess insisted on coming too. She rattled off several good reasons - better cover for me if anyone else from the Themis Center was suspicious, general backup if things went south - but I suspected she was just curious. Suddenly I was on edge again. Yes, we were now blue belts, but she was someone else I had to worry about in a volatile situation.

Sunday was hot, sunny, and sticky, precisely the kind of summer's day I remembered from St. Louis, and which I preferred to spend cowering in the air conditioning. It was Memorial Day weekend, so all the Monday to Friday nine-to-fivers wanted to make the most of their extra leisure day, despite the suffocating heat. Traffic crawled into the suburbs, and I was lucky to grab the last space in one of the downtown Glen Ellyn parking lots. We donned sunglasses and neutral baseball caps, then set off down the Illinois Prairie Path just as 3pm arrived.

I scanned for the orange vests of the Themis Center cleanup crew, assuming Train would be part of that group. I wasn't sure what I'd do when I found them. Lyall, the group's chaperone, had been quick to cut off our first conversation. After he confronted me at Sophie's Books, I'd have few options if he accompanied the group. Jess speculated Train wanted out of rehab, and was being kept there against his will. If I hadn't seen him at the bookstore, I might have scoffed at the idea. But although I thought the entire operation had a cult vibe, I wasn't thrilled with the idea of somehow "springing" Train from their clutches. I knew I didn't want him in my car.

In the end, it didn't matter. We walked about a mile east along the trail, then doubled back and tried the same distance west. We were dripping with sweat and out of water when we gave up. Maybe the schedule had changed, or Train had been assigned to a different shift. Maybe he'd left rehab himself, not needing our help. But after a series of texts from Rosalind announcing their progress through immigration and customs at O'Hare, I decided enough was enough. I didn't want to keep her waiting any longer than necessary. Maybe I'd see Train next time I came out this way for a glimpse of Daniel Hill.

And as if the thought summoned him, I saw Rosalind and Martin's son sitting on a wooden bench by the side of the trail, watching us approach.

Daniel was better groomed than when I'd last seen him. His dark hair was straight and trimmed neatly above his shoulders. He was clean shaven, and he peered up at us through stylish wire-framed eyeglasses. Instead of an orange vest, he wore a plain light-blue t-shirt, khaki cargo shorts, and sandals. He looked like just another local out for a stroll in the stifling afternoon heat. I glanced ahead and to either side of the trail, but as far as I could tell he was alone.

"That's Daniel," I told Jess quietly as he rose from the bench.

"Daniel? Oh! Rosalind's son!"

He grinned as his eyes lingered on her, traveled slowly up and down her body. She giggled as I moved a half step ahead of her.

"D, right?" Daniel said, turning towards me and offering his hand. I hesitated and shook it. Rosalind and Martin were less than twenty miles away, and I was finally talking to their estranged son.

"Hi, Daniel," I said, not knowing what else to say.

He grinned, showing yellowed teeth. "Were you expecting someone else?"

I fought to keep my face free of expression. He knew about Train, and the note. He had to. Who else knew? What was this?

"You're pretty," Daniel said, turning back to Jess with a shy smile. "To whom do I have the honor?"

His accent had no more than the faintest lilt, but that sounded like an expression Rosalind would use.

I wondered if that was intentional.

"I'm Jess," she said, smiling sweetly as she held out her hand. Daniel wavered, perhaps unsure if he should shake it or raise it to his lips. He settled for a hesitant shake.

"You're looking for Bryan," Daniel stated, drawing himself up, full of confidence again. "Although I think you knew him as Train. I'm afraid he won't be joining us this afternoon."

"Why not?" I asked, looking him straight in the eye. "Did he have another relapse?"

Daniel met my gaze, but licked his lips and shuffled backwards. "You didn't get along with Bryan, did you? He told me about the fight you had in prison."

"I had several fights in prison. It came with the territory. That one wasn't special."

"Perhaps, perhaps not. Still, I can't imagine why you'd want to help him."

I shrugged. "I just wanted to talk to him, that's all."

"That won't be possible." Daniel made a show of looking over his shoulder back down the trail. I followed his gaze just as two men stepped out from the tree line about thirty yards away, at a point where overhead power lines cut across the path. They wore orange vests, and I recognized them: Lyall and the other cleanup crew chaperone from last time. Lyall inclined his head in distant greeting, then they turned and strolled away down the trail.

The skin on the back of my neck prickled. The implication was sinister.

"Who are they supposed to be?" demanded Jess, no longer amused or flattered.

Daniel grinned at her, and turned back to me. The kid was living dangerously. "I don't know if anyone else will come looking for Bryan," he said, then paused while a young couple walked past, deep in their own conversation. "His family disowned him, and the friend he worked for in Chicago gave up on him after he entered rehab. No one else cares, D. Only you. And if someone were to stop by the Themis Center and ask questions, that's the story they'd hear: Bryan's old prison buddy, the one he used to fight with, came looking for him."

Despite the almost one hundred degree temperature, a cold shiver trickled down my spine. "What are you playing at, Daniel?" I asked, my voice far calmer than I felt.

"Stay away from us. Don't poke around the Themis Center or pay coincidental visits to bookstores. You don't want to mess with us, trust me."

"You little blackmailing piece of shit," Jess hissed, but I laid a hand on her arm before she could advance on him. She stopped, but I felt her tremble. I willed her to remember her training too.

"Your mother and father are in town," I said softly. "They just landed after visiting your grandfather. He's sick. I'm sure they'd love to catch up. You could join us for dinner tonight if you like."

Daniel's veneer of civility cracked and his face twisted. I couldn't tell if it was anguish or disgust, and I didn't get time to dwell on it before he regained his composure. And then some. There's an old cliche about shutters closing behind someone's eyes, and I watched it happen to him.

"Stay away," he repeated, his voice lifeless. "I don't want to see them. I don't want to see you. Don't come looking for me. I'm no longer in rehab. You won't find me. Don't try."

And with that, he turned on his heel and strode off down the trail. We watched him fade into the crowd, then Jess dislodged my hand from her arm and looked up at me, hands on hips. "So, that went well."

CHAPTER FOURTEEN

AN EXPERIMENTAL APPROACH

Was Train dead?

The thought ricocheted around my skull as the blazing afternoon yielded to a sultry evening. The spreading pall of Canadian wildfire smoke loomed to the north. Threats reared on all sides, and I fought a rising panic.

"Should we call the police?" Jess mused as we hurried back to my Hyundai.

"And say what? All we have are veiled threats and implications. Daniel's right - I don't want any attention from the cops."

"So they get away with it?"

"Maybe. I don't know, Jess. I'm still wrapping my head around one mysterious secret society. I can't handle another one right now."

She grunted, either in frustration or disgust, but bit off whatever she was going to say.

I took her hands and drew her off to the side of the trail. "Please be careful. I know you won't want to drop this. Maybe Daniel was all bluster, but we don't know that. Hell, we're in Chicago, he could be part of the mob!"

Even I didn't find my weak attempt at humor funny. She shook her head in exasperation. "You think I'm not careful? It took me months to find Jamal's emails, because I took my time. I didn't just blunder my way through the dark web like a teenager with their first search engine."

"I'm not saying you did. You're great at what you do, and you can take care of yourself. But I love you, and so I worry about you."

She wrapped her arms around my neck and kissed me. I held her close, inhaling her scent, and she rested her cheek against my shoulder. Panic ebbed, just enough.

We met Rosalind and Martin in the ground floor restaurant of the Metropolitan, a boutique hotel in Wicker Park. I remembered Rosalind saying she preferred bed and breakfasts and smaller hotels, in part because there was less chance of encountering an Imprint. The Metropolitan sported fifty rooms over ten floors, a rooftop bar, and a "comfort food" restaurant. The Hills had taken the train directly from O'Hare, and practically fallen off the elevated station platform into their room.

"You both look tired," said Rosalind, pushing pasta around her plate.

She was one to talk. She'd barely touched her food. Shadows darkened her eyes, I guessed not only from jet lag. Martin didn't look much better, but he'd almost finished his burger, eating like a man who'd found the airline food wanting.

"There's a lot going on," I offered as explanation. Did we really look that bad?

"Agreed, likely more than we can cover tonight. I'm mostly interested in the Henry Lyons Foundation. Have you had any more contact?"

"Yes, actually. Jamal took us to one of their training facilities. Showed us how he imprinted a memory."

"Did he now?" Rosalind set her fork down, abandoning any further pretense at eating. Martin, wiping his chin with a napkin, inspected her half-finished plate, but then sat back and studied the decor. Musical instruments were mounted on the walls and, disconcertingly close, a grand piano hung from the ceiling.

I recounted our visit to Lyons-Strickland Logistics. Jess added commentary, and I wondered if she'd bring up her impression of something watching her. She didn't and neither did I. There was quite enough to tell already.

"Interesting," said Rosalind after I finished. She'd perked up during my tale, her eyes as alert and intense as I'd ever seen them. "And you're sure it was the same memory, the same Imprint that he fixed?"

"I think so. It was the same woman, for sure. I got the impression they'd imprinted lots of memories of that guy."

"I worked with a man like that once," Martin interjected, "back when I was just starting out. The office went through secretaries at a rapid rate, before he was fired."

"Asshole," muttered Jess, looking at Martin with distaste. I assumed her sentiment was directed at his former colleague.

Rosalind laid a hand on her husband's arm and frowned. "It shouldn't have been possible to fix an existing Imprint without erasing it first. Or perhaps I misunderstood what I was told. I haven't received a demo myself."

I leaned forward. Few other tables were occupied this early on a Sunday evening, despite the holiday weekend. But it was quiet, and given how sensitive Rosalind was about using our regular cell phones, the more discretion, the better. "You knew about the HLF before we did. When did they contact you?"

"About a month ago. I was doing another job for Mark Sellars. You remember Mark, my realtor friend? He had potential buyers for a condo in downtown Kirkwood, but the couple in question - Alice and Robert Harrington - complained about strange scents that no one else could smell, sounds no one else could hear. In other words, it was in my 'neck of the woods'." I chuckled, remembering the realtor's go to phrase. "Anyway, the Harringtons insisted on attending the job, which, while unusual, wasn't unprecedented. Afterwards, they asked if they could buy me a drink. I was short on time, but found myself agreeing. And it was over several glasses of strawberry lemonade that they introduced me to the Henry Lyons Foundation."

I finished my own pasta, as she summarized a conversation similar to the one Jess and I had shared with Jamal: a brief history of the HLF and its mission to study the strange, "occult" phenomena witnessed around the world.

"But this is where it gets interesting," she said, dropping her voice lower, as if just realizing we were discussing this in a public place. "You said Jamal and his companions are trying to recruit you, that the HLF is trying to save the world by tethering these 'Intrusions'. Alice and Robert portrayed Tethers as an experimental approach, not as a settled strategy. They used the Imprint I'd just erased as evidence that the approach has side effects, and that very few within the organization are capable of mitigating these side effects. There was much they didn't say, no matter what questions I asked, but reading between the lines I suspect there's a power struggle within the Foundation. Beyond the research, there may be significant philosophical differences concerning how to interpret and act on its results. One philosophy currently dominates, but it hasn't always been that way."

I rubbed my eyes, wondering if and when this would stop getting more complicated.

"So what did they want from you?" asked Jess. "If they didn't show you how to tether an Intrusion, I assume they didn't try to recruit you."

Rosalind smiled grimly. "Oh, but they did. Alice and Robert replaced Jamal as the Foundation's top representatives in St. Louis. They told me that our friends Donovan and Lana are still operating, both on their behalf and doing what they called 'lower quality work' for Steven Rourke on the side. The Foundation wants to bring me in, to train me, as I'm sure they want to train you two. But the Harringtons also encouraged me to 'deal with' the bad Imprints Donovan and Lana are creating. And they were quite insistent that the only way to do so was to erase them. That's why I was surprised when you told me that Jamal fixed a bad Tether."

"To be fair," said Jess, "he has experience with creating Tethers, and you don't. Maybe the HLF just recognizes that and figures it would be easier for you to erase them for now, until you learn to fix them."

Rosalind frowned. The two women locked gazes for several heartbeats. I caught Martin's eye, but his face remained impassive.

Just when I was taking breath to speak, Rosalind sighed and shrugged. "Perhaps you're right, Jess. It could be that simple. But there are too many people involved to believe there is only one agenda at work. Until I learn more, I'm not willing to sign on to anything."

"Oh, totally," Jess said, nodding with a relieved smile. "But I do think we need to learn. And if we learn from people with opposing viewpoints, and compare notes, maybe we'll get to the bottom of it all sooner."

Martin met this statement with a wide yawn that set off sympathetic yawns around the table.

"Sorry, love," Rosalind murmured, nuzzling her head against his shoulder. "I know this must be boring you. I'm fading too. Perhaps we can continue this discussion another day."

I signaled to our server to bring us the check, but Martin snatched it from my fingers and slid my offered cash back towards me. "Take us out later in the week." He smiled, slipping his credit card into the leather sleeve.

"Fine," I said, then steeled myself for the part of the conversation I was dreading. "I need to tell you both something else before we leave. Jess and I saw Daniel again today. Talked to him."

Rosalind and Martin froze, but said nothing, just waited for me to continue. With half an eye out for the server, I hurried through an account of our afternoon encounter on the Illinois Prairie Path. There wasn't much to tell, but I expected a lot of questions. Instead, the Hills just exchanged weary glances, and Rosalind slumped more heavily against her husband.

"Thank you," Martin said. "We don't expect any more from our son. I'm glad to hear he's out of rehab again, at least. I hope he stays out this time. And I hope your suspicions about your friend Train are unfounded."

"He's not my friend," I blurted, then winced at how easily I'd dismissed someone who might have suffered a terrible fate. "I still don't understand exactly what happened, or why you sent us to that bookstore last month."

I looked at Rosalind, but she only grimaced. Jess took my hand in hers. "Let's save that for next time," she said with a sad smile, tugging at me as she stood. "The two of you need rest and some time to yourselves. D's working doubles the next two days, but text me if you need anything."

"Thank you, Jess," said Rosalind, returning the smile.

I allowed myself to be drawn to my feet. I wanted to hug Rosalind, Martin too, but they didn't rise with us, and we left them with an awkward goodbye.

Chapter Fifteen
PSYCHIC SHOCK

I hated driving in Chicago. My blood pressure rose every time I buckled my seatbelt. A reasonable inner voice reminded me that St. Louis wasn't much better, especially during rush hour, but I wasn't in the mood. The reasonable voice scuttled into a corner of my mind as I fumed and muttered curses.

Jess and Rosalind engaged in cheerful conversation as we crawled north on Lake Shore Drive. The Hills had recovered from their jet lag and, setting aside transatlantic family issues, had decided to make the most of their time in the Windy City. Rosalind gushed about the Museum of Science and Industry, which they'd visited earlier that day. Its buildings were the only significant survivors of the Great Columbian Exposition, otherwise known as the World's Fair of 1893. The site in Jackson Park had been bleak swampland on the shore of Lake Michigan, before the labor of countless men transformed it into one of the city's most vibrant green spaces. Cooler temperatures had swept through the region after the holiday weekend, and the thought of strolling through parks and museums sounded idyllic.

Certainly better than being cooped up in a restaurant kitchen for fifteen hours two days running, then discovering this morning that Alessandra, our sous chef, had handed in her notice. She was opening her own restaurant in Los Angeles, offering a fusion of Cuban staples and comfort food from the American South. I joined everyone else in wishing her well, despite mixed feelings that she'd developed a menu based on Cuban cuisine.

I didn't celebrate that half of my heritage, even refusing to eat "Cuban sandwiches". I'd never met my father, or even seen a photograph. He'd abandoned my mother before I'd been born, or so the story went. She refused to talk about him, and had once flown into a rage at my grandfather for telling me the story. As years passed and the rift between us widened, I understood I reminded her of my father, of what must have been a painful time in her young life. I resented her for resenting me, but my teenage rebellion hadn't led me to explore that part of my background. I despised him for what he'd done to her, to us, for he'd abandoned me too.

"You're quiet, D," Rosalind observed after a pause in the conversation.

I grunted, turning north on Clark Street. "I was listening," I said. "Can't talk much while I'm driving in traffic."

"Other than profanity, you mean?" sniped Jess, giving my arm a playful swat. She was in a good mood; the atmosphere at Paragon must be improving.

"Have you seen these idiots?" I said, gesturing to the road ahead.

"Not every other driver is an idiot, love. And he wonders why I won't let him drive to St. Louis," she told Rosalind, with a roll of her eyes.

Rosalind chuckled. "I'm glad you're coming back for the weekend. Your family must miss you, Jess. How's your father doing?"

My mind drifted away from the conversation again. Family. I felt another twinge of guilt for not telling my half-sister Fiona yet that I was coming to town. I resolved to call her that night, assuming we got home at a reasonable hour. I had no idea how long Jamal would keep us.

The Anne Lyons Nursing Center occupied most of a block in the southwest corner of Evanston, a North Shore suburb most well-known as the location of Northwestern University's main campus. James Evans, Jess's grandfather, lived there, further north and closer to the lake, but we wouldn't be calling on him that evening. The nursing home was a bland, three-story building, functional rather than homely. It sat back from the road, allowing a shallow parking lot to span its yellow brick facade. I had no trouble finding a spot, although I suspected that would rarely be an issue. The home's long-term residents were unlikely to draw frequent visitors.

"Did Jamal say why we were meeting him at a home for coma patients?" Rosalind asked, climbing out of my car and stretching. The westering sun silhouetted her riotous blue and yellow sundress, and I caught myself staring a split second before Jess snickered. I disguised my embarrassment by searching for Jamal's white Acura, and spied it lurking next to a silver minivan.

"He said he'd explain when we got here," I said. "Something about showing, not telling."

"Indeed I did."

We turned to see Jamal emerge from the entrance, wearing another of his usual polo shirts, this one salmon pink, and tan slacks. He barely acknowledged me or Jess, giving his full attention to Rosalind. She watched his approach with the polite smile of someone greeting a used car salesman. He extended his hand, which she briefly shook.

"Rosalind Hill. You have no idea how long I've looked forward to meeting you."

"You were at the 5K race," she said, unimpressed. "In Forest Park last year. You accompanied our friends Donovan and Lana. Why not say hello then?"

Jamal offered a wry smile. "Unfortunately, I had been directed otherwise. The Foundation is careful in its approach to freelancers or others sensitive to the phenomena we study. My role, as far as you three were concerned, was to observe and report, nothing more."

"I see. Pity. We might have avoided the unpleasantness at Chouteau Village shortly thereafter. Not to mention D's workplace burning down, obliging my good friends to uproot their lives and move three hundred miles away."

"I had nothing to do with that!"

"Yet you did nothing to stop it, or help in its aftermath. I've witnessed more than enough bullying in my years as a teacher. I have no patience for it, or for those who stand aside and watch it happen instead of speaking up."

Rosalind's eyes were pure cold steel. She was the shortest and oldest of us, but Jamal wasn't the only one to take an involuntary step back. Our Sensei in St. Louis had once described her as a "force of nature" and I understood exactly what he meant.

"You're right," Jamal said at last, turning his hands palms up. "I'm sorry. In my defense, I was lobbying to reach out, to you especially, Ms. Hill. I have skirted HLF protocol before to the detriment, I believe, of my career." A sour note entered his voice, and he lifted his chin. "Yet here we are, and I am doing so again. Faustyn, who supervises our activities in Chicago, knows that D and Jess are with me this evening. He does *not* know that you are, Ms. Hill. I would prefer to keep it that way."

"Oh call me Rosalind," she snapped. "What's with all the cloak and dagger?"

His smile was thin. "It must seem so. There are reasons, some of them good ones. But let's go inside. We only have thirty minutes before visiting hours are over."

After his polite gesture to Rosalind, she fell into step with him, like a queen escorted by a courtier. Jess and I exchanged smirks. We'd both been on the receiving end of "the teacher's look", but had never received such a dressing down. That was worth the drive by itself.

We entered a cool, bright reception area, its pastel blue walls accented with tasteful dark wood trim. A sprinkling of off-white fabric chairs jostled potted house plants, mostly ferns, and led us to a desk against the rear wall. A plexiglass shield towered above the middle half, behind which sat a plump woman in clean white scrubs. Her pale round face was lined with age and care, her graying hair scrunched up into a bun. She offered us a tired smile.

"Which ward, Mr. Peters?" she asked Jamal, giving the rest of us the side eye as she reached under the desk.

"Jennings, I think. Thank you, Ms. Jacobs."

A solid wooden door to our left buzzed, a green light flashing on the electronic lock below its bronze handle. Jamal opened it and beckoned us through. I followed Rosalind and Jess, but not without reservations. Institutions with locked doors made me nervous.

I've spent most of my life inside them: schools, prison, a handful of hospitals. It's amazing how common the architecture is, an almost endless series of identical rooms hanging off of high-ceilinged, crisscrossing corridors. The decor may vary, the scents and sounds certainly do, but my discomfort always increased with every step I took into their depths. I was on high alert for any hint of an Imprint, or possibly an untethered Intrusion, but I sensed nothing, not even a background hum. The entire long room into which we stepped was lifeless.

The Jennings ward occupied one half of the ground floor. The blinds had already been drawn for the night in front of flanking parades of tall windows. Tasteful, rubbed-bronze light sconces punctuated otherwise featureless walls of the same pastel blue hue as the reception area. A faint antiseptic odor was likely just that, antiseptic. Two rows of beds lined the walls, sixteen in total, each with a heavy plastic curtain that could be drawn around it for privacy. All but two beds contained a single sleeping patient.

No, not sleeping exactly. I looked in mixed pity and horror at one patient after another. Men of different ethnicities and ages, whether lying down or sitting up, stared with closed eyes from faces devoid of expression. A simple aluminum-framed chair accompanied each bed, presumably for visitors, and each nightstand supported haunting reminders of a life on pause: family photographs, bowling trophies, children's artwork.

I didn't need the presence of Imprints to feel profoundly disturbed. I halted as soon as Jamal closed the door behind us, and so did Jess, surveying the room with a bleak expression. Hadn't one of her cousins been in a coma once, after a car accident? Only for a few days, though, if I remembered right. I suspected most of these men had been in their present vegetative state for far longer.

Rosalind continued on, pausing by each bed to read the patient's name on the chart hanging off the footboard. About halfway down the ward, she turned back toward us, her expression grim. "I assume you have a reason for bringing us here," she said to Jamal. Despite the piped eighties playlist, her voice carried clearly, along with undercurrents of disapproval and challenge.

Jamal walked towards her before replying, drawing me and Jess in his wake. "If you look up the Henry Lyons Foundation online, you'll find our public face is an organization funding research into coma treatment. That's not just a front. We partner with many distinguished institutions and cultivate some of the finest minds in the world, as they strive to recover those currently lost to us. If the brain has sustained physical damage, our options are limited. But when the precipitating injury is a form of 'psychic shock', we believe there are paths to healing. We just haven't found them yet."

A spasm of emotion crossed his face, and he covered his mouth with one hand. I thought I understood, and looked around with mounting horror. "These men, they all worked for the HLF?"

"No," Jamal said, shaking his head and taking a deep breath. "Perhaps ten percent, mostly new recruits, who attempted too much too soon. Most of these patients, and those in the other five wards, had no idea what they were dealing with. Our model tells us, with a fair degree of certainty, where Intrusions are likely to occur. We cannot predict who, of the dozens or hundreds of people in their vicinity, may be sensitive. Then there are the scores of leaky Tethers forgotten, perhaps created by those whose motives are less than altruistic." His gaze met mine, and I grimaced. "Evidence suggests most sensitives shun these phenomena, much like D once did. We find as many as we can, and recruit those with interest and aptitude. Others try to deal with the phenomena themselves, using only their instincts or even their subconscious. Rarely, if their intuition and mental discipline are strong enough, they survive. More often, they end up here, or somewhere like it."

"How do you know?" asked Rosalind. Her voice had softened and her eyes filled with pity as she surveyed the room.

"Because we investigate every instance where someone falls into a coma without physical brain injury or other obvious medical reason. As often as not, we discover an Intrusion or leaky Tether near where the victim was found. The evidence is circumstantial but compelling."

I met Rosalind's eyes. Was she thinking about our visit to the hardware store on South Grand last year? I'd almost lost myself in a memory associated with an Imprint I was trying to erase, a leaky Tether I was trying to destroy. If she hadn't finished the job for me, could I have ended up in a place like this? If Jamal hadn't stepped in at Garfield Park High School, might I be occupying a bed in this very ward? Might Jess?

"When you say 'psychic shock'," I said slowly, "do you think all these men, all the other patients here, are they still living that memory? Are they stuck in it, like an endless loop?"

Rosalind bit her lip, and Jess laid a hand on my arm.

If anything, Jamal appeared most troubled by the question. "We don't know," he admitted, not meeting my eyes. "We've never been able to wake anyone up to ask."

A wave of nausea twisted my gut. I needed to move, so started walking further down the ward. Behind me, Jess and Rosalind continued to pepper Jamal with questions.

"Are you saying this is what could happen to us?" asked Jess. "Is this supposed to be some kind of warning?"

Of course it was. Jamal's invitation made perfect sense now. Learn how to create Tethers with the HLF or risk making a terrible mistake, one that would ruin our lives. This was the stick to go with the carrot. From the sounds of it, neither Rosalind nor Jess were particularly impressed, but I stopped listening. Point made.

I reached the last occupied bed on the right-hand side, and glanced at its occupant, propped up by a mound of pillows. He had my complexion, but was likely a decade older, his receding black hair streaked with gray. The heavily-muscled arms of a physical laborer peeked out from his standard-issue medical gown, and he looked less gaunt than most. I wondered how long he'd lain there. I checked his chart: Raul Gutierrez, admitted January 13th, scarcely four months ago. If he woke up now, how hard would it be to pick up the pieces of his life? Would he look any different to the woman and children in his bedside photographs? I looked back at his face with sympathy.

It happened fast. His eyes flicked open and gazed directly at me. At the same time, I felt... something, more than just the shock of his animation. Something or someone who was not Raul Gutierrez scrutinized me with his eyes. I flinched, almost stumbling in place, blinking rapidly. By the time I refocused, his eyes had closed, and the sense of another presence watching me vanished as quickly as it appeared. Had I imagined it? My racing heart and the adrenaline-fueled pounding in my ears suggested otherwise.

"D?"

I turned to see Jess leading the others towards me, puzzled concern on her face. I shook my head to clear it, tried to pull myself together. My phone buzzed in my pocket, but I ignored it.

"Did you sense that?" I rasped. Jess stared back at me blankly.

"What did you sense?" Rosalind asked as she approached the bed, frowning at its unresponsive occupant.

"It..." I stopped as Jamal joined us. He avoided looking at the bed. What did he know? What wasn't he telling us? "What is this? If you're trying to creep me out, congratulations: you've creeped me out."

Jamal gave me an odd look. "I'm merely trying to convey the magnitude of the risk—"

"Save it!" I barked, louder than I intended. I balled my hands into fists and forced myself to take a deep, ragged breath. "I need to get out of here. I need air."

Without waiting for a reaction, I brushed past him and strode for the exit. I kept my eyes straight ahead, fixed on the door. I yanked it open, forced myself to offer a tight smile and my thanks to the receptionist, then escaped into the parking lot. I didn't stop until I reached the narrow grass verge bordering the road, then gulped in several lungfuls of air before leaning over, hands on hips, like I'd just finished a 5K race.

I stayed there until another wave of nausea passed, heedless of what passing motorists might think, then straightened and looked back at the nursing home. The setting sun cast ruddy shadows over its bleak facade, and I shuddered. What the hell was that? I hadn't felt this rattled since before I met Rosalind - since before taking up karate to help control my warring emotions at all the weird shit that was going on in my life.

And the universe wasn't done with me yet.

My phone buzzed again, and I dug it out of my pocket in irritation. I was trying to have a panic attack here. It was Fiona, and I saw that she'd tried to call a few minutes earlier. Odd that she'd be so persistent.

"Hi, Fiona," I answered, cupping a hand over my phone. "I was literally planning to call you later. We're coming into town on Friday and—"

"Mom wants to see you," Fiona interrupted.

I paused, wary. She sounded tired, more tired than usual for a mother of two young children. "And why would she want to do that?" I asked, trying to keep the old bitterness from my voice.

Fiona sighed, and there was a hitch to it that told me all I needed to know. "Because she's dying, D."

CHAPTER SIXTEEN

YOURS

"What's he doing here?"

I'd barely crossed the threshold of the red brick bungalow, blinking at the transition from dazzling sunlight to the dim, brooding living room, and Mary was already on my case. She occupied the entire forest-green velvet loveseat, her feet planted wide and flinty eyes narrowed in disapproval. I knew she'd be here, and entertained no illusions as to my reception.

"I could ask you the same question," I snarled. "Get vaccinated yet?"

She opened her mouth to reply, but Fiona cut her off. "Save it, both of you," she snapped, shutting the front door. She stood no higher than my shoulder, gave up a hundred pounds to both me and her older sister, but she shot us a no-nonsense look that she'd likely practiced on her kids for the last couple years. Maybe her husband Eric too.

"Is he here?" A tremulous male voice wafted from the direction of the kitchen, and did just as fine a job of forestalling further bickering. I clamped my mouth shut and surveyed the room. A brown leather recliner shared a scratched-up wooden coffee table with the love seat, both facing a large flat screen TV propped up on the vintage buffet that dominated the opposite wall. Twin stacks of books and magazines flanked a disused white stone fireplace to my left, past which beckoned the entrance to the kitchen and the corridor leading to the bathroom and bedrooms. Paintings and family pictures hung at irregular intervals on the cream-colored walls, and I didn't have to look to know that none of them featured me.

Other than the TV, the only other thing that had changed since I left for college twenty years before was the large wooden crucifix hanging on the wall above it. Mom had never been religious. She'd rebelled against her Catholic upbringing since she was a teenager. She'd never taken us to church, but me and my half-sisters had attended a series of Catholic schools. I suspected my devout grandparents influenced that decision, likely making it a condition of their financial assistance. I was surprised to see such an open acknowledgment of their beliefs in Mom's house.

"Hey, Dad!" Fiona called, leading me through to the kitchen. I wasn't in a hurry to see my stepfather, but in a straight up contest between him and Mary, Patrick Walsh won hands down.

The kitchen was small and functional, and had also changed little since I'd lived there. The entire house was smaller than I remembered, but Patrick was not. Never a small man, he had to weigh over three hundred pounds now. He slumped against the tile-topped kitchen table, sweat beading on his bald scalp despite the ceiling fan whirring desperately above. He drew deeply on a cigarette as we entered the room. The kitchen stank of tobacco, and the large Budweiser ashtray overflowed with half-smoked stubs. I coughed, covering my mouth and almost retching.

"What the hell?" Fiona snatched the still-smoking cigarette from Patrick's fingers, jammed it into the ashtray, then confiscated the half-full packet of Marlboros before he could protect them. "Now of all times, Dad? What were you thinking?"

He laughed bitterly. "A little late for that judgment, Fi." He hacked a smoker's cough and squinted up at me, while Fiona tossed both packet and ash-tray contents into the kitchen trash. She wrinkled her nose and closed the lid firmly.

"That needs to be taken out," she declared, tossing her silver-dyed hair and planting hands on her hips. She and Jess would get on famously. "Can you do that while I take D back to see Mom?"

He didn't answer, just kept staring at me with bloodshot eyes. He hadn't shaved recently, and I wondered if the reek of smoke disguised how long it had been since he showered.

"How many years has it been?" he asked.

I shrugged. "Eighteen, give or take."

He nodded and looked like he wanted to say more, then grimaced. "Try not to wear her out."

Fiona laid a comforting hand on his shoulder, then caught my eye and jerked her head toward the corridor. Two down.

Mom's bedroom was all the way at the end. We passed the door to the basement, where my room had been since I was five and Fiona was born. I left the door, and those memories, closed. The shared bathroom, Mary's bedroom, Fiona's bedroom. With every step, another year rolled back. I'd marshaled my defenses before setting foot in the house, but they weren't flawless. There I was, nine years old, chasing Mary and Fiona down the corridor, brandishing a tree frog I'd captured in the backyard. Three years later, Mary bawling to her father, clutching the Barbie doll I'd decapitated in retribution for her tearing up my Stone Temple Pilots poster. Fiona, in the spring before I left for college, sobbing into my shoulder because the boy she liked had asked another girl to their middle school dance. They were always there, these memories, no matter how deeply I buried them. They'd pop up, unbidden, while I stared into the dark, sleepless, in my prison cell. They had less power over me now than they once did, or so I'd thought. Coming back to this house - this house, not my home - amplified them. They were as potent as Imprints and not so easily dismissed.

Fiona stopped outside Mom's bedroom door. It was cracked a couple inches, enough to leak daylight and a whiff of cedar wood air freshener. I silenced the memories clamoring for my attention. This would be hard enough.

"This might be a bit of a shock," Fiona whispered. "You haven't seen her in a long time, and, well, the last six months haven't been kind." Her lip trembled, and I took her hand.

"I wish you'd told me about the cancer," I started, but she shook her head.

"Not now. What's done is done. Right now she wants to see you. Let me just check if she's awake."

She nudged the door further open and peered around it, then smiled. "Hey, Mom! Guess who's here?"

"Declan?" rasped a low voice I hardly recognized.

"Yep! Go on in, D."

Breathe.

A short, dark-skinned young woman wearing navy blue scrubs stepped out before I could enter. The nurse practitioner nodded to Fiona, gave me a curious look, then yielded the room. It didn't feel like the largest in the house. A queen size bed, a vanity, two wooden armoires and, of all things, a treadmill competed for floor space and crowded the window blinds. The burgundy floral print wallpaper survived, although it was peeling in places. The framed pictures on the nightstand looked recent, one of purple-haired Fiona and her family, and one of all the grandchildren together.

I absorbed all this in a matter of moments, before my eyes were drawn to the tiny, frail woman propped up on her pillows. Shock didn't begin to cover it. I wouldn't have looked twice had I not known this was Mom. She'd always been slim and short, much like Fiona, who most favored her, but lung cancer had taken a heavy toll. Cheekbones jutted out from her bone-white skin, painfully thin arms lay immobile on her lap. A bright pink headscarf disguised what I suspected was hair loss from the chemotherapy, although the vivid red curls I remembered would likely have turned gray by now. Her sixtieth birthday was next month, July 2nd, but she wasn't going to make it. The doctors knew it, she knew it, and now that I saw her, I knew it too.

"Hi, Mom." It sounded lame, but I had nothing witty to say to the mother I hadn't seen or heard from in almost two decades. I'd almost reconciled to never seeing her again.

She looked at me then, and that's when I knew her. If I squinted and ignored her failing body, I could see my mother quite clearly in those quick and expressive blue eyes. Windows to the soul indeed. I'd often seen disdain and disappointment in them, but there had been moments of joy and pride, especially in the early years. Now? Now I saw sorrow and regret.

"Sit," she said, her left hand twitching atop the cover. One of the kitchen chairs had been drafted into service next to the bed, so I sat awkwardly. I wasn't sure if I was supposed to hug her, or if I could, or if she even wanted me to. I wasn't sure why I was there. So I sat and waited.

"I'll leave you to it," murmured Fiona, and she slipped out of the room.

Mom and I stared at each other, the uncomfortable silence broken only by birdsong. We'd always had feeders in our back-yard. I wondered if anyone had filled them lately, and resisted the urge to get up and look.

"Tell me... about yourself," Mom whispered, each word an effort.

"Um, what do you want to know? I assume Fiona keeps you as updated as you want to be."

Irritation flashed across her face. "Tell... me!"

So I did. While the finches and chickadees chattered outside, I told my mother about her estranged son's life. I skipped over my twelve years in prison. I started with Hickory and with Jess, especially with Jess. I told her about running 5k races, and about training in karate. For some reason, she found the idea of karate hilarious: she laughed silently, eyes closed as she trembled with mirth. I was taken aback, but it was hard to take offense when I'd made her laugh for the first time in two decades.

I described our move to Chicago, but I didn't explain why. I left out Steven Rourke, and I certainly didn't mention any unusual problems or their solutions. I claimed our new jobs gave both Jess and I chances to advance our careers, and that wasn't untrue.

"I'm happy, Mom," I concluded. I didn't want to wear her out. "Nothing's ever perfect, but my life is back on track. I think, I hope, I would make you proud."

The last word died on my tongue. Tears I'd doubted would come welled in the corners of my eyes. Hers never left mine. Her hand twitched again, and I covered it with my own. It was so cold, so bony and frail, like antique porcelain.

"Good," she breathed. "Wish..."

"I know. I wish it could be different. Would you like to meet Jess?"

She shook her head, a quick jerk to either side. "Not... like this."

Silence descended again, and I waited for her. The birds had fallen silent, and perhaps they waited too.

"Have not... been... good mother."

I didn't know how to respond. I agreed, but that wasn't something I wanted to linger on at her deathbed. "Mary and Fiona might disagree," I offered at last, and that earned me a sad smile.

"Envelope... on nightstand."

I looked and saw, lying flat next to the picture of Fiona's family, a tattered brown envelope that might once have enclosed a greeting card. There was no inscription or markings of any kind, and I felt a curious reluctance to even touch it. "You want me to look at it?"

"For you."

For me. Steeling myself, I picked up the envelope. It was light, there couldn't be much in it. I lifted the flap and slid out the photograph inside.

I'd seen enough pictures of Mom as a young woman to recognize her instantly. This was how she should be remembered, pretty and vivacious, untamed ginger curls and a winning smile.

She rocked her skimpy black bikini as she slung her arm around a hunk of a man, at least a head taller. His slicked back black hair framed a rugged, square jawed face, and I honestly stopped taking in further details. I knew this face, knew it as well as I knew my own. My heart drummed in my chest as I glanced at Mom, to find her watching me with what I can only describe as dread.

"Dad?" I said, even though I knew the answer.

"Ramon," she whispered.

My middle name. I was even less inclined to use it than Declan. I turned the picture over. "Miami Beach, Sept 1986" was printed in neat letters on the back. I did the math: I would've been conceived weeks or even days after this photograph was taken. I'd never asked, because it really didn't matter to me, but I wondered if I'd been planned and, if not, if that had driven a wedge into their relationship. The couple on the beach looked happy enough.

"More." I almost didn't hear her, lost in my own long-buried thoughts. I looked at her slumping against her pillows, and realized that, as frail as she'd appeared when I'd first entered the room, she'd made a significant effort to rouse herself for my visit. That effort had come at a cost, and she was fading fast. I squeezed the envelope open and spied a small object lurking at the bottom. I dug my hand inside and emerged holding a plain gold ring. A wedding band.

I rolled the hard gold in my fingers. It was too large for Mom; this was his. They'd been married? Of course they had, I'd been given his last name too. A closer inspection of the picture revealed rings on both their fingers. I wondered what she'd done with hers, but there was no way I was going to ask, even if she'd had the energy to answer.

I dropped the ring back into the envelope and slid the photo in to join it. Mom's head lolled against her pillow, but her eyes fluttered open.

"Yours," she said, the rasp to her voice far more pronounced. "Remember…"

Her eyelids closed again as her cancer-wracked body focused on breathing. I watched in silence for a few minutes, wrestling with a spectrum of emotions, then leaned over and kissed her cheek.

"Goodbye, Mom."

The call came the following afternoon, during Madaraka Day celebrations at Jess's parents' house.

Unlike last year's "Kenya Day", marred by storms of both the meteorological and jealous girlfriend kind, this Evans family annual event was full of love and laughter. The hot, dry weather meant Calvin and Zawida could host their three children, partners, and grandchildren on the spacious and well-manicured patio behind their immaculate Clayton home. Jonathan's two older daughters and Kioko's two sons wolfed or picked at their meal, before chasing each other through the back yard in a ferocious game of tag. The food was as delicious as I remembered. I wouldn't tell her mother, but Zawida's Kenyan staples and delicacies were in a league of their own.

Everyone welcomed me with open arms, even frosty Kioko. "My sister's brought the same man two years running," he said as he passed me a beer. "That's a first, man!"

Every time she talked to me, Zawida would tear up and wrap me in a hug. "You take good care of each other," she repeated, and I couldn't tell if that was observation or instruction. I felt guilty about spiriting away her daughter to Chicago, but she was happier than anyone that we were together. For a few short hours, I could set aside my personal and family troubles, and laugh with everyone else at the siblings' good-natured bickering.

My good humor lasted until my phone rang just after we'd finished dessert. Jess had to hunt me down. I'd been talking to Calvin in his study, and had left my phone on the patio table. "It's Fiona," she whispered as she handed it to me, then ushered her father out of the room.

"It's over," Fiona told me when I called back. Her voice was numb, lifeless. I heard muted sobbing in the background.

"I'm on my way."

Jess and I bid hurried goodbyes - she had to tug me free from her mother's tearful hug - and she drove Zawida's Subaru to the Southampton bungalow. Afterwards, I had no memory of that journey. One moment I was collapsing into the car's passenger seat, the next I was climbing out of it again. Mary's and Fiona's cars were parked outside. I trudged toward the front porch steps, while the sympathetic caresses of a soft breeze bathed us in the aroma of the neighbor's lilac bushes.

Fiona let us in, then wrapped me in a fierce embrace. Mary sat on the love seat as if she hadn't moved since yesterday, although her auburn curls hung free around slumped shoulders and she'd exchanged a navy blouse for a black one. She ignored my entrance, dabbing at the corners of her bloodshot gray eyes with a Kleenex as she stared at the pictures on the opposite wall. Crumpled tissues overflowed the waste basket by her feet, littering the scuffed hardwood floor around her sneakers. The box on the table was empty, so while Fiona hugged Jess, heedless of the fact that they'd never met before, I knelt down and collected the debris, then took the waste basket to the kitchen. Patrick sat at his customary place at the kitchen table, fingertips at his temples, and I squeezed his shoulder as I walked past. He didn't speak, but clasped my hand. I emptied the waste basket, picked up another box of Kleenex from the multipack next to the back door, and returned to the living room.

Fiona and Jess held hands as they talked quietly, but Mary continued to stare into space, tears trickling down both cheeks. I opened the Kleenex box and offered her one. Her gaze slowly shifted to it, then to my face, and I suddenly guessed how alone she must feel. She'd lost her husband to COVID less than a year into the pandemic, and was now raising three elementary age children by herself. Mom was her rock, her support and solace. But Mom was gone.

Cautiously, I perched on the edge of the love seat and shook the box. She extracted a tissue and dabbed at her cheeks, her eyes never leaving mine. I realized I still held the wastebasket in my other hand, and offered her that too. She emitted a strangled laugh, then simply rested her head in the crook of my shoulder. I shared a look of astonishment with Fiona.

"I'm going to check on Dad," she said with an unexpected smile. "Need anything?"

"No," I said. I didn't trust myself to say more.

Jess took the basket from me and set it back down on Mary's other side. Then she knelt down beside me, laid her head on my other shoulder, and clasped my hand in hers. As I sat there, between the woman I loved most and the one I'd most detested, sharing our grief, I came to a decision.

"No one's having this, Jess," I whispered, and if Mary heard, she didn't react. "No-one gets to see these memories." I didn't know if there was an Intrusion in the house, or who the Henry Lyons Foundation might send if there was. I didn't care. I didn't care if it was some faceless agent or Donovan Brooks or Lana Gunderson. I didn't care if Steven Rourke heard about it and decided, out of sheer perversity, to coerce them into creating a leaky Tether. I didn't even care if Rosalind saved the day, destroyed the Imprint, and scattered its memory to the four winds. I didn't want any of them to see this. This was private. This was mine. Suddenly, I felt deep empathy for all those souls whose deepest, darkest emotions had been scribed on the fabric of the universe for others, who could, to see. That couldn't happen here. I wouldn't let it.

It was time to talk to Jamal.

CHAPTER SEVENTEEN

DON'T TRUST COINCIDENCES

The funeral was set for Tuesday afternoon, the wake for Monday evening.

Fiona rarely sat down, let alone slept. Her husband, Eric, had been watching Mary's kids as well as theirs the last two days, and looked as frazzled as anyone. He brought them all over Saturday night, shaking my hand and muttering tired condolences. Fiona and Mary hugged their children, who I was meeting for the first time. Fiona's daughter had just started to walk, but only shrank against her mother, wide blue eyes staring at all the strangers. Their three-year-old son had inherited his grandmother's fiery curls, and an impatient stamping of the foot echoed her temperament too. Mary's two boys and girl looked as numb as I felt; this wasn't their first experience with death.

Patrick was too overwhelmed with grief to be of much help. Jess offered to pick up takeout for dinner. Eric and Mary watched the kids, while Fiona appointed herself to do everything else. "I've got to keep busy," she protested over my objections. "I need time and space to grieve properly."

"Let me help," I insisted, wrapping her in a hug as darkness fell. "If you want the wake here, let me handle the food. I know a guy."

Before I could talk myself out of it, I called Mike Szemis, my old boss at Hickory, for the first time since I'd moved to Chicago.

"D! This is a surprise!" The undercurrent of wariness in his voice told me he wasn't sure if it was a good surprise. I skipped the small talk and explained what I wanted. "Of course," he said, with evident relief. "I'm sorry to hear about your mother. This is the least I can do for you. Monday evening, you say? I'll bring it over myself."

While I thought about food, I called Luca, expecting to leave a message during Trattoria Capelli's busy dinner service. When he answered, I stammered out the situation and asked if I could extend my absence for another few days. My new boss was as accommodating as my former one, and had a surprise of his own.

"I was going to tell you Monday, along with everyone else," he said, raising his voice over the kitchen clamor. "Tamsyn's taking over as sous chef, and I want you on meats. You've earned it. And you can mentor Alaska while she takes veggies."

I couldn't believe it. There was just too much to process. I thanked him, hung up, then slumped against the kitchen counter and closed my eyes. A few deep breaths later, I felt an arm snake around my waist, and soft lips kiss my cheek.

"Come on, love," whispered Jess. "Let's go home and give them space."

I'd hoped to meet Colton Lynn and his partner for breakfast on Sunday, but he'd begged off sick with an overnight text: 'COVID again'. Instead, we joined Rosalind and Martin at the Botanical Garden, arriving early to avoid the smothering heat and humidity that had followed us from Chicago.

Rosalind enfolded me in a long, silent hug as soon as we met them in the Visitors Center. One mostly sleepless night had done little to help me sort through the complicated emotions rattling around my brain. I was prepared for her condolences, her offers to help in any way she could. I wasn't prepared for a simple embrace, its intimacy saying more than any platitudes. A single tear trickled down her cheek as I wiped mine away, then

Martin gave me a shorter but no less appreciated hug. And that was all I needed.

"Let's walk," said Rosalind, taking my arm. I glanced at Jess, and she winked back before falling into step alongside Martin. We lingered in the rose garden, Rosalind pointing out varieties that grew in their own yard in Webster Groves, then we sought shade under the trees when the morning sun's relentless heat became too much.

"How is Jess's family treating you?" Rosalind asked. "You know you would have been welcome to stay with us."

"I know and thank you," I replied. "But they've been wonderful. Considerate and understanding. Her mom fusses over me. I'm sure I'll be ten pounds heavier by the time we head back to Chicago."

Rosalind chuckled, and shot me a sidelong glance. "I'd like to meet them someday."

"Perhaps you will. They all seem to think I'll be around for a while. Although we're sleeping in separate bedrooms. They're very traditional that way."

"Quite right too! You're not even engaged yet."

"Engaged?" My laugh was a little uncomfortable, and I looked back to see if Jess had overheard. She and Martin were in earnest conversation.

"...the entire city? How is that possible?"

"They're still not sure. Phoenix has had comprehensive water management plans in place for decades. My bank financed developments out there that depend on them. This could cripple the city for weeks, if not longer."

"What are you talking about?" I asked. Rosalind squeezed my arm. She knew a change of subject when she heard it.

"This morning's big news story," said Jess, rolling her eyes. "You know the news, that thing you refuse to pay attention to."

I shrugged. "I get tired of hearing about the world going to hell, or posturing politicians lying through their teeth. I figure if anything's important enough, I'll hear about it eventually."

"Well, this might be important," Martin said, his face grim. "Someone, likely many someones, poisoned Phoenix's potable water supply. There's a mad run on bottled water in the city, multiple brawls, and at least two shootings. The National Guard are stepping in, while alternative water supplies are organized. It's a big deal."

"Wow, I never understood why people would want to live in a city in the middle of the desert."

"Be that as it may, sabotage on this scale is unprecedented. At least in the US."

"Yeah," said Jess, furrowing her brow. "Didn't this just happen somewhere in India?"

Martin nodded. "Chennai. That city's had a water crisis for years after its reservoirs dried up. They've relied on water tankers driving in, but there aren't enough. They'd just restored one of the reservoirs, but last week discovered it had been poisoned. Hundreds of people got sick, and some died. Those who can are fleeing the region."

Our path crested a slope, and I gazed in wonder at the abundance and variety of plant life surrounding us. Irises of every color imaginable swept in a carpet beneath towering linden trees on one side, while shrubs and tiny-petaled flowers I couldn't name jostled for room on the other. Everywhere I looked, I saw the wonder of the natural world and recognized how lucky I was to live somewhere I could enjoy it. Thinking of thousands upon thousands of people suddenly without access to something as fundamental and life-sustaining as drinking water put my own troubles into perspective. But it didn't make them go away.

I wiped sweat from my brow. "Do they know who did it? Either Chennai or Phoenix?"

Martin shook his head. "Not that I've heard. I'm not sure anyone has connected the incidents, or if they are connected. Melbourne's still without power after hackers sabotaged their electrical grid on Friday. The bank's concerned. My phone was buzzing all afternoon yesterday. I shudder to think what the market's gonna do tomorrow morning."

Rosalind laid a hand on his arm and met his weary eyes. "I know you're worried, love, but please worry about it tomorrow. Let's just enjoy this time with our friends."

Martin grimaced and covered her hand with his. "Sorry," he said, tilting his head towards me, but not taking his eyes from hers. "I shouldn't burden you with my own worries."

I shrugged. "It's what friends are for. You guys are here for me, the least I can do is be here for you."

He nodded, and we resumed walking in pensive silence.

"Can I ask you a question, Rosalind?" Jess said suddenly.

"Of course."

"Why did you send us to that bookstore in Chicago? The one hosting Allen Weston, that Scales of Equilibrium author. I've been meaning to ask for ages. Were you hoping Daniel would be there?"

Rosalind pursed her lips at the mention of their son. "Honestly, I'm not sure what I expected. I've been trying to find out more about that organization, as were you, with little more success. The day before I texted you, I received an anonymous tip."

"What kind of tip?" I asked. Jess flashed me an annoyed glance.

"A text message, from one of those five digit numbers. No idea where it came from. That was when I started worrying my phone was compromised. I'd noticed an uptick of spam before that, but this didn't look like spam."

"What did it say?" asked Jess.

"Let's see, I still have it here." Rosalind let go of my arm to dig inside her purse. She shielded her phone with one hand, while she swiped at the screen with the other. "Here it is. 'If you want to learn more about the Scales of Equilibrium, send your friends in Chicago to Selene's Books. Tuesday 7pm'."

"That's it?"

"That's it. I replied 'Who is this?' but never heard back."

"Weird."

"My thoughts precisely. I debated telling you. I didn't want to set you up for something unpleasant. But I was frustrated and not a little alarmed. I took the risk. Forgive me."

"There's nothing to forgive," I assured her, although I wondered why she hadn't shared that text with us before. "It was another lead, another chance to learn more about Daniel. We were happy to go. It was... interesting."

"Yes, you never did tell me the full story. Daniel wasn't there, but someone you knew from prison was? The man you went to meet last weekend when you saw our son?"

"Yeah," I said. Had that only been last weekend? It seemed ages ago.

I gave a full account of our visit to Selene's Books. I remembered the look on Train's face when we bumped into each other in the restroom. At the time, I thought I'd just startled him, but now I wondered if he'd been afraid.

Rosalind's frown deepened as I finished. "I expect it's just coincidence, you know one of the other patients in the same rehab clinic as Daniel. Just like I'm sure it's a coincidence that multiple cities' water supplies were poisoned around the same time."

"I don't trust coincidences," muttered Jess behind us.

"I don't either," Rosalind agreed, looking at me shrewdly. "Never have."

I didn't recognize half the people at the wake. And I didn't want to talk to most of those I did.

The twenty percent chance of rain fizzled into nothing, so those who couldn't squeeze into the bungalow's living room and kitchen spilled out into the unkempt backyard. Eric and

I had dragged the rickety porch rocker off to one side to make room for three large coolers of beer. We'd made a Costco run earlier that afternoon, disguising our lack of common ground with spirited discussion of the contrasting fortunes of my beloved Cardinals and City SC, the town's new soccer team. Jess insisted on cleaning the house, while Fiona and Mary dug through tote boxes of old photographs. By the time the first guests arrived, the sisters had assembled two science fair-sized collages representing decades of memories. The earliest picture was of Mom and Patrick at their wedding, smiling in dress and tux outside the church. I couldn't help but think of another picture, squirreled away in an envelope at the bottom of my backpack in the Evans' basement.

Mary played music on a pair of Bluetooth speakers, from a playlist she insisted contained all Mom's favorites. I heard a lot of 1980s new wave and punk. I'd forgotten how Mom would lock herself in her bedroom when we were young and raising havoc. Patrick would stalk around the house yelling, mostly at me, while "God Save the Queen" and "I Wanna Be Sedated" thumped through the walls and hardwood floor. I caught myself smiling with Mary during the chorus of "Love Will Tear Us Apart", then we both looked away, embarrassed. A lifetime of frosty enmity may have thawed, but neither of us were quite ready for that first adult conversation. Maybe not hating each other was enough for now.

I smiled, shook hands, hugged without emotion, as waves of relatives and friends washed through the living room. Some appeared happy to see me, most wondered why I was there. Whatever. I'd stopped caring about their judgment years ago. I'd just decided to find Jess and escape outside for a while, when the living room conversation died and all heads swung towards the front door.

Steven Rourke had come to pay his respects.

He was far from the tallest person in the room. Fine lines etched his rugged face, and most of his fiery red hair had long silvered. He wore his elegant charcoal gray suit well, although it couldn't disguise an advancing paunch. Yet his reputation towered over everyone else, and I squared my shoulders as if preparing for battle.

His pale lips twisted into a thin smile as he looked around the room, lingering as his eyes met mine. No one else met his gaze, and everyone took evasive action as he stepped further inside. He halted alongside me, before the picture boards crowded with old photographs. Whispered conversation erupted and trickled into the kitchen, where apprehensive or disapproving faces peered at this new, unwelcome guest.

"I'd forgotten how enjoyable these family gatherings were," he murmured, not taking his eyes from the pictures. His usual faux-British accent had vanished, leaving unremarkable white Midwestern inflections in its wake. "I wasn't sure you'd be here, D. You're only slightly more popular with this crowd than I am."

"I've made my peace, Steven," I answered, keeping my voice as cool as possible.

His lips twitched, and his attention drifted to the collage of pictures before him. "Glad to hear it. My, Siobhan was a beautiful woman!"

"Hey," said Jess, appearing at Rourke's shoulder before circling him to stand by my side. "Everything okay?"

"Sure. Just another mourner, come to pay his respects to my mother."

Rourke smiled, in the manner of a chess grand master acknowledging a good move by their opponent. "Ms. Evans, I presume," he said, turning and giving her a hint of a bow. "It's a genuine pleasure to meet you, albeit in unfortunate circumstances."

"I wish I could say the same," she said, face impassive. I took her hand and twined my fingers in hers.

"I get that a lot, unfortunately. I mean it, for what it's worth." She shrugged, and his smile tightened. He scanned the room again, and his nose wrinkled. "Look at my dear relations. Some fear me. All despise me. What do they think of you, D?"

"No idea. I haven't bothered talking to them. I'm here for my mother."

"Good for you." He looked me in the eye again, as if searching for something. There'd been a time when I'd relished his attention, another when I'd feared it, yet another when I'd resented it. Now I simply endured his regard, just another chore on this difficult day. He nodded, as if finding what he'd been looking for. "Jess, I wonder if I might have a few minutes with D alone. Perhaps we could take a stroll down the block, away from those who despise us."

"D's place is here," Jess began, but I squeezed her hand.

"I'll walk with you, Steven." If for no other reason than to get him out of this house, where he wasn't wanted.

"Excellent!" Rourke beamed, reassuming something of his public persona. He gestured toward the front door. "Shall we?"

"Ten minutes," I said, answering Jess's unspoken question, then stepped out into the late afternoon sunlight. I blinked, looked around and recognized the slim Asian woman leaning against a black Hummer across the street, watching me through circular black sunglasses. Very Matrix.

"It's been years since I walked these streets." Rourke led me east, the sun at our backs, just two men out for a stroll. "It's incredible how little they've changed."

"Why are you here?" I demanded, in no mood to reminisce. "I can't believe you give two shits that Mom passed. What's your angle?"

He tensed, curling his many-ringed fingers into fists before he relaxed. Something sad flitted across his face, before he chased it away.

"Siobhan and I were close once. Back when we were teens. We were both misfits, even then. Comrades in arms, so to speak."

"I never heard that," I said slowly. "Whenever your name came up, she used to scowl and change the subject."

"Well, I can't blame her for that. We had a falling out." We turned a corner and threaded our way through a pack of loudly playing children, spilling out from a too-small front yard. "Did you know I met your father once?"

It was my turn to tense up, and I thought of the man in the beach photograph. "Before or after your falling out?"

"After. I believe I was one of the reasons she fled St. Louis for Miami, she and her friend Elaine. Siobhan showed up to our next big family Christmas Eve gathering with a young man called Ramon Rodriguez in tow. Her husband, she claimed. She was three months pregnant. It was quite the scandal, but then that was Siobhan's style." His smile was wistful. "They stayed about five minutes, just long enough for her to introduce him to me. I think I shook his hand, but I don't remember if we spoke."

Among all the things I'd expected and dreaded about this visit home, uncovering delicate family history with Steven Rourke had not featured. I was tired of it. After years of no contact, except an occasional phone call or meal with Fiona, my emotional capacity was maxed out. I wanted to go home. I wanted Jess. I wanted to stop by tomorrow's funeral, then get on the next train back to Chicago.

"Why are you telling me this, Steven? What do you want?"

He didn't answer immediately. We were three quarters of the way around the block, and I had no inclination to continue our walk after finishing our circuit.

"I haven't treated you as well as perhaps I should. You know I'm not a sentimental man, but I do value loyalty. And you showed me loyalty fifteen years ago. You deserved better of me."

"I can't argue with that."

"Quite. I... have no child of my own, you know."

"Probably a good thing," I blurted. He stiffened, a slight hitch to his step, then grimaced.

"Probably. And perhaps this sudden desire to help you comes from misplaced paternal concern. But you asked me what I wanted, so I'll tell you. I want to warn you."

He stopped on the street corner. I could see Mom's bungalow three houses down, an old couple I didn't recognize walking up the front path. Matrix Girl still guarded the Hummer, and she stood straight and nodded when she saw us.

"What do you want me to stop doing now?" I asked, irritated.

"Nothing. Unless you're far more trusting or gullible than I believe you to be. Beware of the Henry Lyons Foundation. They are not what they seem. They're not even what Jamal thinks they are."

"And you know this because...?"

"Look into a man called Allen Weston. You may have met him once. If your other leads dry up, try that one. But D?"

"Yeah?"

"Be careful. Even I don't want to fuck with these people."

Chapter Eighteen
PERFECT SYMMETRY

"No, not like that," snapped Izzy, sweeping her luxurious black hair over one shoulder and scowling. Given that heavy black eyeliner rimmed her pale blue eyes, the effect was alarming. "Your lines aren't nearly crisp enough. Come on, this isn't that difficult!"

"It's only my third attempt," I protested, panting with exertion. I hated sounding like a sulky child. "This is complicated, and there aren't any diagrams or anything we can refer to. You guys just describe all the steps, and expect us to follow them at a million miles an hour!"

"Excuses," she said, dismissing me with an irritated wave of her hand. "The Foundation's training method has worked for every other agent. Don't blame me, because I can't give you IKEA instructions."

I bristled, wiping the sweat beading my forehead, smearing half of it in my eyebrows. Rosalind might get away with the tough teacher routine, but I was damned if I was going to take it from this arrogant little—

"Perhaps we ought to stop there for the day," said Jamal, rising from his seat at the other end of the conference table. We were back at Lyons-Strickland Logistics, this time in the middle of a powerful thunderstorm that briefly knocked out the power. I'd half-hoped we'd cancel training. I was getting sick of the place, and was really tired of Izzy Fisher.

"Fine by me," she sniffed, picking up her phone and thumbing through notifications. "I have a date to keep anyway."

Poor bastard, I thought, taking care not to say it out loud. Not that she wasn't attractive in her way. Taller than most women, she carried herself with poise and indifference to what others thought of her. Today's black outfit comprised a t-shirt celebrating The Cure and calf-length ripped jeans, complementing her pale but flawless skin. I'd seen Jess sneak admiring glances too. Izzy was a striking young woman, no doubt about it. Pity she was such a pain in the ass.

"Are we just gonna leave the Imprint as it is?" Jess sat halfway down the table, drumming her fingers lightly on its surface. She spoke over her shoulder to Jamal while glowering at Izzy.

He shrugged. "We could. It's not bad, actually. That was your best attempt yet, D." I could almost hear Izzy roll her eyes. "Do you want to take another crack at it, Jess?"

"Or they could try it together," muttered Izzy, texting rapidly as she headed for the door.

"I don't think we're ready for that," said Jamal with a frown.

"Whatever. Good luck, Jess. Hope you fare better than your boyfriend."

I bit back my retort. She *was* trying to help us. I couldn't trust my mouth when I was tired and frustrated. "Will she be at every training session?" I demanded once she was out of earshot. More or less.

"Most likely," said Jamal, stretching the stiffness from his limbs. "Faustyn thinks it will be good for you, and for her. She's one of our strongest field agents, anywhere, the youngest to make Level Five since we devised that categorization system. But she's something of a loose cannon."

"You think?"

The ghost of a smile flitted over his face. "They asked me to take Izzy under my wing, because I do what I'm told and never bend or break the rules."

Jess guffawed. "Like sneaking Rosalind into our nursing center visit?"

"Yes, like that. I don't know if Faustyn knows what I did, but I have a certain reputation within the Foundation. It's possible they've given me Izzy to mentor so they can monitor us both more easily." A note of bitterness crept into his voice. It wasn't the first time he'd alluded to a less than harmonious relationship with the HLF.

"Has she trained others before?" I asked, slumping into a chair that didn't yield at all like I thought it would.

"No, you're her first."

"Wonderful."

"Why?" asked Jess, spinning her chair to face Jamal. "This doesn't seem to require one-on-one instruction. D's right. All you've done over the last month is explain the sequence of steps to create a 'Single-Point Lock'. Again and again. You don't need Goth Girl's help for that. And, newsflash, she's not helping."

"You don't think so? Personally, I think you're both making excellent progress. You could both make Level One within a month."

I frowned. I got the sense there might be another reason, but Jess didn't allow me to call him out on it.

"Level One, Level Five. What does that mean? Sounds like a game."

"It's definitely not that," Jamal replied, favoring Jess with one of his deadpan stares. "The terms recognize an agent's aptitude with locking Tethers, imprinting memories as you call it. The levels also correlate roughly with the types of memory associated with Intrusions. The Single-Point Lock that you master during Level One is sufficient for most types, but is less effective on others. You'll learn more Locks as you progress."

"What do you mean by types of memory?" I asked. "How vivid they are?"

Jamal shook his head. "That doesn't appear to matter much, and varies from agent to agent. It has more to do with the emotions involved. Joy, happiness, or in this case lust, are the easiest to control. An agent reaches Level 1 when they can create an undetectable Tether for such a memory, effectively confining the Intrusion."

"And that's why we're here," Jess said with a crooked grin.

"Exactly. This building has an unusually high Intrusion density, but thanks to a certain philandering executive, many of the memories are ideal to train new recruits, such as yourselves. We also use a brothel in the city, but since it's an active business, we have to schedule around its, um, activities."

"Where in the city?" Jess caught my eye, and I remembered struggling to erase an Imprint recently at a "house of ill repute."

"I, well, that's not relevant right now." Jamal appeared flustered, which was just going to play into Jess's hands.

"They're all Level One?" I interrupted. "Is that common?"

"No, they're not. The memories you've encountered so far are of consensual acts. Of course, it can be more complicated. There are other Intrusions here that you're not ready for, where fear, shame, and self-loathing dominate."

"And are those Level Five?" I remembered Martin's comment about the ex-colleague who'd caused multiple secretaries to quit. From the sober look on Jess's face, I guessed she was thinking about that too.

Jamal looked down at his hands, where they gripped the back of his chair. "You'd be forgiven for thinking so. Fear, especially the terror of assault, or watching a loved one suffer a grand mal seizure, is intense. They're Level Fours, and difficult memories to deal with: Single-Point Locks are rarely enough." He looked up, his expression grim. "When the fear lingers, when it leads to despair, it shades into Level Five. Profound sorrow, all-consuming grief, despair that endures for days, weeks, even years. Those are the emotions we struggle to corral the most."

"I could see that," Jess said slowly, meeting my eyes. She knew what I was thinking. If an Intrusion popped up in my mom's house, would it be a Level Five? All the more reason for me to train with the HLF. Yet Rosalind's caution and Steven Rourke's warning were still fresh in my mind. I winced at the thought: I was going to have to tell Rosalind about all this at some point.

"It's easy to relate to emotions we enjoy," Jess continued. "We struggle with pain and anger, and especially fear, but our defensive instincts force us to engage whether we want to or not. No one likes to think about grief, despair, or depression, not really."

Which was why I'd concealed the envelope Mom gave me in the drawer of my bedside table. The photograph and the ring nagged at my mind.

Jess reached across the table and took my hand. Jamal watched with a shrewd expression.

"I think that's a big part of it," he murmured. "Although not the entire story. Now, do you want to take a crack at this Tether, Jess? Or wait until next time?"

Her eyes searched mine for what I wasn't sure. "I could. But I'd prefer to watch D try again. If you're up for it, love."

Was I? We'd been taking turns, so I'd expected her to jump at another opportunity. Izzy had proclaimed Jess's first attempt that evening was better than mine. Knowing Jess, she wasn't backing away from the challenge. She had some other motive for passing.

"I can do it." I rose to my feet, filling my lungs with the dry, cool air blasting from the vent above my head. She smiled and released my hand, taking deep breaths too.

Jamal sipped from a towering black thermos, then raised an eyebrow at me. "Very well. Are you ready? I'll pick your latest Lock and then—"

"No, let me do it."

"I'm not sure that's wise."

"Why not? It's my Lock, my Catch. I know exactly where it is, and once I remove it, I'll have the memory in my grasp. I won't have to fumble for it like some sort of relay baton handoff. That was my problem last time." One of them, at least.

"Alright. Let's see if you possess the strength I think you do. I'll be here to help if things go awry. Let's review the process again."

"I'll review it. Let me explain it to you. That's how I learn a new recipe: listen to another's explanation once, then explain it back to them."

Jamal nodded in approval. "Excellent. I'm all ears."

I slowed my breathing and organized my thoughts, recalling everything he and Izzy had told us. "I don't have to detect the Intrusion and extract the associated memory this time, since I'll already have it in my mind. The memory has structure. It's a metaphor for the shape of the Intrusion. So the first thing I need to do is find the center, its core emotion or concept. Next, and this is the hard part, I locate its edges, the extent of the memory. Once I do, I have to fold them in perfect symmetry towards the center, repeating this process as fast as I can until it's as compact as possible. Finally, I fuse those folds together." I exhaled noisily. "That sound about right?"

"It does, more or less." Jamal gave us one of his rare grins. "You do make it sound like folding a fitted sheet! But perhaps that's not a bad analogy."

"Give me strength," muttered Jess. She forbade me from folding our sheets; I didn't have the patience to do it right. *Thanks, Jamal, for bringing that up.*

Focus. I stepped away from the conference table and centered myself, shifting my weight to the balls of my feet. I closed my eyes and embraced the sultry warmth and musky scent that suffused the room, for those like us who sensed it. I found the Catch immediately, the almost infinitesimal sphere I'd created during my last attempt at tethering the Intrusion. Although, I saw now that it was far from a perfect sphere: it was distorted in multiple places as if something inside was struggling to escape. I faltered, wondering for a moment about the presence Jess had sensed here before. I'd just have to deal with that if and when it happened.

Unlike others' Imprints, I knew exactly where the Lock was, the point at which I'd fused the folded memory together. I didn't need the usual brute force approach Jess chided me about. All I needed was to pick open the fusion point, then corral the unfolding memory so I could manipulate it again. Easy to say, harder to do. But I wasn't going to back down now.

I probed the fusion point like a surgeon wielding an invisible scalpel, or indeed like a thief picking a lock. With an abrupt snap, the memory released like a time-lapsed movie of a flower bud opening, rows of petals expanding one after the other. I tried to track the edges, but unlike a flower, the memory stretched asymmetrically, almost as if using a couple spare dimensions. I blocked out everything else: Jess's anxious breathing, Jamal's shifting weight on his creaking chair, the remembered grunts and moans of the executive, Barker, and his latest lover, sprawled over his large wooden desk. The desk, and its panting, half-dressed female occupant, were the memory's core, so I fixed the shape of them in my mind and decided where to start folding. This was the vital moment. Once you started, you couldn't stop, or the memory would spill out chaotically, just like in an Erasure. And there wasn't a magic number of initial fold points. It was a judgment call based on experience or, in my case, instinct.

Well, four fold points hadn't worked very well last time. *Your lines aren't nearly crisp enough.* Simplify. Try three: there, there, and there. Only one way to find out.

I grasped the edges of the memory and folded.

Imagine you're a security guard, studying camera feeds on several rows of screens. You can't stare too long at one for fear of missing something important on others. You learn to scan them rapidly. It takes intense concentration and swift analysis. Now, imagine that each time your focus shifts from one screen to another, you drag the first one with you, forcing the others to shift and squeeze together to accommodate it. If you do this right, if your chosen focal points are in perfect symmetry, you end up with one vanishingly small screen, superimposed on all the others.

That's more or less what I did, except with a three-dimensional historical event. And each drag, each fold, cost me a stab of pain between my eyes, pain that built into a steady throb beyond any headache I'd ever known.

I found three focal points easier to manipulate than four. My mind wove a series of equilateral triangles around the Intrusion in a steady dubstep beat. I imagined myself on the dance floor back in the day, blinding lights flashing in time with the bone-shaking bass drum, my head pounding with every bpm. I'd been just another raver in the crowd, but now I was the DJ, spinning sick beats to lock away memories with.

Once I'd compressed the memory to "Catch size", it resembled a tiny, perfect sphere. I knew I'd got this one right. Resistance increased, like a collapsing star reaching its upper limit of density. Ignoring the skull-splitting pain, I made one more fold, held it, and poured all my remaining will into that single point, fusing the edges together.

And then I let go. I staggered, saving myself from an embarrassing tumble to the floor by clinging to the back of my conference room chair, a drowning man clutching floating debris from a shipwreck. I rested my forehead against the chair's cool, faux leather and tried to will the pain away. I heard echoes of a prior conversation: *we're messing with our minds here*.

"Well?" I croaked, cracking open my eyelids. Nice to see that dehydration was as much a side effect of imprinting memories as it was of erasing them. I pawed at my water bottle on the table, then Jess was at my side, solicitous, one arm wrapped around me while she guided the rim of the bottle to my parched lips.

"That was amazing," she whispered in my ear, and I rested my throbbing head against hers.

"Do you sense it? The Imprint?" All I could feel was her warm body next to mine, her breath against my cheek; all I could smell were the hints of jasmine in her perfume.

"No," she said, louder this time. We looked down the table at where Jamal sat, steepling his hands, a thoughtful look in his eyes. "I can't sense a thing."

"It's there, but very faint, indistinguishable from the background," he said, and a satisfied smile crept over his face. "Well done, D. That was remarkable, especially for your second effort of the evening. I take back what I said earlier. You won't be making Level One within the month: you're already there."

Chapter Nineteen
PUBLIC DISORDER

I closed our apartment door behind me, then scratched at the stubble on my chin. Should I take a shower now or wait for the morning? But that would just be a ploy to avoid the conversation I knew we should have.

"What am I doing, Jess? What are we doing?"

She sprawled across the couch and rested her head on one hand. "Hopefully you're about to fix me dinner. I'm starving."

I grinned despite myself. "Let's see if I can scare up some pasta."

I raided both pantry and fridge for ingredients, then boiled a pan of water while I sliced chicken breast and broccoli. Simple, mechanical tasks I could do in my sleep.

"You don't seem as impressed to make Level One as Jamal thought you would be." Jess's voice floated into the kitchen from the living room, but I waited until dinner was simmering, before walking back through and replying. I hated trying to have a conversation by yelling from one room to another.

"Part of me feels guilty," I admitted. "It wasn't a perfect Imprint, and if I have to make Level Five before I can protect the memories I care about..."

She patted the couch cushion next to her, and I perched on the edge. "You're worried what Rosalind would say." It was a statement, not a question, carrying more than a hint of challenge.

"She's our mentor. I know we agreed to pursue independent investigations into the HLF but I can't imagine she'd approve of this."

"You need her approval?"

"No, but..." I ran my hand through my hair and tightened my ponytail. "It just feels like a betrayal. Because I don't want to stop. I want to learn these skills. I need to learn these skills, for me and for others."

"Then explain it to her. If she's the friend we think she is, give her the chance to hear you out."

I sighed, and the kitchen timer went off. "I know." I collected our food into a pair of bowls and brought them back into the living room. Jess was frowning at her phone, but set it face down on the coffee table before accepting her dinner.

"I'm proud of you," she said, a forkful of pasta poised before what I recognized as her serious face. No hint of mischief or gentle mockery. "I know I surprised you by passing on my turn. That took a lot of strength and discipline."

"Thank you." I wasn't always sure how to handle Serious Jess. "It helped when Izzy left for her date." I cracked a grin that wasn't reciprocated.

"She really bothers you, doesn't she?"

"She annoys the crap out of me. I can handle criticism. You don't survive in a kitchen if you can't. But she's so dismissive and arrogant all the time. It doesn't bother you?"

She shrugged. "I can handle Izzy. Don't let her get under your skin. If she's as good as Jamal says she is, we can learn a lot from her." I didn't argue, not least because I wasn't sure Izzy's style of instruction was the only issue here. We chewed in silence for a minute before Jess continued. "Did you sense anything this time? Something or someone watching you?"

So that was why she'd passed on her turn to tether the Intrusion.

"Not really. You?"

"Not this time. Not like last week." That time, as I followed her attempt to imprint another voyeuristic memory, we'd both gotten the distinct impression of another consciousness, silent, observing. I'd guessed it was Jamal or Izzy, both monitoring the entire process. But Jess wasn't buying it. "I don't understand why we sense it sometimes and not others," she said, stabbing at her last remnants of chicken. "Maybe it's all in our heads, a side-effect of certain memories no one's told us about."

"I'm surprised you haven't asked."

"I'm surprised you haven't, especially after what happened back at the nursing home."

I could still visualize the coma patient opening his eyes for one split second of terrifying recognition. It haunted me every day. I'd only confided in Jess. She already knew I was crazy.

"There wasn't any Intrusion," I said slowly. "It felt different."

"Was that because you knew it wasn't me, or Jamal, or Rosalind? What's going on there? Don't you find it strange they have an entire facility full of, allegedly, casualties of Imprints or Erasures gone wrong?"

I did. Even though the Henry Lyons Foundation funded research into coma treatment, why set up a private nursing home just for those who got lost in an Intrusion's memory? More than one home, if I'd heard Jamal right. Were they studying their patients? Or something more sinister?

I'd become awfully trusting of the HLF now that I wanted something from them.

I dialed Jamal's number before I could change my mind.

"Hi, D. What's up?" His voice had a tinny, breathless quality, and I hesitated.

"Am I interrupting something?"

"Just my evening run along the lakeshore. Trying to get it in before dark."

"Good for you," I said, trying to remember how long it had been since my last run. "We've been meaning to ask you something for a few weeks now."

"Yes?"

Ask, dammit. "Have any HLF agents reported being watched during tethering, by someone or something not physically present? Have you ever experienced that?"

There was a long pause, during which I could only hear Jamal's labored breathing. Someone called "On your left!" in the background.

"Nothing credible," he said at last. "It might be a side effect of the mental state required for the process. Those who've reported it don't usually remain agents for long."

"Why not?"

"I'm not sure I can tell you that." Because he didn't know or wouldn't say?

"What about your nursing center? Has anyone observed anything there?"

"Well no. Those poor people are unresponsive, D."

I looked at Jess and must have had the question in my eyes, because she gave me the thumbs up. "He looked at me, Jamal. Raul, the patient in the last bed. Just for a split second, almost too fast for me to notice. But he looked at me and he was *aware*! Or something was."

The sound quality changed, as if Jamal now spoke directly into his phone. His voice brimmed with accusation. "You never mentioned that before. You don't think that's something his doctors would want to know?"

"I was a little distracted by my mother's deathbed request to see me," I countered, standing up and pacing my living room.

"Fair enough," Jamal said after another pause. He sounded chastened, if not penitent. "I'll pass that information along. If it's a sign he's waking up, then that would truly be momentous."

Chicago wasn't St. Louis hot, but it was still Midwestern hot. And humid. Lake Michigan didn't help nearly as much as I'd hoped.

I'd fallen away from my running routine. Jess wasn't really a routine kind of girl, and it was all we could do to attend regular lessons at the dojo, not to mention practice outside of them. But running was more about clearing my head, putting my brain in neutral while my body ate up the miles. I had a lot of thoughts competing for attention, and decided running might ease the pressure. I drove out to Lincoln Park on my next evening off and tried to run along the lakeshore, but pulled up gasping far short of a 5K distance. The breezeless eighty-plus degree heat smothered me like a heavy blanket, thumbing its nose at Chicago's reputation as the "Windy City".

"No more evening runs for me, not during summer at least," I whined to an amused Jess after I slunk back through our apartment door.

I broke that promise less than a week later, just not in the way I imagined.

My birthday fell on the second Monday of July. We'd talked about a long weekend away, but neither of us had much paid time off left after our St. Louis trip. Jess's grandparents invited us for dinner instead of our traditional Sunday lunch, and Jess herself suggested we try a well-regarded steak restaurant recommended to her by a coworker. Both options had merit, but I wanted something more intimate this year.

"Let me cook us dinner," I told her over the weekend. "I've been wanting to try my hand at something new, paella maybe."

"You want to cook on your birthday?" she said, incredulous.

"For you. For us. Let's spend an outrageous amount of money on a bottle of wine and bring the romance to our apartment."

"We don't already have romance here?" She embraced me, running her hands under the back of my shirt and proving we did.

Nevertheless, I started prep work as soon as I got home from my lunchtime shift. I played one of my college-era playlists on our Bluetooth speakers, bobbing my head and singing out of tune at all the right places. I washed rice, shelled shrimp, diced chicken, and cut vegetables, never once feeling like I'd brought my work home. If you couldn't enjoy cooking for pleasure, your cooking for work would suffer. That's what Mike Szemis had always told me, and I'd taken it to heart. As promised, Jess texted me when she left work. I turned on the burner, stirred the pot, and waited.

And waited.

Where are you? I texted for the fifth time, the paella long turned down to warm. I'd received only one reply, about thirty minutes ago: *Working on it.* I tried calling, but she didn't answer. I checked the Chicago Transit Authority website, but there were no delays on the Red or Brown Lines. Was she walking home? What was going on?

A key rattled in the lock, and she stumbled through the door, panting, sweat streaking her face and matting her hair. She shed her backpack, tossed it on the couch, then hurried over to the living room window. We usually kept the blinds closed, since they faced the street and the morning sun baked the apartment otherwise. She teased two of the slats apart and peered between them.

"Jess, what's going on?" I demanded.

"There he is," she breathed, and beckoned me over. "Look across the street, underneath that oak tree, in front of the house with the wrought iron fence."

She swayed backwards so I could see through the gap in the blinds. Our house cast shadows across the street that just reached the fence in question, two doors down to my right. Standing under the tree, one hand stuck in the pocket of his khaki cargo shorts, while the other supported his phone, was a thin man wearing a White Sox jersey and ball cap. The visor was turned forward and hid most of his face. His arms were dark, as was his short hair. He could be anybody. I watched him swipe at his phone a few times, then I turned to Jess.

"Who is he?"

"Damned if I know." She released the blinds and sank into my arms. "He followed me all the way home from work."

"What?" I leaned back to see her face clearly. "How do you know? Or when did you know?"

She grimaced at my self-correction. "I noticed him when I left Paragon. I was aggravated about something at work - someone else's code I'm trying to fix - and just happened to look up as I came through the doors. He was chatting with a taller guy, both holding coffee cups. I assumed they were waiting for a friend to go to the ball game. But they both looked right at me for a split second, before turning back to each other. It got my attention. You develop instincts as a woman in a city, especially a woman by herself.

"I kept my head down and got to the subway platform as fast as I could. I figured I'd lose myself in the crowd. Thought I had too. But after I squeezed onto the train, I saw this guy slip on further down the car. Didn't look at me, but I didn't like the coincidence."

"I wouldn't either. Just him? What about the other guy?"

She shook her head, and wiped her face with my shirt. "I didn't see the taller one, though he might've done a better job of hiding."

"And you didn't call me? I could've met you at the North/Clybourn station."

"I thought about it, but I knew you were working on this fabulous dinner I've been looking forward to all day. There are enough people out and about this time of night. I didn't think I was in any danger. But I wanted to be sure, so I got off the train at the Chicago station. Just stood there on the platform and waited while the other commuters headed for the exit. And he got off the train too, at the last second."

"Holy shit, Jess."

"I can take care of myself," she said, drawing herself up, daring me to say otherwise.

"I know, but... What happened after the platform cleared?"

She laughed, but there wasn't much humor in it. "We just stared at each other. No pretense. He didn't approach or say anything, but he didn't back down either. And neither did I. There were a handful of people waiting for the southbound train, so we weren't alone. Then we couldn't get on the next couple of trains north. I mean, they were jammed. I walked down the platform, hoping I could jump in somewhere at the last second and leave him stranded but it was ridiculous. That was when you started texting me.

"I got on a train finally, but so did he. I texted you back while considering getting a Lyft from the station, but I didn't want to wait around any longer. As soon as I got to street level, I kept to Halsted as long as I could, then ran when I turned on Wisconsin. I didn't look back to see if he was still following me, but it looks like he did. Fuck knows why."

"Then let's find out," I growled, letting go of her.

"Wait, D..."

Too late. I didn't even grab my wallet before I marched out of our apartment and into the street. Yes, Jess could take care of herself. She'd gotten herself home, unharmed. But I wanted answers.

For someone who'd demonstrated such good powers of observation, Jess's stalker didn't notice my approach until I was almost across the street. Warned by some instinct, he glanced up, dark eyes widening in alarm. Then he fled, and I chased him.

He had five or six steps on me, but my strides were longer. By the time he rounded the corner, heading towards Halsted Street, I'd started to gain. He dodged around a middle-aged man walking his dog, yanking at the guy's leash arm as if to fling him in my path. I swerved with a muttered apology, scanning for other pedestrians. My lungs began to burn, despite how much I gulped down the hot sticky air. I needed to end this sooner than later.

He dodged in front of a minivan as it edged forward at a cross street. Its driver hurled curses at him and then me as I pursued, levering myself off the hood. A three step gap became two, but then I spied an elderly couple walking arm in arm towards us maybe twenty yards ahead. This was gonna hurt, but I saw no other way. I leapt forward and tackled the stalker to the ground.

My arms wrapped around his thighs as he hit the sidewalk, so his legs cushioned my face and chest from the impact. Pain lanced through my elbows and knees as the uneven asphalt shredded my skin. I shuddered, but held on. Blood poured from his mouth after his chin smacked off the ground. He kicked feebly while his hands scrabbled for purchase, his phone having skittered several yards ahead. The couple stopped in alarm, the old man stepping in front of his partner as years of protective instinct kicked in. *Good for you*, I thought, then focused on my quarry.

"Who are you?" I hissed, fending off his attempts to punch my head as I pinned down his legs. He snarled, but didn't reply. Asian, but not Japanese, and he didn't look Chinese either. Korean? I caught hold of his wrist and yanked it to the side, twisting his arm behind his back. That earned a satisfactory cry of pain. "Why were you following my girlfriend, asshole? Touch her and I'll rip this arm off, you hear me?"

There was a pause, a moment when clarity and reason tried to corral my adrenaline-fueled rage. My captive twisted his head to the left, and I glimpsed a tattoo behind his left ear, a set of uneven scales, a design I recognized but couldn't place. A crowd grew around the elderly couple, some protective, others fascinated, with maybe a dash of bloodlust. I wondered what Sensei would say, and groped through what I'd learned of karate that might apply to this situation. I was pretty sure losing my cool, running down an unknown man to the ground in front of a bunch of strangers, lying prone and vulnerable, wasn't the best strategy. And in that split-second of realization, I was kicked in the head.

My peripheral vision, and my captive's widening eyes, gave me the briefest of warnings. I flinched, but the toe of an athletic shoe drove into the hairline above my left ear, snapping my head to the side. Fireworks exploded behind my eyes and I rolled away, losing hold of Jess's stalker as I sought to defend myself from multiple assailants. My back hit a low brick wall; I was trapped, semi-dazed and cursing myself. I'd learned nothing since prison. I braced for blows that never came.

Shouts. No words, white noise. Movement. Too much of a blur. *Pull yourself together, man.*

When I could focus more on my surroundings than the pain, I caught a glimpse of two White Sox fans lumbering in the direction we'd come. A taller man supported Jess's stalker, who covered his mouth with one hand, blood trickling down his forearm. Two guys wearing Cubs jerseys followed them halfway down the block, goading them to come back, then lost interest after they turned north at a cross street. I dragged myself into a sitting position, and that was when I saw the cops.

The crowd of remaining onlookers parted as two of Chicago's finest strode forward. A man and a woman, they looked fresh out of the academy. The male cop hung back to talk to the witnesses, including the elderly couple, while his partner squatted down a discreet distance away from me. On the stocky side of slim, she moved with a sure fluidity that told me she'd hold her own in a fight. Green eyes squinted at me above flushed cheeks, and thin lips set in a tight line. I forced myself to remain calm and return her gaze, suppressing my fear of the police, or rather what they'd once represented.

"Are you okay, sir?" Her voice was deeper than I expected, expressing polite concern. I was just another brawling troublemaker, and the night was young.

"Got kicked in the head," I said, probing the sore spot and wincing. No blood on my fingertips though, so that was something.

"Care to tell me what happened?"

I hesitated, but I wasn't thinking clearly enough to tell anything other than the truth, or most of it. "Some guy followed my girlfriend home from her office, downtown. I wanted to know why, but he ran, so I ran after him. Then another guy kicked me in the head. Then you got here."

She nodded, expressionless. "Do you know them?" I shook my head. Carefully. "I see. And where is your girlfriend now?"

"Inside our apartment. On Bissell." At least I hoped she was. I resisted the urge to look back in that direction.

"Good." The cop held my gaze for another few seconds, then rose to her feet and extended her hand. I took it and levered myself up off the ground with a mumbled "Thank you." She glanced at her partner, who shrugged. Most of the crowd had dispersed, save the couple who glared at me for disturbing their evening walk.

"Try to keep the public disorder to a minimum, Mr...?"

"Rodriguez." Dammit.

"Mr. Rodriquez. Tell your girlfriend to call us if she's ever followed again. We take that kind of thing seriously."

Chapter Twenty

Let's Show Them What We're Made Of

"Your first mistake was forgetting about the second man," Sensei Ryuichi told me gravely. "You let yourself be lured into an ambush. When considering a lesser threat, do not neglect the greater one."

Thursday's karate lesson had not gone well. I was out of sorts, tentative and sloppy. My headache had lasted two days, my embarrassment even longer. I'd slunk back to our apartment an hour after abandoning Jess, and our romantic evening proved more challenging to recover than my stodgy paella. She'd sympathized with my wounds, while telling me in no uncertain terms what she thought of my impulsivity. And I agreed with her. I was almost grateful when Sensei took me aside before we left the dojo.

"And my second mistake?" I didn't sound petulant. Not at all.

"Going to ground after catching your quarry. You left yourself exposed and vulnerable. Worse, you did so in a public place, before a crowd of people."

"So I should have caught him on my feet, held him where I could see everyone else?"

Sensei pursed his lips. Rosalind claimed he was a fifth-degree Master, and while I wasn't familiar with the term, her reverent tones were all I needed. Anything he didn't know about combat probably wasn't worth knowing.

"You wished to learn about the men following Jess, yes? One stood outside your home, watching. What might you have learned by watching him? What might you have learned by following him home? Sometimes victory in battle is best achieved without fighting at all."

I was humbled. Not for the first time, I'd learned that karate was about much more than physical combat. I needed to be smarter, more disciplined, and more aware of the situation in order to beat my opponent.

I slumped on the couch when we got home, and found the end of the Cardinals game on TV. Jess curled up next to me with a book, and the sound of turning pages entertained me more than the baseball. I was getting tired of watching the boys in red give up ninth-inning leads.

"You should read this for yourself, you know. Especially since you're the one who bought it."

Jess waggled the book under my nose after I turned off the TV in disgust. I noticed it was *The Gaia Contract* by Allen Weston, the copy in which Train concealed his hasty plea for help. Jess must have fished it out of my nightstand.

"Is it any good?" I asked.

"Not particularly. It's like a crusty old Victorian academic and a zealous evangelical pastor had a love child, who joined a hippy commune and wrote while tripping on some really good shit."

"Way to sell it, but maybe you can give me the highlights when you're done."

"I can give them to you now. The man's written the same chapter twenty times, just with different anecdotes. Modern human civilization is destroying the world, and the world is fighting back. We can either fight with it or face annihilation."

"The End is Nigh?"

"Basically. But Allen Weston's not just some crackpot carrying a protest sign outside the G7 summit. You remember the applause he got from almost everyone at Sophie's Books?

His writing skills are suspect, but he's a charismatic speaker and clearly has a following. I looked him up. He used to be a respected academic, taught environmental law at Harvard, then Columbia. About ten years ago he lost his tenure and vanished for a while. He reappeared just before COVID as the director of The Themis Institute."

Hello. "What's the Themis Institute? Any connection to the Themis Center, Daniel's rehab clinic?"

"Maybe. I haven't found anything yet. The Institute is an 'environmental think tank', but doesn't have a physical head-quarters. Seems to be more of an online movement."

"What's the 'Gaia' reference about? I've heard that name before."

"Greek goddess, or rather the Greeks' personification of the Earth. Some guy in the 1970s used her name for his hypothesis that all living and nonliving things were part of one symbiotic, self-regulating system. Spawned a resurgence of the ecological movement, although it's considered more new age religion than good science these days."

"So Weston doesn't think humans are holding up our end of the bargain?"

"Something like that. He thinks the system is unbalanced and calls for action to help restore that balance."

I ran a hand through my hair, dislodging my ponytail in the process. I'd considered cutting it short, a more professional look, and perhaps less of a target for potential assailants. Jess had vetoed the idea, professing her undying adoration of my long hair. So the ponytail stayed.

"That guy I chased had a tattoo behind his ear. Scales of some kind. I saw it on someone at the Themis Center too."

Jess lay the book flat on her lap. "Are you sure?"

"Pretty sure. Scales of Equilibrium, perhaps?"

"Could be. Themis was a Greek goddess of justice and so-cietal order. I looked that up as well. I saw statues where she's holding a set of scales. Getting tattoos sounds a bit cult-like. Maybe they're keeping tabs on us after the Train thing?"

"Or maybe they know you're snooping after them. I wonder if we should warn Rosalind."

"I thought I was being careful. Guess I'll have to be more careful. So should she."

Another memory resurfaced, a conversation with an old adversary. "Steven Rourke told me to look into Allen Weston. At the wake." I hadn't shared much of that conversation with her. I still had mixed feelings about most of it. "He warned me about the HLF, implied they weren't who we thought they were. I'm still not sure what I think about them, but he gave me Weston's name as if that might help me understand."

Jess set the book on the coffee table and turned towards me. "He thinks there's a connection?"

"Either that or he's fucking with me," I said, then drew her in for a kiss.

Faustyn joined us for our next Tether. He climbed stiff-legged from the passenger seat of Jamal's Acura and dusted down his suit, greeting our surprised expressions with a curt nod.

"No Izzy today?" I asked, trying not to sound too happy at the prospect.

"She's here already." Jamal gestured towards the elevator lurking in one dingy corner of the concrete parking garage. "We'll meet her in the lobby."

Jess and I exchanged puzzled looks. We'd already been surprised by the summons to Polk Medical Center, a hospital in Chicago's Medical District, not far from Garfield Park High. Now the head of the Henry Lyons Foundation's operation in the city had decided to attend our training.

"There's much interest in your progress," explained Faustyn. "I wanted to see it for myself. Please don't mind me." Jamal couldn't quite suppress a scowl.

Nothing could persuade me to get in that elevator, so Jess and I took the four flights of stairs down to street level. Besides, it was too much for Faustyn's gimpy leg.

"Something's off," I told her as we descended, avoiding litter and pungent pools of dubious origin. The early evening sunshine deferred to caged fluorescent bulbs that flickered without conviction from the ceiling. I sensed a background buzz of otherworldliness, of Intrusions or imperfect Imprints, but that wasn't what I was talking about.

"Yeah," she muttered. "I thought we'd be staying at Lyons-Strickland until I reached Level One."

"Jamal's not happy Faustyn is here. I wonder if they found out about him meeting Rosalind."

"Who knows? Office politics. Faustyn might be one of those bosses who micromanages his employees, stands over their shoulder while they work."

She sounded bitter, and I paused on the last flight of stairs. "Everything okay?"

Her expression soured. "Conor's been pestering me all week about finishing my code for our next release. Getting on my last nerve. Then he takes a personal day today; you know, the day before that release. Fucking hypocrite."

I squeezed her arm. Volatile Jess wasn't going to help anything. "That's work, love. Forget about it for now. We're doing something else. Let's be ready."

I could feel her tension ease as we stood together, breathing slowly, staring into each others' eyes. Her other hand found mine and squeezed back. It amazed me sometimes how, after being together for almost two years, intimate moments like this snuck up on us.

We emerged into a brightly-lit lobby to find Jamal, Faustyn and Izzy deep in conversation next to a nearby potted fern, as

far as possible from the bustling throng of visitors, potential patients, and staff. Since they hadn't noticed our arrival, I paused,
a finger to my lips.

"...what happened last night, we need to move things along,"
Faustyn was urging Jamal, who continued to look unhappy.
Izzy, who'd gone full Siouxsie with her makeup, smiled to her-
self.

"I understand the need," Jamal acknowledged. "After
months of delay, I welcome it. But it helps no-one if we burn
them out."

"That's why you're both here. If we lose..."

Faustyn's head snapped up as he saw us standing by the stair-
well door. I made a show of walking forwards as if we'd just
arrived. His eyes narrowed.

"Everything okay?" he asked. I surveyed the scene. This
wasn't the Emergency Room, yet there was an edge to the way
everyone stood, how they walked, how they looked at each other
or kept their heads down. It was still a hospital, a place for the
sick and the injured. It was still a large building full of doors,
corridors, rooms, and stairwells, and I liked it no more than I
ever had.

"Everything's great," I lied, plastering a smile across my face.
"We just wanted some time to prepare. We'd expected Jess to
work on reaching Level One at Lyons-Strickland this week."

Jamal's eyes flicked towards Faustyn, but his expression was
stone. "That was the original plan. But we think there's a good
Level Two candidate here, and don't want to pass that up."

"You train recruits at a working hospital?" An incredulous
tone crept into Jess's voice.

"Only with adequate supervision," Faustyn said stiffly. "We
have an arrangement with the hospital administrator." I glanced
at Izzy, who rolled her eyes. She perched on the back of a cracked
vinyl bench, and though her gaze was friendlier than usual, I
detected a spark of hunger too.

"So what now?" I focused back on Jamal. "Do we wander the corridors looking for the Intrusion? Or do you have a better plan?"

"Yes and no. We need to wander some corridors, but we've narrowed it down to the lower two floors of the East Wing. This floor and the basement."

"Which is?"

"Surgery. Maternity."

"And they're just gonna let five strangers walk around operating rooms and birthing suites?"

"Of course not. We'll have an escort."

Jamal gestured towards a short black woman with a graying buzzcut who strode towards us from the direction of the elevator bank. She wore a neat, silver-colored skirt suit with a fresh white flower pinned to one lapel. The lanyard around her neck barely moved as she walked. Given the air of authority she projected, I'm sure it didn't dare. She studied each of us in turn, lingering on me and Jess, and it was all I could do not to stand at attention. In terms of stage presence, she rivaled Rosalind.

"Must this be tonight?" she demanded, wheeling on Faustyn. "Hell's gates have opened, and the Lord God knows we're already stretched thin."

"I do apologize, Doctor Hammond," Faustyn said, spreading his hands in placating fashion. "But we have something of an unusual situation on our hands. I beg your indulgence."

She raised her eyebrows. "Now you have an unusual situation? That's all you folks ever have."

"It's delicate." Faustyn licked his lips and glanced at Jess of all people. "Suffice to say we wish to expedite the training of our two new recruits."

She speared me and Jess with a skeptical gaze. I couldn't fault her. I tried to project a calm and authority I didn't feel.

"Doctor Alisha Hammond," she introduced herself, offering a robust handshake, first to Jess, then to me, as we gave our names. "I am, of course, forever grateful to the Henry Lyons

Foundation for their patronage, without which my hospital would struggle to survive. But that does *not* give you the right to run around wherever and whenever you wish. You want to train here? You make an appointment with me first. And you never leave my sight while you're here. Is that clear?"

"Yes, ma'am," I said, resisting the urge to salute.

"Of course," Jess added, and Doctor Hammond nodded in satisfaction.

"Good. Do as you're told, and we won't have a problem. Now, where are y'all headed this evening?"

Jamal told her, and she frowned. "All of you?"

"Izzy and I are training them," he said, the least fazed by her brusqueness.

"And what about you?" she demanded of Faustyn.

"I'm here to introduce D and Jess, and to impress upon you the gravity of—"

"Fine, you can stay here. The rest of you follow me."

I suppressed a grin as we left Faustyn spluttering in our wake. The grin vanished as Doctor Hammond buzzed us through a pair of double doors. Either the occasion was getting to me, or the ambient level of strangeness took a step up.

"Put these on," she said, proffering boxes of surgical masks and nitrile gloves. "Don't touch anything, and for the love of God, don't breathe on anything. We'll start with maternity."

"Be alert," muttered Izzy. "I can find the Intrusion if I must, but we'd rather you do it. Both of you."

"We've got it," Jess assured her with a defiant tilt to her chin. Izzy's eyes twinkled.

We followed Doctor Hammond down a long corridor of whitewashed walls, sprinkled with unused machines and the dull, repetitive beeps of their employed counterparts. Something herbal tempered the antiseptic scent I always associated with hospitals. Doors on either side hinted at cluttered rooms where expectant mothers endured the final stages of labor, sometimes surrounded by family, sometimes alone. I'd never expected to find myself in a maternity ward, and I risked a glance at Jess. Her eyes were half-closed in concentration, which reminded me of what I was supposed to be doing.

As we'd learned at Lyons-Strickland Logistics, an Intrusion wasn't like an Imprint. It didn't radiate heat, chill, scent, or sound in the same way, and was much more localized. Most people wouldn't notice an Intrusion if they stood right on top of one. Even those of us more sensitive didn't detect more than a slight increase in emotion, a raising of our hackles, until we got close, until we focused the right way. It was like one of those optical illusions where a two-dimensional picture resolves into a very different three-dimensional reality after the slightest change in viewpoint.

We'd just passed the last pair of rooms before the corridor turned to the left when Jess's step faltered. She gasped, and an instant later I felt it too. Goosebumps prickled my skin, my heartbeat thudded like drums in the deep, and I convulsed as sudden pain ripped through my abdomen. We reached for each other, our eyes wide.

"Shit," rasped Jess. "I thought this might be more intense, but... wow."

Doctor Hammond stopped and gave us a wary look, then turned to Jamal. "This is it?"

Jamal, a step or two behind, opened his eyes and nodded.

"Wonderful." She gestured into the room to our left, and the pain sharpened. I guessed that's where the memory would be. "This poor child has been in labor for ten hours. Her momma can't be here for another two, until she gets off work. I forbid you to make things more difficult for her than they already are."

"We won't need to enter the room," promised Izzy, with a confidence I didn't share. "We'll be quiet. She won't even know we're here."

"She'd better not." Doctor Hammond scrutinized me with the full force of her skepticism, and I was suddenly tired of it.

"We're up for the job," I told her. "Perhaps you can spare a few minutes to comfort her while we do it."

She arched her eyebrows, but the corner of her mouth twitched. "Telling me what to do in my own hospital. Now there's a brave one." Then she strode into the birthing suite, and her voice morphed into something soft and soothing as she addressed the woman within.

"Right, you two," snapped Izzy. "Don't make a liar out of me. You need to work together on this one."

"What do you mean?" retorted Jess, quieter and quicker than I could.

"Can't you feel it? This Intrusion, the memory associated with it, is far more potent than anything that horny douchebag did back at Lyons-Strickland. You won't get away with sloppy lines this time. You need each other."

Jamal laid a hand on her arm, but rested his gaze on me. "D did much better after you left, Izzy. Lines as clean as yours. But this is a step up, so soon after your first Level One Tether. We know there's a connection between you two, a connection you've used effectively to destroy leaky Tethers—"

"Not to mention rip my shields to shreds," grumbled Izzy.

"—and we want to see if that same connection helps you create as well as destroy. It's your choice. If you'd rather tackle this alone, either of you, we're here as a safety net."

Jess snorted. I stared down Jamal, and although he didn't look away, his feet shifted.

"I would have appreciated seeing the game plan in advance," I said in as cool a voice as I could manage around my twisting insides. I turned to see Jess still fuming at Izzy, who returned her regard with arrogant amusement. "What do you think, babe? You want to give this a try together? Or just walk away from the whole damn thing?"

Jamal blinked in alarm, and Jess chuckled. "What the hell. Let's do this. Let's show them what we're made of."

We faced each other and tried to block out everything else. Deep breaths hurt, but I did what I could to find my inner calm, the internal focus I needed. I half-closed my eyes and extended my awareness, searching for Jess, for that part of her consciousness that I'd somehow connected with before. For a few frantic heartbeats, I fumbled alone, but then there she was, as familiar, strong, and intoxicating as in real life. We danced for a moment, two ethereal dolphins chasing each other's tails through an invisible ocean.

"Let's see what we're dealing with," I muttered, and led her towards the Intrusion, stepping sideways in some extra dimension to reveal the reality behind the three-dimensional image of the hospital corridor.

I'd been sucker punched before. I liked to think I was more aware of myself and my surroundings these days, but I wasn't prepared for whatever force slammed into my gut as we probed the Intrusion. I heard Jess wince, saw her body double over as mine did, our connected consciousness recoiling, then circling, protecting, regathering. We clutched each other, straightened up and pushed back. We were stronger than this. Better. We wouldn't be surprised again.

I'd encountered other memories of stressful labor, most notably at Chouteau Village almost a year earlier. This sweating, moaning woman, writhing on sodden sheets, was older, strands of gray running through the hair plastered to her dark face. Her legs were raised up and spread wide as two nurses worked between them, talking in low, urgent voices. "The baby's breached," I heard one say, and pain stabbed my gut again, as if invisible hands wrapped my internal organs with my intestines, tying them in knots. Through watering eyes, I noticed the balding man, a husband or partner, standing with his back to the far wall, horror, pity, and anguish battling for control of his ashen face. I didn't want to see this. I didn't want to *feel* this.

We needed to do our job, and quickly.

"Wanna lead?" I asked through gritted teeth.

"Sure," said Jess, and her spirit enfolded mine, channeling my strength alongside hers. I could sense what she sensed, but I was a silent partner, hers to command. I'd never been so vulnerable.

There was someone else there, watching us from the sidelines. We tensed, but it didn't feel like before, the strange presence brooding behind the memories. This was smaller, hungrier. This was...

"Back off, Izzy," growled Jess. The other woman made a noise that could have been a gasp or a stifled laugh, but our awareness of her faded.

We reset. *Go get 'em, Jess.*

She identified four—

Four? Okay.

—focal points on the edges of the memory. We gathered our strength—

Oh, crap! She's looking at me! The woman in the bed is looking at me!

—and we folded. One, two, three, four. Again. Fold met fold—

Gone, it's gone now.

—precise lines, in rapid succession. Smaller—

Did you see, Jess?

—and smaller—

Yeah, I saw.

—until they formed a perfect infinitesimal sphere. Hold—

Quick!

—focus—

Don't let it see us again!

—and fuse.

And we locked the new Tether in place.

After all the preamble, all the study, imprinting the memory had taken seconds. I crumpled to the floor as if I'd just run a marathon. Jess sank to her knees next to me, chest heaving, hands shaking as they rested on my shoulders. Our foreheads met as our exhausted spirits reluctantly disengaged.

I didn't know what had shocked me more: what we had done or what we had seen.

"Wow." Izzy stood above us, hands on hips, hunger in her black-rimmed eyes.

"That was… remarkable," breathed Jamal next to her, his expression unreadable. "A near perfect Level Two Tether."

No one knew what to say next, so this was the scene that greeted Doctor Hammond as she emerged from the birthing suite: Jess and I sprawled on the floor before our fascinated trainers.

Her lips pursed in distaste. "Is it done?" she demanded, and Jamal nodded. "Great. Now get the hell out of my hospital."

Chapter Twenty-One
SHE DESERVES TO KNOW

The good doctor hustled us back to the lobby without celebration, although she tossed Jess and I bottles of water as we passed the nurses' station. I was every bit as parched and exhausted as when erasing an Imprint, but stumbled along as best I could.

We found Faustyn waiting for us in one corner of the bustling space, as conspicuous with his Santa Claus beard and suit as a sunflower standing in someone's front lawn. A smile played over his face as he bounced a yo-yo in front of two elementary age boys, who gaped in delight at a skill not tied to an electronic device. A broad-shouldered woman sporting a cascade of blonde dreadlocks watched warily from a nearby chair. Faustyn's smile tightened as he noticed our approach.

"Do you want to try now?" he asked, passing the yo-yo to the taller boy's tentative hand. "You can keep it if you like. I have many more where that came from."

The boy accepted Faustyn's gift reverently, and made an uncertain and unsuccessful attempt to set the yo-yo in motion. His companion sniggered, but Faustyn told him to slow down and practice. Then he nodded at the woman and joined us, eyebrows raised in question.

"Perfect," said Jamal quietly. "I can't remember the last time someone perfected a Level Two Tether at their first attempt."

"And they did it together?"

"They did."

"Good. I'll be interested to hear the details." Faustyn steered us towards the elevator, but Jess didn't move.

"What's going on?" she demanded, folding her arms. I planted my feet next to her. It was time for answers.

Faustyn paused and looked at Jamal. Izzy stood off to the side, her usual cockiness replaced by something more somber.

"Well, someone speak," I said. "Enough with the mystery. There's something you're not telling us, and don't claim we don't need to know. It sounds like we took a risk for you back there, and you're going to explain why, right now."

"Very well," murmured Jamal, tearing his gaze away from Faustyn. "But let's go somewhere less public first."

"Right now," emphasized Jess.

"Just tell her," Izzy said. "She deserves to know."

Jamal took a deep breath. "We lost one of our agents yesterday. He'd almost reached Level Five. He's the third Chicago agent we've lost this year."

"What do you mean 'lost'?" I said, although I thought I knew.

"He's alive but unresponsive. He's been taken to the Anne Lyons Nursing Center."

"Fuck. I'm sorry." He grimaced. He was sorry too.

"Tell them all of it," said Izzy, hands clutching her arms over her chest. She was trembling. "Tell her, or I will."

"Izzy..."

"It's Conor, Jess. Conor McKee. He's the agent we 'lost' yesterday."

Jess glared at Izzy, then Jamal, then Faustyn, then shook her head in disgust. "You *fucking* people," she snarled, and stalked off towards the garage.

I thought of and discarded several follow up comments and questions, then simply hurried to catch up with her. We reached our car at the same time, and I fumbled with my key fob trying to unlock it.

"Take me there," seethed Jess, eyes bright in the garage's gloom. "Please."

We swept past the elevator as Faustyn and Jamal emerged. Jamal probably guessed our destination. Lake Shore Drive traffic had receded from its evening peak, but the drive to Evanston still took most of an hour. Save for a flurry of texting, Jess stared out the passenger-side window in silence. I couldn't think of a single thing to say or do, other than get her where she wanted to go as fast as possible.

Conor's wife and daughter waited for us in the nursing home's much smaller lobby. I'd spent most of the drive racking my brain for their names, before giving up and asking Jess as we pulled into the parking lot. Michelle, dressed more soberly than at their house party in a white blouse and charcoal pants, stood to greet us. Her eyes were puffy and haunted, and a quiet sob escaped her as she collapsed into Jess's embrace. Esmeralda stared up at me shyly - I wondered if she remembered the ten minutes I'd spent pushing her swing at the party - then tugged at Jess's shirt.

"Hey Princess!" Jess smiled and crouched down, pointing at the iPad clutched in the girl's hands. "Playing anything cool?"

"Bluey!" Esmeralda tilted the screen towards her with a toothy smile.

"That is cool! Can I watch with you?"

Jess climbed into the seat next to her and made a show of looking at the screen, but not before catching my eye.

"I'm sorry," I said to Michelle. I wasn't sure whether to embrace her too, and my arms dangled without purpose. "We're both sorry. If there's anything we can do..."

She forced a smile and raked her short blonde hair. "Jess already offered her child care services," she said in a hoarse voice. "I might take her up on it, especially if... well, no one knows, or is saying, how long..." She couldn't finish the thought, and I didn't make her.

"What happened?" I asked gently. Perhaps she didn't want to talk about that either, but I suspected she wouldn't have been told the real story, unless she was part of the Henry Lyons Foundation too.

"No one's really sure. Conor said he had to work late last night, because of this week's big software release. A janitor found him slumped over his desk around 8pm and called 911. He's alive, no physical injuries, but..." Tears welled in her eyes, and I wrapped cautious arms around her. She sobbed into my chest while joyful music blared from her daughter's iPad. Jess's expression, looking at me over Esmerelda's head, was bleak.

Michelle detached herself from me with an embarrassed smile, wiping her eyes. "Sorry. And thank you. It's overwhelming. Visiting hours are over, or I'd take you to see him. Not that there's much to see. He just sleeps. Nothing I or Ez do gets a reaction." She lowered her voice, but Esmeralda appeared engrossed in her show. "She doesn't understand. She's mad at him, thinks he's playing a game. I... He must be so frustrated, wherever he is. The man I love is in there."

She raised her chin in defiance, and I was all out of responses. Fortunately, Jamal made his entrance.

We all turned as he stepped inside, his face grim. I saw Jess stir out of the corner of my eye, but she said nothing. None of us said anything. The silence stretched until he finally strode forward and stood before Michelle.

"Any change?" She shook her head. He sighed, then glanced down at Esmeralda, who ignored him. "Hello, Jess," he murmured. "I'm surprised to find you here."

"Are you though?" she snapped back.

"I didn't think anyone on Conor's team knew yet. The company wanted to respect the family's feelings before making an announcement."

"I bet you did." She started to rise, but Jamal held up a hand to stem the flood of vitriol. To my surprise, it worked. I think Jess was surprised herself.

"Can I get you anything?" he asked Michelle. "A ride home, perhaps? No? Please, Michelle. You have my number. The company takes care of its own. Call me any time, day or night, okay?"

Michelle nodded, deflated and exhausted. She began wheedling Esmeralda to leave, but the girl refused, demanding she finish her show. Jess stepped in smoothly to head off a full-blown tantrum.

"I'll ride home with you," she offered Michelle. "D can pick me up on his way home."

"D?" Jamal extended his hand. "Jamal Peters. I'm Conor's boss."

"So I gather." I gripped his hand harder than I meant to, and earned a frown for my trouble. We stood in silence as the women wrangled Esmeralda out to the parking lot, then I rounded on him.

"Conor's an HLF agent?" I hissed. "When were you gonna tell Jess?"

"Maybe never," Jamal said in a cool tone, rubbing his hand with exaggerated care. "There are certain benefits to minimizing contact between field agents, especially when something unfortunate happens."

"What really happened? No more bullshit, or I'm done with you and the HLF."

We stared each other down, but he blinked first. Suddenly he looked tired and defeated, little better than Conor's wife. "I wasn't there, you understand," he said with a half-glance at the duty nurse, absorbed with her phone. "I heard this from Faustyn. Conor's been close to completing Level Five for a while. He and his mentor identified a likely candidate Intrusion last night, in the offices of Paragon Insurance. There was... interference. The mentor called for backup, and decided to leave Conor in his office for the cleaning staff to find."

"You have got to be kidding me," I spat. Jamal held his ground, but his eyes widened and his feet shifted. Easy, D.

"Someone falls into a coma and you just drag them to their office for someone else to find? He could've died!"

"Not my call. His mentor was in bad shape too. They needed assistance."

"But not 911?"

"Not immediately. Not for this."

"Why not?"

"Really, D? Would you want to explain what happened in a way that would actually help any random paramedics? The Foundation understands comas, and the particular conditions that cause these kinds of comas, better than anyone."

"So why leave him?"

"Because we can't just abduct someone. Leaving Conor in his office when the cleaning staff were already making their rounds gave us precious time to put our own paramedics and support team in place. Unfortunately, this wasn't our first rodeo."

I scowled at him, but it made a kind of sense. Something else about his story bothered me, though. "You said there was 'interference'. What did you mean?"

He didn't answer immediately, taking off his eyeglasses and polishing the lenses with the hem of his shirt. I guessed he'd let something slip, and was weighing how much he could get away with revealing. Or not revealing.

"We think," he said at last, replacing his eyeglasses and blinking as his eyes readjusted, "that other sensitives may be interfering with our own, somehow trapping their mind inside the Intrusion. We're not sure exactly how it works. Trying to understand helped us devise the shielding technique Izzy used on you and Jess earlier in the year."

"Lovely. Who are these other sensitives? How long has this been going on?"

"Months? Years?" Jamal gestured to either side of and above us. "We've only recently detected the interference, thanks to Izzy and other strong, capable agents like her. As to who these people are, and why they're doing this, I can't tell you. We simply don't know enough, not yet."

I wasn't sure I believed him, but I decided not to press the point. Not yet.

"Other sensitives? Someone did that to Conor on purpose? Who?"

I winced as yet another light turned red on North Avenue. I just wanted to get home. I wished Jess had stayed around for Jamal's explanations, so I wouldn't be forced to recite them. It'd been a long night, and I just wanted to collapse on my couch and stare at the TV, until either my brain turned to mush or I fell asleep. Either was fine by me.

"They're still trying to figure that out, apparently."

"Uh huh. And you trust him?"

"Not particularly, but I'm sick of the lot of them right now."

My phone buzzed in my pocket for the third time during the short drive from the McKee's house. I slapped it in irritation.

"Yeah, me too," said Jess. "I wanna talk to Conor's mentor, find out what really happened. And I'm wondering..." She tailed off, and I caught a hitch in her voice.

"Wondering what?"

"I'm wondering if I got that job at Paragon just so the HLF could keep tabs on me."

I wanted to tell her that was paranoid, but was it? Did they have an agent among the staff of Trattoria Cappelli? Was it Luca himself? He'd hired me sight unseen after all.

"I think you got that job on your own merit," I said at last. "And you've been killing it, haven't you?"

"Perhaps," she said with a smile, then her eyes widened as we turned onto our street. "Oh! What's Rosalind doing here?"

I was hunting down a parking spot, so it took me a moment to spot Rosalind. She stood next to a wheeled carry-on bag in the shadows of our front porch, far enough from the wall sconce to go unseen by casual observation. She wore one of her skirt suits, including a jacket despite the heat, and studied her phone while petting Jasmine, the Millers' cat.

"I apologize for the even shorter notice," she whispered as we hugged. "Can we go inside?"

"Sorry for the mess," I said after showing her through our apartment door. I scooped up stray blankets from the living room floor, while Jess cleared mugs and plates from the coffee table. "We weren't expecting you. Obviously."

She waved away my apology and helped straighten the couch cushions. "It was a last minute decision. Did you not receive my texts, or was the spam filter on your phone extra vigilant tonight?"

I dug out my phone and saw I'd missed three messages, all from a 636 number I didn't recognize. "You doing burner phones after all, Rosalind?"

"Today I am," she confirmed. "The longer it takes certain people to realize I'm here, the better."

"What's going on? Is Martin here too?"

"No, just me. Do you mind if we sit down?"

We huddled around the kitchen table, and Jess poured three large tumblers of ice water. Then, because it was late and none of us had eaten dinner or felt like cooking, we ordered a pizza. Rosalind insisted on paying, since she was our "unannounced guest".

"Where are you staying?" Jess asked as I used her laptop to place the online order.

"I was hoping I could crash here for the night. I'd be happy to pretend I'm at Uni again and sleep on the couch."

"Nonsense. D can take the couch, if you don't mind sharing a bed with me."

"Now that definitely reminds me of Uni!" Rosalind laughed, and Jess batted her eyelashes. "Thank you. I'll try not to be a bother. If I'm here more than a day or two, I'll make other arrangements."

I caught Jess's eye. Rosalind was rattled, and that didn't bode well.

"Everything's okay with Martin, right?" Jess asked her.

"Oh, good Lord, yes!" Rosalind grimaced. "It's nothing like that. Not that we haven't argued about this, but we decided it was best for him to stay in St. Louis. He's not happy about it, but he's fearfully busy with work, and I still have most of a month before the new term at Gold Cross."

"Well, it's great to see you, all the same," I said, sliding her credit card back to her. She briefly covered my hand with hers. I'd forgotten how much I missed her.

"Likewise," she said. "I wish it was purely a social call, but I do bring tidings of a strange and alarming nature. And I want your news too. I haven't heard much from you since your mother's passing. How are you?"

I squirmed in my chair and avoided looking at Jess. Mom's death wasn't the only awkward topic of conversation looming over us. There was a reason I hadn't shared much with Rosalind.

"I'm fine," I said before the silence stretched too long. "I talk to Fiona at least once a week, and she's coping. Mary too, from the sounds of it. She and I aren't at the telephone conversation stage yet, although we're all in a family group on Snapchat. Fiona thinks Patrick should consider moving, but he and Mary are mad against it. Still family drama."

I allowed myself a wry grin. Six months ago, I wouldn't talk to anyone in my family except Fiona. I'd be video chatting with Steven Rourke next.

"You will let me know if there's anything we can do?" prodded Rosalind. "Grief takes time, even when... well, it just takes time. Any news about the Scales of Equilibrium? What inroads have you made with the Henry Lyons Foundation?"

"Some," I said, and licked my lips, wishing the pizza would arrive so I could dodge the question longer. She watched me intently, a teacher asking her student a question she knew he could answer. And I hadn't had time to revise.

"We're learning how to make Imprints," Jess said quietly. "We're actually getting good at it."

Rosalind blinked, but held my gaze. Her voice turned cold. "Explain."

So I did. I shook off my paralysis, my fear of offending my friend and mentor, and recounted our lessons with Jamal and Izzy. I told her about Lyons-Strickland and Polk Medical Center, but I also emphasized the *why*: my conviction that certain memories shouldn't be visible to anyone who was sensitive enough to detect and erase Imprints. Some things were private and deserved to stay that way. If I ever thought my childhood home might harbor an Intrusion, I wanted the ability to lock that damn thing down so that no one, not even Rosalind, was any the wiser.

She frowned while my floodgates opened. I couldn't tell if I'd disappointed her, if she felt betrayed, or was just trying to understand. Or maybe all of it together. The pizza arrived, and we went about the mechanics of passing out plates and choosing slices while she processed it all.

"I see," she said at last, cutting into her pizza and forking a bite-size piece into her mouth. I'd never seen anyone eat pizza with a knife and fork before. I would've teased her, but it didn't seem like the time. She chewed, swallowed and sighed: a deep, soul-expelling exhalation that seemed to sap most of her remaining energy. "I understand your choices, even if I disagree with them. It's unfair of me to hold you to the same standard to which I hold myself."

"Is that the only fair standard though?" Jess objected. I paused with a new slice of pizza halfway to my mouth. Rosalind turned her scrutiny on Jess, who was uncowed. "Believe me, we're far from thrilled with the HLF, but could they not have this right? Isn't it better to lock these memories, these Intrusions, away? Could breaking those locks be dangerous? What if there *is* something out there, trying to get through?"

Rosalind's face, if possible, turned paler. "What do you mean?"

"Haven't you ever felt it? Something, someone, some sort of presence or awareness behind these memories?"

"These aren't ghosts, Jess—"

"I'm not talking about ghosts!" Jess's fist thudded the table, and Rosalind's silverware rattled in alarm. "This is something else, something bigger. I've felt it and D has too." She speared me with her gaze, and I nodded, setting my drooping pizza slice down before it collapsed over my shirt. "What if these Tethers, these Imprints, are actually stopping something terrible from happening? And what if, by erasing them, we help it happen?"

Rosalind looked long and hard at Jess, who simply bit into her pizza and chewed, unflappable. I remembered asking questions, earlier in my apprenticeship with Rosalind, that she'd seemed uncomfortable answering. I'd never pursued it, but then I hadn't noticed the watchful presence Jess described until recently.

"I've been erasing Imprints for eight years," Rosalind said at last. "I've never experienced anything to convince me there's more to this than memories and my own imagination."

"What if there is, though?" I asked, determined to show a united front. "I don't know what it might be, or if it's actually bad." Jess frowned, but I rushed onward. "I'm not sure what the Foundation knows, or if they'd tell us. But every time I get answers about any of this, more questions follow. We have to keep going, and keep asking."

Rosalind forced down another bite of pizza, then discarded her silverware. "Do you want to know why I'm here? Why I skulked into town and why I'm holing up in your apartment? Donovan Brooks is in a coma."

Jess and I exchanged startled looks.

"When?" I asked. "How?"

"Sometime over the weekend. Martin and I decided to train at your old dojo Monday night, and Sensei Allen told us. Donovan's girlfriend, Lana, was inconsolable. I know we had our differences, but I wouldn't wish that on anybody." She cocked her head, clearly detecting something in our reactions. "As to how, no one seems to know for sure. But I heard something yesterday that concerned me, enough to send me scurrying up here to see you in person.

"You remember the Harringtons, the new Foundation representatives in St. Louis? They've been lax about training me on how to imprint memories, or create Tethers in the HLF vernacular. We've discussed the theory, but mostly in the context of helping me erase the bad Imprints Donovan and Lana leave in their wake. That changed last night. Alice showed me how to create a Tether. When I asked why, Robert told me Donovan was out of commission. And the way they *smiled*, D! It gave me the creeps. It was all I could do to maintain my composure until I got to my car afterwards."

"Shit," breathed Jess, and I knew she was thinking the same thing. Were some HLF agents turning on their own? Was the power struggle that real?

"There's something else," Rosalind continued, and suddenly her eyes were moist. "I heard from Daniel."

"Is that... good?" I hardly dared ask the question.

"I'll let you be the judge. He sent two texts last night, just to me." She woke up her phone and tapped the screen rapidly. "The first reads 'Tell your friends to leave Chicago by August 1'. The second..." She tailed off and gathered herself. I held my breath. "The second reads 'Tell D that Bryan was a bad man'."

Chapter Twenty-Two
PLAYING WITH FORCES

"We fight back!" Jess declared. "We set bait for the bastards, then D and I take them out. Just like we broke Izzy's shields, except we break them!"

I glanced around Polk Medical's cafeteria, but none of the few remaining diners paid us any attention. Counter service had closed for the night, and we figured this was as good a place to have the conversation as any other.

Jess's emphatic statement earned a mixed reception. Rosalind had already heard the idea and made her objections clear, but she had a lot on her mind. Since arriving five days ago, she'd observed several Tethers. Following a poor Level Two effort of my own, Jess nailed her Level One at Lyons-Strickland under Izzy's supervision, and we'd just combined on another perfect Level Two. My failure had reinforced Rosalind's misgivings, despite Jamal's assurances that I was far ahead of most trainees at this stage. She'd tried to talk us out of tonight's attempt, and was now processing the complete absence of any detectable Imprint after we'd used our connection to create the Tether.

Jamal sat back in his chair opposite mine, brow furrowed in thought. Izzy's calculating eyes gazed at Jess above a greedy smile.

Faustyn was horrified. "Are you suggesting mental warfare?" he hissed, leaning over the table. "I cannot condone that. The Foundation's mandate is to research and mitigate Intrusions, not use our skills to attack others."

"Tell that to Michelle McKee," snarled Jess. "Tell that to the loved ones of other agents you've lost to comas. This is self-defense! How can you expect anyone to create Tethers when they risk not waking up afterwards?"

"Everyone understands the risks, Miss Evans."

"Do they? Because I don't remember D and I getting the lowdown before we joined your little training program."

Jamal coughed politely. "That's not entirely true, Jess. I made you both aware of the dangers of creating and erasing Imprints. That's why I took you to Anne Lyons Nursing Center."

"But you never mentioned your suspicions about other sensitives putting your agents in comas," I pointed out.

"Because they're only suspicions," Faustyn insisted, earning a frown from Jamal. "We have people working that theory."

"Who?" interjected Izzy.

"I'm not at liberty to say. But I am at liberty, and have a responsibility, to forestall anything as dangerous and foolhardy as what Jess is suggesting."

"And how do you intend to stop her?" Rosalind asked as Jess bristled. "You have no authority over us. We haven't signed anything. We accepted your guidance, some with more skepticism than others, but we're not beholden to your decrees over what we should and shouldn't do."

Faustyn stared at her. It was his first time meeting Rosalind, and I might have spared a shred of sympathy if the guy wasn't being such a jackass.

I stood, scraping my chair backwards, to break the tension. "I'm going to the restroom," I said, trying not to act like I was interrupting class. "This water's going straight through me."

"Look," Faustyn tried again. "Think about what you're saying. Do you really want that on your conscience? There are other ways..."

In the restroom, I splashed my face with tap water and gazed into the smudged mirror above the sink. Bloodshot eyes stared back, and I thought I could detect wrinkles forming at their corners. I looked almost as tired as I felt. For the first time in a while, I yearned for a normal life, a life without the HLF, Imprints or Erasures, a life where I could just make my way in the world like everyone else. A life with Jess. Would it be as exciting as dealing with paranormal phenomena? I thought it might. She'd rescued me from the mundane, and we didn't need the thrill of battling forces we barely understood to enliven our relationship.

I was so engrossed with my own thoughts that I almost ran into Izzy as I left the restroom. She stood with her back to the wall, one foot raised and flat against it, arms folded. I halted and uttered the default Midwestern "ope" for such awkward situations. She tilted her head and smiled. It lit up her face, black eyeliner and all.

"Didn't mean to startle you," she said. "I wasn't adding much to the conversation, so I thought I'd check on you. So many Tethers in one week takes its toll."

"I'll be fine," I assured her with far more confidence than I felt. "It's all part of the plan."

"Yes, Jess told me. For what it's worth, I like the idea. It's about time we took the battle to these people. It was hard enough getting Faustyn and the other brass to acknowledge they existed."

Her eyes looked haunted for a moment. I wondered what she'd seen in her young life, and during a Foundation career much longer than mine.

"When did you know?" I asked. "And how?"

"About a year now, since before Connie and Raul were attacked. Have you ever sensed wills other than your own when you're locking a Tether? Or destroying one?"

"Maybe," I said cautiously.

"I put it down to overactive imagination at first. Then one day I was creating a Tether down in Hyde Park and sensed two of them, just as I was about to start folding. It was like they were trying to smother me, to wrap me and the memory in some kind of cocoon."

"Holy shit."

She grinned, and took a step towards me. Today's t-shirt was sleeveless with a deep V-neck, and I tried not to dwell on how much skin it revealed.

"I was too fast for them," she said, regaining some of her cockiness. "Too strong. But other agents weren't as fast and strong as me. I'm exceptional, you see."

She took another step towards me, and my body became very aware of hers. I could smell her scent, musky with hints of dark chocolate, and something else I couldn't place. I shot a quick glance down the corridor towards the cafeteria. "Izzy—"

"But you're exceptional too," she went on, inching closer. "You and Jess. With your connection, you can be so much better, so much faster and stronger than I am by myself. If anyone can fight back against these assholes, it's you."

"Izzy, listen," I started, backing up a step.

"We're all fascinated by your connection, you see. They weren't sure, back in St. Louis, but Conor confirmed it when you destroyed the Tether at Paragon. No-one can agree on how you do it. Nothing other agents try works anywhere near as well. But I think I know."

"What do you know?" I asked, curious even as I sought to evade her.

"You love each other," she said simply, her upturned face inches from mine. "You're physically attracted too, of course, but that's easy. It's the emotional connection that makes a strong relationship, when one person's hopes, dreams, and fears align with another's. You and Jess are emotionally codependent. That's what makes you so powerful."

It sounded plausible. It explained the Foundation's interest in us, and in accelerating our training. I wondered what other agents had done to try to replicate our connection. Izzy was giving me some idea.

"I can help," she breathed, reaching up and resting her forearms on my shoulders. The swell of her breasts pressed against my chest, and I froze. It had been a long time since a woman had come on to me so aggressively. Sure, I'd sometimes flirt with a waitress or cashier, often under Jess's amused scrutiny. But this was more than flirtation.

"Izzy, no." I grasped her wrists and lifted her arms off my shoulders. She pouted as I took a more purposeful step back.

"We could be even stronger," she whispered, raw hunger in her eyes. "You, Jess and me. The three of us could be stronger than anyone in the history of the HLF! We could do anything!"

"From what I've heard, you're already as strong as you need to be. Exceptional, wasn't that the word you used? Jess and I are trying to catch up. And we're together, Izzy. You said it yourself. We love each other. We're partners, we're committed to our relationship, outside of all this crap. And I can't betray that. I won't."

She searched my eyes with her own, then looked down at where I still held her slender wrists in my hands. "I don't see a ring on your finger. Hers either."

"No, well, we haven't got there yet."

I released her and turned towards the cafeteria. I hoped to all that was holy, Jess hadn't seen any of that.

"It doesn't have to be a betrayal, but my offer stands," Izzy said with a crooked smile. "I'll help you guys in any way I can. Let's see if Jess has sold Faustyn your plan yet."

I was rattled, but if Jess had noticed or suspected anything while Izzy and I were both absent, she didn't mention it. She was planning logistics with Jamal, while Faustyn watched stony-faced. Rosalind stood some way off, talking on her phone.

We dispersed soon afterwards, with some details still to be ironed out, like where and when. Faustyn wanted nothing to do with it, which bothered exactly no one. Jess tasked Jamal with finding a candidate Intrusion, and demanded his and Izzy's schedules. Whatever outrage she harbored from discovering Conor was an HLF agent was eclipsed by a fierce determination to make his attackers pay. I admired her for it, even as I worried where it might lead.

Rosalind wasn't wrong. She made another appeal as we drove back to her Streeterville hotel. "Why the counterattack? Why this insistence on brute force, on blowing things up like we're in some Hollywood action movie? You both have more control than that. Or you should. Why else are you training at the dojo every week?"

"So we can 'blow things up' with precision, if it comes to it," said Jess, unmoved. "Look, I'm first in line to figure out not just who these people are, but how they're doing it. But in the heat of the moment, we may not have time for analysis. And, if I'm honest, I want to make these people pay for what they did to Conor and his family."

"And that's what worries me. You're making this personal, Jess. You're letting it cloud your judgment. Why not let the Henry Lyons Foundation deal with this? They're the ones under attack, not you."

"But they aren't dealing with it," I pointed out. "Faustyn wants nothing to do with this. I don't know what he and his bosses are waiting for, but people are getting hurt."

Rosalind leaned forward. "Let's just say you succeed. Let's say you stun these attackers, rather than damage them irreparably, and that you're undamaged yourself. Let's say you find them, identify them, and scare them off. What then? Does it stop there? This might be the work of a few rogue sensitives, which is disturbing enough. I think it's more likely they're part of something bigger, within the Foundation or without. You'd be putting a target on your back."

"You don't think we're already targets?" Jess scoffed. "It's just a matter of time before they'd come for us anyway."

"Not if you stop. Not if you walk away from the HLF and go back to erasing bad Imprints, or just walk away, period. No-one's asking you to do any of this."

I glanced at my rear-view mirror. Rosalind's expression matched her earnest tone. Was she afraid? That wasn't the woman I knew: calm, composed, wielding quiet authority, and ready to back up her words with force if necessary. What had she been doing since she'd arrived in town, other than observe our Tether training?

"It's a little late for that," Jess murmured before I could ask. "Knowing what we know... We can't just walk away. We're nobody's pawns, but we want to do what's right."

"This is so much bigger than we ever thought, back in St. Louis," I said, turning onto Ohio Street. "I think we need to see it through, but I understand your concern. I don't expect you to join us if you're against it."

Rosalind sighed as I stopped in front of her hotel. "No, I'll come. I rather think you might need me, one way or another. As long as you schedule it before August 1st."

I got out of the car and opened the back door for her. She smiled and took my hand as I helped her out.

"You still want us to leave town by August 1st?" I asked quietly.

"I think it would be prudent. At least for a few days."

"What do you think will happen if we don't?"

She shook her head. "I really don't know, D. But I'm worried. If my estranged son broke years of silence to warn me, it can't be good."

"Out with it," Jess barked as soon as we got home. "You've been brooding ever since we left the hospital. Are you having second thoughts? Do you agree with Rosalind?"

She stood, hands on hips, chin raised in defiance.

"Not at all," I said, taking my lovely firebrand in my arms and kissing her. She stiffened, then melted into my embrace. "She's right to be worried, but this is one hundred percent the right thing to do. I'm tired of reacting and playing by others' rules. If we have this rare talent, this connection, let's put it to good use."

"I agree. Thank you, love." My shoulder muffled her voice, but her arms coiled around my back, drawing our bodies even closer. "Then what's on your mind?"

I stirred against her, but it didn't feel right. I had to confess.

"Back at the hospital," I began, then drew back until I could see her face. "When I stepped out to go to the restroom, Izzy followed me. We talked, but... she came on to me. Nothing happened, and I set her straight, but I thought you should know."

Jess gazed up at me, one eyebrow raised. "She has been acting friendlier," she said slowly. "Got a little handsy at Lyons-Strickland, but I thought it was just camaraderie after I made Level One."

"You didn't tell me that."

"Sorry, love. I honestly didn't think anything of it. But now I do. You think she's after a threesome?"

"Jess!"

"What? Wouldn't be my first one." She grinned as my jaw dropped, then her expression sobered. "But as attractive as she is, no. You're the only one for me, D."

I cradled her cheek with one hand and took my time. "And you're the only one for me, Jess." We kissed and held each other. The silence was momentous.

"I think she's after more than that though," I said at last. "She envies this connection we have, how we use it to erase and create Imprints. She wants in."

"Ha! Well, she'll just have to figure out another way. But we may need the help, if things get as bad as Rosalind fears. Now, help me set a trap for the assholes who put Conor in a coma."

The idea was simple enough: Jess and I would offer ourselves as bait. According to Jamal, all four Chicago agents attacked that year, including Conor, were some of the best and brightest. Only Izzy had survived. We weren't in that league yet, but we'd turned heads and earned a reputation because of our connection, which had catapulted us to Level Two in record time. We needed to make an even bigger splash, go after a Level Three Tether immediately, and trust our faceless adversaries couldn't resist the temptation.

The problem was finding a candidate Intrusion in a suitable location. We believed the other sensitives had to be close for their wills to have sufficient effect. Our chief evidence was Izzy's account of the HLF's experiments with the shielding technique she'd used against us.

"They flew me over to HLF headquarters in England for two weeks," she'd told us before we left Polk Medical, unembarrassed by our encounter. "It's a big-ass manor house. They trained me on constructing a Shield the first day, then spent the rest of the time moving me from room to room, seeing how far I could get from the target before the Shield failed. All day, every day. Tedious as hell. And the food was terrible."

"I think I saw you once," I said. "In the apartment building on Austin Boulevard."

She gave us a rueful grin. "Yeah, I got in trouble for that. But I wanted to see who I was dealing with. I couldn't have been much closer. I was in the apartment underneath, and you blew through my Shield anyway."

So, assuming Izzy was one of the strongest agents in the Foundation, we had to find an Intrusion where our assailants could conceal themselves nearby. I was hazy about what resources Jamal had at his disposal, but by the weekend he'd found a likely candidate: the bar next door to the Great Lakes Hotel.

"You're kidding me," was my reaction when I called him back just before Saturday dinner service at Trattoria Cappelli. Tourist season was in full swing, and I was clinging on to my new role in charge of meats. It didn't help that I suspected Chef Luca might be an HLF agent, despite Faustyn's assurances to the contrary.

"I know you have history at the hotel," Jamal said. "You destroyed a Tether back in March, but there's been a relapse, a reoccurrence of the Intrusion in the bar next door. There's a cafe opposite the hotel lobby, which would be a perfect place for our targets to loiter while we're in the bar."

As long as I avoided the hotel itself, I figured I'd be fine. The Great Lakes held a dread fascination for me, the site of a recent triumph and a prior failure. I didn't want the staff to recognize me as "fire alarm guy" or someone promising unusual solutions to unusual problems.

Jess begged off work early on Monday, three days before Rosalind's August 1st deadline. She grumbled about her interim team lead as I walked her to Fedora, the bohemian watering hole adjacent to the Great Lakes. We gave the hotel a wide berth, aided by a family of five struggling to unload their luggage from the minivan parked at the curb. We dodged bickering siblings and waved off an apology from the tired-looking mother before slipping into the bar. It was much darker inside, and we stood blinking as we searched for anyone we recognized.

"Over there," said Jess, at the exact moment I spotted Rosalind's waving hand towards the back of the deep but narrow room. She sat at one end of a semi-circular booth, its studded crimson leather wrapping around a scooped tabletop of reclaimed wood. Jamal and Izzy sat beside her, all nursing cocktails.

"Drinking on the job?" I inquired as we reached the table.

"It's a bar," Izzy said, raising her glass. "Can't occupy a table and just drink water, can we?"

"I suggest you order your own drinks from the bar." Jamal gave us a significant look. "From this end of it."

Fedora's bar stretched most of the length of the room. Jess and I had sat at it during our previous visit, part of our ill-fated weekend trip the previous year. She disliked the layout, I remembered. I thought I recognized the bartender, a tall, clean-shaven man with friendly eyes but little conversation. He was currently pouring beers for a pair of older couples, all wearing identical Gary Numan T-shirts and likely attending a concert later.

Jess and I headed towards a free chair at the end of the bar, and I was in touching distance when the hackles rose on the back of my neck. I was prepared for the sharp stab of sensation as I passed by the Intrusion, but it was no less unpleasant.

"Now what?" I set my Goose Island IPA and Jess's White Russian down, while Jess slotted in next to Izzy. They exchanged a meaningful look before Izzy turned away, sipping her cocktail. "This place is hopping. We're going to look weird standing spaced out in the middle of it."

"Only one of us has to engage the Intrusion, though," Jess pointed out. "You'll be five yards away. We can connect easily over that distance."

"So I'm the one who gets to stand there looking foolish?"

"Of course!" she laughed. "It's the role you were born to play!"

We were nervous, and everyone knew it. I sipped my beer and slowed my breathing, seeking my inner calm.

"Speaking of roles," said Jamal, "Level Three Intrusions are typically associated with memories of rage or violence. They're much more volatile than anything you've tried to tether so far, and a Single-Point Lock is not always adequate. Once you've dealt with our presumed adversaries, you may not have the remaining strength or skill to create the Tether. If Izzy or I take over, let us. Understood?"

I nodded, then looked at Rosalind, who watched the rest of us with disapproval.

"I'll be here to clean up any mess," she said, for all the world like she was the only adult in the room. "I still think you're playing with forces you don't understand."

"Only one way to find out," I muttered. The bartender was busy with another group nearer the door. I rose to my feet and exhaled a lungful of air. Showtime.

I found the Intrusion again, reached for Jess and found her too. Establishing our mental connection got easier every time, as simple as holding hands. I basked in its power, the power of our mutual love if what Izzy believed was true. I paused, waiting for signs of other consciousnesses, but sensed nothing. Fine. Steeling myself, I focused on some indefinable direction and pushed forward.

I thought it hadn't worked at first. The bar looked the same, packed with tourists. My first clue that this was a memory was glimpsing the dark-skinned, female bartender. My second was the drunk guy lurching toward me from the restroom, a college-age, frat boy type, sporting close-cropped hair and a linebacker physique. As he passed a smartly-dressed young couple at the bar, he leered and slid behind the woman to grope her breasts. She recoiled and struggled to free herself from his pawing hands. Her partner sprang off his barstool and punched the drunk in the face, and that was, presumably, when all hell broke loose. I didn't see much more, because that's when I felt the other consciousnesses.

They were quite different from what we'd started calling The Presence, the unknown but unmistakable intelligence that Jess and I occasionally encountered. We'd felt its scrutiny, but no hint of action, malicious or otherwise. Now, I sensed two hostile wills flanking me, less powerful but full of ill intent. As I grappled with the vision of drunken mayhem, they built walls around me, cutting me off from physical reality. I knew with strange certainty that if they completed those walls, my mind would be trapped inside. I'd relive this memory forever, while my body languished in a bed at the Anne Lyons Nursing Center, next to Conor McKee. And maybe Jess too.

That thought spurred me into action. I'd taken way too long to recognize and assess the threat. The walls were almost complete. Jess's alarm and panic resonated with mine. I channeled it. These walls were just another barrier, not unlike Izzy's Shields. I had no time for finesse, or solving any puzzles. I might only get one shot. I could sense the origins of these walls, the points from which they spread. In one smooth action, I locked onto those points as if they were Catches in a Two-Point Lock, gathered all our combined strength, and hurled it against them.

Everything fell apart.

Chapter Twenty-Three
A Falling Out

My shoulder cannoned off someone's back, and I caught the indignant "Hey!", although I was too blind with head pain to see who it was, much less apologize. Images of violence flashed before my eyes, the stench of blood filled my nostrils, and I regretted taking even one sip of my beer.

Hands grabbed me under my shoulders as I sank towards the floor. Words of comfort burbled through a torrent of agony. More hands, lifting me. A seat. Oh god, a seat felt so good! I sank into it, cradled my head in my hands, and waited for the end.

Instead, my piercing headache ebbed, enough for my surroundings to blur into view. I was back at our table. Jess slumped against Izzy, and Jamal was on his phone, panting and blinking rapidly. Rosalind was nowhere to be seen. Curious heads turned our direction, and I caught more than one disapproving comment. I wondered whether I'd yelled or done anything equally alarming.

I turned to ask Jess, cradled in Izzy's arms, and my pounding heart skipped a beat. She was unresponsive, eyes closed, jaw slack, a line of saliva trickling from one corner of her mouth. Izzy held her wrist and counted silently.

"Jess!" I croaked. I could hear Jamal talking to the 911 dispatcher, but all I cared about was Jess. *Wake up! Please, wake up!*

"Her pulse is fine," murmured Izzy, shifting Jess's weight to prop her up. "She collapsed as soon as you launched your attack. We all felt it, like a shock wave. The HLF brass will be very unhappy with you."

"Don't care," I snarled, then almost passed out from a coughing fit that bounced my brain around my skull.

The bartender arrived with a pitcher of ice water, reproof and concern. I noticed we'd been given a wider berth by his other customers, and I didn't blame them.

"Is there a problem?" he asked.

"She's had some kind of fit," Jamal told him, cupping his phone. His voice betrayed an edge of panic. "It's happened before. I called 911. Paramedics are on their way."

The bartender glanced at me, and I flailed for how to excuse my behavior, but he simply nodded before turning to face the room. "Someone's taken ill back here," he called. "Paramedics will arrive shortly. Please make way for them and give my other guests some privacy."

After a brief flurry of rubbernecking, everyone decided to do the right thing. Jamal stood by the front of our table, holding his phone to his ear.

"Where's Rosalind?" I asked him, and he pointed towards the door.

"She got to you first, while Jamal and I dealt with the Tether," Izzy explained. She wiped the saliva from Jess's cheek with gentle fingertips. "It was a doozy. I'm not sure you could have managed it, connection or not."

"That wasn't really the point, was it?" I snapped, between long, slow gulps of water. "We lured those bastards here, and I hope I got them worse than my girlfriend."

Izzy met my eyes, and for the first time I saw genuine respect in hers. "We'll find out soon, I hope. Rosalind went to check next door."

All I could do was wait, and endure the pain and anxiety. I took both of Jess's limp hands in my own, willing my life into hers. I couldn't voice the question that terrified me: was she in a coma? I couldn't handle that. I wasn't the praying sort, but I mumbled fervent appeals to anyone who might be listening.

A mild commotion announced the paramedics' arrival. A stocky woman with spiky blond hair took in our group at a glance, then asked me to make room. I wobbled as I climbed to my feet, and her companion steadied me. He was taller, wiry, and looked like he was still in high school.

"Easy there, my friend," he said, escorting me a couple steps away. "You need to sit back down?"

I shook my head and almost regretted it. "I'll stand," I muttered. "Just got up too fast."

He surveyed the table and formed an obvious conclusion. "You guys been here a while?"

"First round." I tried to smile, but God only knows what that looked like. "We'd only sipped our drinks, believe me."

I heard a moan and looked down to see Jess wrinkle her nose in disgust. Her eyes were glassy and unfocused, but open. A million tons of weight dropped away from my heart. The paramedic pocketed whatever she'd held under Jess's nose and shone a penlight into each eye, moving it from side to side. Jess struggled to follow along, then groaned and slumped against Izzy again, eyelids fluttering.

"She's got a concussion, a pretty bad one," the paramedic announced. "We need the stretcher." She asked if we had a hospital preference, and Jamal immediately answered with Polk Medical Center. She didn't ask how Jess could have sustained a concussion sitting at a table. I suspected we might hear more about that later, and I wasn't wrong.

Rosalind appeared at my side as they helped Jess onto the stretcher. She nodded, but now was not the time for an explanation. Jess was too groggy to talk, but she gave me a weak smile and squeezed my hand as they wheeled her out to the ambulance. A couple other patrons wished us well, but most watched our sad parade in awkward silence.

The three ambulances parked at the curb were joined by a Chicago PD cruiser as we emerged from Fedora. Two hassled-looking police officers jumped out, one heading into the hotel lobby and the other making a beeline for us.

"Get back, get back," he barked at the crowd, although the gaggle of onlookers had given the paramedics plenty of space. "Are you with her? Then I need to talk to you. Don't go anywhere." He ducked into Fedora, and Jamal's scowl followed him.

"Dammit, he's not one of ours."

I tried not to think about the HLF owning cops. "I'll come find you at the hospital," I promised Jess, kissing her softly.

"You better," she mumbled, forcing a smile.

Our hastily agreed-upon story was that we were as confused as everyone else. One moment Jess was sitting there, the next she'd keeled over in her seat. The returning cop, a brusque white guy sporting an extravagant white mustache, was unimpressed. However, since there was no evidence or report of assault, he scrawled down our names and disappeared back inside.

As we stood there answering questions, two stretchers were wheeled out from the hotel and lifted into the remaining ambulances. I wasn't close enough to see much, although both occupants appeared to be men. Rosalind touched my arm and waved her phone. She had pictures.

"Let's get off the street," Jamal suggested, and we followed him into the parking garage around the corner. I climbed into the passenger seat of his Acura, while the ladies slid into the back. There was no question that we were all going to Polk Medical.

"I'll have to report this to Faustyn eventually," Jamal admitted. "But it can wait until we get an official diagnosis of Jess's injuries."

"Surely they should check you out too, D," said Rosalind.

"I'm fine," I assured her, willing it to be true, and knowing it likely wasn't. "Tell us what you saw next door."

She tsked at my brush off, but didn't pursue it. "The hotel security guard had just found them when I arrived. Two men lay sprawled on the cafe floor, almost on top of each other. I asked what happened, and he said he didn't know, just that he heard them fall. I offered to check vital signs while he called 911, and when his back was turned, I snapped some quick pictures."

"They were definitely breathing?" I asked. Rosalind's misgivings echoed in my mind. What if I'd killed someone?

"They were." Her tone was gentle, devoid of judgment. "One had an impressive bump on his head from the fall, but otherwise they appeared much like Jess. The other man began to stir after the security guard got back, so I said I needed to find my husband and left."

Something in the way she said this got my attention. "Did you recognize either of them?"

"Not exactly. Take a look."

She passed me her phone, and I swiped through a half-dozen pictures of two unconscious white guys, or rather their heads and shoulders against a gray tile floor. The younger man was blond and pale, with an impressive aquiline nose. I didn't recognize him, but I did his companion: the lump on his forehead couldn't distract me from that long, pointed beard. It was Marcus, Jess's former colleague at Paragon. She was going to go ballistic.

There was more. Rosalind had been rushed, and the lighting hadn't been ideal, but she'd caught sight of the tattoos behind each man's left ear. Marcus's was indistinct, but I recognized the other man's: a set of uneven scales. The Scales of Equilibrium.

I blinked at the phone and tried to ignore my headache. I needed to think. I hadn't pursued the Scales' connection to the Henry Lyons Foundation since Rosalind arrived in town. Was this it? Were they a rogue faction, or an unrelated group? Why were they attacking Foundation agents? What did that have to do with radical environmentalism?

Izzy made a noise of impatience in the backseat. "Does anyone else get to look? Did they kill JFK or something?"

I passed her Rosalind's phone. She thumbed through the pictures and gasped at the last one. "Oh shit."

"What is it?" snapped Jamal, impatient with the downtown Chicago traffic, as well as waiting until last.

"They're Scales."

He didn't visibly react, navigating another busy intersection. Why hadn't he taken the Eisenhower? I could see the main tower of Polk Medical a few blocks ahead.

"You know of the Scales of Equilibrium?" I asked.

He pursed his lips and nodded. "We do."

I waited, but he clearly wasn't going to volunteer more. I decided to ask the big question.

"What can you tell me about a guy called Allen Weston?"

One advantage of asking a question of someone driving a car is they have nowhere to go. They either have to answer or stew in silence.

I thought Jamal had taken the second option, but just as I prepared to repeat myself, he cleared his throat. "The first thing I can tell you is that the man is dangerous. If you know about the Scales of Equilibrium, you know they hold some fringe beliefs. Those beliefs, and more besides, derive from him. How do you know about him? What do you know?"

So the HLF wasn't omniscient. I took a certain smug satisfaction in their ignorance of this one part of our lives. My peripheral vision caught Rosalind shifting in her seat.

"We know they're snooping around with even less subtlety than you lot. They've threatened us verbally and physically."

"Then you must have been asking too many questions. I would strongly advise you to stop. We're aware of Weston and his group's activities."

"But not that they are responsible for attacking your agents," Rosalind pointed out. "At least Izzy didn't, if her reaction was genuine."

"Genuine as fuck," Izzy bristled. "Jamal, tell me you didn't know it was them."

"I didn't know it was them," he said smoothly. "I give you my word. I'm still processing the implications, believe me."

"So how do you know Weston?" I persisted, as we entered the hospital's parking garage. I wanted a straight answer before he escaped from the car. "What is he to the HLF?"

Jamal visibly wrestled with himself as we circled the concrete ramps looking for a space. "You understand that the more I tell you, the more reasons they have to harass you?"

"Mr. Peters." Uh-oh. Rosalind was going full British. "My son has been ensnared in this man's organization for at least a year. I have spent most of that time trying to understand what trouble he may be in. He refuses to communicate with me. The least you can do is help a worried mother put more of the puzzle together, especially if the Henry Lyons Foundation has something to do with it."

Jamal sighed. "Very well. He was one of our top researchers, worked closely with Emma Astbury for years until they had a falling out."

"Who's Emma Astbury?"

"She's led the Foundation's research program for the last two decades."

"What did they fall out over?"

"No one knew for a long time. Astbury isn't the gregarious type. Weston was always passionate about the environment, about humanity's impact on it. He theorized that the disproportionate concentration of Intrusions in urban areas was some kind of 'immune response' to our species' activities. They argued about it - a lot - but it was never personal."

"So if not that, then what?" coaxed Rosalind.

"We don't know what causes the Intrusions." Jamal was forcing the words out. "There are many theories, most of them untestable for all practical purposes. Astbury and others are convinced they're natural phenomena, something to study and manage. Weston believes an intelligence is behind it. Specifically, that some spirit of the Earth is enacting retribution for humanity's mistreatment of the planet. He began advancing his 'Agency' theory, and that's when everything blew up, just before the pandemic. He left the Foundation and has been flying under the radar ever since."

My skin prickled as I tried to absorb it all, so I could tell Jess later. But something still didn't add up. "Why?" I asked. "Why should a different theory cause their falling out? I thought scientists tolerated each others' ideas."

"They do, up to a point." Jamal's tone was grim. "But Agency Theory doesn't just postulate the Intrusions as a sort of biblical plague, inflicted on civilization by an avenging angel. It advocates joining forces with it."

The hospital kept Jess overnight for observation. We couldn't describe how she was injured, and even in Doctor Hammond's hospital, we weren't about to discuss mental connections, much less any kind of psychic attack. So, after running a battery of tests, from vision and hearing to reflexes and memory, the on-duty physician prescribed acetaminophen and bed rest.

"I can't rule out some kind of seizure," Doctor Rafiq told her, stern and authoritative, despite standing scarcely taller than Jess as she laid on her hospital bed. "If you have another in the next ten hours, I want to be here to see it."

I offered to stay, even though there wasn't much room in the overcrowded ward into which she'd been shunted. I felt terrible. We'd focused on how to repel and incapacitate our attackers, with only passing concern over the risk of backlash. It didn't help that she'd asked me to be the trigger man. "You were always better at dealing with Izzy's Shields," she'd admitted. "I'll set up the hit if you carry it out."

I had, and it almost blew up in my face.

I told her about Marcus and what Jamal had revealed about Allen Weston and the HLF, but I could tell the information wasn't sticking. Her eyes drifted, unfocused, and twice she interrupted me with questions about work. I decided to try again in the morning.

I found Rosalind, Jamal and Izzy in the waiting room, each busy with their phones. "We share the blame," explained Rosalind. "How is she?"

"Recovering," I said, and repeated what the doctor had told me. "Did anyone see Marcus or his accomplice come in?"

Jamal shook his head. "It's possible they were taken to another hospital. But even if they were brought here, we're not family. It would take a while to get any information about them."

"And how are you?" Rosalind asked me for about the fiftieth time.

"Fine. Tired." Too tired to keep the irritation out of my voice. She gave me a wintry smile.

"I think we'd all be better off resting at home and out of the way," she said, looking over at Jamal and Izzy. "I presume you two need to follow up with your Foundation peers, yes? I owe my husband a phone call. And D needs to sleep."

Jess didn't object to me leaving, but I'm not sure she completely understood. I hoped she'd be more lucid the next day. I had to stop by the restaurant first thing in the morning for some prep work, but I'd have time between that and dinner service to visit and, hopefully, take her home. Our apartment felt strange without her. I was no longer used to sleeping alone, and slept little for all that I was exhausted.

I stumbled bleary-eyed through my morning routine, and struggled to concentrate as I marinated cuts of chicken and pork. The Blue Line took me most of the way to the hospital, but the white noise and swaying of the rail car threatened to send me to sleep in my seat. I stood, wrapped myself around one of the steel poles, and thumbed through my phone's news feed.

I almost missed it, the headline registering just after I'd swiped it offscreen. I dragged my feed back down and stared at my phone in horror.

"BODY FOUND NEXT TO GLEN ELLYN TRAIL"

The two paragraphs following the headline added few details. A body had indeed been found earlier that morning. The police had acted on an anonymous tip, and were pursuing leads based on it. That didn't sound good at all.

I kept my face down as I hurried to the hospital, flinching at every glimpse of blue uniform. I hoped to get in and out quickly, but Jess was still waiting for discharge, and had even less patience than I did.

"The doctor told me I could go home an hour ago," she complained as soon as I arrived and gave her a hasty hug. She looked much better, more alert, despite the dark smudges of exhaustion under her eyes. "Oh, did you see this? They've been looping back to it all morning."

She gestured to the wall-mounted TV in the room's far corner. It was muted, but I could read the familiar headline on the scrolling banner underneath uninspiring footage of a taped off section of trail. About twenty yards from the camera, a half-dozen black-clad figures decorated with emergency yellow clustered under the trees lining the right of the path. I could only imagine what they saw and what they were saying.

"Just saw it," I muttered, glancing around to see who else might be in earshot. I showed her the article from my news feed.

"Do you think this is retaliation? For what we tried to do at Fedora? How did that end up, by the way? I was paying even less attention than usual to you last night."

She spoke lightly, but I knew that was a defense against her own vulnerability. I repeated my account of events after she lost consciousness, and this time her eyes flashed when I mentioned Marcus.

"Seriously? I knew something was off with that asshole. I bet that's what he and Conor argued about that day, and nothing to do with work. I need a new job," she finished with disgust.

"First things first," I said as a nurse entered with a clipboard of paperwork. "Let's get you home."

We had time to take the train back to Lincoln Park, but now I felt too exposed. While the nurse walked Jess through post-concussion symptoms, and what she should and should not do over the next few days, I called a Lyft. The poker-faced driver, who picked us up outside the hospital's front entrance, was the silent type, which suited me just fine. I happily endured his 70s playlist.

Rosalind texted me during the ride, asking if I'd seen the headline and if we were home yet. She was waiting for us when we arrived. Jess waved off my solicitous attempt to help her inside, but accepted an embrace from Rosalind.

"How do you feel?" Rosalind said, scrutinizing Jess's face.

"Better," Jess replied, detaching herself. "And please don't say 'I told you so'."

"I don't think I need to. We seem to have stirred up the hornet's nest. Have you heard from anyone about this body, D?"

"It's Train," I said, louder than I meant to. Get a grip now. "It has to be. And no, I haven't heard from anyone, but that's only a matter of time. Assuming this is Scales' recrimination for yesterday, carrying out Daniel's threat."

Rosalind winced, then gazed at me for a long time before speaking. "It was the Scales' threat," she said, a hint of pleading in her voice. "Daniel was just the messenger."

"Was he? And if the police do come asking and I tell them about that conversation, what will they think?"

It was as if I'd slapped her face. "My son may be many things, but he's not a killer."

"Are you sure about that? I'm a killer, Rosalind. We're good friends and I love you, but I've killed a man. Dragged a knife across a stranger's throat. Would you have known that about me if I hadn't confessed it to you?"

She looked thunderstruck. I felt awful, but also an adrenaline-fueled panic that was increasingly hard to suppress. I took a deep breath. "Look, for what it's worth, I don't think Daniel is a killer. But if it comes to it, I can't keep that conversation quiet. It depends how ruthless they are."

And that's when the police knocked on our door.

My fight or flight instinct dithered over its options, with the end result that I froze. I tried to recall my training, the self-control I'd been practicing for the last year at two different dojos.

"Remember you're innocent, love," Jess murmured, squeezing my arm before opening the door.

Three figures crowded onto the porch, two uniformed cops flanking an older man wearing a white button-down shirt and gray suit pants. His slicked-back charcoal hair had just begun to silver above his ears, and fine lines etched his pale, angular face. His expression wasn't unfriendly, but this wasn't a social call.

"Good afternoon, ma'am. Is this the address of Declan Ramon Rodriguez?" What a fantastic start.

Jess looked them up and down. "Who wants to know?"

"Detective Pappas with the Chicago PD," he said in a grave voice, displaying his badge. He looked past her and saw me standing at the top of the stairs, Rosalind at my shoulder. I caught his eye and nodded.

"Just let them in, Jess."

"Thank you," Pappas said as she stepped aside. He climbed the stairs, followed by the female cop. "Mr. Rodriguez, I presume?"

"D, please." *I'm innocent! I've done nothing wrong!* "How can I help you?"

"May we talk in private? I'd prefer not to trouble you with an invitation to one of our stations."

"We'll be right outside," said Rosalind, taking a reluctant Jess's arm on her way out. I gestured towards the kitchen table, and the Detective and I took chairs opposite each other. I rested my half-folded arms on the table and forced them still.

"D?" he said, raising his eyebrows.

"I never much cared for my given names," I explained, not for the first time. "'D' was a clean break with parts of my past I regretted. But I expect you already know that."

He nodded. "I always applaud someone's efforts to remake themselves, to lead a better life. I'll get right to the point. What can you tell me about Bryan Liggett?"

I frowned. "I don't know that last name, but I have met a Bryan or two."

"I believe he once went by 'Trainwreck', during his incarceration at Missouri Eastern Correctional."

"Ah. I knew him as 'Train'. Not that I knew him well. I didn't socialize much while I did my time."

"But you did know him. Did you ever get in a physical fight?"

I dug my fingertips into my forearms, and once again replayed Daniel's words from our meeting on the trail: *If someone were to stop by, that's the story they'd hear: Bryan's old prison buddy, the one he used to fight with, came looking for him.* They'd been buzzing around my head for hours.

"I did, once. Not just him, either. Spur of the moment things, forgotten as soon as they were done."

"Really?" Pappas's eyes narrowed. "You didn't hold a grudge? You didn't move to Chicago six months ago to look for him?"

"No and no. What's this about, Detective?"

He continued to study my face, then sat back in his chair. "Have you seen the news? We found a body buried next to the Illinois Prairie Path in Glen Ellyn."

"I did see that. Are you telling me that's Train?" I knew that was a mistake as soon as I said it. He sat up, alert.

"Why would you think it was Train?"

"Why else would you be here asking questions about him?"

"He's apparently been missing for weeks. I could just be here asking if you knew where he was."

"A detective?" I scoffed. "And you didn't ask that. You asked if I held a grudge because of a decade-old prison fight."

He looked at me shrewdly, then nodded to himself. "Very well. We don't have a positive ID yet, but other evidence points to the body being Train. And we do have reason to believe you sought him out recently."

"Was that part of your anonymous tip?"

Irritation flashed across his face. "I'm not at liberty to divulge the source of my information. Is it true?"

"Not exactly." I unfolded my arms slowly, and laid my hands flat on the table. I was going to have to tell him almost everything. Without naming names, I told him about an out-of-town friend asking me to check up on their son, who was in rehab at the Themis Center. I told him about my stakeout and about following the cleanup crew along the Illinois Prairie Path, about how surprised Train and I had been to see each other. And then I told him about the bookstore, and once again unexpectedly bumping into Train outside the restroom, about him asking me for help, and about his no-show when we went to Glen Ellyn to meet him. But I didn't yet tell them about Daniel's threat, or about Lyall and the other Themis Center chaperone emerging from the tree-line as Jess and I talked to Rosalind's son. I'd keep Daniel out of this if I could.

Pappas didn't interrupt my story, simply jotted notes in a black moleskin journal as he listened. He pondered them in silence for a minute after I finished, then shut the journal and clipped his pen to it.

"We're trying to track down the owners of the Themis Center," he said. "All we know is that's where Train was last seen."

I frowned. "You can't just knock on their door like you did mine?"

"We tried. The building is vacant. There's a "For Lease" sign in the window."

I gaped at him. The bastards had covered their tracks well.

Pappas stood and, after hesitating, so did I. He adjusted his shirt and cricked his neck before picking up his journal. "Thank you, Mr. Rodriguez. I think that will be all for now. I'd like a quick word with your partner if you don't mind, in case there are any additional details she remembers."

I shrugged. If I minded, what could I do that wouldn't look suspicious? I trusted Jess.

"Oh, one more thing," he said as I went to get her. "Don't plan on leaving town in the near future. I want you right where I can find you."

Chapter Twenty-Four
YOU PERCEIVE ME

I shifted uncomfortably in the back seat of my car. I'd never ridden there before, but Jess and Rosalind agreed it was best if I kept a low profile. They had agreed on a lot in the thirty-six hours since the police knocked on our door, most notably that the best time to break into the Themis Center was late Wednesday night.

Detective Pappas had not talked to Jess long. "He just wanted to know if I'd seen Train at the bookstore and why we'd gone looking for him in Glen Ellyn. He seemed okay with my answers, but I still think you're his number one suspect."

She'd taken a sick day and suggested I do the same, but as rattled as I was, I decided to go to work. "I need to act normal," I explained. "Hell, I need to *be* normal for a few hours. Forget about Train and Henry Lyons and the Scales and all that shit - just cook and give my mind a break."

It made sense at the time, but I was twitchy and paranoid all day, suspecting even the busboys of ulterior motives. Luca pulled me aside, and I excused my behavior with the simple truth that Jess had been in hospital overnight.

"What are you doing here then?" he demanded, to which I'd mumbled that a friend was looking after her. I held down my part of the dinner service, but couldn't leave the restaurant fast enough.

I was surprised to find Rosalind still at our apartment when I got home around 11pm. But that was nothing compared to my shock at the reason.

"Hi hon," Jess said, greeting me with a kiss. "We've decided we're going to break into the Themis Center tomorrow night!"

"Is that a joke?"

"It's not," Rosalind assured me. She rose from the kitchen table and stretched her back. I noticed her overnight bag was stashed in a corner of the room. "Allow me to summarize our reasoning."

"This oughta be good," I muttered. She fixed me with a baleful glare, so I shut up and listened.

"I haven't stayed in Chicago just to avoid my Henry Lyons handlers back home, or try to prevent the Foundation from luring you two deeper in. I've been trying to understand the meaning of Daniel's texts, primarily the warning about August 1st."

"This Thursday?"

"This Thursday. It seems likely that the Scales of Equilibrium are involved. At first, I believed his warning was directed at you two specifically, an escalation of their threat to leave them alone or else. After we discovered their involvement in the incapacitation of HLF agents last night, I wondered if that was it, but Jess flushed them out. Without her plan to entrap your attackers, they may not have had the opportunity to try anything before Thursday. So, I'm thinking Daniel was warning me about something else entirely. Something much bigger."

"Like what?" This sounded more like an explanation than a summary. I wanted to collapse on my couch, but that risked falling asleep.

"Have you been following the news about all these urban infrastructure breakdowns? Poisoned water supplies, power grid disruptions, highway collapses, et cetera? Just today, they evacuated Charlotte's financial district after HVAC system contamination made hundreds of bank workers ill: nausea, fainting, even paralysis. Martin has friends there - he's close to panic. Phoenix still doesn't have a reliable clean water supply, and people are leaving in droves. It's chaos. And that's just this country. The entire city of Cardiff lost electricity yesterday after coordinated attacks on multiple substations. They could be without power for weeks."

"Cardiff. That's in England, right?

"Wales, actually. My point is that almost every day, some city somewhere in the world falls victim to sabotage or unattributed infrastructure failure. Everyone blames the usual suspects: Russia, China, Jews or Muslims, depending on how ignorant and racist they are. But you've read Allen Weston's book, or at least Jess has. He thinks modern civilization is a plague destroying the natural order. You've personally heard him say we need to fight back, to restore 'equilibrium'. As for 'scales', with what else do you associate that metaphor?"

"Judgment?"

"Exactly. Our cities, and the institutions that drive their prosperity and growth, have been judged and found wanting. I think the Scales of Equilibrium is more than one man's environmental crusade. I think it's a well-organized, worldwide terrorist organization with roots in the Henry Lyons Foundation. For some reason, they want to stop all Imprints, want today's HLF to leave Intrusions alone."

"Because they think Intrusions are manifestations of Gaia's power," Jess murmured, catching my eye. A chill ran down my spine.

"As to that, we are truly speculating," said Rosalind with a frown.

"But you think the Scales are planning an attack here, in Chicago?" I asked, trying to wrap my mind around it all. "Some kind of mass disruption, like Phoenix or Charlotte? And Daniel knows about or is part of it?"

"That's my fear, yes. I think a date has been set and Daniel... I don't know how involved he is, but he had at least enough conscience left to warn us."

"Unless we were actually on the scent, and he was trying to throw us off," Jess pointed out.

Rosalind pursed her lips and shook her head. "Either way, we're running out of time. We have twenty-four hours to leave town or try to stop this attack."

I almost laughed. "In case you've forgotten I can't leave town. If I do, I just convince the Chicago PD that I killed Train."

"That was the final piece of the puzzle. Why was Train killed? He asked you for help, D, and couldn't speak freely either time you saw him. The Scales didn't want you poking your nose into their business, and they especially didn't want you anywhere near the Themis Center."

"You think that's where they planned the attack?"

"Perhaps. Or recruited foot soldiers to carry it out. Or both."

"But it's closed now, according to the detective."

"Convenient, don't you think? It's a long shot, but it's possible we forced their hand in more ways than one. Maybe there's evidence somewhere in that building to confirm our suspicions, possibly save lives. And maybe even prove your innocence."

I couldn't stand it - or stand - any longer, and slumped onto the nearest kitchen chair. So much for soothing myself with the comforting mechanics of a restaurant kitchen. My mind was spinning worse than before I'd left for work.

"So why not tell the cops? They want to talk to the Themis Center folks, maybe already have."

"What do we tell them?" Jess laughed without humor. "Our theory rests on unexplained paranormal phenomena and the nebulous connections between two shady secret societies. Who's gonna listen to that? Would you have believed us eighteen months ago?"

I had no answer. I couldn't think of another option, other than ignoring the problem and hoping it went away. Rosalind had decided to crash at our place instead of finding yet another new hotel, but she insisted on taking the couch. I tossed and turned in my own bed that night.

I left the co-conspirators to plot the details of our burglary - Jess took another sick day - and joined the tail end of the morning commute. Bright morning sun fought off a spreading pall of darkening cloud, a harbinger of the possibly severe thunderstorms in the forecast. Neither my fellow commuters nor the flocks of tourists, heading to the museums, Millennium Park, or Navy Pier, looked worried about the state of the world or the attacks on American cities. How could they not care? Were they all just as blissfully ignorant as me, too caught up in their own lives? What was going to happen tomorrow, to them and to Chicago?

Jamal called as I walked from the station to the restaurant. "We're on hold," he told me. "No more Tether training until further notice. And, if I know Faustyn, not until a serious discussion of our actions, and our reflection on their consequences. That goes for me and Izzy too. Guilt by association."

He couldn't hide the bitterness in his voice. I wasn't sure if he was mad at me and Jess or at Faustyn. "Did you tell him the Scales were the ones attacking his agents?"

"I did. That's the good news. He took that very seriously. I don't know the details, but I believe the Foundation has access to Marcus and his companion, and that we have people investigating further. Top men, presumably."

I wondered if the HLF knew about my visit from the cops, but decided not to ask. "So, just keep our heads down for now?"

"I would. Focus on your day jobs, don't draw attention to yourselves. I'll be in touch as soon as I know more."

Got it. Nothing says "don't draw attention to yourselves" like squatting in a Hyundai Elantra, parked on the edge of downtown Glen Ellyn as the seconds ticked down towards midnight. Rain still pattered on the roof and windows, an afterthought of the deluge that had swept through Chicagoland earlier that evening. The streets were deserted when we arrived, and we worried we were too conspicuous, but no one appeared to have noticed us. We were just waiting for any final stragglers to leave the bar two blocks down from the former Themis Center.

"It's 11:45," Jess announced at last. "I think it's time. The longer we sit here, the more we risk being seen."

"I agree," said Rosalind. She was almost unrecognizable in her long-sleeved black shirt and pants. She claimed she'd gone through a "goth phase" in high school. I thought of Izzy and immediately offered money to see those photographs. "You ready, D?"

I shrugged, and yanked at the fabric of my own matching shirt. I hated long sleeves. "Sure. It's not like the plan is super detailed."

"The best plans are simple ones. Get in, see what we can find, get out."

"And you're sure we can get in? I'm still fuzzy on that detail."

"We told you we explored earlier," Jess said, tapping her reserves of patience. "Walked around, peered inside the Themis Center just like we did its neighbors, lunched at that coffee shop you told me about. It poured afterwards. I doubt anyone saw me slip into the side alleyway and check it out. The basement door's the way to go."

"There's no alarm system?" I couldn't keep the skepticism out of my voice.

"Not that I can tell. I couldn't see any sensors or control panels anywhere. I'm only half-certain it has electricity."

"We can't be certain," added Rosalind. "But we're out of options and time. I trust Jess's judgment enough to take the risk."

And what are you *risking?* I thought sourly. *I'm the first one they'll throw the book at if we're caught.*

But she was right. We were out of options.

Just for fun, the rain started to pick up again. Even hurrying as much as stealth allowed, my sodden cotton shirt clung to my skin as I followed Jess into the alley between the Themis Center and its neighbor. A single streetlamp glared over its empty parking lot, and we hunched over as we ran past into the alley's menacing shadows. Sheer brick walls rose above us on both sides, offering a handful of dark windows but little shelter. Everything was dark, soulless. A flight of concrete steps led down to the Themis Center's basement door, almost flooded by a puddle of rain clogged with discarded food containers. I wished I hadn't worn my work shoes, but they were the only black footwear I owned.

The women huddled on the final step as I squelched and examined the door. Instead of the solid wood I expected, it looked like a typical house's back door, its upper half a lattice of glass. It practically invited burglars. I peered inside, but it was too dark and the glass too grimy to see much.

Straightening, I took out the hammer from my jacket's inside pocket. I'd wrapped its head in a dish towel before leaving our apartment. "Here goes nothing," I mumbled and struck the glass above the door handle, sharp and hard.

Part of me hoped the glass wouldn't even crack, or that its shattering would trigger the alarm and just get the whole thing over with. We'd have no choice but to hightail it back to the car and come up with Plan B. But nothing happened, other than the faint sound of shards tinkling on the floor inside. I cleared out enough jagged pieces of glass so I could grope inside for the deadbolt, found it, slid it back. The door opened inward with only a modest creak of protest.

"Impressive," said Rosalind.

"I'm an ex-con after all," I quipped. No-one laughed, least of all me.

"Go on then," hissed Jess. I stooped to clear the short lintel and shuffled into utter darkness. As when entering any building for the first time, I extended my senses to pick up any Imprints. I came up blank, but pitch black basements of empty former hotels and rehab clinics gave me the creeps all by themselves.

I replaced my hammer and dug out my other piece of equipment: a slim flashlight with a red filter, the better to preserve my night vision. I swept the room with its beam, but there was little to see. A stack of empty and decrepit metal shelves huddled against the wall to my right. An ancient-looking furnace squatted against the back wall, just visible past a flight of wooden stairs. Jess and Rosalind turned on their flashlights too, but a minute of cautious exploration turned up no more than a long-dead mouse caught in an old-fashioned spring trap under the stairs.

"We didn't expect to find much down here anyway," said Jess, still sounding disappointed. "Let's go up."

"Fifty bucks, that door's locked," I muttered, tiptoeing up the creaky staircase. Sure enough, when I turned its handle and pushed, the door at the top refused to budge. "Now what?"

"We can't turn back now." Jess looked at me expectantly.

"Fine." I threw my weight against the door, but it only shuddered in its frame. Shooing the women back down the steps, I stopped halfway, turned, and sprang back up, hurling my shoulder at the wood immediately above the brass handle. With a screech and a sharp crack, the frame splintered around the lock, and I flailed to stop myself tumbling through the opening. The door swung and cannoned off the wall behind it. I froze. Surely that had been audible outside! The seconds ticked by, but all I heard were footsteps padding up the stairs behind me.

"Fool of a cook," whispered Jess with a playful punch to my side. "Let's hope the orcs aren't coming."

"What?"

"Never mind."

We fanned out, careful to keep our lights away from the windows. I recognized the double glass doors leading to the street outside and gave them a wide berth. Rosalind investigated the reception desk, while Jess and I explored the rest of the floor. One long room, perhaps where hotel guests might once have dined, occupied half of it. It was gutted now, as empty as the basement. A kitchen, restrooms, and what might have been an office rounded out the main level. We weren't sure what we were looking for, but there was nothing to see. No furniture, no picture frames disguising wall safes, no loose floorboards belying secret compartments, no slips of incriminating paper wedged under counters. The Scales of Equilibrium had done a good job cleaning up after themselves.

"I suppose we should try upstairs," Rosalind said, evidently frustrated. For want of a better plan, we followed her up the switchback main staircase to the second floor. A short corridor ran across the width of the building, before turning towards the rear in a "U". A series of doors, mostly open or ajar, led to what had been guest rooms, and more recently housed the residents of the Themis Center.

"Let's split up," suggested Rosalind. "Don't smirk, Jess."

I took the wing to our left, four rooms total. Unlike the main floor, they'd left the furniture in the residents' rooms: a twin bed, a plain wooden desk and ladder-back chair, and a dresser. No frills here. I scoured all the drawers, looked under all the mattresses, checked the medicine cabinets in the tiny ensuite bathrooms, but failed to turn up so much as a loose penny. Rosalind and Jess had no better luck. Dispirited, but determined to see it through, we trudged up the last flight of stairs to an identical-looking floor of guest rooms. Without a word, we split up again. I'd just turned the corner of the corridor when I heard a gasp and Jess's low, urgent "D!"

I hurried back to the room right before the turn. She stood inside next to the desk, eyes closed. I saw Rosalind hurrying back from her wing, and as I waited for her, I thought I heard a sound from below. After listening for several thudding heartbeats, I convinced myself it was just an old building talking to itself.

"What have you found, Jess?" asked Rosalind, stopping just inside the door, but I passed her and took Jess's hands. And that's when I felt it.

"Whoa!" The Intrusion was powerful, if only a few inches in diameter. It hurt to breathe, my convulsive swallowing was agony, and cold sweat erupted across my forehead and the back of my neck. I wrenched myself away, Jess staggering with me, and we stared at each other in the muted streetlight seeping through the window. I wondered if my eyes betrayed the same spark of fear as hers.

"What is it?" demanded Rosalind, stepping toward us. "An Imprint or... ah!"

She shivered as she passed through the space near the front corner of the desk, her face twisting through a mix of pain and terror. Her hand sought and found the back of the desk chair to steady herself. When she opened her eyes, they were clear and calm.

"They're quite different from Imprints, aren't they?" she said. "Much more localized. I still wonder how I've never encountered them before."

I licked my lips. "We should probably leave it alone. We barely survived at Fedora two nights ago, and this thing feels a hell of a lot stronger than that."

"We probably should," Rosalind agreed. No one moved.

"I mean," said Jess, in the tone of someone trying to convince themselves, "whatever it is, whatever memory it manifests, the chance of it being relevant has to be almost zero."

"How long has it been here?" I wondered, stretching a hand towards the unremarkable space where the Intrusion lurked. "Does the HLF know about it? Did the Scales know about it?" I looked back at Jess.

"Is it a trap?" she whispered.

Suddenly, I felt the press of time. Over thirty minutes had passed since I'd forced open the basement door. We were riding our luck, and it made me jumpy. We'd found nothing and had no reason to expect anything different from a conventional search of this floor. What was one more risk?

"I'm gonna try to tether it." Jess and Rosalind stared at me, neither rushing to berate me for recklessness or foolishness. "Even if it's another Level Three or higher, the worst that could happen is I create a shitty Imprint. Do you think you could erase it if I do, Rosalind?"

"I can certainly try," she said, voice and expression grim. "But we all know that's not the worst that could happen."

"We'll do it together," Jess insisted, linking her hand with mine. "I think we could've handled the Fedora Intrusion if it hadn't been for Marcus and his fellow asshole."

"You're still recovering from that night," I protested. "You just came home from the hospital and you're still complaining of headaches. I can't ask you to risk more damage."

"But you're not asking," she said. She threw her arms around my neck and kissed me. "I'm volunteering. It's my decision. I know the risk. And, not gonna lie, I'm terrified. But we need answers. There's a whole city of people out there who could be hurt, or worse, by whatever the Scales are planning tomorrow. If there's anything I can do to prevent that, even if it means another concussion or... or worse, I have to try.

"Besides," she added with a glint in her eye. "Those scaly bastards are trying to frame the man I love for a murder he didn't commit. I'll take any shot I can against them."

I didn't like it, but I'd already lost the argument. I returned her kiss and then disengaged. We all prepared ourselves in a now-familiar routine: breathing, seeking inner clarity, and heightening awareness of our surroundings. We turned off the flashlights and joined hands, forming a circle of three. Jess and I connected our wills - hers was as strong as ever - and I convinced myself I sensed another, presumably Rosalind's. Then we leaned into the Intrusion and hoped for the best.

And struck gold. Or rather, as Jess proclaimed afterwards, embracing her inner nerd, we struck mithril.

Three men occupied a room almost indistinguishable from the one in which we stood. An olive green comforter covered the bed to the right, on the edge of which sat Daniel Hill, hands in his lap. He looked the same as when Jess and I met him on the Illinois Prairie Path two months before, well-groomed and self-assured. He kept pushing his eyeglasses up his nose while he spoke, as if they didn't quite fit. Train sat on the chair in front of the desk, facing the bed and looking nervous, foot tapping as he listened to Daniel. Lyall stood in the corner behind him, near the door to the ensuite bathroom, watching with careful, cold scrutiny. I could tell things weren't going well for my fellow ex-con.

"We've been training for months, Bryan," Daniel said. "You knew what you were getting into."

"What choice did I have?" whined Train. "I needed help. You guys took me in, helped me when no one else would. I'm grateful, I am."

"Of course you had a choice. Not every patient here has joined the cause. But most do, as you and I did. Once you saw the righteousness of our mission, you didn't hesitate."

Train licked his lips and half-glanced behind him, but stopped short of meeting Lyall's implacable gaze. "I believe in the cause. Of course I do. Who doesn't want a better world, or to atone for the evils of civilization? Atone for my own evil. But what you're asking me to do..."

A dull throb began behind my eyes, followed by sharp pulses of pain across my connection with Jess. I felt her wilt, then regather her strength, and together we tried to block out the discomfort. I guessed this was due to staying inside the Intrusion for so long, and that the risk increased with every second. But we couldn't stop now. We'd stumbled across something vital, and I couldn't imprint this memory until we'd seen it play out. I gripped hers and Rosalind's hands tight, and felt them both return the gesture.

"Sacrifices must be made," Daniel said, leaning forward. "You know that. The longer we wait, the worse it will be. You've killed before, for no good reason. Now you have one. Not for me, or for Lyall, or even Allen. Do it for Gaia."

"I can't! I—"

In one fluid motion, Lyall stepped forward and sliced through Train's throat with a hunting knife. Blood fountained from his tattooed neck in a grisly arc and splattered over Daniel's horrified face. Train's eyes bulged, and he gurgled illegibly as his arms thrashed in a belated and futile defense. Lyall staggered, clutching the back of the chair with one bloody hand, then grabbed his victim's shoulders and heaved him like a sack of flour onto the floor. Train twitched feebly while his lifeblood oozed out, then lay still.

"He was trying to leave," Lyall explained in a reasonable tone, wiping the blade on his shirt. "Tried to get his old prison buddy to help him. But no one leaves the Scales of Equilibrium so easily. Come, Daniel, help me with the body."

I'd seen enough.

"Help me, Jess," I croaked, and tried to find the edges of the memory, to fold it away. She swayed alongside me, and I realized the Intrusion had sapped too much of our strength. We had to get out, now. As the shocking scene replayed, I focused on Rosalind's fingernails digging into my palm. I sought her spirit, her will, a beacon to lead us out of the mire, but just when I thought I'd found it, something else blocked her out. Huge, indomitable, and fiercely intelligent, The Presence regarded us with the dispassionate curiosity of a child studying a colony of ants. I tried to turn away, felt Jess do the same, but in the opposite direction, and we cringed, frozen and helpless before its scrutiny. Never before had it made itself known with such force and clarity. I thought I was staring into the face of Death itself.

:: YOU PERCEIVE ME ::

The words were not spoken individually. The idea was planted, fully-formed, into my brain with the force and precision of a surgical drill.

"No!" I cried, whether aloud or just in my imagination. "No, no, no, no, no!"

The universe ripped in half.

One moment I cowered before something vast and incomprehensible, clinging to my connection to Jess with all my failing strength. The next I was splayed on the floor in the dark, twitching like Train in his death throes. Somewhere nearby Jess was retching, but when I looked up, all I saw was Rosalind kneeling next to me. Tears ran down her face and blood trickled from her lips. She met my eyes, haunted and anguished, then lowered her head and vomited.

I hauled myself to my knees, despite what felt like every nerve end in my body misfiring in an internal fourth of July fireworks display. I used the hem of my shirt to wipe Rosalind's chin, then lifted her upright. She rocked in place, gripping my forearms for support. I turned to Jess, to find her sitting slumped on the floor, back to the bed, and breathing hard. She reached for me and I reciprocated, our fingertips touching in silent affirmation that we were still alive, and there for each other.

"Rosalind, what did you do?" she croaked.

"I'm not sure," Rosalind said, wincing as the words caught in her throat. "Water. Any water in this place?"

Good question. I dragged myself to my feet and stumbled into the bathroom, hoping the water hadn't been cut off. The faucet sputtered, and distant pipes groaned in protest, but finally I had a steady stream running. I cupped my hands and drank, then made way for Jess while I helped Rosalind up and into the bathroom for her turn. I was alarmed by how frail she was; for the first time, she looked every year of her age.

"Do you need to sit?" I asked after she'd drunk her fill.

She shook her head with exaggerated care. "I'll be fine. I've always been a fast healer."

"You sensed it, didn't you?" whispered Jess, leaning against the wall tile. "The Presence. Did you hear it?"

"I sensed... something," Rosalind admitted after a lengthy pause. "Something I couldn't explain. I was frightened, Jess."

"I think we all were," I muttered. I shuffled back into the bedroom, replaying the memory of Train's murder. If it was real, if that had been a true memory, Train died in this room two months before. He hadn't been a friend, he'd been a nasty piece of work to be honest, but he hadn't deserved to die like that. My hands flexed convulsively, and my gorge rose again.

"Oh Danny, what have you gotten yourself into now?" Rosalind's mournful voice rescued me from revisiting other, older unpleasant memories. I recalled the look of horror on Daniel's face as blood showered it. *Tell D that Bryan was a bad man.* No, Daniel wasn't the killer. But he'd talked about killing, about sacrifices.

"He's in deep, Rosalind. At the very least he's an accessory to murder. And he's clearly involved in whatever the Scales are planning tomorrow. Today, now."

"I know." Her voice was small, helpless, and she stared at the bed with such a bereft expression that it tore my heart. I'd just lost my mother, never to see her again in this world. Rosalind had just as surely lost her son. I wanted to comfort her, but couldn't imagine anything to say that could.

"At least we know D's innocent," said Jess. "I mean, we know who really killed Train."

I gave a hollow laugh. "Yeah, but how do we prove it? Testify that we tuned into some supernatural recording that conveniently showed us what really happened?"

"I wonder..." Jess took hesitant steps towards the desk, towards the Intrusion. She stopped and closed her eyes, then they opened wide with surprise. "It's gone!"

I joined her, but, try as I might, I couldn't sense the Intrusion. The room was as normal as any other.

Rosalind was as shocked as we were. "Whatever I did, no one else can see that memory now, Jess, if that's what you were thinking."

A worried frown crept over Jess's face, but then something occurred to me. "Maybe they won't need to." I knelt down next to the desk chair and turned my flashlight to white light. I found what I was looking for on the underside of the ladder back's top rung. "I doubt that would have convinced the cops, but this might."

I shuffled backwards to give Jess and Rosalind space to crouch down and examine what my flashlight illuminated. A bloody fingerprint.

"Got you!" Jess breathed in triumph.

"Well, that was an unfortunate oversight."

We leaped to our feet and spun around to face the doorway as two black-clad men entered the room. My night vision had taken a hit from the flashlight, but I recognized the taller one from his build and voice. We'd just watched him cut out Train's throat: Lyall, the Themis Center's chain gang chaperone and, apparently, much more. I couldn't be sure in the gloom, but his companion, barely reaching Lyall's left shoulder, might have been Jess's stalker, the guy I'd pursued through our neighborhood a few weeks before. Both stood casually just inside the door, blocking our exit.

"I really ought to thank you," Lyall continued. "We thought we'd removed everything even vaguely incriminating from this building. Lesson learned. Hand over that chair."

"What are you doing here?" I asked. I crouched slightly and got my breathing under control. I sensed the ladies do the same behind me, Rosalind on my left, Jess on my right, and hoped one of them would think of something clever. "Did you follow us?"

"Nothing so heavy-handed," he chuckled. "Our alarm system's still online. It notified us as soon as you broke into the basement. Glen Ellyn PD should be here any moment. That won't look good on your record, will it?"

"What about you? Your lease is up. You're trespassing too."

He laughed, and suddenly there was a gun in his right hand, something long and sleek, and pointed at me. "The chair, please. Then we'll leave you to face the music."

The words were barely out of his mouth when I caught a flash of movement to my left. Lyall grunted and recoiled, staring in shock at the remaining five spikes of a Chinese throwing star embedded in his chest, just below his left shoulder.

What I was most proud of, afterwards, was being first to react. I sprang forward, jamming the star in and upwards while I grabbed the wrist of his gun arm. The gun went off, a muted compression of air followed by the shattering of window glass behind me. I smacked my free elbow into his jaw and tried to wrestle him down. His gun hand caught on the bed's footboard, and I didn't hesitate. I brought down my fist like a hammer on his forearm, and bones snapped with a sickening crunch. He yelped in agony as he collapsed to the floor, the gun skittering away from his powerless fingers. He thrashed as I landed on top of him, trying to buck me off, so I drove my shoulder into his chest.

"Stay the fuck still, you murdering piece of shit!" He fell limp.

Curses and scuffling nearby reminded me, belatedly, of his companion. I turned to see him lying on his stomach, Rosalind pinning his legs and one arm, while Jess twisted the other high above his back. I recognized him now, not just from the uneven scales tattoo behind his ear. Jess did too, and gave his wrist an extra quarter turn as her knee clamped his head to the floor.

"That's the last time you follow me anywhere, asshole," she growled.

"You'll regret this," hissed Lyall. "You think we're coming after you now, just wait—aargh!"

"What do we do now, D?" asked Rosalind in a conversational tone, none too gently extracting another throwing star from the stalker's arm.

Police sirens wailed outside, followed by the sound of multiple slamming car doors and footsteps on the stairs below.

"We talk to the cops," I said.

"And what do we tell them?"

She and Jess both waited, looking to me for answers. Lots of people were looking for lots of answers.

"I think we tell them the truth."

Chapter Twenty-Five
LET'S DO THIS

I started awake as Detective Pappas opened the door to the interview room, using his foot to close it behind him. I rubbed my eyes and sat up straighter, my back and buttocks protesting about the hard, uncomfortable chair in which I'd spent most of the night.

"Coffee," he said, setting two white styrofoam cups down on the gray laminate tabletop. "I didn't use creamer. They only have the nasty powdered crap here." He sat facing me and placed his moleskin journal in front of him. I glanced at my Fitbit: 04:49.

"Where are Jess and Rosalind? What about Lyall and his buddy? How long—"

"You know," Pappas interrupted, one eyebrow raised, "the way this works is that I ask the questions. Pretty sure that's the protocol."

I stifled my impatient retort and sipped my coffee. It scalded the tip of my tongue and was utterly tasteless. No caffeine was worth that.

Pappas's mouth twitched as I pushed my cup to one side. "Jess and Rosalind are enjoying Glen Ellyn PD's hospitality in adjacent rooms. Ms. Hill is something of a celebrity, on account of her shuriken."

"Her what now?"

"Shuriken. Japanese throwing stars. Did you know she carried a pair of them on a belt under her shirt? Palmed them while you chatted with Lyall?"

"No, I didn't." But I wasn't surprised. Jess was gonna want some for sure. I scratched at the bandage, covering the cuts on my hand where I'd pushed the star further into Lyall's chest, then made myself stop.

Pappas leaned back in his chair. "She prefers hira-shuriken, which are flat, lightweight, and ideal for quick, efficient throws from different angles. The samurai used them primarily as a distraction, as did she."

"Sounds like you're an expert."

"No, but after listening to Rosalind's history lesson, I'm gonna nail the samurai weaponry category at our next trivia night."

I chuckled, then remembered where I was and risked another question. "How much longer are you keeping us?"

He took a sip of coffee, then grimaced. "You've answered my questions and those of the Glen Ellyn PD. You, Jess and Rosalind have been very helpful, but you also made strong allegations about an imminent terrorist threat to my city. I notified the FBI, and we're waiting for them to get here."

I groaned. I wasn't worried about work, but I was very conscious of the date. Whatever the Scales of Equilibrium were planning, it could happen at any moment, but I guessed that was his point.

"I'd never dismiss such allegations out of hand," he continued, opening his journal and then closing it again. "Given what's been happening in this country and the world this summer, I'm inclined to take you seriously. My sister works for First Bank in Charlotte."

"My god! Is she okay?"

Pappas nodded. "Thanks for asking. My nephew has strep, so she worked from home yesterday. But many of her co-workers got sick, and some are still in the hospital. I don't want that to happen here."

"Did Rosalind...?" I clamped my mouth shut. I couldn't speak for her.

"She showed me her son's texts, and shared her concerns. And Ms. Evans corroborated your conversation with Daniel on the trail. Why didn't you share that with me before?"

"Because I didn't want to implicate Rosalind's son, not if I didn't have to. I don't think he had anything to do with Train's death. But he's neck deep in whatever the Scales are planning."

Pappas opened his journal and frowned slightly as he examined it. "I'm gonna leave that to the Feds. My case is Bryan Liggett's murder."

"Am I still a suspect?"

"We're still running tests on that chair. The fingerprint matched, we're just waiting for DNA results. I've got a squad of uniforms ready to comb through that building, assuming the Feds don't get in my way. But even if the blood matches the victim, that isn't enough."

"But it's better than a decade old prison skirmish and an anonymous tip, isn't it?"

"Perhaps. I take anonymous tips at face value. Some are genuine: folks are scared. Others make trouble, neighbors tattling on each other. A few are misdirection. Now, this tip pointed us to the body, so someone knows something. It also implicated you, but, as you say, with no tangible evidence."

"Because I didn't do it. I didn't even know he'd been killed that day on the trail. I thought the Scales were just being assholes, lurking around the treeline like that."

"They've certainly taken a dislike to you." Pappas regarded me with a thoughtful expression, while I considered another sip of tasteless coffee. "There's something I still don't understand. You broke into the former Themis Center looking for evidence of a planned attack on Chicago. You go floor by floor, room by room, and turn up nothing. Then, in one of the twenty-eight bedrooms, you happen to discover a bloody fingerprint on the back of a chair, a fingerprint that might exonerate you from a serious crime. That seems fortuitous to say the least. Mad detective skills. When, and if, you're no longer a person of interest in my case, I may hire you. Care to elaborate?"

We hadn't had time to discuss how we'd explain what we'd learned only from the Intrusion. I was confident neither Rosalind nor Jess would attempt to tell that particular truth, but I couldn't know what they'd told Pappas. I had to gamble, and say as little as possible.

"We were focused on today's attack, it's true," I said slowly. "Finding evidence of Train's murder was a bonus goal. I'd be lying if I said I checked the back of every chair, but I checked that one. Call it a hunch, or maybe I'm just lucky. Maybe there's more evidence in that room, if you check."

"Oh, I'm gonna check. We'll go with a hunch then."

He wasn't satisfied, so I tried to redirect. "What did Lyall have to say?"

Pappas scowled and scratched the end of his nose. "Nothing. For one thing, he's still in hospital getting his arm fixed. No word on whether he'll prosecute you for assault."

"He threatened us with a gun!"

"Which you could use to justify self-defense. I really don't know. His lawyer arrived before you did, and forbade him and his buddy from saying anything. The good news is the property owner isn't pressing charges for your forced entry, or any damages during your unauthorized visit. I might have made pointed comments about the building's poor security draining local police resources."

"Oh! Thank you."

He shrugged. "They may have had other motivations. Once you've talked to the FBI, you're free to go home. For now. Don't leave town, D."

"And if this attack happens, whatever it is?"

"Then we'll be in it together."

Special Agent Carmella Jones arrived at the Glen Ellyn police station with the rising sun, and questioned us well into the morning. Where Detective Pappas had presented an air of conversational civility, the young, ebony-skinned agent was direct and no-nonsense.

"Tell me what you know about the Scales of Equilibrium," she demanded, crossing her arms. I shared what I could, avoiding anything supernatural. She tapped one finger against her bicep throughout, as if there were other places she'd rather be. That made two of us.

"We've been watching them for a while," she said, giving me a curt nod when I was done. "They're careful, but not that careful. We picked up credible chatter about an imminent threat to Chicago. We didn't know about the Themis Center though. Thank you. I'll tear the place apart and see if we find anything."

"That's it?"

She arched an eyebrow. "Unless there's more you're not telling me, there's not much else I can do. I couldn't evacuate Chicago in a day, even with a concrete threat."

What else could I tell her? Would Marcus know more? Would he tell before any lawyers stepped in? I didn't know where he was, just that the Henry Lyons Foundation "had access" to him. I had no idea what the FBI knew or thought about the Foundation, but I saw no advantage to stirring up that hornet's nest just yet.

Jess, Rosalind and I all hugged when they finally let us leave. We were itching to compare notes, preferably after finding breakfast.

"And then what?" asked Jess as we climbed into my Hyundai. The local cops had driven it to the station for us, and probably searched it.

I stuck my fist in my mouth as I yawned for the hundredth time, and started the engine.

"Now we wait," said Rosalind grimly. "What else can we do?"

We waited, huddled in our apartment after calling in sick, for nothing. We heard no explosions or sirens, saw no news alerts. The worst thing that happened to Chicago was the high-flying Cubs' embarrassing 12-1 home defeat by the Pirates, and I didn't count that as a disaster.

We felt like we'd dodged a bullet. The tension of the last week didn't melt away, but it subsided to a level I'd come to associate with our new normal, walking a tightrope between two warring secret societies. However, there were still far too many unanswered questions, too many aspects of our lives over which we had too little control. And so I made a decision.

"Do you think we stopped the attack because Lyall and my stalker were being interrogated?" Jess asked a few days later. She looked lovely. I'd insisted we dress up for our first date night in a while, and she'd gone out and bought a sleeveless, form-hugging black dress that hung no longer than most of her shorts. Add in a delicate silver necklace, dragon-head earrings, and a rare touch of make-up, and she put most runway models to shame.

"It's telling that they skipped town as soon as they were released," I said, once again smoothing my button-down shirt. It was the only one I owned, but even accompanied by dress pants, I still felt underdressed. I sipped my Pinot Grigio, and cast another wary glance around Trattoria Capelli's main dining room. This had sounded like a much better idea when I planned it. Even at a corner table, I felt too exposed.

"I'm sure they were involved," said Jess, tearing chunks from our loaf of bread, but not eating any. "Maybe Marcus too. I wish

Jamal wasn't being so tight-lipped about him. I wanna give that guy a piece of my mind."

"Perhaps that's why Jamal's being tight-lipped." I grinned, but Jess wasn't amused.

"We're the reason they're talking to him, so we deserve to hear what he's said. We've taken risks for the Henry Lyons Foundation. They want something from us? Fine. But they need to give us something in return."

"You sound like Rosalind."

"She's not wrong. This is a business relationship, not an apprenticeship. We've got something they want, they have something we want. I've been too eager to learn in the past, too willing to accept others' demands of me in return. She's helped me understand how to value myself."

"Pity she's gone back to St. Louis."

"Yeah." She flashed a mischievous grin. "Although I'm not sure you could've handled her sleeping in our apartment much longer."

"Oh please," I protested, though I knew she was teasing. "Rosalind's just a good friend. Besides…" I tailed off, and was saved by the timely arrival of our entrees. "Besides," I continued, after resetting. "I know she missed Martin and they have a lot to discuss. In person, not just over the phone. Plus, she has to meet her new HLF handler in St. Louis, now that the Harringtons have been recalled. How's the chicken?"

"First bite was great," Jess said, allowing herself to be redirected. "Is it this good when you cook it? I'm still surprised you took me on a date to your workplace."

"These people have been good to me, Jess. They've helped us find a foothold, in Chicago, in our new life together. I know the future's uncertain, but—"

"I'm worried about Rosalind," she interrupted, twirling pasta around her fork. "On top of all the HLF and Scales nonsense, she can't let Daniel go. She knows she should, but she can't. It's eating her up inside."

I cursed as garlic butter squirted onto my shirt while I pried open a mussel. Perhaps seafood linguine hadn't been the best choice of entree. "Can you blame her? I don't know much about being a parent, but he's her only child. What's she supposed to do?"

"Daniel's made his own choices, good or bad. I think she needs to let him deal with the consequences of those choices. He's a grown man now. You never know. He may return to her and Martin eventually."

"If he doesn't help blow up the world first."

"Well, quite. Did you hear what happened in Paris today?"

The conversation drifted towards less personal topics. For a while, we were content discussing the end of civilization as we knew it. The FBI and their partners across the globe may "have their eyes" on the Scales of Equilibrium, but the pace of urban infrastructure attacks hadn't changed much. Jess believed the Scales were part of a wider network of righteous and disaffected terror groups. I urged caution, once again, against poking her nose into places that could draw unwanted attention.

"I *am* careful, love," she assured me, more amused than irritated. "I do know what I'm doing, but I could really use the Foundation's resources, and get the full background on Allen Weston."

"You're thinking of accepting their offer then? To meet with their top brass in the UK?"

"I am, and I think you and Rosalind should too. We could all benefit. They're desperate to learn more about what we can do, and what happened at the Themis Center. About The Presence. You could tell that shook Jamal, as well as Izzy and Faustyn."

It had. We'd met our HLF buddies the day after the attack that never happened. I'm sure Faustyn had intended to chastise us for our reckless behavior at Fedora, but we'd pre-empted him by owning up to yet another unsanctioned operation. Only Izzy, unusually quiet, accepted our claim that some intelligence had crashed our attempt to tether the Themis Center Intrusion, and communicated with us. Jamal was skeptical, but couldn't quite meet our eyes. Faustyn, I believed, was wishing he'd never heard of us. However, he'd obviously reported our claim back up the ranks, because both we and Rosalind had received invitations to fly to the Foundation's headquarters in England. Someone was taking us seriously. I had my reservations about going, but if we got some answers and helped stop the Scales of Equilibrium, then Jess was right.

"Yeah, I think we should go, as long as the Chicago PD are cool with it. I need a passport though."

Jess stirred the remnants of her pasta, lost in thought. She claimed her headaches and fatigue in the aftermath of Fedora had all but gone, but she still looked tired to me. Jess had always been a loud and lively creature of the night, always brimming with energy whenever I'd returned from a dinner shift. Not so much these last few days.

"What have we stirred up?" she asked, raising those emerald eyes I adored so much. They looked haunted now. "No one even wants to talk about it."

"I don't know," I admitted. The Presence, the indescribable entity I'd never allowed myself to believe in. The boogeyman. The ghost that didn't exist. "But we all heard it speak, if you can call it speaking. It wasn't part of the memory. I can't believe others haven't encountered it."

"Unless there's something about us, or what we're doing, that's attracting it. Or making communication easier."

"Maybe. We won't really know until we try to access another memory, Intrusion or Imprint."

She pursed her lips. "If we can."

"What do you mean?"

"I've been thinking about what Rosalind did, at the end. She cut off all contact, not just with The Presence but with the memory, the Intrusion. What if she didn't just sever that connection? What if she somehow erased our abilities, our sensitivities? What if we can never tether another Intrusion or erase another Imprint again?"

I reached for her hand, found it, squeezed with what I hoped was reassurance. "We won't know until we try. And if she did, would that be such a bad thing?"

"You tell me."

We gazed into each others' eyes and hardly noticed when Jordan, our server, arrived to clear our plates. His discreet cough snapped me out of my reverie, and I found him looking at me expectantly. "Sorry, what?"

"Are you ready for dessert tonight?" Jordan repeated. He played it straight, I'll give him that. I took a deep breath and pulled myself together. Unknown intelligences, lost paranormal abilities, and global terrorism would have to take a backseat for a few minutes.

"Yes, Luca made something special for us," I told him. He nodded and set off for the kitchen.

"Something special, huh?" Jess made a show of patting her stomach. "If I eat anything else, I may not be able to get out of this dress later."

"Oh I'm sure we'll find a way," I said with a grin. I was anxious again, for a different reason. The mood wasn't what I'd hoped for. Doubt and worry overwhelmed romance and relaxation. But perhaps that made this even more important.

Luca brought the dessert himself, along with a beaming smile for Jess. He set the covered plate down with a flourish, then retreated, but only as far as he had to. I saw Jordan, Tamsyn, and other kitchen staff peeking through the room's open doorway. I'd expected nothing less.

"What is this?" Jess said slowly, although I think she'd guessed. *No guts, no glory, D.*

I lifted the cover to reveal a silver-colored box sitting in the middle of a white plate. Then, because I was determined to do this properly, I slid out of the booth, went down on one knee and took her hand.

"Jess, I've turned your life upside down. I've torn you away from friends and family and the city you called home. I've dragged you into a strange world where we can see Imprints of past lives, where we wield almost magical powers to erase or tether those memories. I've mixed you up in a conflict with both human adversaries and some power we don't understand."

I was very conscious that everyone in the restaurant was watching me. This was a terrible idea. What had I been thinking? This was hard enough without inviting a room full of strangers as an audience.

I opened the box. The modest diamond within glittered in the light from our table lamp. I hoped she didn't mind me picking it out. I heard her breath catch, so I plowed onward.

"But you turned my life upside down the day I met you. When we ran that first 5k in Forest Park, when you flirted with me in the bar afterwards, when you demanded my phone number. I never imagined, after the life I'd had, that I could be with anyone, much less someone as smart, funny, and beautiful as you. I never expected to date again. And I definitely never expected to fall in love. But I did, that day and every other day since, all over again.

"I don't know where the world's headed right now. I can't see what happens next. All I know is that wherever our lives go, I want them to go together.

"Marry me, Jess."

My rehearsed speech delivered, exactly as I'd written it, I held Jess's hand and waited. Eons passed. She stared down at me with an inscrutable expression, lips slightly parted. What was she thinking? Terror gripped me, terror that she would laugh in my face, or storm out of the restaurant, or just give me a sad smile and say no. I was as exposed as I'd ever been.

"I never expected anyone to propose to me," she said at last, and the smile that followed was anything but sad. "And I never expected to say 'Yes' if they did. Oh, D! Let's do this!"

Mobile phone screen capture received by federal law enforcement via anonymous tip.

09:28

8/1 CHI aborted

Tartarus
Explain

Too many disruptions.
Actors compromised. Best to wait

Tartarus
That is disappointing

Agreed
Not the end of the world
Time is on our side

ACKNOWLEDGEMENTS

I claimed *Imprints of the Past* was "four decades in the making". It certainly took several years to write, rewrite, edit, edit again etc. I was determined to put my best foot forward. For this sequel, I couldn't take as long without losing the interest of anyone who read the first book. I needed all the support and encouragement I could get, so it's a good thing I received so much, from so many people.

I joined a vibrant indie author community when I dipped my toe into social media promotion. Many of the authors with whom I've connected are also just starting out, while others boast an admirable back catalog. To a person, they are generous with their time, criticism, and encouragement. We're all on different trajectories, but we're one big writing group, holding each other accountable, and celebrating each others' successes. This community is a big reason why you're reading this second novel now, and not in several years time.

This book is far better for having been read by many more people, much earlier in the process. I am eternally grateful to those who offered to read early drafts, and who provided valuable written and verbal feedback: Geri Drilling, Enrique Serrano, Rhiannon Davies, Aimee Keener, Arielle Keener, Tina Sellers, Kristy Sellers, and Rick Wurl. Each of you challenged me in different ways, inspiring significant changes in the characters and/or the narrative. Collectively, you drove me to discover and reveal their "truths". And again, Rick curated all the violence.

Gareth Clegg resumed editorial duties, and polished the final text into this finished product. It's fascinating to discover one's tics as a writer through professional editing. With my first book, I egregiously used adverbs to unnecessarily describe speech and actions. This time, despite my best efforts, and after entreaties from at least one beta reader, I fell short by several hundred commas. I compensated through antiquated or inappropriate use of compound words: no-one (sic) should do that. We never stop learning, and I'm grateful to have someone watching my back.

Michele Guarnieri designed the covers again, following up her work on the first book. I'm thrilled with the result. Although the genre prefers covers featuring only one character, I insisted on including Jess along with D, as this book revolves around their partnership more than his personal journey. Michele captured the mood perfectly. And yes, that was covers, plural: ebook, paperback, and hardback covers are all a little different, especially if you include dust jackets for the latter.

Finally, my wife, Sherri, deserves recognition as my greatest supporter. She and her sister, Keri Ousley, designed and produced all the bling for *Imprints of the Past*, initially for its launch party at the Novel Neighbor, one of St. Louis's great local bookstores. Sherri doesn't shout it from the rooftops, but she'll tell anyone who'll listen that her husband wrote a book. She indulges my random, frequent conversations about characters and plot points, and her thoughts have been as influential as my beta readers. Most importantly, she gives me the stability and space to write. When she asks "What are you doing?" and I reply "Book stuff", she generally leaves me to it, and it's almost always true. I'm a very lucky man.

ABOUT THE AUTHOR

Gareth Ian Davies was born and raised in the south of London, during which time he wrote many terrible things and dreamed of becoming a novelist. Instead, he earned a degree in Physics from the University of Bristol and didn't quite know what to do with it. After moving to the American Midwest he flirted with a career in nuclear engineering before taking the somewhat safer path as a software architect. He spent the next three decades writing code and technical documentation, before finally realizing his dream by publishing his first novel.

Gareth lives in St. Louis with his wife, her sadly declining fish population, two cats, and a cockatiel.

ALSO BY GARETH

OF IMPRINT AND ERASURE
Book 1 – Imprints of the Past

STAY CONNECTED

Want to be one of the first to get all the latest news? Check out Gareth's socials and sign up for upcoming announcements, first looks, and more!

Facebook:
Gareth Ian Davies

TikTok
@garethiandaviesauthor

Website
garethiandavies.com

Milton Keynes UK
Ingram Content Group UK Ltd.
UKHW010635290424
441924UK00005B/289